PRAISE FOR *Uncontrolled Flight*

"*Uncontrolled Flight* is a compelling read overloaded with turbulence — emotional, historical, and literal. Peck masterfully braids three strong and divergent voices into a robust narrative urged forward by the burning landscape and the mysterious, simmering ambitions of her complex characters. As I read, I found myself switching allegiances many times and questioning the choices we all have to make under obvious and invisible pressures."
TARA MCGUIRE, author of *Holden After and Before*

"Compelling from start to finish. Tangled webs . . . well woven."
DAVE PADDON, storyteller, author, and retired commercial pilot

"Masterfully crafted, with a complex cast of flawed and wholly relatable characters. Peck skillfully weaves multiple narratives into a riveting story that is part tragedy, part mystery — and totally impossible to put down."
J.T. SIEMENS, author of the Sloane Donovan mystery series

"In *Uncontrolled Flight* Frances Peck skillfully navigates a taut tale of firefighting pilots, air crash investigators, and dangerously spiralling lives against authentically drawn BC settings. Her characters — tough, damaged Nathalie; young, compromised Will; and heartbroken Sharon — gleam with originality and passion. As they career through the loss of the heroic man who connects them all, their lives break open to reveal dark secrets and betrayals, but also treasures of courage, loyalty, and inspiring human potential for growth."
KAREN HOFMANN, author of *What Is Going to Happen Next* and *A Brief View from the Coastal Suite*

"*Uncontrolled Flight* is just what the title suggests: a fast-paced arc that leaves you both afraid of what's inevitably coming and yet unable to look away. Its deft complexity is like the aircraft so central to its storyline — seemingly simple on the outside, yet packed full of connecting parts that all play a crucial role in the unfolding plot. It captures the conflicting feelings of those facing horror and loss inordinately well."

RUSSELL WANGERSKY, award-winning author of *Burning Down the House: Fighting Fires and Losing Myself* and *Whirl Away*

"Frances Peck's new novel is so compelling and accomplished it's easy to forget that it's only her second. *Uncontrolled Flight* is a beautifully paced, intimate look at BC wildfires, and the casually courageous aerial firefighters who risk their lives attempting to control them. As in her debut novel, *The Broken Places*, Peck's characters' voices are multidimensional — I flew through the pages, enjoying all the nuance of their thoughts and desires. Peck's descriptions of BC and note-perfect dialogue are equally precise. I can't recommend this book or her writing highly enough."

DANILA BOTHA, author of *Things That Cause Inappropriate Happiness* and *For All the Men (and Some of the Women) I've Known*

"*Uncontrolled Flight* begins with a plane crash that sets off a complex, emotional ride. At turns tense, sexy, and heartbreaking, each page drops us deeper into the world of Rafe, the experienced pilot who seemed to have it all, and the loved ones left grappling to understand what went wrong, who to blame, and who to protect. As their stories converge, guilt and resentments, secrets and lies, twist into a knot that no reader could stand to leave alone."

GENEVIEVE SCOTT, author of *The Damages*

PRAISE FOR *The Broken Places*

"A beautifully written and terrifying story ... [t]he central characters are wonderfully complex."
GLOBE AND MAIL 100 BEST BOOKS OF 2022

"Not a soul emerges unscathed in this intense and absorbing drama."
VANCOUVER SUN

"Peck deftly weds second- and third-person perspectives, flashbacks and flashforwards, epistolary interludes and enough literary *amuse-bouches* that the form of the novel is as compelling as the content."
ALBERTA VIEWS

"Rather than concentrating on disaster ... Peck, in compelling and at times moving prose, is more concerned with asking the question, what will you do in a crisis?"
SUBTERRAIN

"The novel is intense, the situations extreme and yet so many moments of masterful writing and sensory engagement are on offer for readers."
WRITESCAPE.CA

"It is the way that Peck focuses on the human suffering that no doubt will make the biggest impact on most Vancouverites reading the book ... Peck digs deep. For pages at a time, she submerges us completely in the minds of one character before moving on to the next."
THE BRITISH COLUMBIA REVIEW

"Wow! What a thrill of a read from debut author Frances Peck. I'm absolutely in awe to read such a magnetic and bursting debut novel. Peck's writing style is absolutely gripping and electrifying ... [A]n excellent and compelling read, I would highly recommend this new voice in the Canadian literature landscape."
WORN PAGES AND INK

"*The Broken Places* is not really about an earthquake — it's about humanity: how we live; how we interact; how we grow."

"What I love about this book is that it's not a heartwarming, let's-all-work-together-to-overcome type of a scenario. It's real and grueling: the death toll; the fires; the terror and confusion; the selfishness; the regret; and the loss of innocence ... But it's not all grim: some of the characters have moments of connection and growth. There's love and kindness and forgiveness."

Uncon

trolled

Flight

UNCON TROLLED FLIGHT

a novel

FRANCES PECK

NeWest Press

Library and Archives Canada Cataloguing in Publication
Title: Uncontrolled flight / Frances Peck.
Names: Peck, Frances, author.
Identifiers: Canadiana (print) 20230150918 | Canadiana (ebook) 20230150942 | ISBN 9781774390757 (softcover) | ISBN 9781774390764 (EPUB)
Classification: LCC PS8631.E355 U53 2023 | DDC C813/.6 — DC23

NeWest Press wishes to acknowledge that the land on which we operate is Treaty 6 territory and a traditional meeting ground and home for many Indigenous Peoples, including Cree, Saulteaux, Niitsitapi (Blackfoot), Métis, and Nakota Sioux.

Editor for the Press: Leslie Vermeer
Cover and interior design: Natalie Olsen
Cover images: (trees) Jonatan Hedberg/Stocksy.com, (plane) Matt Photography/Shutterstock.com, (fire) Login/Shutterstock.com
Author photo: Rebecca Blissett

  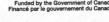

NeWest Press acknowledges the support of the Canada Council for the Arts, the Alberta Foundation for the Arts, and the Edmonton Arts Council for support of our publishing program. We acknowledge the financial support of the Government of Canada through the Canada Book Fund for our publishing activities.

NeWest Press
#201, 8540-109 Street
Edmonton, Alberta T6G 1E6
NeWest Press   www.newestpress.com

No bison were harmed in the making of this book.
Printed and bound in Canada   27 26 25 24 23   5 4 3 2 1

FOR TRAVIS SHELONGOSKY

Prologue

SHE ASKS WHAT I REMEMBER. Thursday morning, July 18, 2013. Walk me through it, from the very beginning, she says. Whatever you recall.

As if there's any part of that morning I could forget.

The first thing, if we're going to get technical, was guitar. The riff that kicks off "Barracuda," the hard-rocking seventies song my dad plays on repeat whenever he needs a lift. It's a solid tune, though I'm convinced my dad likes it because of the two smoking-hot sisters who fronted the band. As an alarm tone, it'll wake you up no matter what shape you're in.

Next thing I remember: Gracie, grabbing my pillow to drown out the alarm, one long leg slung outside the covers. She'd shown up in the wee hours, after her shift at the Hound and Hearth, smelling faintly of beer. Her knock on the door made my heart jump. Okay — to be honest, it was another part of me that snapped to. I'd texted Gracie a few days earlier when we shipped in to Quesnel, told her I'd missed her since last summer (true), that we were on high alert so I really, really had to sleep (also true), but that if she had nothing better to do she was welcome to visit (nothing truer). I closed with a few smiley faces, a lame way of saying that if she had better things to do, I'd understand. Six-foot-three Gracie, Kenyan turned Canadian, full basketball scholarship in the States until she tore her ACL. She's unlike any woman this Interior town has ever seen. She does not lack for better things to do.

My next memory, besides Gracie brushing her lips against my cheek as I told her goodbye, is how hot it was. Not at first. Like the day before, and the day before that, the morning started off bearable, the smell and feel of nighttime still hanging in the air, cool and sweet. I hit the gas, blasting the Foo Fighters in hopes that more guitar would clear my head, guzzling the biggest coffee they'd sell me at the motel restaurant, desperate for the caffeine to kick in. I'm never a morning person, not even when the shit's going down, and I was sorely missing the couple hours sleep I'd lost to my athletic visitor.

As I tore down the highway, leaving the storied gold-rush town of Quesnel behind, the sky thickened, daylight barely leaking through. I'd shut the Tacoma's windows tight to keep out the soot and burnt air, but it did no good. Even with the AC set to recirculate, the whole cab smelled of it: a forest of century-old fir and pine, giving way tree by tree.

By the time I made it to the runway, just before eight, the day was brewing up hot and dry, like every July day so far of this record-breaking year in this corner of the British Columbia Interior. A handful of pilots and mechanics milled around, doing precious little from what I could see, mostly burning off nervous energy before we got the signal to go. In front of the fire centre — *centre* a fancy term for two Atco trailers yoked together by a rough front porch — three guys from the ground crew sprawled in the shade, scarfing down coffees and fistfuls of Timbits. Crazy bastards. Every minute they're not humping loads of protective gear and hoses and pulaskis up the slopes, they're stuffing their faces, and even then some of them lose weight. No wonder, trying to keep up with the fire's punishing pace.

I saw him as soon as I parked the truck. Off to one side near the tarmac, head tilted skyward, still as a photo, taking it all in. Rafe Mackie, whose air tanker I'd soon guide in for a drop. Oddly for the most genial pilot on our team of cranky loners, he stood by himself. His hulking frame, slimmer than usual now that we were a couple of months into the season, cast an exaggerated shadow against the dingy vinyl siding of the maintenance shed. He stood motionless, like he was anchored there, staring up. My chest hitched a little seeing him that way, huge and alone. A solitary giant surveying an empty sky.

I downed the last of my coffee, stepped into the smoky heat, and jogged over, willing my body to wake the rest of the way up. At first Rafe didn't see me, gazing as he was into the smoke-tinged blue, but when I called his name he turned. I waited for the broad grin that said you were the best thing he'd seen all day, except for maybe his wife on the lucky mornings he opened his eyes at home. It didn't come.

"What's with you? Didn't get your Wheaties this morning?"

One corner of his mouth pulled up, unconvincingly. "Nah. Tired. Didn't sleep worth shit."

"Yeah. Same here."

Was it a look in my eye, or the way I hitched up my jeans? Who knows, but like that he was on to me. "Young Will. Don't tell me you had company."

I ducked my head. "Might've."

"Jumpin' Jesus, boy. You're gonna wear it off you keep at it like that." He shook his shaggy head. "Gonna get yourself in trouble one day."

"Nah. I'm always protected."

"That's not the kind of trouble I'm talking about." He trailed off, scanning the sky again. He was there but not there, it seemed, his mind on something else. Probably the intense day we had ahead.

"I'm always a hundred percent upfront," I said. "They know it's just for fun, no getting serious. Not till I'm an old guy like you." I elbowed him, hoping to provoke the grin.

He frowned. Something was eating him for sure, but it was too good a morning to go digging into anyone's bad mood. Whether it was the afterglow of long-legged Gracie or the certainty that we were going to tame this fucking fire, I was pumped and ready to roll. So we compared notes on what lay ahead: the wind, the weather, which direction the fire was headed, and our aircraft, which despite their advanced age and peculiarities we loved like the memory of our first girlfriends. Rafe still seemed out of sorts — nothing major, just a few beats behind. Lost in his thoughts maybe. Or, like he said, tired. We were all tired.

But when it came time he clapped my shoulder twice for good luck, our decade-long ritual before every flight, his broad hand as powerful as always.

"Gonna treat us to a bull's eye today?" I asked.

"Ah, William. You're the finest kind." Seeing my puzzled expression, he shrugged. "Something my father used to say." He hesitated and I thought there'd be more, but instead – finally – he grinned. It was like the sun breaking. It told me everything would be fine.

I turned away and trotted off to my plane, moving smoothly now. Oiled up. Ready to go.

Next came the walkaround to make sure my well-worn Aerostar was shipshape. Ferrari of the skies, the Aerostar's sometimes called, and the reputation is well earned. A Ferrari, even a beat-up one, is in a class of its own. Partway through my inspection Ernie showed up with a rag and started cleaning the windshield and the props, rubbing off yesterday's insect guts. "What's the last thing to go through a bug's mind before he dies?" he asked. I waited obligingly. "His ass!" It was a joke he'd told a dozen times before, but it made him cackle merrily just the same.

The sun was searing now. By the time I finished the walkaround my hairline dripped with sweat. My little speedster looked as good as it ever does in the middle of action, and one of the mechanics had fuelled it up earlier so we were set to go. By the time Ernie and I got the thumbs-up to climb into the cockpit, my favourite white shirt, the cotton worn so thin you could see through it, was stuck to my back and soaked through the pits.

"Gonna be another scorcher," Ernie said as he wiped his forehead. "Good day for a few cold ones, eh?"

The question was purely rhetorical, what with Ernie being a tee-totaller and beer like all other alcohol being strictly off limits for us pilots. For days we'd been alternating between yellow and red alert, meaning ready to fly in either half an hour or five minutes. Twelve hours bottle to throttle is a rule you break only if you're looking for a career change. Sometimes I wonder if local iced tea sales spike whenever a wildfire brings out the air crews.

Ernie and I taxied out, made the usual radio calls, and took off. As we banked toward the fire, I remember wondering how many more times we'd have to do this. It was our fourth straight day in the Cariboo, and even though we'd wrestled countless blazes under control, new ones kept springing up. It was one of the sprung-up ones we were off to now. It hadn't started crowning yet, and a good thing too. When a fire starts jumping treetop to treetop, it's moved from a walk to a sprint and you've gotta race like stink to catch it. We definitely wanted it in the walking stage.

I remember how, as we came up on our coordinates, the smoke billowed up from below, a thick and suffocating mass that you'd swear no living thing could survive, and I guess not many can. We did a quick flyover to get a feel for what we were up against, then a second, slower pass so Ernie could do his assessment. When he was ready he radioed Rafe in that unhurried drawl you might mistake for uncertainty if you didn't know Ernie was the best air attack officer in the province. Once Rafe had positioned his Tracker over us we did the dummy run, tracing the exact circuit he needed to fly. Then we waited for the Tracker to descend and Rafe's drops to start. It wouldn't be long.

Sure enough, in a minute or two there he was. For me, watching Rafe come in over a fire was like feeling his hand clap my shoulder. It meant we had it covered, that even the hungriest blaze would soon be tamed. Rafe Mackie was our best tanker pilot, fast, confident, always accurate, so he was often first up in the rotation.

I remember, too, what Ernie said as the Tracker closed in on the tall stand of trees: "Here we go. Stunt time again."

Ernie was right. Rafe was coming in awfully low, so low that we both knew what was up next. It was a game he played after he'd had a couple of stellar days in a row, days when every drop was a bull's eye and his plane could no more resist his command than his fingers could ignore a mosquito bite. Never content with the simple path, or the everyday riskiness of what we do for a living, Rafe was going to dance with the treetops: swoop in just close enough for a kiss, then pull up at the last minute.

We waited, ready for his genius move.

He closed the distance. A bit more, then a bit more. He didn't pull up.

"Show-off," muttered Ernie.

A couple more seconds. Still he didn't pull up.

Ernie let out a long exhale.

As the gap between the tanker and the treetops narrowed, I remember how my stomach churned from the large black coffee I'd tossed back. For a second I thought I might puke. I swallowed hard to keep it down. Goddamned gut — always ahead of my dumb-ass brain. Somehow it knew the ending when I wasn't even sure yet what had started.

"Holy shit," breathed Ernie.

What I remember then is the cold. It came on fast, like I'd stepped into a meat locker. In spite of the blistering sun and the waves of heat coming off Ernie, I shivered.

I remember Ernie's voice floating over us in the cockpit. "Fuck, fuck, fuck" was all he said, over and over, the words low and dropping lower until they disappeared under the noise of the engines.

That's the end, I tell her. That's all I remember.

Are you sure? she asks. There's no more?

I'm sure.

It's important to be truthful, I've always believed that. The truth is, there's other stuff I could tell her. About what I saw and felt. About how my throat burned with acid, and how Ernie at the last second screamed like a trapped animal. But it's none of her business, that stuff. It's too much. It belongs to me, and to Ernie too. Not some stranger.

I could also tell her, but I don't, that even though I was right there when it happened, I never saw how Rafe Mackie went down. Because while Ernie sat beside me, sweating and screaming, I did the only thing that came naturally, the one thing you never do when you're in the cockpit of a small prop plane, not when you are the person flying it.

I shut my eyes.

PART ONE
CRASH

ONE

Eleven days after

THEY ALWAYS SAY HOW IMPORTANT it is to see someone at a time like this. By someone they mean a professional, a stranger who knows nothing about you but is going to forage around in your deepest thoughts anyway, and root out the ones that don't belong, and leave you refreshed and fixed. And empty.

What do I know? To me, during that first long week after the crash, the most therapeutic course of action was to hunker down, sleep a lot, and occasionally ask myself what the fuck happened out there.

Granted, there were signs this might not be the wisest approach. For one thing, sleep didn't come easy, though surely that's to be expected when your best friend and mentor smashes like an egg right in front of you. For another, I was behind in the personal hygiene department. I'd given up shaving and laundry, and daily showering seemed excessive now that I was avoiding the gym. I was also drinking every chance I could, and there were chances aplenty during the week-plus I was off work for what Jeff called recovery time. When beer failed I helped it along with whisky, and if that didn't do the job I rounded the edges with good old BC bud. I could get away with it, temporarily. It's not like Jeff was going to slap me with a urine test the minute I got back. Near the end of my restorative time off, I was partaking of this three-course meal every afternoon and topping it up through the evening. The toxic table d'hôte, my neighbour Melody called it.

In those first days, seeing a counsellor to talk about my air-quote feelings was the last thing I wanted. What *did* I want? Exactly one thing: to be left alone. So I let the calls go to voicemail, ignored the texts and emails, and basically rode it out.

God knows, there were enough people I was supposed to be in touch with. Like the crash investigators who showed up the afternoon it happened. Besides taking a stunned statement from me, they called a few times later to confirm some random detail or another, always reminding me that an in-depth interview would follow. There was also Jeff, who thank God was playing the hard-ass boss and keeping the media away from Ernie and me, for which he was rewarded with a full-time hounding himself. *How could this tragedy have happened? Did a mechanical problem contribute to this tragedy? What does this tragedy mean for your company?* For supposed specialists in communication, our intrepid reporters have a limited vocabulary, every question hanging off the same tired word.

Then there was Melody, my building's resident hippie chick, who floated onto her next-door balcony every time I ventured out on mine. Whether she was curious, lonely, or just lured by the waft of bud, I don't know, but I couldn't sit out there two minutes without her materializing and quizzing me through the railings. *Don't you ever work?* I wanted to ask. But I never did. I didn't want to forge any bonds that I'd have to escape from later. Our passing acquaintance, based on a few words in the lobby every week or two, and the one time I lent her my stepladder to clean cobwebs off her ceiling, was more than enough.

"You sure you're okay?" she asked for like the eightieth time on Tuesday evening, five days after the crash. "You haven't left your apartment since forever."

She leaned out, the balcony rail pressing into her middle. She had on this long skirt, a Stevie Nicks skirt my buddy Andy would call it, and her hair was like a clump of Spanish moss. She used to go around with it in dreadlocks until someone told her it was cultural appropriation.

"How would you know where I've been?"

"I know. Your front door. You always slam it when you leave, then you run down the stairs, boom, boom, boom. I haven't heard that for two days, could be three."

"Well. Maybe I'm quieter now."

"You're not."

This is why I steer clear of Melody. Besides being a granola girl, so instantly not my type, she's a know-it-all, an expert on the best way to do everything from knocking down spider webs to recycling flyers to locking a bike.

"You should try crystals," she said. "I got this awesome set down in Santa Fe last year? You can borrow them. I'll walk you through it."

Why hadn't I brought my book from inside? Even though I'd long ago lost the thread of the story, who'd been killed and who the suspects were, I'd have something to look at to signal how uninterested I was in this kooky girl and her magic rocks.

She continued, undaunted. "You're hurting, Will. What you've been through, it's so not normal. And what you're doing now … IMHO? It might feel good in the moment but it's only toxifying. It's just gonna make it worse. You know, long term."

IMHO? There was nothing humble about my neighbour's unrelenting opinions. How hard would it be to find a new apartment, I wondered idly. I still had a few days off. Then again, it was 2013. What were the chances of scoring another one-bedroom under fifteen hundred a month, pest-free, with parking, less than an hour's commute to the airport, preferably still in the Commercial Drive area?

Just thinking about it exhausted me, so I settled for re-entering the hovel I already had. "Later," I muttered as I shut the sliding door. Melody may have said more, but she was too late. I was in. Safe.

∧ ∨ ∧

WHAT IT BOILS DOWN TO is that in those first few days, I wasn't handling things all that well. What's the right way to behave, anyhow? It's not like I've got experience to go by. Sure, I lost my mom, but that was twenty years ago and we knew it was coming. Ernie, the only person

I could really compare notes with, got time off from the ministry of forests and went to the Okanagan to be with his people. For some kind of spiritual healing, smudging or something? I didn't ask, didn't want to intrude. Whatever his recovery looked like, I knew there would be no toxic table d'hôte in it. Ernie's one sober dude, has been all his life.

It was Jeff who kept pressing me to see someone. Eventually I started screening his calls too. At that point I was convinced that if one more person asked how I was doing, I would punch something – or worse, someone. But Jeff is nothing if not tenacious. A week after it all went down, he knocked on my door, loud. Twice. I didn't need x-ray vision to see Melody plastered against the membrane of wall separating our apartments. No one had visited me in ages. This would be a treat for her.

I let Jeff in and mumbled something about the place being a disaster. Luckily I was only on the appetizer (beer) course of the daily menu. Jeff stared pointedly at the half dozen empties on the coffee table. "You know your blood alcohol has to be zero before you're up in the air again. Zero."

Of course I knew. We all knew.

"Have a seat," I said, sweeping a tee-shirt, workout shorts, and an empty Doritos bag off the lone armchair. Underneath it all was my iPad – I'd been wondering where that was – which I tossed onto the coffee table. "It'll never be on the cover of *House and Garden*, but I call it home." I settled into the least cluttered corner of the sofa.

"Right." Jeff gingerly adjusted himself, his butt barely making contact with the worn seat, as if he were settling onto some squalid toilet instead of my expensive (at one time) recliner.

Posture is the first thing you notice about Jeff. The rumour around West Air is that he was forced to take ballet when he was a kid. There in my stale garbage heap of an apartment, after days of stressful media appearances and general crisis management, face haggard and eyes burning, he sat perfectly aligned, ankles crossed, like the headmaster of some upper-crust prep school. He looked around, his head turning levelly. "So this is how Vancouver's most eligible bachelors live."

"Ha ha. I warned you it wasn't pretty." I scratched at my facial growth, which was days beyond fashionable.

"Few would call you Prince Harry at the moment." As always, I squirmed at the nickname the guys had slapped on me a few years back. The resemblance is faint at best—I personally think the royal Harry looks kind of goofy—but when you're a ginger there's a limited pool of famous look-alikes out there.

"Seriously, you look like shit. And you smell like some kind of waste product too. Perhaps more than one." This was Jeff's idea of humour. "It's no way to tempt the ladies."

"Yeah, well I'm taking a break from the ladies right now."

"What about the rest of the human race? You planning to issue gas masks at the front door?"

"I'm taking a break from everyone."

In one smooth move Jeff rose and crossed to the sliding door, which was cracked open to the breeze. He stood there, his back to me. "There's someone out there," he said quietly. "On the balcony next door."

"That'd be Melody. Wearing a bunch of layers? Hair like a bird's nest?"

"More or less." Jeff stared out the door, erect as an officer of the Raj. "She's going back inside. I believe I startled her."

"I doubt it. She doesn't startle that easy."

Jeff turned to face me. "Will."

Here it comes, I thought. No more chit-chat.

"This accident has shocked us all, but you and Ernie, you've been hit the hardest." He resumed his perch on the recliner. "Witnessing such a tragedy, well, it's impossible to know how that might affect a person. It's regrettable when such a tragedy occurs, and I will call upon all possible resources to help you overcome the challenges ..." He must have heard himself uttering media-speak because he gave his head a shake. "Look, I know how close you and Rafe were. You worked together so well, and so long. But you won't pick up the phone, no one's seen you since the accident, you didn't even show up at the funeral yesterday. It's like you've vanished, and people are worried about you. *I'm* worried about you. I think you should start seeing someone."

"Impossible. I have my commitment-free bachelor reputation to protect."

"You know what I mean."

I played with the TV remote, pushing the illuminate button, waiting for the lit-up controls to go dark again, repeating the sequence. "Fuck," I said eventually.

"There's a counsellor we bring in for this sort of thing. You should call her."

He nudged a business card onto the coffee table, next to the foothills of paperbacks, flyers, takeout containers, empty beer cans, and several — Jesus, *five?* — balled-up socks, then pinched it back between his fingertips and brought it to where I sat. "Here, take it." He bent over me while still somehow giving the impression of standing perfectly straight.

They say the boss is always right. I took it.

∧ ∨ ∧

THAT'S WHY I SPENT lunch hour today, my first day back at West Air headquarters, where I'm basically quarantined for a week or two until I'm deemed fit for the skies, staring down a yellow file folder instead of, say, a toasted chicken wrap. The folder sat neatly aligned and, interestingly, never opened in front of The Counsellor, an earnest-looking lady who couldn't have been anything but a therapist with her thick-rimmed glasses, artsy scarf, and head cocked at an "I'm concerned" angle every time she asked me a question. And asking is all she did, for one hour minus a lot of silence. The answers were supposed to be my job.

It was a job at which I sucked, to put it mildly. She kept prodding me to describe my feelings, but I had nothing for her. I could describe the day's events, which I did, but every time I tried to focus on how I felt, I got stuck on how good a pilot Rafe was and how what happened, his plane dipping lower and lower and then just plummeting, makes no sense at all. If instead of digging inside myself I tried to imagine other people, like Sharon, who must be truly falling apart, my thoughts just skated away.

It's been like that since it happened. Whenever I replay the accident or the hours leading up to it, the minute I get to the Tracker closing in on the treetops, the video stops. My mind jumps away and turns to other things.

It's exactly what happened during exams in high school, and later university, especially if essay answers were involved. I'd sit there checking my watch and telling myself, as it got later and later, that I had to concentrate, I had to get to the heart of the question, I couldn't afford to think around the edges anymore. Then I'd zone out. Ten minutes later I'd come to, look at my watch, lecture myself again but get nowhere. Finally, in the last fifteen minutes I'd write a few paragraphs in a big burst, whatever came to mind, usually an incoherent bunch of facts with nothing to tie them together. I was a straight-C student in every subject except math and English, and the only thing that kept me from the Ds I deserved was my "inexplicably perfect," to quote my history prof, grammar and spelling. For that I thank my mom, who was a translator, and my dad, who's an electrician but reads anything between covers, even the dictionary. It was only genes and a house full of books that squeaked me through two years of post-secondary before I chucked it for good.

It should've been a hard decision, leaving the BA program halfway through, but it wasn't. As second year ended, this profound restlessness came over me. It was a perfect April afternoon, the day before my last exam, when I realized what the unsettled feeling meant.

I'd just had lunch on the beach at English Bay with my buddy Andy, a foot-long turkey bacon with everything from Subway and a cold root beer. In those days I ate the same lunch at least three times a week. I still order it now and then, a nostalgia thing. We were sitting, our backs against one of the driftwood logs that line the sand, our stomachs bulging like bellows. I belched, a loud, fragrant one. Andy, a hard-working Scottish Presbyterian not to be outdone in any endeavour, let rip a quieter but riper fart.

"Jesus," I said. "What are you, like, twelve?"

"You started it." He grinned proudly, as a guy will when engulfed in a stench of his own making.

"You're gonna gross out any girl who walks by. You're like a rancid hex."

"Naw. I'll say it was you."

He would too, and the kicker is, the girl would believe him. One look at Andy's light blue eyes, which he'd fasten on her as if oblivious to every other distraction, one glance at his chiselled face and wavy blond hair, his six-pack artfully enhanced by a skin-tight tee-shirt (the fart having conveniently deflated his stomach), and she'd believe every fictional syllable that spewed from the guy's mouth. As long as I've known him, Andy has gotten away with the most outrageous lies and the most transparent pick-up lines, seriously lame shit like *Wait, you're her, the girl from my dream last night* or *I'm leaving for two months' climbing in the Himalayas – I would love someone to come back for.* Or my personal favourite, spoken to me or whichever other guy he was with: *Will, call 911 because my heart just got stolen.* Words that would earn the rest of us anything from a bitter smirk to a slap across the face would get Andy laid within the day. I witnessed his technique time after time and didn't learn a thing from it – another missed opportunity in a youth of wasted education.

That afternoon, as the sun shone and Andy's fart slipped out to sea, for the first time in weeks I felt drowsily contented. I closed my eyes and imagined days of this: lounging on the sand, smelling the salt breeze, waiting for the right girl to pass by on her run along the Seawall. Her long hair would fly, she'd glow with vanilla-scented perspiration, she would notice the intriguingly laid-back, lightly freckled guy beside the god that was Andy. And suddenly I knew. I could not squander another year in classrooms and auditoriums, bathed in fluorescent light and the B.O. of liberal arts misfits.

"I'm quitting," I announced. The sun on my face felt glorious.

"Huh?"

"University. I'm quitting. Tomorrow's my last exam and after that I'm done. I'm not going back in the fall."

Andy sat up and trained his piercing gaze on me. I sensed a deeply genetic work ethic stir inside him. "Quitting? You can't quit."

"I can."

"But you've done two years. You're halfway there. You can't quit now. You've gotta finish."

"Why?"

"What do you mean, why? Because you've gotta *finish*."

"What's the point of finishing a thing if you're not getting anything out of it? I'm only in school because my dad made me."

Andy shook his head. "Quitting. It's so ... dumb. It's weak." He punched my arm. "C'mon, you're not that guy. You're not some slacker who takes the easy way out. You, like, *care* about stuff and shit."

I flicked sand on top of a tiny crab shell beside me, covering it in a crumbly drift. "It's not the easy way out. I'm gonna catch holy hell. My dad'll stop talking to me for a week or two, and the guilt trip will last all summer. Believe me, there's nothing easy about it. I just don't want to be a student anymore." Once the crab shell was buried, I smoothed the sand over it, erasing all signs that it had ever been there. "I want to fly."

"You already fly," said Andy. It was true. I got my private pilot's licence when I was sixteen.

"I mean for a living. Full-time."

Andy went quiet. We looked out at the grey-blue bay studded with white sailboats, the occasional kayak skimming along. It was the kind of breezy, clear afternoon the weather gods concoct just often enough to keep us in love with our soggy city. Overhead a Beaver thrummed into view, its chug-chug-chug filling the sky as it shuttled commuters across the Georgia Strait to Vancouver Island. I pictured myself in the cockpit, wearing the crisp white shirt, making the radio calls. Why not? I had tons of time now to get my floatplane endorsement.

After some minutes of gazing at the horizon, the mountains of far-off Vancouver Island tracing a humpbacked line in the sky, Andy turned back to me. He nodded thoughtfully.

"I get it," he said. "You want more pussy."

TWO

July

"MEDIA TRAINING?" Nathalie slammed a stack of files onto her desk. "Fuck that noise, I'm not going. Look at all the records I've gotta go through. Plus I'm waiting to hear from the coroner. He promised me the preliminary report from the pathologist this afternoon. And the GPS analysis could come in anytime. I'm not wasting an afternoon in the boardroom listening to some suited-up sleazebag tell us how to dodge reporters' questions and look the public in the eye while telling them fuck all."

"Nonetheless, methinks you must go." Lyndon leaned against the flimsy fabric-covered divider that passed for an office wall in the space-and cash-strapped world of the Canadian government. He peered down at his petite colleague, nearly a foot shorter even in high-heeled boots. "It's part of the regional training plan. We have to go. You know that."

"And *you* know I've got a rich helicopter pilot and his new wife dead, journalists crawling up my ass, family members to meet next week, and no clue what happened. I don't give a flying fuck about the regional training plan. Why doesn't Mr. Hugo Boss from Ottawa make himself useful and go deal with the media for us? That'd be a lot better use of the taxpayers' money than another PowerPoint nap in the boardroom."

"Nathalie Girard, the people's watchdog." Lyndon smirked. "Not a single one of us wants to go to this, but if you play truant Tucker will march over here and haul you in, and make a spectacle of it too. You know how he is."

"Tucker the Fucker. Then I won't be here to haul." Nathalie gathered up the files and slung her laptop case over her shoulder. "You do not know where I am."

"Fine, but this I do know: shit shall come your way if you are not in that boardroom. If not from Tucker, then from head office."

Nathalie tossed her dark curls. "Oh, spare me. Head office is too busy writing pointless emails and organizing retirement dinners to pay attention to what we actually do out in the regions." She grabbed her keys. "I've got my cell. You can always call if anything important comes up."

"Have it your way, mam'selle." Lyndon gave her a shallow bow before sauntering off, his mannerisms like his speech accented by his abiding love of choir and sherry, or so she presumed.

After a quick glance to make sure Tucker was nowhere in sight, Nathalie scooted up the hall, received the daily squint of disapproval from Luanne, the unibrowed receptionist, and crossed the parking lot as fast as her high heels would take her. Moments later she nosed her small blue Miata out of the parking lot and into the sun-washed street. A single finger-push and the roof opened to a breeze that cooled her cheeks and flew her hair like a pennant. It had taken her years to save for and track down a hard-top convertible Miata, the more common soft-top a ridiculous choice for the rainforest that was Vancouver, and she drove with the top down whenever she could.

Zipping in and out of lanes, putting every slowpoke in her rear-view mirror, Nathalie sped toward the place she always went at times like this, when the office drudgery or frenzy wore her nerves and kept her from concentrating. She thought of it as her secret workspace, the soaring, atrium-like lobby of the aerospace building at the British Columbia Institute of Technology. BCIT was not her alma mater. That was SAIT, in Calgary, which had generously overlooked her math and physics grades and welcomed her into the aircraft maintenance engineering program seventeen years ago, when they were bending over backward to recruit women. But BCIT felt familiar just the same, all those AME and other aviation students counting down the months till they could enter the real world of flight, the world she now called her own. Her Transportation Safety Board pass entitled her to free parking, and once inside the high-ceilinged common area she always found a spot she could make her own. With her Starbucks travel mug, her diminutive frame, and her casual Gap wardrobe, she was all but invisible to the students and instructors who crisscrossed the space, just another technical geek in their midst.

After snagging a bench seat beside the giant bank of windows, Nathalie opened her laptop and felt the world fall away. The screen played a slideshow of stills from her latest crash, a Robinson R22 helicopter that had gone down three days earlier, unwitnessed, in the Coquihalla Canyon. With it went a newly married couple en route home to Vancouver after a week's honeymoon in Kelowna: the husband a wealthy sixty-four-year-old who'd been flying since his twenties, owner of a gated one-acre compound on the West Vancouver mountainside; the wife a twenty-eight-year-old personal trainer whom he'd met in Hawaii and whom he married, Nathalie would bet, as soon as he'd tucked his dick back in his pants and had the pre-nup drafted, reviewed, inked, and notarized — not that the courtship timeline was part of the evidence gathered so far. And who knew? Maybe it was true love. Just because the lithe, tanned blonde could have stepped off the cover of *Trophy Bride Quarterly*, just because she was six months younger than the pilot's oldest daughter, just because she was promoted to wife number four after a stint as fiancée number six — none of that proved that the pilot, James Stanhope III, was shallow or easily infatuated. Maybe he had an unusual capacity for love. Maybe he was the one heartlessly tossed aside at the end of each failed relationship. The only thing Nathalie knew for sure was that he was smart with his money. How else could one man afford four wives?

Don't speak ill of the dead, Scrapper, came her grandmother's voice, *or they'll make ill for you.*

Yes, Mémère, she murmured. She refocused on the photos, willing them to tell her something, anything, about why this helicopter with a long-time pilot at the controls abruptly fell from the sky, slammed into the mountainside, and exploded, the resulting debris field covering hundreds of metres of sloped terrain. For one full day Nathalie and a colleague had combed the area, fighting to stand upright on the steep-sided ground, plucking rotor blades from the salal and engine components from the trees. The newlyweds were similarly scattered, thanks in part to the impact and in part to the wolves and foxes, often the first responders at a wilderness crash. It took hours before the coroner and two grey-faced RCMP rookies finally zipped the body bags and airlifted out the newly wedded remains.

It's got to be mechanical. Nathalie studied the close-ups of the buckled wreckage, so much aluminum foil crushed in the fist of fate. No way was it weather, the usual culprit in the famously windy, socked-in Coquihalla. The day of the accident was still and cloudless, hot but not too hot, perfect for flying. The crash happened just before noon, so they weren't heading into the sun. Stanhope had gassed up before leaving Kelowna and was airborne only an hour before crashing, so he hadn't run out of fuel. There was no other air traffic in the vicinity and, given their flight path directly above the canyon, no terrain or other obstacles in the way. Was it a medical event? Heart attack or stroke topped the list whenever you got an older pilot plus sudden loss of control, but in this case a health emergency seemed unlikely. Stanhope's last checkup, two months ago, depicted a man in top shape: blood pressure normal, heart rate excellent, weight ten pounds less than at his last exam — one of the many benefits of screwing a twenty-something personal trainer, no doubt. The guy had no medical conditions or risk factors of any kind. Which left mechanical.

"Nat?"

The deep voice, right behind her, made her jump. Instinctively she shut her laptop, heeding years of privacy training, and twisted around.

"Nathalie Girard. It *is* you. I'd know that hair anywhere."

"Jake?" Her pulse revved. "Holy shit. This is a surprise." Jake Behrend. She hadn't laid eyes on him since AME school. "What are you doing here?"

"Job interview." He crossed to the bench seat directly across from her. "I'm teaching these days. Started a few years ago. Got my first gig at SAIT, actually. You'd hardly recognize it now, it's expanded like crazy. Anyhow, I heard they're looking for a full-time instructor here, someone in structures, so I figured what the hell, throw my hat in the ring."

"Structures, huh? The tough stuff." He'd aged remarkably well. Hair a little thin on top, a touch of grey at the sides, but no flesh hanging over his belt. Probably still played hockey; he was religious about not missing a game back then. Still, the first thing you noticed, the sight you had to make yourself stop staring at, was that face. Hot damn, Jake Behrend, the original stud. Years later and still a specimen.

"I kind of fell into structures after we graduated," he was saying. "It wasn't the plan. Avionics looked better back then. But you go where life takes you, right?" He leaned forward over the low table that separated them, and Nathalie's insides liquefied as that face neared, rugged and tanned, its impossibly perfect angles sidelit by the tall windows. It was the kind of face you saw in celebrity pics, not real life.

"So where'd you end up?" he asked. "Still in aviation I'm guessing, if you're here."

"Hell yeah. I didn't slog through two years of training with all you shitheads just to leave the field." She could see, as if it sat on the table between them, their class photo, thirty-seven fresh-faced AME grads, herself and the other two women bunched like flowers in the middle. She wore a calf-length summer dress from Sears that she'd bought with a money order from her grandmother. *The strongest woman fits best the clothes*, Mémère had said on the phone, another in her long line of faintly accented, usually cryptic sayings. During the same call, Mémère reminded Nathalie that the strongest woman did things alone. Nathalie understood. Her grandmother could not afford both a dress and a trip to Calgary for the ceremony.

"You haven't changed a bit, Nat. Still tough as nails."

No one called her Nat — she loathed the bug-like syllable — yet Jake always had. She let him get away with it because he was such a damned stud. And *tough as nails* — that was what he said every time he asked her out and she said no. He was dogged back then, but so was she. Not once did she cave, not even when her saliva ran with wanting him.

It was hard enough to convince the students and instructors – the *male* students and instructors – that you could do the work, could be one of the guys as everyone put it, without shredding your reputation by dating one of them.

Falling into her old approach, she ignored Jake's teasing. "I'm with the TSB now." She couldn't mask the pride in her voice. "Technical investigator for the past six years. I was just running through photos of that R22 crash the other day in the Coquihalla."

"Well, didn't you win the prize. I thought you had to be a fifty-something commercial pilot on the long glide to retirement to get on at the TSB."

Nathalie shook her head. "It's true I'm the youngest, at least in our region, but only half the investigators are pilots. The others are regular-joe AMEs like us. Most crashes we team up, a pilot to look into human error, fatigue, decision-making, the operational stuff, and an AME for the technical and maintenance side."

"So how'd you snag a cushy government job?"

Nathalie gave him the quick version: hired out of SAIT by Howe Sound Air, a small carrier in Squamish where no one seemed fazed by a female apprentice and where she mostly serviced floatplanes; then four years later an offer from Mainland Air, a bigger company at Vancouver's south terminal, where she expanded into helicopters and made crew chief three years in.

"Nice going," said Jake. "Not too many crew chiefs who don't come with smelly armpits and three days' growth."

"You're telling me. I was the first female chief ever at Mainland. Guess they forgot to put stubble and stink in the requirements." She opted not to add that once the congratulations had died down, word went around that the company had pocketed a nice chunk of change from an employment equity program that placed women in male-dominated trades. She had shut her ears to the rumour, refusing to let its implication, that she was anything less than qualified, get to her. Crew chief was a plum job no matter how you landed it, and for three years she demanded meticulous work, favoured no one, took no shit, and stayed out of trouble.

And got restless. Once the novelty of promotion wore off, it dawned on her that she'd pretty much reached the pinnacle of her trade. Unless some miracle occurred and she made director of maintenance, she'd stay crew chief all her life: draw a middle-income paycheque, endure the deprivations of shift work, hopefully fend off injury and arthritis, and eventually, if she was lucky and the company didn't go belly up, retire with a small pension that she'd have to supplement should she crave the occasional T-bone. Unless she set up her own maintenance company, a venture she had neither the stomach for nor the bankroll, there was nowhere else to go. She was energetic and successful, and she was bored.

Then she met Lyndon Johnson, the Pres, as he was known. He showed up at Mainland Air one morning, flashing his TSB card, to interview a recently arrived AME whose former employer had lost a Beaver floatplane in a rainstorm. The new hire, who'd been shaken for days after hearing about the accident, so distracted that Nathalie pulled him off duty, asked her to sit in on the interview. From the moment Lyndon started to draw out the nervous mechanic, taking him step by step through the maintenance he'd done before the crash, asking for explanations of technical terms — even though, she later discovered, Lyndon was a licensed AME himself and knew every tool and procedure — Nathalie realized that this was what she wanted to do.

Two weeks later, after the mechanic was cleared of any wrongdoing, she invited Lyndon for coffee, flirted enough to prime the pump, and collected every detail she could. What qualifications did she need, how would she apply, what should her résumé emphasize, how could she stand out among the dozens of hopefuls?

Once again, as Mémère used to say, it was good to wear a dress. The feds were pushing to recruit more women and visible minorities for jobs traditionally held by white men, and the Transportation Safety Board was high on the list of agencies in need of more diversity. After a night course on report writing, a skill Lyndon warned her she'd be tested on, Nathalie found herself shortlisted, interviewed, examined, and hired inside of two years — record time, sniffed Lyndon, who'd spent nearly half a decade pestering the regional manager to even review his application.

And once again Nathalie found herself the lone woman in an office of men. Fortunately the TSB guys welcomed her politely, domesticated as they were by wives and daughters and government harassment policies. They helped her as she felt her way into the job. They gave her space when she went silent on seeing her first dead bodies, then mocked her mercilessly about it afterwards. They taught her tricks for assessing cockpit gauges and GPS tracks, and strike patterns in the ground and trees. They shared accounts of past accidents and theories about current ones. Nathalie countered with a mix of tomboy toughness and carefully doled out feminine wiles. She took criticism without complaint, teased the guys as much as they made fun of her, laughed at their dirty jokes and told a few of her own, tossed her curly black hair and made liberal use of heels. Now, six years later, she knew the ropes and could relax a little. She knew what she was doing, enough that the TSB had added *senior* in front of *investigator* on her business card.

Most of the time she knew what she was doing. As always, whenever the question of competence came up, she felt the Cessna 172 investigation knife her as sharply as it did a year ago when the whole debacle unfolded.

None of this would she share with Jake. "I got the TSB job the same month I turned thirty" was all she said. "Best birthday present ever."

"No kidding. Great pay, fat pension, no more nightmares that you forgot to check some belt on a plane that's flying out in the morning." Jake rubbed the back of his head. His hair, cropped short and slightly gelled, was jet black apart from the greying temples. "Did you get those bad dreams in your overalls days?"

"Didn't we all?"

"Every AME I know. That's why I got into teaching. That, and my wife hinted as how it'd be nice to get the grease out from under my nails before we had a baby."

Nathalie sighed inwardly and took the cue. "You've got kids?" She prayed for a short answer.

"Two girls, seven and ten. My sweethearts." He reached for his back pocket.

She stood up. "Listen, would you wait here a sec and watch my stuff? I need another coffee." After two steps she turned around. "Can I get you anything?"

"Nah, I'm good."

How many times had she made a move like this to fend off the litany of descriptions, recollections, and vomit-making stories about other people's kids? Lately she'd given up all pretense of politeness. Why not? How polite were *they*, rambling on about babies and toddlers and teens she knew nothing about and cared nothing for. It always went like that. Get people onto the subject of their sweet little tykes and that was it. They'd be at it, like a used-car dealer hell-bent on selling you something, anything, until they saw the back of your head.

When she returned from the cafeteria, travel mug freshly filled, Jake stood. "My interview. I gotta go." He stepped in and gave her an awkward hug. He wasn't much taller than she, Nathalie remembered as they came together. For a moment all she was aware of was hard, compact muscle and the scent of a soap not her own.

Jake released her but held her at arm's length. "Great to run into you, Nat." He eyed her up and down. "You sure look good. Haven't changed a bit. If I said pretty please, would you show me around Vancouver tonight? My flight home's not till noon tomorrow."

Nathalie pulled away and laughed. "You haven't changed a bit either. Still sniffing where your nose doesn't belong."

"Come on. I don't see any wedding ring."

She looked pointedly at his hand. "I do."

"We have an arrangement. What I do on the road is my own business."

"Yeah, well I have an arrangement too. Don't fuck where you work."

Jake's smile was even and dazzling, his eyes snappy with banter. "Come on, Nat. After all these years? It's not like we're in the same office. We're not even in the same province. Give a guy a break."

"Safe flight home."

He shook his head, resigned. "Tough as nails, Nathalie Girard. You always were." He gave her shoulder a final squeeze. "Good luck with the investigation. Maybe I'll see you around."

As Jake disappeared into the cavernous building behind her, Nathalie sat down, her body zinging, her resolve crumbling. Good thing he left when he did, the cocky bastard. Fifteen years since she'd laid eyes on the guy and still he got to her. Briefly she wondered if she should have capitulated when they were both single, but it wasn't worth dwelling on. When she'd started AME school she made a solemn promise to herself, and her grandmother, not to get involved with anyone there. *Time enough for the boys after you finish with the college,* Mémère said, her powdered jowls set firm. *They come sniffing around, you don't have to let them lick, you get my point?* Nathalie got it. Not one to mince words, her grandmother.

Willing her hormones to subside, Nathalie opened her laptop and wrenched her attention back to the R22 photos. She clicked on an image of James Stanhope, like Jake a rugged Eddie Bauer type, virile and carefree. Yet one morning, his new bride by his side, something went horribly wrong, an error or a misjudgment or a moment of bad luck that in an eyeblink rubbed out his joyous future.

It's got to be mechanical. She knew it, felt it in her gut. Not that knowing narrowed the range of possible causes much. She frowned as she clicked through the photos, urging them to tell her something, to betray some clue that would crack the case, even though that almost never happened, not in the world of accident investigation. The story wouldn't start coming together until she'd paged through the maintenance logs. Was the fuel screen recently cleaned? The engine overhauled? Annual inspection done on time? She'd check for service bulletins and airworthiness directives on the ten-year-old helicopter and see whether the required refitting was done. With luck the wreck would give up some secrets during the engine teardown, a procedure whose name was in this case a dark joke, the engine already torn into more pieces than she could count. Still, the exercise would force her to examine every component and to separate the damage caused by the crash from maybe, just maybe, some flaw that existed before the flight.

What happened to you? Nathalie silently asked James Stanhope, zooming in on his confident profile. *What chain of events lined up to snuff out your life, poof, like that?*

And where was the pathologist's report that the coroner had promised? She rechecked her email but found nothing, just a long-winded invitation, first in French and then in English, to a potluck lunch in Ottawa (sure, it's only five thousand kilometres away, I'll be right over) and a terse one-liner from Tucker asking why she wasn't at the training.

Her phone rang. The display showed it was Tucker, not the first time her prescient manager had called while she was reading an email from him. She debated letting it go to voicemail, then thought again. Better catch the shit straight on.

"Hey," she answered. "Sorry I skipped out on training, but I've got so much to do on this R22 crash what with the media and —"

"Nathalie."

"No, really. I'll get one of the guys to fill me in on what I missed, I promise. I'll read the manual or the slides or whatever got handed out, I'll take a test after if you want —"

"Nathalie, stop. Listen to me." Tucker paused. Great. What else could she be in trouble for?

He cleared his throat. "There's been another crash. We just got word. It happened an hour ago, that forest fire near Quesnel. An air tanker went down. A Tracker."

"You need me to go?" With her free hand, she shut the laptop and set it on the table in front of her. "I can be ready in an hour, my gear's all —"

"Nathalie, no. No." He paused. "It's Rafe."

Her elbow jerked and the travel mug spilled the last of its contents onto the table, spattering droplets onto her laptop. She watched the mess spread, unable to move.

"He's dead."

THREE

October

SHE STANDS BY THE WINDOW, staring out at the side yard where in a few months, January or February, the witch hazel will jeer at nature and push perfumed yellow blooms into a winter sky. How long has she been here? A few minutes? An hour? She looks around the kitchen, hoping for a clue. She came in here for something but can't remember what. A cup of tea? A tissue? An apple?

Retrace the steps that brought you here. Colleen shared this trick with her in the summer, when such moments occurred all the time, her feet taking her along a path her mind could not chart.

She was in the den, emailing Sheldon and Nancy that everything was fine, she wasn't selling the townhouse until spring, she couldn't spend Christmas with them in Halifax but what a thoughtful invitation.

Yes. Christmas.

She riffles through the stack of unopened mail and pulls out the brochure. "Cruising for Christmas" spans the cover in a baby-blue cursive that suggests teenage girls or fundamentalist Christians. She flips the pages and, seeing no evidence of pyjama parties or the Lord, settles into the wicker chair in the alcove to read.

No matter what the material — menus, mysteries, the latest *New York Times* bestseller, her secret baby books — the act of reading anchors her, gathers her in a bundle, a warm quilt around her shoulders. It is healing, she assures herself, to read so much. Reading will pull her through. Plus it is a duty, in a sense, to stay current in case she goes back to the library one day.

The cruise brochure offers not one Christmas but many. Christmas Aloha Style departs sunny Los Angeles for an unforgettable expedition through the exotic Hawaiian Islands. Christmas Fiesta will treat her to unlimited margaritas and guacamole as she explores the Mexican Riviera. Caribbean Christmas promises languid circles around the Bahamas, accompanied by the soft strains of a steel drum band.

Do people really do this? Sharon tries to imagine it: packing her bags, stepping aboard a floating hotel, mingling with strangers, disembarking when instructed in select port towns. She would need a second bathing suit, a pedicure, a bikini wax. A crash course in world events to prepare for small talk at the dinner table. And a lot of books. She could get some serious reading done on a cruise.

Unlikely as the whole enterprise seems, she knows people take such trips all the time. She need look no further than her own sister. Colleen was a convert from the moment a decade ago that she boarded a five-star Princess Line vessel destined for her own wedding in Barbados. The trip was Gord's idea. A golf pro thirteen years Colleen's senior, he had the nut-brown skin, etched lines, and frequent nakedness of a man at home in the open air. Colleen fit his lifestyle like a bill snugged inside a wallet, and now she lives for their twice-a-year voyages, dropping references to Martinique and Aruba the way others speak of the mall or their favourite brunch spot. Now her tanned arms and chest are a season or two away from leathery, her tennis whites and pastel sun visors billboards for the country club. Colleen has not just married Gord but merged with him, the pair as in love with their comforts and routines and the picture they make as they are with each other.

Sharon sets down the brochure and hugs her waist, fingertips sinking into the nubbly grey pile of the cardigan she reaches for every morning now that the weather has cooled. Where is the Widow's First Christmas cruise? The Bahamas for the Bereaved? Conspicuously, no single people of any variety grace the pages of her cruise pamphlets. There are only couples. White couples, straight couples, the occasional mixed-race couple. Couples playing shuffleboard, couples in evening dress, couples hand in hand on beaches and under palm trees and on wide open decks. A widow in such surroundings is unthinkable. She would cast a pall, her solitude a thick cloak that would smother any spark of merriment among her fellow passengers. *Widow's weeds* – the phrase suggests actual vines snaking up the sides of the gigantic ship, twining through portholes and over pool chairs, creeping over buffet tables and tennis courts, choking everything in their wake, pulling the ship and its carefree cargo slowly, relentlessly, to the ocean floor.

She stands up and again regards the witch hazel. Not a tree, really; a shrub. Rafe planted it in the spring of 2003, soon after they moved into the townhouse, declaring that they must add one bit of greenery to make the small yard their own. She had never heard of witch hazels, but Rafe came home from West Air one day intent on having one. "They flower in winter," he said. "Can you believe it? They give off this scent, like it's spring." That weekend he drove to a nursery in the Fraser Valley, chose a small specimen, and tamped it into their tiny plot the same day. Imagine, planting a shrub in early April, he had marvelled, proffering another benefit of west coast life for his reluctant wife to admire. You'd never dream of it in Toronto, where April and sometimes May could still bring snow.

What would Rafe say to these cruise flyers? She knows. He would snort and roll his eyes and ask how so many lazy slobs could be duped into forking over their savings to do a whole lot of nothing in captivity. It's not far off her own opinion, though she used to find herself mildly defending those who "choose to cruise," as Colleen puts it, partly to stand up for her sister, whom Rafe mocked too freely, and partly to remind Rafe, because he needed reminding, that his opinion was not the only one.

Outside the window the branches of the witch hazel sway, stirred by a breeze that, according to the weather channel, will build to a gale by afternoon. Another grey, miserable day in the unending series offered by this cheerless city. She cannot wait to leave, to go home to Toronto where she belongs. However, now is not the time. There is too much to work out first, not just about the summer but what led up to it. She must figure out the before of her life before she can begin the after.

The storm is gathering, but at least she has a to-do list, another strategy that Colleen urged and she adopted without protest, knowing that with her sister it's easier to relent. Dry cleaner, yoga, lunch with Rachel, library, farmers market, latte on the way home — each item laid out in a logical progression to get her out of the house, moving, interacting, to steer her gently but firmly away from grief.

Those were Colleen's goals. What her own might be Sharon cannot say, and finding herself unable to summon up a single authentic desire, she accepts her sister's. Is that why she is accumulating cruise brochures that she'd ordinarily recycle with the other junk mail? Now that her own life has vanished is she going to slip, unresisting, into the mould of her sister's? With Rafe no longer here to structure her days will she float off — literally — into a vast, timeless ocean?

The witch hazel sways more vigorously now. The storm is coming. There is some comfort in knowing she will complete every task on the day's list, that no wind or rain can shift her course.

Yet she wonders, as she has begun to do since Rafe's death: what would happen if she went off course? If she ignored the day's agenda? What if, and it is such a peculiar notion that she can scarcely articulate it, she simply stopped the errands, the routines, the lists? What would happen to her then? What, if anything, would be left?

FOUR

Twelve days after

"IF YOU CAN'T TALK about how you're feeling, then tell me how you met." Those were The Counsellor's instructions today after our second lunchtime session kicked off with another round of looming silence. Her voice stayed level and pleasant – they must practise that at therapist school – but the lines around her mouth hinted at exasperation. I stared at today's scarf, the colours more sedate than yesterday's. I'm not hiding anything, I wanted to tell her. I'm being as honest as I can. If I don't know how I feel, how can I say anything about it?

So I told her about meeting Rafe. I remembered the details more vividly than I'd have thought. Especially the car. As soon as I pulled into the West Air lot I saw it: a silver Honda S2000, top down, taunting the April rainclouds but giving me an eyeful of its sweet red-and-black leather interior. It was fresh from the showroom, the 2003 model built on the new AP2 chassis. Andy and I had been daring each other to take one for a test drive to see if the auto magazine hype was right.

I circled the car slowly, wondering who the lucky owner was. The vanity plate, FL1ER, didn't narrow it down any there at the hangar.

Inside the office, a knot of pilots had gathered up front, most of them holding coffee cups, all of them listening to Jeff, who was nodding toward a tall, thickset man I didn't recognize. "I tell him, 'You want challenging terrain? We can arrange that.' Now here he is. What do you say, Rafe? Ready for the mountains?"

"Let me at 'em," the big man said, rubbing his palms together. Jeff clapped his back, hard, and the new guy grinned so wide his eyes just about disappeared into the flesh around them. He surveyed the eager circle around him. "But I've got a lot to learn from the rest of you."

So. This was our new air tanker pilot, due to start next week when training began. He must've heard about the unofficial tradition of showing up a few days early to mainline caffeine and swap a season's worth of gossip.

I gave him a quick once-over: ruddy face, powerful torso, hands that dangled like boxer's gloves from wrists as big around as fir branches. FL1ER, my ass. Classic bully was my guess, athlete gone to seed who drinks too much and fucks around and is the hero of every flying story he tells, and he tells a lot. For him that car was about the impression it made, not about beauty or finesse or performance, and immediately I resented him for it. He didn't deserve that sweet little ride, the beefy, self-centred asshole.

I like to think I can size people up pretty well. From the get-go I can tell you what they're like at a party, how they react to stress, what kind of jokes and stories they'll tell, whether they're careful or sloppy, how they are with their dates and spouses. Yet on every count, especially the last one, my first impressions of Rafe were utterly wrong.

My reassessment started right away. I edged closer to the group while Rafe, at Jeff's urging, ran through his abbreviated résumé: flying since he was twenty-one, commercial licence at twenty-six, early career at Canadian Airlines, eight summers fighting wildfires in northern Ontario, first moonlighting during his regular job and then going full-time when Canadian got swallowed up by Air Canada. The more Jeff probed the more Rafe addressed his shoes, which he scuffed constantly, as if digging himself a trench in the floor. Maybe he wasn't as in love with himself as I thought he was.

As soon as Jeff paused, Rafe flipped the spotlight. "What about the rest of you? How long you all been at this gig?"

Everyone took a turn reciting his tally sheet, ranging from Bernard, an old-timer with twenty-eight years of bird dogging, to Simon, who'd come on as a tanker pilot three years ago. Despite my certainty that Rafe was a limelight hog, his body relaxed every second the attention was off him. When it came to me I admitted to being the newbie: two years as a part-time bird dog before being hired on for real this year. I glanced at Rafe. "That your Honda convertible outside?"

"So it is." His eyes sank again into the fleshy squint of a grin.

"Looks pretty new."

"Less than two weeks. Got it soon as I moved out here. Now that I'm in Lotus Land, no winter and all, I thought I might as well. You like it?"

"From what I've read, yeah. I've never been in one."

"We can change that." He turned to Jeff. "There's nothing official going on today, right?"

"Right."

"Then let's go, bird dog." Rafe tossed me his keys.

You can guess some of what came next. The car ... Jesus, I loved that car. I couldn't believe he would let me, a total stranger, drive it; I'd have been happy just to sit in it awhile. It handled like a dream, better than anything my sorry carcass had ever driven. At Rafe's suggestion I headed out to Highway 99 and let it rip, pushing it to 150, 160 K. That little honey never broke a sweat. Makes me shiver even now to remember it. The way it hugged my body, it felt like it was part of me. I only had to think a thing and the car would respond, instantly and effortlessly, like the lover you always dream of.

Being with Rafe, it turned out, was like driving the S2000. From the minute he jammed himself into the passenger's seat (I questioned why a burly guy would choose such a glove-tight vehicle until I hit third gear and all was explained) our conversation just happened, natural, flowing, fast. First we talked cars, then aircraft. By the time we stopped for coffee at the Blenz off Westminster Highway we'd exchanged the basic personal stats. Me: twenty-six, single, no serious girlfriend because why choose one if you can have many, no dog because it's wrong when you don't have a yard, Vancouver born and bred, wannabe surfer, lifetime snowboarder and hiker. Rafe: forty-four, married thirteen years (for freakin' ever, as he put it), no kids (though not for lack of trying, he said), grew up in Nova Scotia but spent most of his adult life in Toronto, into weightlifting (no shit), hated the snow so was thrilled to be in Vancouver.

"Yeah, but there's all the rain." I blew on the black coffee that had for ten minutes defied all laws of physics by never dropping below scalding, even at the outdoor table we were forced to sit at. The seats inside were fully occupied, a few by workers on break but most by the students who camp there all day with their books, devices, layers of clothing, cups of yogurt, and the occasional stuffed animal, texting, surfing the net, streaming, entertaining friends, and basically treating the café as their own personal dorm.

"Who cares?" said Rafe. "If it's not snow, I'm happy. There's no shovelling the rain."

"Shovelling snow's good for you. It's muscle work, like going to the gym."

"Christ, boy, spoken like a west coaster. You got no idea what it's like to creep home on a road that's scarcely been plowed, sniffing the arse of the car in front of you, after you been flying all day and at the gym after, only to find fifteen centimetres you gotta clear out of your driveway before she turns to sleet and the whole goddamn mess freezes in place."

"So get a snow blower."

"Snow blowers," he snorted. "They're for pussies and professors. If you're a man and not petrified of getting your hands dirty, you shovel your own goddamn snow. It's a point of honour. Ah Christ, I hated every second of it."

I pondered his explanation, in which lurked a puzzling contradiction I couldn't quite grasp. "Whatever," I said, taking another burning sip.

"This winter I'm gonna stay warm every night, eat supper, watch the news, heat things up a little with the missus. All that energy I'd spend shovelling I can put to good use. The *finest* use." He winked at me over the small metal table. "So you're not married. Ever live with anyone?"

"Nah. I like to keep my options open." I pried the plastic lid off my coffee cup and thought how my buddy Andy had nailed it all those years ago: flying gets you laid, a lot. You don't even have to dress up or really work for it. Someone mentions you're a pilot and suddenly there are women, plural, who want to know everything. What's it like to fly a plane? Do you ever get scared? Is it hard to work the controls? Isn't it dangerous, flying over forest fires? Aren't you afraid you're going to die? If you smile a lot, throw in a little sly humour, and wear short-sleeved shirts as much as possible, you're in. Honestly, that's all it takes. Some days you look at all the lonely guys who are just as fit as you, just as decent, with just as good a personality and paycheque, and it hardly seems fair.

"Understandable when you're a young fella like yourself," said Rafe. "I'm telling you, though, there's nothing like it. You come home after a couple weeks on call, draggin' your butt, pickled in smoke, and she's waiting for you, cold drinks in the fridge, clean sheets on the bed. Then before you know it, *you're* in the bed, a nice homecoming and all. I'm telling you, that's hard to beat."

Slowly I shook my head. "I can't see it, not for me. If you're happy, great. It's just ..." I flashed to the day I came home late from school, a few months after mom died, and found my dad on the kitchen floor, curled up in a ball in the dark, no lights on. He had my mom's rattiest old apron wrapped around his head. I left before he knew I was there. "It's not for me. Too much like serving a life sentence."

"True, your life's tied up once you get married. But not tied up like a prisoner's tied up. More like a present with a bow on top." Rafe glanced over at the parking lot, and I looked in time to see a long-haired girl in thigh-high boots slide into a black Lamborghini, flashing a tantalizing glimpse of the shadows beneath her short skirt.

"Jumpin' Jesus," Rafe said.

I chuckled. "Hong Kong's finest. Young, gorgeous, and loaded. Richmond's full of them."

Rafe stared as the girl draped herself over the driver, a guy in dark glasses who didn't even put down his phone, too cool to acknowledge his own arm candy.

"God, what is she? Like, fourteen?" I said.

Rafe turned back to me, his face gone dark. "Yeah. Fourteen going on twenty-four."

"See? You feel guilty just looking. That's what marriage does to you."

Rafe shook his head, stood up, and crushed his empty coffee cup with one hand. "Whaddya say we hit the road, bird dog." He overhanded the cup into the trash bin ten feet away. Bull's eye.

∧ ∨ ∧

AFTER THAT I GOT ACQUAINTED with Rafe pretty fast. He was easy to know, open and friendly. Far from being the self-obsessed superstar I'd pegged him for, he was a humble guy who spent more time drawing out others than talking about himself. That's a rare quality, almost unheard of among pilots.

During refresher training, even though Rafe mingled with the others, asked about their lives, and made them laugh, he mostly stuck around me. Jeff must've noticed because he paired us up for practice drops, me in the bird dog plane guiding Rafe in the tanker. Mind you, we were both new to West Air and without long-time flying partners, so maybe it was inevitable we'd form a team.

Being rookies, we got stuck with the oldest heaps in the hangar (the *vintage* models, Jeff insisted on calling them), the Piper Aerostar for me, the Grumman Turbo Tracker for Rafe. I'd logged some hours on the Aerostar over the past two years of part-time flying, and despite its age I found it an agile little plane, just what you want for scouting, flying in low for a look at the fire, then guiding the big tankers in for the drop. Rafe's Tracker, on the other hand, a surplus military plane from the fifties converted to turboprop firefighter in the eighties, was, to put it politely, an airborne slab of sidewalk, thick and heavy, gouged and scratched, stuffed to the nuts with clunky mechanical instruments and ancient gauges – everything his Honda S2000 wasn't. Our planes were so close to obsolete there weren't even simulators to train on like for the other aircraft. We had to fly for real. It was one more reason we became a duo.

Rafe took it in stride. The fact was, he had more fire experience than many at West Air, but he understood the pecking order. You earned your cred and graduated to better aircraft based on your time with the company. Gigs with other outfits—like Conair, our biggest competitor, where I'd racked up some hours—didn't count for much. Experience in other parts of the country, like Rafe's, was worth squat. No one could convince a western firefighter that other regions offered anything close to the technical challenges we faced here, with our treacherous cocktail of mountains, dry and windy desert, and weather that changes as quick as you can sneeze. Where else in Canada does the terrain, which is ordinarily the ground below you, rise right up to your flight altitude? Where else can a single lick of lightning tear through hectares of parched land the way it does in the BC Interior? The point is, Rafe, like me, was starting at square one that year, and he seemed okay with it.

Funny thing—if anyone had asked us back then whether we'd be flying the same planes now, ten years later, we'd have laughed till we pissed. Yet that's exactly what happened. My Aerostar's a no-brainer. It's a performer in spite of its age, and until West Air buys me a jet I won't get anything better. As for the Tracker, even though its life dragged on from middle-aged to decrepit, some part of it needing repair or adjustment after nearly every flight, Rafe not only tolerated the old clunker, he loved it. His loyalty was the force that kept that plane aloft, and the Tracker became an inseparable part of the legendary Rafe Mackie, bull's-eye king. Put the man and his plane side by side and you could see why: both of them hefty and overbuilt, highly experienced, worn around the edges but rock-solid all the way.

And now, gone. Both of them. Gone.

FIVE

A decade earlier

PEOPLE CALL IT LOTUS LAND, but Sharon never saw the appeal. The moment Rafe mentioned that West Air was searching for pilots, she felt perturbed. She was a Toronto girl, born and bred. Her whole family lived in the city, all her friends and co-workers too. Every summer her four closest friends from high school threw her a birthday party; some years it was brunch on a chic patio, some years a gourmet picnic in leafy High Park. Toronto boasted the country's best restaurants and theatres. It was the centre of art and fashion. It was New York with universal health care, Chicago without the crime. Who in their right mind would decamp more than four thousand kilometres to a city cleared out of a rainforest, barricaded from the rest of Canada by the Rocky Mountains, where the only thing higher than the cost of living was the average pot-smoking twenty-something?

"What does West Air have that you can't get at Thunderbird?" she asked Rafe one evening as they sat in the big Adirondack chairs, sipping decaf, wrapped in sweaters against the chilly October twilight. By then he'd worked Vancouver into the conversation enough that she knew the move was no idle fancy. "It's the same job. You're still fighting fires. It's the same terrible hours and mostly the same pay even though it costs so much more to live there."

"It's the flying." He leaned in, his face shadowed by twilight. "They don't get as many fires in BC as northern Ontario, but the ones they do get are in all kinds of terrain — mountains, valleys, desert, coast. Some of them get right near where people live, not like up north where the only thing you'll ever see move is a moose. You gotta get in there and hit fast before the fire spreads, and you got a lot of obstacles to watch for."

"So it's more dangerous."

Rafe was quiet. She knew he was thinking of how to say it. "It's harder, that's the thing. The flying's technical. Seat-of-your-pants stuff. The finest a pilot could hope for."

Gathering the collar of her sweater, Sharon took in their back-yard, the lawn thick green under a drift of autumn leaves. From the side flowerbed towered purple asters, their blooms a nostalgic nod to summer. She remembered kneeling in the rich topsoil three summers ago while Rafe was up north, patting the transplants in place, dreaming of colour that would last until fall when he'd be home again. She loved Toronto, loved their yard, loved everything about their house, a solid brick two-storey that Rafe had renovated over the years, replacing the kitchen, adding a powder room downstairs, building this deck they sat out on most non-winter evenings. They lived in a home and a city that her husband had always seemed grateful to return to. Now she wondered.

"Is this some kind of … midlife crisis?" It came out halting. "Do you need something, like … more thrills in your life?"

The breeze picked up and stirred the neighbour's big maple.

Rafe reached for her hand. "I love what I do, Sharon. You know that. But we all need to try new things, right? To stay fresh. Eight years I been at Thunderbird. It's too much of the same. Those fires up in the boreal, miles and miles of jack pine, after a while they all turn into the same damned fire. I could fly over one of them with my friggin eyes closed." He thumbed her palm, deep and gentle. "I like having my eyes open, you know? Actually think about what I'm doing. Besides, wouldn't you like to put the boot to winter?"

"They have winter in Vancouver. It's just rain instead of snow. People can't take it, everything grey and wet for months on end. They get depressed. That's what I hear, anyway."

The dark was coming on, their trim garden shed a mere outline at the rear of the yard. In the distance a siren wailed, a faraway crisis in a different neighbourhood. Here in their corner of the city, life was peaceful and still. Familiar. She liked the sameness of it and the certainty it brought.

She pulled her hand out of Rafe's and plunged it into her sweater pocket. "I don't understand why you'd want to leave all this. Our house, God, you've worked so hard on it. It's just the way we want it now. The deck, the yard — it's all perfect. And our friends are here, our family."

"It's not that I want to leave. But West Air's not gonna come here."

An evening bird brought forth a mournful note as they sat, a quiet married couple, dusk falling around their shoulders. Sharon bit her bottom lip. It was like coughing up a pebble to say it, but she had to. "Would it be different if we had kids?"

"Oh, honey." Rafe twisted toward her. "That's not it." He reached for her hair, looped a strand behind her ear.

She gazed at this man, head like a boulder, eyes of a golden lab. How well she knew him, the way he tidied up, shut things neatly in drawers. How he needed to fix whatever was broken.

"Maybe it is," she said. "Maybe this is your way of ... filling the void." He shook his head but she continued. "You know it's not over, Rafe. It's just a matter of time. The doctors keep saying so. Don't give up yet, okay?"

"Sharon, listen to me." He took her hand again, pulled it right out of her pocket. "This isn't about kids or no kids. It's not about this house or our life here. I love our life. You're the best thing that ever happened to me, you know that. My life only got going when I met you." He gazed at her as the evening bird repeated its low note. "This is about the flying. Right now it feels like when I left the airline, remember? Like everything I do is programmed in here" — he balled her hand into a fist, rapped her knuckles against his head — "and all I do is follow the program. That's no way to be. I need to think, make some real decisions. It's gotta be exciting. Otherwise what's the point? I may's well retire and get fat."

Sharon knew how he felt about the flying. All summer he'd jittered through his days of leave, edgy and unsettled, suggesting outings then changing his mind, starting projects and abandoning them, roaming from house to yard to garage as if his weeks on the job barely tapped his boundless energy. Relax, she told him. It was like telling a bison to heel.

She also knew he was lying when he said his restlessness had nothing to do with kids. So long and so diligently they had tried to make a baby, to be rewarded with nothing: no false positives, no miscarriages, not even a missed period. Nowadays, though they still performed on schedule whenever Rafe was home, they spoke of pregnancy less and less. Gone were the what-if conversations that used to entertain them for hours: would their child be good at math or art? be untidy or neat? love horses if she was a girl? join Little League if he was a boy? Now they saw less of their friends who had kids, and it seemed impossible to catch Rafe's eye when a baby smiled in the checkout line. Never mind the doctors' optimism; Sharon knew her husband's was dwindling. She had taken to hiding the baby books she borrowed from the library, signing them out when no one was around and reading them in private, like an alcoholic sneaking from the bottle. After ten years of effort there was failure in the air, and Rafe Mackie, superlative pilot and eternal fixer, didn't do failure.

"We don't know a single person in Vancouver," she said. "It's so far away."

"We move out there and they'll descend on us in droves, just you wait. It's the most beautiful city in Canada — hell, North America. It's always at the top of those polls. People will be lining up to stay with us. We'll get a big guest room with its own bathroom, maybe a view of the mountains."

She took a deep breath and let it out silently.

It was done. They would discuss it again, he would work harder to enlist her support, but it was over. They were going, and she could offer no compelling argument for why they shouldn't except that the life she knew, the people she needed, her job at the glass-fronted library a pleasant twenty-minute stroll away, her time with Colleen, not just her sister but her closest confidante, this green backyard that spread peace through her days — all of it would disappear, in its place a frightening and desolate future.

∧ ∨ ∧

IN THE END THEY GOT the guest room, with its own tiny yet modern three-piece bath, but did without the mountain views, which would have added hundreds of thousands to the price. As it was they were stretched tight by the bloated Vancouver housing market and the paltry salary Rafe would pull down during his two probationary years at West Air. Gone was their detached brick house with its airy, high-ceilinged rooms and expansive yard; it sold in three days for full asking price. Now home was a two-bedroom vinyl-sided townhouse at the end of a row of identical units, with a small patch of grass to one side and a cramped back patio that barely held a single Adirondack chair.

Rafe was also right about the visitors. Colleen and Gord, still in the vigorous newlywed phase they managed to draw out for a decade, made the trip twice a year, once in August, when Rafe was off fighting fires and Sharon was desperate for company, and once in March, when Rafe was home and the mild air, daffodils, and cherry blossoms made Colleen swear she couldn't return to Toronto, where late winter reigned, grimy and grey. But return she did, every time, leaving Sharon lonelier than before, the mantle of solitude resettling on her shoulders.

That first Christmas Rafe's brother Sheldon, a laughing, thickset man who even a passing stranger could see came from the same gene pool, made the long flight from the east coast, with Nancy, his tiny firecracker of a wife. "Surprise!" they yelled when Sharon opened the door to find them on the steps, their two teenage boys, Peter and Aaron, looming behind.

"Jesus, girl, it's all green here." Sheldon wrapped Sharon in a wrestler's embrace. "But we'll make a Christmas out of it anyways. Won't we, boys?" Peter and Aaron nodded shyly and the four of them trooped into the small townhouse, which shrank further with so many big men inside.

"Don't worry, Sharon," Nancy said as the women made tea. "We booked a hotel room nearby."

"No, no, you must stay here with us. There's the spare room, and the living room sofa folds out – the boys can stay in there." Sharon loaded a plate with homemade shortbread cookies, thankful Rafe had talked her into baking something for Christmas even though it was just the two of them.

"Those boys are Gullivers," Nancy said. "They take up a lot of space." She bustled around the narrow kitchen as if organizing a military campaign instead of laying out cups and saucers. The phys-ed teacher at a junior high in Halifax, she naturally took command. When things got hectic, she plucked the front of her blouse, feeling for the whistle that dangled there throughout the school day.

"Tell you what," said Rafe, who had slipped soundlessly into the kitchen. "I'll run out and buy one of those big air mattresses. We'll set it up beside the sofa. Then the boys can each have a bed."

"What about your Christmas tree?" said Nancy. "There's no room for that and an air mattress."

"We'll move my armchair to our bedroom and just push the tree into the corner. Piece of cake. Or shortbread." Rafe reached over Sharon's shoulder to snatch a cookie. "Like the lady says, you're staying with us."

"How're you going to buy an air mattress if you won't darken the door of a Canadian Tire?" Nancy asked, trying to hide a smile. Rafe's hatred of the national chain was legendary. "Do the ladies have a trip to the hardware store in their future?"

"Cheeky thing. She's not here fifteen minutes, eh, Sharon? Already ridin' me."

"Well, Raphael, my question still stands." Nancy waited, hands on hips, a tiny terrier facing down a mastiff.

"Don't you worry your head about it. There's a London Drugs a few blocks away sells stuff like that. I'll pick up more mix while I'm at it. Those boys drinking rum and cokes now like their dad?"

"Rafe Mackie! Those boys are fifteen and seventeen. I better not find a drop of rum in their cokes or we're flying straight back to Halifax, even if it's Christmas Day."

"Now Nancy, you don't believe for a minute that those boys aren't drinking. Especially in Halifax. One pub for every three citizens or whatever it is."

"If they are drinking they're doing it the right way, in secret, without my knowledge. They know if I smell liquor on their breath they join the ranks of the homeless." Nancy hefted the tea tray. "Now get out of the way, you big galoot. We temperance ladies need our tea."

As Nancy brushed past, Rafe winked at Sharon. "I knew you'd be pleased to see them. What with Colleen and Gord out on the high seas, this is the best family Christmas I could come up with." He took both her hands in his. "I know it's hard, sweetheart. Making a new home out of nothing's one of the hardest things there is. But I'm gonna make it better for you, just you wait and see. I'll fix it all up."

The kitchen glowed warm as he spoke, and the voices swirled around her, and her limbs began to loosen. On the rainy west coast, multiple time and climatic zones from nearly everyone she loved, Sharon felt for one brief interval as if she were home.

SIX

July

NATHALIE DEKED THROUGH the sluggish Richmond traffic, taking every shortcut she knew between the BCIT aerospace building and the Transportation Safety Board, and arrived at an office buzzing with industry. Media training had apparently halted: the boardroom was empty save for the instructor, who sat frowning at the conference table, his media savvy no longer a desirable commodity. Nathalie rounded the corner and burst into Tucker's office, where the boss stood talking with three other investigators. The air practically vibrated.

"There you are." Tucker barely glanced her way. "We need you to hold the fort here for the rest of the day. Lyndon and Joe are heading to Quesnel, to the crash site. Roy and I are off to the south terminal to interview the head brass at West Air. I'll be on my cell, Roy has the field phone. When the media starts calling, which should be any minute now, direct them to me. Transport Canada and RCMP inquiries go to Roy. Anyone else, just give them the bare facts and say we'll follow up later."

"What are the bare facts?" Nathalie looked from one investigator to the other. "What the hell happened?"

"We don't know much," said Tucker. "The details are still pretty thin. We know the Tracker went down around oh-nine hundred, plus or minus a few minutes. The airplane registration, lat-long, all that's on your desk. So's the weather at the time of the crash, the Cariboo Fire Centre emailed it in. No reports of mechanical difficulty beforehand as far as we know. No distress call from the cockpit. Apparently the plane was coming in for a retardant drop when it clipped the trees, lost control, went down. No guesses as to why. Good news is there should be plenty of witnesses. Besides the two in the bird dog plane — the pilot and the ministry of forests guy — we've got a dozen ground crew who were just outside the drop area waiting for the call to move in. They'll have seen something and they'll definitely have heard the plane. If the engines weren't running right, they'll know."

She looked straight at Tucker. "Are we sure he didn't make it?"

He nodded. "There was a post-impact fire, small but confirmed. One of the helicopters got in and doused the flames, then went down for a look-see. He never made it out of the cockpit."

"Christ," she whispered.

"We're not sure when the coroner can get in, or our guys for that matter. Depends what happens with the fire. Last we heard they had it mostly contained, but the forecast is for hotter temps, increased wind, and no rain. The area's bone dry, and the accident site's only a kilometre out from the active fireline. We don't know when it'll be safe enough for anyone to go in."

"We can't just leave ..." Nathalie swallowed. "We can't leave the wreck to burn up. We need all the evidence we can get. A post-impact fire is bad enough, but if the wildfire closes in we won't have anything."

"There's nothing we can do. What happens, happens. The ground crew will try to keep the blaze under control, and other air tankers are on the scene if they're needed." He looked at her steadily. "Everyone wants us to get in there."

Lyndon spoke up. "Tucker says you and the pilot were acquainted."

Nathalie studied the framed certificates that lined Tucker's beige walls. "A little."

"I met him once," said Roy, smoothing the top of his grey crewcut. "A few years back, at a conference here in Vancouver. I sat with him at the banquet, his wife too. One of the other West Air pilots gave this talk on aerial firefighting, and he kept leaning over and giving me insider details, funny stuff. You wouldn't think a single thing about forest fires could make you laugh, but he had some good stories." Roy shook his head.

"Seemed like a straight-up guy."

The group fell silent, the only sound a delivery truck rumbling past outside Tucker's window. The afternoon sun shone hard, barely filtered by the open blinds. It was a glorious day, the kind you never want to end, the kind when workers recall vague errands for which they must leave work immediately. But at the TSB it was not a day for playing hooky.

Lyndon broke the spell. "We better get a move on. There's a flight to Quesnel at three ten. Luanne's holding two seats for us if you think we should leave right away."

"Absolutely," said Tucker. "Get up there as soon as you can. If you're lucky you might get to the site before dark, at least for a first look."

Lyndon, Roy, and Joe headed out the door, Nathalie on their heels.

"Nathalie, hold up a second."

Reluctantly she turned back. Tucker waited until the others were out of sight before he spoke. "After today, you are not involved in this investigation. Not in any way. Is that clear?"

She looked at the floor and nodded.

"I mean it. You've got your hands full with the new helicopter crash, and they're still stewing at head office because of that Cessna 172 business. You need to be available for their questions on both cases. Your workload's too heavy to take on another investigation right now. Anyone asks, that's why you're not on this one. Understood?"

She brushed her hand over her eyes. "Understood."

"Like I said, the information we pulled together so far is in your office. Roy and I won't leave for another ten or fifteen minutes, so you've got some time to walk around outside or freshen up if you need to."

"I don't need any time."

She went straight to her cubicle, passing a line of deserted desks. Lyndon and Joe were up front; she could hear them finalizing their travel with Luanne. On the desk in front of her computer monitor were the notes written by whoever had fielded the calls – Lyndon, by the look of the elegant cursive. She tried to read but managed only a few words before the light dimmed and the words swam. She shut her eyes.

Steady, Scrapper, she told herself. Steady.

SEVEN

Thirteen days after

IT'S NOT WHAT THE COUNSELLOR wanted to hear because it's not *feelings*, but my sharpest memories, the ones I was willing to relive during today's wasted hour, are from the first season I flew with Rafe.

The summer of 2003 is still the worst fire year I ever worked, and I hope to God it stays that way. We've had dire seasons in British Columbia since then, some with more blazes and more hectares burned, but none that ever wrung me out like the summer of oh-three.

It was cooking hot for weeks and the forests were choked with dead-wood, a little thank-you gift from the armies of pine beetle gnawing their way through the BC Interior. It was a deadly combination, and the fires would not stop. That year over a quarter million hectares burned in BC. I looked it up once. More than ten times the average. Some days there were hundreds of fires going at once. It was the year our life's work seemed impossible. We'd contain one blaze only to have another break out a hundred kilometres away. We'd get the new one under control, then find out the wind had fanned the first into trouble again.

Anyone who lived in BC then remembers the nightmare part.

It started with lightning, same as it often does. There must be a god or goddess of lightning. It's not Zeus, he's thunder. Maybe a member of his extended family? Maybe The Counsellor knows. I should ask her during one of the long, drawn-out pauses when she's waiting for me to break down or dredge up some deep revelation.

It was mid-August 2003 when lightning touched down in Okanagan Mountain Provincial Park, just south of Kelowna. In no time that freak bolt became the worst firestorm the province had ever seen in a populated area. When all was said and done, thirty thousand Kelowna residents got evacuated, every one of them scared shitless would be my guess. Two hundred and fifty houses went up, just like that. One heart-breaking loss was the dozen wooden railway trestles in Myra Canyon. They burned up in early September when amazingly that fuck of a fire was still going. For anyone like me who'd cycled along the old Kettle Valley Railway, losing those testaments to the sweat, brawn, and sheer engineering balls of an earlier century was the final blow.

By the time the Okanagan Mountain fire took off, our crew was already shit-kicked. For weeks we'd been on at least yellow alert, with long stretches of red alert and its princely five minutes' notice thrown in for variety. We'd been called out so many times our piss smelled like smoke. The last days of July and first week of August we tried to tame the McLure fire, which swept along the North Thompson Valley above Kamloops and took the Louis Creek settlement and the sawmill that employed just about everybody. That bastard jumped the North Thompson River more than once; the whole town of Barriere had to leave. At times the wind whipped the flames so high that we were called off, air and ground crews alike. It's hard to explain to someone outside the business, I can't seem to get it across to my dad or Andy, but ask anyone who fights fires — nothing makes your gut hurt more than to stand back, with all your equipment and your specialized training, all your goddamned bravery, and watch the world burn. It's the least brave thing you can do.

So we were dragging our butts, even the couple of us in our supposedly fresh twenties. Our three days off in thirty in no way offset the giant energy deficit. But not Rafe. Was he trying to prove himself that first season, or was he truly made of tougher stuff? He used to say the Maritimes produced salt-cod pilots: hard and leathery, no expiry date. Whatever it was, while the rest of us turned flat and hollow-eyed, he was *on*, like some kind of amped-up flying machine.

When the call came we were at our base in Kamloops, finishing breakfast. We normally pooled our meal allowances to buy groceries, and we had a couple of great cooks in our midst (me not one of them), so our breakfasts usually rivalled those at any logging camp, and those are renowned. I was so exhausted that not even blackberry pancakes with maple syrup, venison sausages, and a steady stream of espresso could get me going. But Rafe was stoked. He was in the middle of a lengthy joke about a blonde, a brunette, and a Newfie when the horn went off.

Calloway poked his head through the door. "We're up, boys. New fire in Okanagan Mountain Park and it's spreading fast. Wind's bad, from the southwest. They want us all."

We never learned the Newfie's fate. En masse we rose, draining our cups of the last precious drops, knowing we'd need that caffeine to carry us through the coming hours.

Rafe had stayed my partner since training that spring. After stuffing our overnight bags with the essentials for a couple of days off base, we walked to the tarmac. "What're we in for?" he asked, scanning the sky as if it might offer a slideshow of the days ahead.

I hoisted my duffel bag higher. "It's not gonna be pretty. It's a big interface area down there. Lots of houses near the park, lots of people. A southwest wind is bad news, it pushes the fire toward Kelowna."

"Ah, Jesus. North Thompson Valley all over again, eh?"

"Except way more people. But it might not come to that. We get in there early, lay down some good retardant lines, maybe we can keep it in the park."

"Let's hope so," he said, and angled away toward his squat hunk of plane.

It was not to be. By the time we arrived the wind was gusting, the fire mowing down all in its path. The park, a wilderness area on the east side of Okanagan Lake that had been protected from logging, was chockablock with deadwood and duff, and the flames ran through it in no time. "Thank the fuckin' treehuggers for that," a grizzled Kelowna firefighter told me days later. "Think they're saving the forest and they end up levelling it."

Over the next few days we dropped load after load of retardant and water, were even joined by the Martin Mars bomber, that behemoth of a flying boat, but we may as well have been dribbling spit. Flying overtop the destruction, about all we could do was watch — and in the case of Ernie, whose home turf was just a ways up Okanagan Lake, strain like a shackled prisoner in the seat beside me and swear — while hectare by hectare the wildfire ate its way toward Kelowna, a hunter scarfing snacks before digging into the big prey.

By the time the flames hit the city, heightened by winds up to seventy-five kilometres an hour, we had a true firestorm on our hands. It took everything in its path and then some, tossing frisbees of flaming debris kilometres from the main blaze. I can only imagine what it was like for the poor bastards grunting it out on the ground — the provincial wildfire crews and municipal firefighters too, hundreds of them working the perimeters, hosing down roofs, doing what little they could to save people's homes. Residents gathered in the safe areas to cheer them on, and for weeks afterwards plastered the region with homemade posters and thank-you signs. But there are times in the face of fire when even the most superhuman efforts amount to nothing. Night after night the skies raged red while we sat by, transfixed and helpless.

There was one bright moment for the aerial crew. It rallied our spirits briefly, and cemented Rafe Mackie's reputation forever.

The fire centre had gotten a panicky call from a goat farmer in the wine country hills above Kelowna. The fire was closing in. As far as he was concerned it could take his land, buildings, and equipment, but not the animals. A friend had made it up there with a horse trailer, and between that and the farmer's own vehicles they'd loaded up the goats. But the road out collided with the fire's path, and the flames were picking up speed by the minute.

When the call came we were on the ground, in theory taking a breather, in reality giving in to the impossibility of fighting this motherfucker of a fire.

"Let's do it, young William," said Rafe.

"Do what?"

"The drop."

"Are you insane? There's not one part of that hill that's not burning. We can't see through the smoke let alone find a farm. Even if we spotted this guy's place we couldn't get close enough to do anything."

"We've got the lat-long. They just said it on the radio."

I stared at him. This fire was history-making and it was pulling the stuffing out of us, but up to now we'd been holding it together mentally. Not anymore. Rafe had finally gone batshit.

"Come on," he said. "We can at least try."

"No fucking way! It's a suicide mission. We'll never get the okay for it. I like my job. And, you know, being alive."

Rafe waited a moment, as if daring me to change my mind, then jogged away.

The next time I saw him he was fending off the mass of reporters that had swarmed our makeshift airbase. In the scramble of lights, cameras, mics, and impeccable hair, I could barely make him out, his ball cap pulled down so low you wouldn't recognize him, sunglasses hiding his eyes even though the smoke created a perpetual twilight. You'd never know it was Rafe. How had I ever thought he was an attention hog? He gave a single statement: "This is a team effort. It's not about me or what I did. If you refer to me by name or turn this into a story about me, I will never cooperate with you again and neither will West Air." And then he left.

It was an outrageous comment. Rafe had no authority to speak for the company, and I knew that when word got to our boss, monitoring events from the comfort of Vancouver, Jeff's posture would remain perfect but he would forget to breathe. And yet Rafe's ploy worked. When the story hit the news, it starred the valiant firefighters of West Air, who risked their lives in the deadliest conditions to save land, buildings, strangers, and, heart-rendingly, goats. Rafe's name was never uttered and his face never appeared. As a team we were instant celebrities.

And Rafe? Once word of his solo adventure spread in aviation circles — and spread it did, well beyond the borders of the province and even the country — he was a legend.

Where did that leave me? Pretty much where you'd expect to find a confirmed coward and disloyal partner: wallowing in shame.

Around eleven o'clock that night, I was slouched in the lobby of our hotel, watching the TV coverage. Wrung out as I was, I knew sleep was a ways off, and pacing in my room or rereading the same paragraph of my paperback wouldn't bring it on faster. The lobby, really a small corner outfitted with a leather couch and a couple of armchairs, was empty. The TV was on mute and the closed-captioning told the jerky, misspelled story of the day's events — houses engulfed in flame, cars consumed in their garages, wild-eyed residents checking in from whatever friend's house or community centre they'd fled to. The hotel intercom was playing a Muzak version of Guns N' Roses, someone's sick idea of soothing late-night tunes. I'd been sipping a 7Up to stay hydrated, but I couldn't hold it steady and had set it aside. I'm ashamed to say I was not at my best.

Then Rafe was on the sofa beside me. "What's up, bird dog? Can't sleep?"

I shook my head, stared at the TV, and tried for all I was worth to keep it together. I couldn't talk to Rafe or even look at him, couldn't relive the scene between us earlier or imagine flying with him again in the morning.

"I ever tell you why I took up air tankers?"

It was a story I'd heard several times, but that didn't deter him.

"You know I was with Canadian Airlines for a stretch, better part of a decade. The pay was hard to beat, but by Christ the job numbed the mind. Good thing you never went that way yourself, the big commercial planes. Fly them for a living and you're no more than a taxi driver in a nice shirt and hat. It's drudgery. Sheer friggin drudgery. Well, one day I get home after doing Toronto to Calgary and back for the five hundredth time and I tell Sharon straight out, that's it, I'm done. I'm calling my buddy at Thunderbird Air and I'm getting on the wait list.

I just wanted to fly again, you know? Use my hands and my eyes, my brain, all the tricks they teach you when you're starting out. Feel the adrenaline now and then. And if I could put out fires at the same time, so much the better."

"We're doing a shit job of that," I mumbled. On the TV screen a man welcomed a bologna sandwich like it was a ribeye. Ads, Jesus — a shiny surface that hides a bunch of lies. Like the fake allure of commercial aviation. Like the failed work of phoney heroes.

Rafe cracked his knuckles, the pops loud in the silent lobby. "Ever wish you had a brother?" That was Rafe: when he really wanted your attention, he'd come at you from left field.

"What's that got to do with anything?"

"Just wondering. Being an only child like you, Christ, I can't imagine it. No one to share stuff with when you're growing up."

"No one to beat on me is more like it."

"Well, I can't argue that. Sheldon and I traded a fair few jabs when we were young. More often than not he got the best of me, least until I turned sixteen and started to fill out. But as many times as that bastard slapped the shit out of me, he stuck with me when I needed him." He played absently with the wedding ring that cut into his fleshy finger. "The stories I could tell you, young William. He bailed me out big time in those days. Always looking out for his little brother."

It was hard to imagine Rafe Mackie needing to be bailed out, harder yet to picture him as anyone's little anything. Childhood was a time he never spoke of, apart from the occasional joke about the Maritimes. This was the first I'd heard of a brother.

Then Rafe's hand surprised me, a big warm mitt on my arm. "Will, I'm gonna say what a brother would if you had one. Look at me." Reluctantly I turned away from the TV. "You can't let it get to you, what's happening out there. All we can do is fly the circuits, make the drops, repeat as required. If we do that every single time, and we do it right, we give 'er all we got, that's as good as it gets. We're doing everything in our power to fix it."

I looked at my lap.

"You know," he said, "since I've been at West Air I've never seen you fly less than your best. Every time you're up there you give it a hundred percent. You're calm, you're in charge, you fly that plane like you were born to fly it. But the fire, that's the part you can't control." He leaned closer. "You hear me? You control everything you can, but there comes a point when you've gotta accept that it's out of your hands, it's over to Mother Nature and there's not a goddamn thing you can do."

"Yeah, well fuck Mother Nature."

Rafe laughed. "You're not the first man's ever said that. That's not how it works, though. It's Mother Nature that fucks us." He leaned back against the sofa cushions. "You hear that?"

"What?"

"That song. I love that damn song."

It drifted around us from the intercom, the simple strumming and drumbeat, the honey-smooth voice that could break your heart crooning about sitting on the dock of the bay. I felt the air lighten minutely. "That's right up your alley all right. That Motown shit."

"That's not shit, boy. It's better than that heavy metal screechin' you got on all the time, the Foolish Fighters or whatever they are. Listen. It's great."

Like the story of how Rafe got into flying tankers, I'd heard the song many times, piped into the department stores and waiting areas of life, but I'd never really listened. When the music ended, I threw him a bone. "It's catchy, I'll give you that."

"Here's a piece of trivia for you. A few days after Otis recorded that song he got himself killed. Plane crashed into a lake in Wisconsin. He was twenty-six. Same age as you."

"That's creepy."

"Not creepy—tragic. It's what makes the song so great. Here he is giving his all, singing the tune that's gonna make him a household name, which he has no clue about when he's recording it. Everything's going great for him, his life's about to take off, and he has no idea — *no idea* — that in a few days, bam. It's gonna be over. There's something … I dunno, haunting about that."

I glanced at Rafe. He was serious.

"It's a good way to die," he said. "Quick, painless. Flying one minute, snuffed out the next. It's how I'd go, given the choice." He slapped the leather arm of the sofa. "All right, enough of this bleak shit. We'll both end up crashed in the lake if we don't get some sleep tonight. Let's go, bird dog."

He pushed himself up and headed to the elevator, his steps long and swinging, me following his lead, the way it always went when we were on the ground.

EIGHT

October

THE LUNCH CROWD HAS THINNED by one thirty, when Sharon escapes the fall breeze for a table at the Left Coast Café, yet it takes the waiter, thirty going on eighteen, hair boyishly tousled, teeth disturbingly bleached, a good ten minutes to glance her way. By the time he finally saunters over with a menu and a mumbled greeting, she feels invisible, a speck on the floor rather than a paying customer. She orders a glass of pinot gris and pulls out the book she has brought along to fill the wait.

Rachel, always late and never apologetic about it, is nonetheless a good and constant friend, one of the few Sharon has made in Vancouver. She's also one of the few who stayed in touch through the unbearable weeks after the crash. Every few days she would phone, text, or email. Just checking in, she would say, no need to reply, a thoughtful gesture that ironically inclined Sharon to reach out to Rachel more than anyone except Colleen during that dark time.

It's been eight years since the women first met at a twice-weekly exercise class that Sharon joined in hopes of finding one place in this chilly city where she might belong. They progressed from nodding hello to comparing favourite workouts (racquetball for Rachel, yoga for Sharon) to grabbing a coffee after class to meeting occasionally for lunch. A single, childless real estate agent — the Countess of Condos, as she wryly dubs herself — Rachel is the master of her hours, short and crammed with multitasking though they are. Sharon had no job back when they met, thanks to a local glut of library technicians, and almost no friends, so between Rachel's showings, open houses, and frantic shoring up of sales that threatened at the last minute to collapse, the women had ample time to get acquainted.

"There you are," says Rachel now, striding toward the corner table as if she has been waiting for Sharon instead of the other way around. "You look nice. All glowing and healthy."

In her stretched-out grey cardigan, lips chapped, complexion patchy, hair clipped up into an untidy spray, Sharon knows that *nice* is a stretch. She plays with the stem of her wineglass as her friend settles, emanating a faint spicy scent that envelops the table. "I'm just flushed from yoga," Sharon says.

"Well, it suits you."

Rachel doles out compliments the way she distributes condo flyers, indiscriminately and with the confidence that whatever she's selling is something people want to buy. Yet she dismisses others' praise so swiftly that Sharon has learned not to bother. Besides, why state the obvious? The Amazonian Rachel Zarya, swinging black hair, luminous brown eyes, legs as long as an Arctic day in summer (Rafe's description) is at all times, under all conditions, dazzling. It is a fact that Rachel accepts yet seems to value lightly, treating her beauty as an unremarkable circumstance of birth, like an outie belly button or a knack for math. To Sharon, who has laboured over her appearance since puberty, when a sour aunt once compared her to a Russian shot-putter, such nonchalance is unfathomable and is the one thing about her friend of which she is deeply, intractably envious.

"A glass of whatever she's having," Rachel tells the waiter, who appears instantly at her elbow, beaming as if starstruck. "Then the scallop salad with a side of grilled asparagus."

"I think I'll have the mushroom risotto," Sharon says. "And another glass of wine?"

The waiter scuttles off and Rachel leans in. "*Two* glasses of wine? At one thirty on a Tuesday?"

"It's nearly two o'clock for those of us keeping track, and I'm not driving anytime soon. After lunch I've got the library and then the farmers market. Lots of time to walk it off."

"There better be. All we need is some lurid headline in the *Province*: 'Pilot's widow arrested for drunk driving – still grieving.'"

Rachel's irreverence is one of her best traits. It reminds Sharon of her Toronto friends. "Would that be any worse than 'Condo Countess caught with underage boy – parents horrified'?"

Rachel rolls her eyes. "I told you, he wasn't underage. He was twenty. Shaved daily, drove a car, had his own place."

"Yeah, a basement suite in his parents' house that he shared with some other student. He was still living with mommy and daddy. He was a *boy*. What was his name? Jared? Jason?"

"Jordan. Believe me, he was a man in all the ways that matter." Rachel crosses her legs. "Mommy and daddy were just in the wrong place at the wrong time. They had no right to let themselves in like that, you know, not without notice. He had a proper rental agreement in place and he was mighty annoyed that they broke it."

"Like they were mighty annoyed to find their only child with a naked forty-year-old woman on the kitchen table. At least that's what I hear from a supposedly reliable witness."

"Oh God. They had no sense of humour. The whole thing was hysterical. They kept going on about it, in *our* house, in *our* house, how could you do something so inappropriate in *our* house, when it wasn't really their house, it was *his* apartment. And I'm not forty! Not until March."

"Well, you're in cougar territory, that's all I can say."

"Speak for yourself, girl. You got five years on me. You're the cougar in this café. Except you haven't exactly been ..." Rachel shakes her head. "Anyway, it was time to end that particular liaison. He was texting me constantly, like eight or ten times a day, asking me what I was doing, what I was wearing, was I thinking of him the way he was thinking of me – God, all this juvenile sexting crap. I've got no time for that. I just wanted to order takeout once in a while, you know? Not buy the restaurant."

The waiter, who has silently materialized during this last assertion, places Rachel's salad in front of her, adjusting the plate just so, lingering long enough to make it clear that she need only say the word and he will supply her with as much takeout as she desires.

"He offered a really big menu, though," says Rachel, taking a delicate sip of wine. "A huge, long menu, if you know what I mean." She doesn't acknowledge the waiter, who has unburdened himself of Sharon's plate and stands, beguiled and empty-handed, a man-child awaiting instruction.

"Rachel!" Sharon's face burns. "You're impossible."

Rachel's head turns a fraction. "That's everything, thank you." The waiter slinks off, Converse sneakers trailing soft disappointment all the way to the kitchen.

Sharon watches him go. "That was mean."

"Not. Guys like that need to be put in their place. A pretty face, a full head of hair, some Crest Whitestrips, they think that's all they need to bring to the table. They don't even try, those pretty boys. No banter, no seduction, no cleverness. They just stand there like some Roman statue, expecting to be admired and eventually pleasured." She cuts into a scallop. "At least Jordan had charisma. He knew how to flirt and he understood the art of conversation. He put some effort into it, you know?"

"And effort should always be rewarded."

"Well, sure. I'm all about rewards."

Sharon spears a slice of porcini mushroom. "You really never wanted to get married? Not even when you were a teenager?"

"Nope. The white dress always looked like a straitjacket to me. You can disguise it with lace and beads and a veil, but it's still an instrument of torture." Rachel toys with a leaf of watercress. "For me, I mean. I know it's not that way for everyone."

Sharon chews slowly. "No."

"Did you always want to get married?"

"I guess so." Sharon lays down her fork. "When I was five or six I was the flower girl at my older cousin's wedding. It was this huge outdoor party in a botanical garden in Toronto. Blue sky, flowers everywhere.

My mom kept telling me that one day I would be the bride, I would be the one up there getting the ring and the kiss and the attention. After that I daydreamed about it all the time. I was so young when I met Rafe, I never had a chance to change my mind."

"How *did* you two meet? I can't believe you never told me that story." Rachel searches Sharon's face. "Only if you're okay talking about it."

"There's not much of a story. It was in Toronto, of course. I was twenty, practically a child. Same age as your ... plaything." Sharon takes a generous swallow of wine. "We got into a fender-bender, if you can believe it. Rafe didn't want to report it, he was worried his insurance would skyrocket, so he said why don't we sort it out privately over dinner. Normally I'd have said no way, I didn't know him from Adam, but he was so ... eager. He wanted to make it right, to fix everything up."

"He was drop-dead handsome too, right? All muscle back then, I bet."

"He had such big brown eyes, they were so kind. A year later we were married. It was the big wedding I'd always wanted, the amazing dress, my own flower girl. Just like I imagined."

Rachel is smiling, which means Sharon has developed the picture well. It may be the most enduring lesson Rafe taught her: how to retouch life's negatives to mask their flaws.

A tinny rendition of Pachelbel's Canon begins, and Rachel paws through her oversized Fendi bag. "Sorry, I better take this. Yes...? Well, it should work. No, no. What? Never mind. I'll be there in fifteen." She drops the phone back into her bag and frowns. "I've got to run. There's a showing on one of my Yaletown listings and the agent can't open the lockbox. The place has been on the market for two weeks already. It's not moving. I better look after it." She roots through her bag again and slaps forty dollars on the table for her share. "Next time we'll do it right, okay? A leisurely meal, no interruptions." And with a neat high-heeled pivot, Rachel is off and out the door.

Sharon pushes aside the remnants of her risotto – too soupy – and sips more wine. A moment of intense quiet always follows Rachel's exit, a sound-swallowing stillness like the inside of an underground parking garage.

A few late-day customers linger inside the café. A young couple at the front with eyes only for each other. Two white-haired matrons chatting quietly and sipping tea. A middle-aged woman with grey hair past her shoulders and a smock top adorned with what appear to be — Sharon looks again — yes, there are CDs sewn onto the top's wide sleeves, a cascade of silver donuts glinting in the light. Dear God. Only in Vancouver.

At a table across from her sits the other remaining diner, a dark-haired man around her age, suit jacket on the chairback behind him. Obviously in business or banking; no one else wears a suit in this town. He is off work but also *at* work, eating lunch but preoccupied with his phone, texting or emailing or surfing, extracting maximum productivity from his thirty minutes away from the office. Though he is seated at an angle to Sharon, she can see him work the phone. His hands are those of a farmer or a builder, too chunky for such a slim instrument, yet they handle it gracefully. That is the beauty of large hands on a man: they can palm a football or clobber a thief; trace a woman's cheek or cradle an infant's head.

Stop. Don't think about that.

Rafe's hands were as big as that man's, and as symmetrical. Sharon finishes her wine, tepid now, and remembers how it felt to slip the wedding ring onto his finger. The gold band was the broadest they could find, to match the thickness of his finger. "No point putting some girl's hoop earring on this meat pipe of mine," he joked.

The ring was among the few belongings returned to her. It came in a small plastic baggie, the kind that would hold a sandwich or grapes. Whether it was the CSI-like presentation or her muffled state of mind, Sharon did not at first recognize the ring, perhaps because she'd so seldom seen it off Rafe's finger. He used to brag that he never removed it, not even at the gym, where he wore padded gloves to keep it from digging into his flesh.

The businessman is nearly finished. He spears the last cherry tomato, eats the last bite of fish. A healthy lunch. She admires that. Few men choose wholesome fare when left to their own devices. He probably works out. He shifts in his chair, the fabric of his trousers snugging a muscled thigh. No, he definitely works out. Like Rafe did.

The pain, when it comes, is always a surprise. Even now, so many months later.

She married a man who was often away — long shifts as an airline pilot; three or four months in the bush as a firefighter — so she is accustomed to living alone. It got harder once they moved to Vancouver, with no job to fill her days, no sister nearby or close friends to visit, but she managed and for the most part didn't mind the solitude when it came. Which is why she is blindsided by the crater that Rafe's physical absence has blasted into her life. Even in the last years, when their togetherness changed flavour, she drew comfort from knowing he was there, or soon would be. Now he is nowhere. Not in the house, not in the yard, not on her phone. There are no scrawled notes slipped under the coffee maker, no giant knees filling up the space under the breakfast table, no broad palms to open the pickle jar.

She comes to as the man near her stands up. When he removes his jacket from the chairback, she gets a full view. He is tall and solid, but his face is pointy and fox-like, its planes blank, without expression, silent as to what sort of man lives inside. His eyes, small and flat, sweep past Sharon. She is once again a speck on the floor.

He is nothing like Rafe, not even close. Unguarded and wide, her husband's face was a billboard that flashed his emotions before his tongue formed words. And his brown eyes always saw her. Even at the end, when the face he looked at was not the one he wanted to see, when what he really wanted was to turn away — even then, he saw her.

NINE

July

FOUR THIRTY ON THE DAY of the Tracker crash and Nathalie was alone. One by one, her co-workers from the marine and rail divisions had trickled out, lured by the lazy, sun-drenched afternoon. Tucker and Roy, their visit to West Air over, had hightailed it to a hastily arranged press conference. The accident would lead the evening news. Plane crashes were often top stories, but a fatal incident connected with this year's wildfires, themselves a headline grabber in recent weeks, was a shoo-in for the number-one spot.

Now that the phone calls had dried up and she'd done her bit to arrange the media session, Nathalie had little reason to stay in the office. Yet she was reluctant to leave, to expose herself to the bright day. She kept hunting for tasks – email, photocopying, shuffling through the R22 helicopter photos – to take her mind off the drumbeat of questions: Is he really gone? Where is his body? What the hell happened out there?

An hour earlier the coroner had finally emailed the preliminary findings from the R22 crash. Cause of death for both the pilot and his bride: blunt-force trauma as a result of impact. As Nathalie had expected, the report contained no suggestion of a heart attack or other physical incapacitation. It was looking more and more like a mechanical problem, as her gut had been saying all along. The next step: a thorough inspection of the wreckage whenever the heap arrived by tractor-trailer, and after that the engine teardown.

Heart attack — is that what took Rafe down? He was a big man with a big personality, Type A for sure. Like all the other firefighters, he'd been working a schedule and a half this summer, grunting out the hours, days, and weeks with little time off. Yet nonstop wildfires didn't change the duty limits: West Air, like most companies, capped a pilot's flight time at eight hours a day. What's more, Rafe haunted the gym with a regularity that put her own sporadic regime to shame. He was healthier than most men half his age and his paperwork would prove it: being over forty, he needed two medicals and one ECG a year to keep his licence.

Did he misjudge his distance from the trees, then? Possible, but not probable. Rafe Mackie had battled fires for nearly two decades and was famous for his timing and accuracy. No West Air pilot scored more bull's-eye drops than he did. His plane was like an extension of his body, he once told her, like a hockey player's stick or a fencer's sword, and he knew exactly how to position it in relation to anything around him — terrain, other aircraft, objects, people.

It's got to be mechanical, she told herself, just like the R22 will be. Sure, Trackers were as tough as army tanks, but they were manufactured decades before she was born; there was only so much mechanics could do to keep them airworthy. A couple of the big companies, like Conair, had already scrapped the model in favour of newer turbine-powered craft, whose spare parts could be ordered from a supplier instead of cobbled together, Frankenstein-like, by resourceful AMEs.

Concentrate, Scrapper. The R22. She had her own investigation to worry about.

She eyed the photo folder on her laptop, yet her right hand chose the browser icon. In the search pane she typed "West Air Flight Services," and when the site opened she hit "About Us." There he was, trademark grin, big shaggy head, broad shoulders packed into the leather bomber jacket he'd owned nearly half his life. He faced the camera straight on, eyes direct and without guile.

She zoomed in, lost in the pixelated features of a man she'd seen up close, in real life, many times. A man who no longer existed.

"I fucked it up, Rafe, didn't I?" she whispered. "Like everything else these days. Fucked it right up."

^ ∨ ^

EVERYTHING ELSE, for the most part, meant the Cessna 172 accident, the investigation that threatened to follow Nathalie the rest of her career, like a sex scandal trailing a preacher. *Fucked it up* was Tucker's concise analysis of how she'd mishandled the case.

The crash, near Prince Rupert on the north coast of BC, was a fatal one, killing the pilot and both his passengers, a father and son who were long-time friends of the pilot's family. It was a boys' adventure turned nightmare, especially for the two wives left behind. The plane went down in early April of last year, but as usual when the cause wasn't immediately apparent, it would take months to gather enough evidence for a credible report.

From the beginning Nathalie, the lead investigator, suspected a mechanical malfunction. Nothing about the Cessna's upkeep inspired confidence. The so-called maintenance logs were a stained jumble of papers she discovered five days after the crash, stuffed into a plastic grocery bag beneath a mound of oily rags in the hangar. Once she got the records in order, they yielded sketchy information at best. Small wonder, she soon learned, seeing as the logs were kept and the maintenance done by the pilot's brother, a licensed AME who was also a raging alcoholic, a scratch-and-win addict, and a household name with the collection agencies. The Cessna's last annual inspection never happened, according to the logbook (completed in full, said the brother); the fuel strainer gasket, a rubber seal declared defective by the manufacturer, was never replaced, according to the logs (was most definitely replaced, insisted the brother). Sure enough, when Nathalie examined the wrecked airframe a week later and found the gasket with a chunk missing, she knew she had her culprit.

"Just what I expected," she told Tucker that very day. "Not only did that slimy bastard not replace the gasket, he didn't even know it was supposed to be swapped out. Sure as I'm standing here. First time we interviewed him, he said there wasn't a single airworthiness directive for the plane in the last three or four years. Later, when we showed him the AD on replacing the gasket, when we shoved it right in his greasy fat face, he changed his story, said he *did* do the work. But there's no record of it in the logs, no record of a new gasket being bought, no receipt, *rien*. The lazy, lying scumbag – he doesn't deserve to be called an AME. He needs his wrists broken and his licence pulled, and the families need to know what he did."

"Easy, Nathalie," Tucker said. "I get that you want this wrapped up, but the lab has to check the gasket to make sure the break didn't happen on impact. They're backlogged at least a month. What else is new, right? But you know you can't skip that step. You've got to hang on till the results come back. Then crack your whip."

"A month? Jesus. It'll be summer by then, the lab will empty out. The families, what are they supposed to do? Sit around the Canada Day picnic roasting wienies and swapping theories about what could've happened? While, I might add, that shitpile of a brother sits there, mouth shut, except when he's drinking of course. The pilot's widow, is she supposed to spend the whole summer wondering if her husband's to blame, worrying that she married a screw-up who stole the life of an innocent kid and his dad?"

"There's nothing we can do. Without the lab report, you can only speculate. Besides, you've still got to look at whether it was water in the fuel. If the fuel was bad, that's as likely an explanation as a defect in the strainer gasket."

She shrugged. "Sure, I'll look into the water thing, but that's so hard to prove. Especially because there wasn't a drop of fuel left in the tanks by the time we got to them. With the gasket, there's a known defect. There's an AD out on it, for God's sake. How much more of a warning light do we need?"

"My point is," said Tucker, exaggerating every syllable, "you still have a ways to go before you can pinpoint the cause. So cool it on the incompetent AME angle for now, okay? Tell the families we're waiting for lab results and can't conclude anything until then."

"How about we put some pressure on the lab, get them to bump us up in the queue?"

"Not a chance. I already pulled the only string I had getting them to analyze that crack in the propeller hub on Lyndon's Piper Navajo. They've got every other investigator in every other region putting the screws to them, and as you said, summer holidays are coming."

"Yeah, which they'll draw out for fucking months, the lazy slobs."

"Be that as it may ..."

There it was, Tucker's signature line. Shorthand for *this conversation is over.*

All summer long Nathalie had seethed and simmered, emailing the lab in Ottawa every Monday morning only to receive the same reply: "We have not yet conducted your analysis. We will contact you when we have further information." *Merde*, she muttered, railing at her powerlessness. By mid-September the lab had quit replying, an insult that drove her back into Tucker's office.

"It's been more than three months now." She tried to control her voice. "That is unacceptable."

"Nathalie, I've told you. There's nothing we can do to hurry them up."

"Then get the gasket back from the lab. We'll take it to Cohen's, get it looked at here in town. They'll give us an answer in a day or two."

"You know full well we don't have the budget for an independent lab."

"Come on. How expensive could it be?"

"It doesn't matter. No budget means *no budget.* I guarantee you, the cost will not be zero."

"Then we need to make an exception, ask the board to —"

"What? Give us special treatment? This is the federal government, Nathalie, not the private sector, not some reality show on TV. There is no special treatment. We are all equal, we all receive the same mediocre treatment, and that means we wait our goddamned turn."

"But the widows are on me every week, phone calls, emails, *what do you know? when will we hear something?* The pilot's wife, God, she's like a cancer victim. She must've lost twenty pounds and she was not a curvy lady to begin with."

Tucker took a long breath. "Nathalie, if my French was better I'd say it in French. There is nothing we can do."

As so often happened when her stress level skyrocketed, Nathalie heard her grandmother's voice, faintly accented from a girlhood in St. Boniface, before she met and married the suave anglo who left her a widow and mother of four at age thirty. *You know, Scrapper, only a nutting does nutting.* It was a necessary saying in Nathalie's family, a franco-Manitoban clan plagued by adversity, not the garden-variety difficulties that life tends to dispense but a steady, crushing grind of misfortune that ruined every business venture, parted most marriages, snatched loved ones prematurely, and doled out staggering portions of illness and deformity.

True to her destiny, Nathalie, an only child, lost her parents in any icy car crash the winter she was six, leaving Mémère to raise her the only way an arthritic woman who had gratefully released her children into the world years earlier could, which was to say with many rules and no excess affection. Scrapper, Mémère called the little girl, because she was always in trouble at school. Small wonder given the snotty kids Nathalie had to rub shoulders with. Her temper would flare and before she knew it she'd have shoved some prissy princess or slapped a bully's face. Mémère did nothing to correct this impulsiveness; if anything, she encouraged it. *Better to hit than be hit* was her motto.

Two months out of high school Nathalie left her grandmother's care a rougher, less adored version of the fragile orphan who'd entered it, but she left as a woman, ready to do battle, imprinted with the family credo of hard work and willpower, clad in the armour of a fuck-you attitude.

Which was why Tucker's do-nothing instructions only inflamed her. After months of nothing she had to do something, and at the end of September she did. She met the two widows at a nearby Starbucks one blustery Monday afternoon, rain slanting against the plate glass, and told them what she had so far: a cracked fuel strainer gasket that should have been replaced and records that contradicted the AME who insisted he'd done the job.

"We don't know for sure," she told the women — she *knew* she had prefaced her remarks this way, would swear to it later when Tucker grilled her — "but we think the defective gasket may have caused the engine to fail in midflight, and that's why the plane went down."

The pilot's widow, bundled inside a black fleece jacket, stared at Nathalie, her sunken cheeks deep dents punched into her face. "You mean it wasn't his fault?"

"The information we have to this point suggests there was no pilot error." *Suggests* — she knew she had couched her answer that way. She would never, ever say anything definitive without solid evidence to back it up, had been trained not to, knew instinctively not to. All she wanted was to reassure the widows that the evidence so far pointed to mechanical failure, a hidden flaw that no one aboard the airplane that day could have possibly overcome.

The widows did not hear *don't know for sure*. They did not hear *suggests*. What they heard was *no pilot error* and that was the message they took to the media the next day. By evening the *Vancouver Sun* and the local radio and TV stations were carrying the same story: "Pilot not to blame for Cessna 172 crash."

"Goddamn fucking vampire reporters!" Nathalie was in full fury when Tucker summoned her to his office the next morning.

"I just got off the phone with Harold Winterfield." Her boss's voice was icily precise. "I've had fifteen minutes of being ... disembowelled by our esteemed chairman, who wants to know why in God's name Vancouver news stations are broadcasting conclusions that the board hasn't even seen let alone approved."

"CTV was the only station that called me, and I told them we knew nothing for certain. I was one hundred percent clear about that."

"Nathalie, what the hell were you thinking? What possessed you to meet with those widows? What possessed you to tell them *anything* about the conclusions of this investigation, conclusions we haven't even reached yet?"

"But I didn't —"

"No." Tucker held up his hand. "I don't want to hear it. I have no idea how you could do such a thing, and I'm not interested in your excuses. There *is* no excuse for grossly poor judgment and misleading statements. What you've done—you are an embarrassment to the TSB and your fellow investigators. You've cut corners before, Nathalie, jumped to conclusions before we've gone through all the evidence. Lyndon has talked to you about that, and I have talked to you about that, and we agreed to chalk it up to training. But now you know better."

"But Tucker, I only—"

"Don't you get it?" Tucker's voice dropped dangerously, rapids over a cliff. "This time you fucked it up. Do you hear me? Fucked. It. Up." He sat back in his chair. "Now get out of my office. In fact, I don't want to see you for the rest of the day. Go somewhere and think about what you've done. I've got a colossal stinking mess to clean up."

It was a mess that even Tucker, with his steely poise, instinct for damage control, and high-level contacts, could do no more than mop the edges of, and his attempts to correct the story only provoked more damning coverage. Headlines like "TSB backtracks" and "Investigators waffle on cause of crash" assaulted Nathalie in the long days that followed, until she quit scanning the daily papers and online news sites and turned her car radio to country and western instead of the all-news channel.

At the office it was harder to ignore the fallout. For the rest of the week Lyndon, Roy, and the other air investigators gave her a wide berth. No one followed her into the kitchen when she made the coffee, a task she'd shouldered soon after joining the TSB and sampling its bitter swill. Lyndon no longer offered to pick her up a sandwich on his daily walk to Bread Heaven. The guys didn't gather outside her cubicle in the afternoon to recap the day's events. Screw them, she told her own image day after day in the mirror of the women's washroom. Since when do you need anyone's approval? But every afternoon at quitting time, when she slid into her sleek Miata, the sky leaden and the September rain falling in sheets, she was exhausted, her body and mind ground down by unwanted consequences.

By the end of that punishing week the media, with reliable fickleness, moved on to other stories. After a solitary weekend of drinking too much wine and watching too much late-night TV, Nathalie headed for the office kitchen on Monday morning to make coffee and toast a bagel only to find Lyndon behind her, asking if she'd heard about the cargo plane that skidded off a Detroit runway on Saturday. It was the first tiny ray of light.

After that, bit by bit, work life resumed its normal rhythm. The other investigators sought her opinion on rates of climb and propeller pitches. Roy borrowed her to adjust the graphics in his latest report. Lyndon brought her a turkey panini for lunch and threw in a banana, no charge.

Only Tucker kept his distance. Never again did he mention her botched handling of the Cessna 172 investigation, not even to take her off the case, a move she had fully expected. But neither did he ask for updates, bounce ideas off her, or even inquire how her weekend went. Months later, when the lab report confirmed her theory — loss of power due to a failed fuel screen gasket that should have been replaced as per the relevant airworthiness directive — Tucker remained silent. Nathalie knew, as surely as if she'd seen a printout, that in the precisely ordered spreadsheet of Tucker's mind her name now carried a thick black mark. What she could not work out was how to erase it.

TEN

Thirteen days after

THE COUNSELLOR WAS SO THRILLED to hear about the Kelowna fire, to hear anything that involved multiple sentences, that before today's hour was up I also threw her my first visit to Rafe's house. It was an odd day, that one, the day I first met Sharon, his wife. His widow.

After the summer of 2003 kicked the stuffing out of me, I did like most of my co-workers and took the winter off: hit the ski hills, tried some cold-water surfing in Tofino, caught up with my friends outside the stick-and-rudder world, got reacquainted with the ladies, basically chilled and regrouped. The previous two winters I'd worked here and there, mainly flying relief for small airlines to keep up my skills, not to mention my bank account. I'd made a few more bucks helping my dad with the occasional job, just the grunt work that required no electrical know-how. But by 2003 I was on West Air's payroll full-time and making a real income — still a probationary amount, still at the bottom of the pay scale, but double the coin I'd earned as a part-timer. Enough to keep a single guy with beer tastes and a crappy apartment afloat.

Rafe, on the other hand, worked steadily that winter. Like me he was on a beginner's salary at West Air, pulling down a fraction of what he'd made in Ontario, and like me he was waiting for the payoff. If you survive two years of probation your salary soars, then edges up every year after that. All of us rookies were pumped to stick it out until we hit top pay. Then you could afford a whole winter's rent in Whistler and spend all your time on the slopes. Or buy a boat, head down to the tropics, and duck the season completely. Rafe had a mortgage to pay, an obese Vancouver mortgage, and his wife hadn't found work in her field, something to do with libraries, so he needed money, the more the better. He was good with his hands; by then I'd seen photos of the house he renovated in Toronto and the addition he helped build on his brother's place in Halifax. So I put in a word with my dad, who set him up with a residential contractor. The pay was good — the outfit worked mostly in West Vancouver, where the appetite for renos is as bottomless as the trust funds — and the nine-to-five schedule left Rafe some decent home time. Which he needed because he and Sharon were trying hard for a baby.

They'd spent most of their marriage wanting kids, Rafe told me. He blamed his schedule, which only got worse when he left commercial flying for firefighting, a job that apart from occasional days off kept him in northern Ontario three to five months a year. When he was home they tried, valiantly, as he put it, but even though they both checked out medically, nothing happened. I figured they'd adopt eventually, but later Rafe told me it wasn't an option. "You take on someone else's kids, you got no idea what you're getting. Their past, their family history — it's all a blank. You're just asking for trouble." Then he changed the subject, as if it didn't matter. I knew different. Being childless felt like failing to him. Like the one bull's eye he couldn't pull off.

That first winter was when I really got to know Rafe. We talked on the phone some evenings, went for a beer once in a while, ate eggs the occasional Sunday morning at a six-booth diner near my place. It was usually Rafe's idea to get together. Not because I didn't want to — I did, he was funny and easy to be with — but because he always beat me to it. I think he was lonely that first year in Vancouver, maybe lonelier than he let on.

We covered a lot of ground: flying, travel, hockey, women, micro-breweries. Deeper stuff too, like my mom's death, which I rarely hauled out in the open. His fear that Sharon would never feel at home in Vancouver. I described growing up here and how the city seemed different back then, seen from a bicycle seat, smaller, less cosmopolitan, safer. He talked about Toronto and the stripped-down beauty of the northern boreal. A little about the old days in Halifax, where he worked construction with his brother and learned to fly. Never a word, though, about Cape Breton, where he grew up. His younger years were like a chapter gone from his life, like he'd skipped boyhood altogether. He never mentioned his parents either, not until that first time I came to his house.

It was a wet, cold Saturday in early March, the 2004 flying season not yet begun, and I'd promised to help Rafe replace their hot water tank. I steered the Subaru beater I drove in those days through steady rain, renewing my daily vow to replace the worn wipers. As I pulled up to their townhouse, I gave thanks that Rafe's Honda s2000 was stowed inside the garage. No need for it to amp up the ugliness of my rustbucket in their neat suburban driveway.

Before I reached the top step, Rafe opened the door. He looked like shit, I remember that. Pale and ... I don't know, solemn. But he gave me the gears as usual. "Come in, young William, come in. Jesus, where's your raincoat? What is it with you?"

"I'm not some wimp from Tarrana, hides under an umbrella every time there's a drop or two."

"Drop or two? It's a friggin monsoon out there. Here, let me take ... What is this, polar fleece? It's soaked through. Honest to Christ, you locals."

"You must be Will." Her voice was smooth and musical, a violin to Rafe's rasping fiddle. I looked up from unlacing my shoes and saw a face I knew only from pictures. Sharon, calm and immobile, stood in the vestibule as if she'd been there all along (she hadn't), as if she'd been teleported instead of moving like an ordinary mortal.

On the surface she looked no different from the creased photo in Rafe's wallet: shoulder-length hair somewhere between blond and brown, pale skin with spots of colour high in her cheeks, unusual light grey eyes. A bit old-fashioned looking, like a woman in an oil painting. *Ethereal* was the word that sprang to mind, maybe because I was reading my way through one of my dad's favourites, Wilkie Collins. What you couldn't know from any photo was how still she was, how composed. Inside that stillness was a warmth I felt immediately. Like when you round a corner on the Sea to Sky Highway at night and are suddenly hit with the full moon.

Rafe made the introductions and I shook Sharon's hand, noting how soft it was. "Let's get started," he said. "We'll have tea and a visit later."

He led me to a small utility room, more of a closet really, off the neat white kitchen. The old tank was wedged in there tight; the new one, still in its cardboard box, stood over by the fridge.

"The tank's drained, the water and the circuit breaker are off. We should be good to disconnect her."

I'd helped my dad with this job before and knew the drill. So did Rafe. He handled his tools easily, not in that clumsy way of guys whose do-it-yourself expertise extends to stringing up Christmas lights once a year. They were good tools, too, and well cared for. "You get a truckload deal with Snap-on or what?" I asked.

"A tool is like a woman, young William. Get the best one you can and look after it forever. You'll find none of that Jesus Canadian Tire crap in my house."

"No wonder my dad likes you. He won't set foot in a Canadian Tire. If I go there I have to keep it a secret from him, like it's a drug deal or something."

"Wise man, your father. You should keep him."

"I *will* end up keeping him if he spends the rest of his life shelling out forty bucks for a new screwdriver, a *single-head* screwdriver. Old Age Security can't support someone who shops like a billionaire."

"Forty bucks?" Rafe snorted. "You tell him from me, wait for the sales. He can land a decent screwdriver for thirty-seven, thirty-six if he's lucky."

"Uh-huh. Thanks for the tip. Ready to tackle this bastard?"

Together we heaved the old tank out of the closet, Rafe lifting his end like it was an empty soup can, and set to work installing the new one. A couple of hours later, after some last-minute fiddling and swearing at the ground wire, we were done. Rafe turned the water main back on. "How about some tea while we let her fill up? If you got time, that is."

"Sure. I don't have to be anywhere until tonight."

"Well, then. A hot date?"

"Maybe."

"Remember, treat her like a tool." He winked. "Better yet, treat her *with* your tool."

"Very funny. She's not what you'd call a tool-oriented girl. More the mani-pedi type."

"Mani-pedi?" Rafe swished boiling water in the teapot, dumped it out, and dropped in two teabags.

"Manicure, pedicure. You know, a girlie girl."

"Huh." He covered the teapot with a quilted cozy that looked out of place in his rough hands. "Not the type I'd picture you with."

"Oh? What's that supposed to mean?"

"Now don't go all snotty on me. I see the attraction. I just imagine you with someone . . . I don't know, more hardy than that, kinda natural and outdoorsy. Someone who'll go off with you on all those surfing and hiking trips."

"I do that stuff to get away from everyone. I take a girl and she'd want me to talk the whole time, take her everywhere I go, say her bathing suit doesn't make her look fat, that type of thing. No thanks. Anyhow, outdoorsy doesn't do it for me. I like someone who wears a dress, holds onto my arm. Who can, you know, have fun without getting too serious."

"But what about the next morning? Or after two weeks in Butthole, BC, when you're tired and filthy and just want to talk? Believe me, there comes a time you need more from a woman than just looking good on your arm or doing you-know."

"He's too young to care about that."

Again Sharon had soundlessly appeared, this time in the kitchen doorway. Exactly when she'd arrived I wasn't sure. I cringed, first at the thought that she'd heard my comments on womankind and written me off as a superficial moron, and second at the realization that that's basically what I was.

"Is there enough tea for me?" she asked Rafe.

"Plenty." He poured three mugs, pushed one toward me, handed another to Sharon. "What do you mean he's too young? You were twenty-one when we got married. Will's older than that."

"But I'm a woman. We mature faster." She smiled and sipped her tea. "You were thirty when we met, remember? Thirty-one when we got married. Would you have us believe that when you were young, you ever took good company over you-know? I don't think so."

As she said this, something happened that I'd never seen before: Rafe went beet red.

"Don't get me wrong," I said, gripped by a strong urge to save face, Rafe's and mine. "I've got nothing against good company. I wouldn't spend time with someone I didn't like or couldn't have a conversation with. She just doesn't need to be, like, my soulmate or anything."

From the pitying look Sharon cast me, it was clear I'd only dug myself in deeper. I took a gulp of tea. It burned as it went down.

"William, William." Rafe, still flushed, spoke quietly. "You are so full of shit. You play it all cool and laid-back, no ties, no commitments. But one day it's gonna hit you. You mark my words. Inside that lanky body is a heart that's gonna swell so big it'll knock you flat. That's the day that'll change your life." On the last word, his voice actually broke.

I stole a glance at Sharon, who was frowning.

"Life is short," he went on. "So goddamn short. The only thing that matters is the ones you love. We all learn that in our own way. I did, and God knows my ma and da did. One day you will."

"Rafe, honey —" Sharon stood up.

"Tell you what," Rafe said, ignoring her. "Help me haul the old tank out to the garage and we'll call it a day. You can go get spruced up for your meaningless date. Lord knows, you need all the time you can get."

He winked, as if to say he was back to himself again. His voice, flat and melancholy, said different.

ELEVEN

October

RACHEL WAS RIGHT. Two glasses of wine with lunch, especially when lunch consists of a few forkfuls of thin risotto, is over the limit. As Sharon exits the Left Coast Café, leaving behind the Peter Pan waiter and a fifteen percent tip, which she considered reducing before timidly dismissing the idea, her hip bumps the wooden bench outside the café door. Definitely too much wine.

One bracing inhale of the autumn air and she opts for a salutary stroll outdoors instead of a bleary-eyed ramble through the library stacks. Yet her wooziness clings to her as she walks the trendy, tree-lined boulevard, barely noticing the designer shops, yoga outfitters, artisanal bakeries, and latte bars that supply the sundries of this well-heeled part of town. Her head swims with thoughts of Rafe and weddings and the taut, vacant man in the café whom she'd fooled her-self into admiring.

The lies we tell ourselves. So many lies.

For starters she lied to Rachel about how she and Rafe met. Not the how, when, and where, those details were accurate enough, but the story suffered from a certain amount of distortion, or rather omission.

The fender-bender, for one thing. That was completely her fault. Stuck on the Don Valley Parkway in stop-and-go traffic, a construction zone having stretched the normal rush hour well into the evening, she'd leaned forward to turn up the radio — she loved that song about Jack and

Diane — then looked up to see that the vehicle in front of her, a black sports car with a beetled rump (a 1972 Porsche 911, she later learned), had pulled well ahead. Free at last! She tromped on the gas and spent the next two decades wondering whether to blame the boppy music, her scant experience behind the wheel, or the sheer joy of advancing more than a foot for her out-of-control acceleration. The car ahead stopped suddenly, too suddenly for the worn brakes of her battered Mazda, and she plowed into its sporty little rear, crunching the metal and fixing the course of her life.

She also lied about, or at least fudged, the part about Rafe being eager to please. Not at first he wasn't. He lunged out of his car like an uncaged fighter, shoulders rounded for a bruising, face thunderous. "You gotta be fuckin' kidding me!" he yelled as he strode toward her. "We're in a fuckin' traffic jam! We're going slower than a toddler on training wheels! How in the fuckin' fuck could you possibly rear-end me?"

Sharon, freshly twenty and still very much a girl — what's more, a daddy's girl who lived at home, deferred to her parents, and kept a stuffed animal (maybe two) on her coverletted bed — did what a girl sometimes does in a catastrophe: she burst into tears. Gripping the steering wheel with both hands, she gave herself over to it, fat drops of panic and shame rolling down her cheeks and onto her blue-jeaned lap.

"Jesus, girl." Rafe peered through the rolled-down window. "Don't do that. Don't cry."

She sobbed harder.

"Aw shit. I didn't mean to yell. I'm just … Lord thunderin', my *car*." He glanced mournfully at his vehicle. "Look, we can't stay like this, blocking traffic." Behind them snaked a line of Toronto commuters, tense at the best of times but now stoked to maim and destroy. "There's a Subway off the next exit. We'll park in the lot and figure things out. Okay?"

Sharon nodded, still crying. A string of salty snot crept down her upper lip.

"Buck up, girl." Concern had filed the ferocious edge off his voice. "It's gonna be fine. Just follow me. And no funny stuff. I got your licence plate number."

She was too shaken to do anything but what she was told. In the smallish Subway lot, she was relieved to see no two spaces together; at least she'd be spared the mortification of swiping the sports car a second time while trying to park next to it. She pulled into a spot several down from Rafe's dented vehicle and sat there, breathing raggedly, trying to compose herself. Within seconds he rapped on the car roof. "C'mon, get out and stretch your legs. You'll feel better."

She obeyed. Though the clock said evening, the air shimmered as if it were midday, the parking lot a giant sponge for the July sun. Her tight jeans stuck to her legs; her sleeveless blouse hung damp and wrinkled as a hanky.

"I'm sorry," she mumbled.

"No, I am. I shouldn't have yelled at you. I'm a big galoot."

She pushed her long hair out of her face. "A what?" She forced herself to meet his eyes, big brown eyes—that much of what she told Rachel was true—but she didn't find them, or their owner, attractive. All she saw was trouble. Trouble that she had caused.

"Galoot. A big galoot. That's what my ma used to call me. Name's actually Rafe. Rafe Mackie." He produced a half-smile. "Though under the circumstances you can stick with galoot. And you are?"

"Sharon. Talbot."

"Okay, Sharon Talbot. I shouldn't have let my mouth run away on me. But my car." He gestured toward the black Porsche, hunched low in its space as if nursing wounds. "Christ almighty. I only bought her a month ago and I been fixing her up ever since, I just put the new chrome onto her, and now ..."

Sharon lowered her gaze. "It was my fault. I thought the traffic was moving again and I went too fast. We don't need to argue about what happened. Just tell me what to do."

Rafe suggested she pay him directly for the damage and leave the insurance companies out of it. Then she wouldn't have to admit fault, her parents needn't find out (she could say she swiped a fire hydrant or something), and no one's premiums would go up. Sharon agreed immediately, in part because he offered to repair both vehicles himself, charging her only for materials, but mostly because she wanted the problem to disappear.

It was also true that Rafe asked her to dinner, right there in the parking lot, her cheeks still tear-salted. But contrary to what she told Rachel, she'd refused. Besides being too rattled to eat, she wasn't sure she trusted this man, charging like a pit bull one minute, backing down the next. Only when he downgraded the invitation to coffee did she agree. "There's still a hellish drive ahead," he pointed out. "We should both unwind before crawling back into that mayhem."

Gradually, over wretched coffee at the Subway — his treat, he insisted, since he'd be taking her money soon enough — she began to relax. Rafe, a man of appetites as she would learn, went back for a refill, then a foot-long sub, then two chocolate chip cookies. Sharon, who refused all food and abandoned her coffee after the first sip, watched as he inhaled it all. He drank her in too. *Intense* was a word people used about Rafe Mackie, and his unwavering gaze and fascination with each detail she offered, at first unsettling, disarmed her bit by bit. In the busy restaurant off the parkway, a steady queue of sandwich-seekers in and out the door, a boisterous trio of house painters at the corner table, Rafe noticed nothing and no one but her. It was as if he'd drawn a translucent curtain around the two of them, created an intimate nook from which life outside remained visible but with its edges blurred and sounds muted. Sharon, never before singled out in a crowd, never special to anyone beyond her family, warmed in the spotlight. Who could withstand that kind of attention? she would ask herself later. Who could dodge the high beams of a big-hearted galoot?

From the time they started dating until they married the following summer, a year and two weeks after their fateful accident, Sharon heard repeatedly from her family and friends, and from Rafe's friends too, that she'd scored big when she landed this man. Her father, a suit-and-tie insurance man, applauded Rafe's occupation, all the more impressive next to the career choice of Colleen's boyfriend, the evening clerk at a video rental store. A pilot, her father said, has his head in the clouds but his feet on the ground. Her mother rejoiced that Rafe was ten years older, the perfect age gap and not coincidentally the precise interval between herself and her beloved husband. "He's a hunk and he's obviously crazy about you" was Colleen's assessment after Rafe's first dinner with the family. "He couldn't take his eyes off you all evening. It's like you put a spell on him." Sharon's girlfriends concurred: he was a first-class catch in every way. Does he have a brother? they asked. A cousin? In the onslaught of approval, Sharon could think of no reason not to let this man join his life to hers, fashion her a future, and give her a family.

When it came to his own family, Rafe was strangely tight-lipped. His father, he reported when Sharon pressed, was dead. His mother, a crotchety Scotswoman old beyond her years, would not attend their wedding owing to a lifelong inability to step off Cape Breton Island. They were the first and almost the last details he ever parted with about his parents or his faraway birthplace. Like Sharon, Rafe had only one sibling, a brother who at the time worked nonstop in the Alberta oilfields and didn't meet Sharon until the rehearsal dinner. "Whoa," Sheldon said, holding her at arm's length after Rafe had introduced them. "Now I see why you're in such a hurry to marry this one. Do it, boy. Shove a ring onto her finger before she finds out that under that pilot's uniform is nothing but an oversized knucklehead."

Everyone agreed: fortune smiled when it brought these two together. The wedding unfolded with no histrionics or rancour, no ancient aunt grousing about how the youngsters were ruining their lives, no old flames getting soused and blubbering over broken hearts, just sunshine and leafy shade and the sprawling Muskoka summer home of a pilot friend of Rafe's.

After the ceremony but before the food and drink, as guests mingled on the back lawn, a rumble shook the air. Thunder? Sharon thought. Please, not today. Gradually people fell silent, and one by one they craned their necks as, below the wispy clouds that threaded the bluest sky, there appeared an airplane, swooping in low and towing a banner. As the plane neared, levelling out over the lake behind the property, the message streamed out for all to see: "Sharon, you make my heart soar."

On cue Rafe raised a champagne flute and clasped his new wife's waist. "To the loveliest bride a man could ever dream of," he said, and everyone drank as the banner of love vanished beyond the trees.

Is that when the lies began? Sharon's distorted reflection peers at her now from the window of a high-priced handbag shop she will never, in a million years, enter. Did the deceit take root there, among the people she loved and should have been honest with? Was she truly happy that day, stepping into a future she genuinely wanted? Or was she assuming a role, the young bride mouthing lines that others had written, beside a man whom others had cast, believing that if you speak something often and convincingly, it will turn into truth?

TWELVE

Thirteen days after

THREE DAYS I'VE BEEN BACK at work, or more accurately marking time at the West Air office until I'm allowed to properly work again. Three noon hours I've sat cooped up with The Counsellor, who keeps bringing the empty yellow file folder, maybe so I'll have something to focus on while I'm avoiding eye contact. I'd like to say we've made progress on what she calls my coping skills, but from where I sit now, on my sagging sofa, piled high with takeout containers and wrappers and unlaundered clothes, progress is not what I see.

It's not The Counsellor. She's doing her best. In fact, her monotone voice and concerned eyebrows are, in a weird way, starting to grow on me. She just doesn't have much to work with. I've never been one to articulate my feelings, as she puts it. It's a failing that every girl I've dated longer than six weeks has helpfully pointed out before dumping my sorry ass.

Probably I haven't had the best models. After my mom died my dad went quiet for a long time, like the bulk of my teenage years. Looking back, I know he missed her so much that words weren't up to the task. Instead we worked on projects: finishing the solarium he'd been framing when the cancer was diagnosed; fixing up an ancient dirt bike, a junker he promised would work by my sixteenth birthday (it did); camping on long weekends, which threatened us with their unscheduled days. When we found ourselves indoors, driven there by bad weather or nighttime, we got lost in other people's stories, my dad drawn to thick paperbacks by Leon Uris and Charles Dickens (any book with a plot like an intestine, as he'd put it), me graduating from Archie comics and Hardy Boys to sci-fi trilogies and crime novels. Some evenings he'd pull out the chessboard and try, as if this time the outcome might be different, to interest me in the game. For his sake I pretended we were not engaged in the slowest, most numbing pursuit known to man. I knew he was only looking to distract me, and probably himself, from the unthinkable admission that we had lost her.

Still, we got through that time, my dad and I, and we did it without the breakdowns or soul-baring monologues you're told you should go through to straighten out the twisted shit life drops in your lap. Like stealing your wife when you're forty-two and still deeply, publicly in love with her. Like leaving you without a mom when you're fourteen and can't picture the world without her in it. Since then my dad's come around enough to have a few lady friends, none of them serious but all of them kind, and for a time diverting. For me, although I still miss her, it's a far-off loss, like a bone you broke long ago that aches now and then.

I'm proud of how my dad and I handled things, quietly and on our own, and I still, maybe more than ever, believe that feelings are meant to be felt, not narrated and shared in excruciating detail for months and years until the wide world around you, with all its people and experiences, shrinks to a pinhole at the end of which lies your own pathetic navel.

I believe too — not that I'll treat The Counsellor to this theory — that for a guy it's more natural to skip the guided tour, to deal with crap your own way, on your own time. It's what Rafe did after the death of his mother, his last family in Cape Breton.

The day after we replaced the hot water tank and he went all quiet and strange, he called me. It was a dismal afternoon, still cold and thick with rain. I'd gotten next to no sleep the night before (the date was indeed hot) and almost blew him off when he asked me to meet him at the pub, but some echo of his moroseness from the day before changed my mind. By the time I slid into the corner booth, he was half-cut and bleak as shit. Not so much sad as pent up, like he'd take a swing at the first loser to look at him wrong.

He would not go to the funeral, he declared after ordering a double round of scotch. His brother could handle that nonsense. Nor would he waste another day moping around. He would drink one toast to his ma and that would be the end of it.

Now that I had some idea what the hell he was talking about, I raised my single malt along with him. "To the finest woman that ever was," he said. "May God rest her soul." He tossed the shot back, twenty bucks' worth in one go, and shuddered as it hit. "I'm going to say this one time, young William." He spoke with exaggerated slowness. "For what I put that woman through, the trouble, the loss ... ah Jesus, the shame of it, I will never forgive myself. Ever. I fixed it up as best I could, but at what price, eh?" He slid his empty glass to the centre of the scarred wooden table. "Imagine it. Never go home again. Never see your only ma again." I waited for more, but when I started to ask he held up a hand. He was done.

It was the last I ever heard about the mother of Rafe Mackie and the last he ever said of his childhood past. The gloom possessed him for weeks. It muffled his voice whenever we spoke, which was less often that spring. He didn't feel like going out, he said. He turned down jobs from my dad, stopped answering the phone for a spell. But things ran their course, and by the time fire season rolled around he was himself again. Whatever grieving he did, he did it in private, without fanfare. He didn't sign up for years of therapy or declare every emotion as he experienced it. Several stiff drinks, one short speech, a stretch of time, and it was done.

My point is, privacy counts for a lot. In the feeding frenzy of social media and reality TV and tell-all talk shows, there's something noble about keeping your business to yourself.

If only I could get that across to the people who keep hounding me. The Counsellor has no choice; it's her job to harp on this "talk about your feelings" crap. But it's not my neighbour Melody's job, even though she has declared it her "personal mission" to "free my awareness" so that we can "share and compare" what has happened. How she's in a position to either share or compare is beyond me. Both, to my mind, involve an exchange. How can she give her side of an event she had no part in?

Something I didn't share (or compare) with The Counsellor is that starting last week, a few days before I was due back at work, Melody took to tapping on my door around noon before heading to Granville Island, where she fills in afternoons and evenings at (it's almost too obvious) an aromatherapy shop. After work she'd stop by again and pull some food-like item out of her wicker basket, curried lentil soup one night, daikon-carrot slaw another, something called an omega-3 muffin at one point — exotic offerings that prove, ironically, her deep adherence to convention. No matter how outrageously she dresses, how many tattoos and holes and henna patterns speckle her body, Melody is a small-town Ontario girl, taught that to draw a man from his shell you show an interest in him and, when the going gets tough, bring food.

The night of the muffin, which I chucked onto the coffee table, where it landed like a cow patty next to two empty Red Bull cans, Melody pushed her way in. No invitation, no hesitation, just barged past me into the living room, where she took a dramatic sniff. "Your lair" — as she has since taken to calling it — "is getting … um … funky. You know, stale." Her nose quivered as only a trained aromatherapy nose can.

"It's a donair from earlier." I stood, feet apart, in the middle of the room, praying that her small-town manners extended to never sitting down unless invited. They didn't.

"It's not a donair." She arranged herself in the armchair with her legs pretzeled, arms straight out, hands twisted together, no doubt some kind of yoga pose.

"Yeah, I think it is."

She brought her hands in to her chest, then pushed them upward, exhaling noisily so I would know this was not a random movement but a practised, meaningful sequence. "Will, you are so confined. Your inner self is all closed off. When was the last time you left this apartment? Like, days ago? It's a beautiful summer night out there." She swept one arm toward the balcony. "Come out with me, breathe the air, look at the stars. You need to get some perspective, connect with the universe. That's why you're so bottled up. Come on, just around the block."

"No thanks." I inched toward the door, praying she'd take the hint.

"Come on! There's a secret place down the street, I bet you've never seen it. The courtyard at the Arbutus Arms."

"That dump on the corner? With the missing stucco and the Pepto Bismol shutters?" I hovered near the door, poised to usher her out.

"A highly negative person might describe it that way. There's this garden you can't see from the street. You have to go through the gates, they're never locked, then under the archway. Once you're inside it's like a different world." Like a fawn she leapt off the chair, grabbed my wrist, opened the apartment door, and pulled for all she was worth, which wasn't much seeing as she's five-foot-nothing and lives on leaves and pods. I didn't budge.

"Come on." She tugged my wrist with both hands.

With her brow all furrowed and her nose scrunched up, she could have been a mouse pulling on a Clydesdale. I couldn't help but laugh. "Okay, you win. But just a few minutes. Then I must re-enter the lair."

Melody bounced down the stairs ahead of me, setting off a chaotic jangle from a wristful of bracelets and what I swear were little bells on her long skirt. Wherever we were headed, our entrance would not be stealthy.

I lagged behind, my first day of pre-work sobriety making it surprisingly difficult to negotiate the stairs. As I stumbled on the bottom step, I wondered how I'd manage the Aerostar controls in a week. Maybe I'd underestimated how long it took to detox.

True to her word, Melody guided us to the scuzziest building on a block not known for architectural wonders. She pushed open the flaking wrought-iron gate, then led me under the archway and down a short concrete path.

The first thing that struck me was the size. Enclosed by the wings of apartments, the courtyard opened up generously. Floodlights illuminated the central area, planted with trees and shrubs and flower borders, but didn't reach the corners, which bled into darkness and made the space seem bigger. Melody headed for a bench beside a laceleaf maple. Once we sat, I registered the splash of running water behind us and the twinkle of white lights in the branches above. The air smelled sweet, a little canvassy. I hoped my verbalizing neighbour would stay quiet for a while, and she did.

Evening sounds slipped through the apartment windows, many of them open to the summer night. Someone was putting away dishes, and a clatter rang out as plate slid onto plate. Voices drifted from a balcony several floors up. A guy sat on the sill of a second-storey window smoking, the grey wisps suspended in the floodlit air. Behind us faint music mixed with the sound of the fountain.

It was beautiful, this courtyard, its fragrant plants, damp air, and soft light, the sounds of life being lived all around us.

Gradually the music built and the tune, a vague melody at first, took shape. Acoustic guitar and a skinny snare drum and then, as the volume rose, a voice like the fur of a big, soft dog.

No, I thought. There's no way. Of all the songs, at all the times, it couldn't be. But it was.

As Otis filled the air I heard Rafe, the big grin audible in his voice, say how much he loved this damn song, and every point of pain inside me gathered into one fierce spot. In the second verse, Otis's voice broke soulfully on a syllable and the song pulled me down with it, my head falling into my hands, my body caving.

"It's okay, Will." Mingled with the music and the fountain, Melody's voice was so low I might have imagined it. "It's okay," she said again.

She didn't touch me. In spite of all her flakiness and need to share, she knew not to touch me. She just sat there, feet grazing the ground.

In that moment, hearing that song and remembering all it meant to Rafe, and all that Rafe meant to me, I knew that Melody was wrong. It would not be okay. Not now, not for a long time.

PART TWO

INVESTIGATION

THIRTEEN

July–August

THE THREE WEEKS FOLLOWING the Tracker crash unfolded like a deck of aces, one perfect sunny day after another. Only twice did it rain, both times waiting until night, the fortuitousness of which buoyed local forecasters, accustomed to delivering gloomier outlooks in this famously waterlogged city. From Wreck Beach near UBC to Ambleside on the North Shore, every patch of sand was layered with bare, lotioned bodies. Every eating establishment with a patio and craft beer list was mobbed from noon till closing.

Day after day, the clear skies filled with aircraft. Weather like this beckoned weekend warriors, green pilots who logged a few amateur hours on Cessnas and homebuilts that seldom ventured beyond the hangar. Hikers, campers, hunters, and anglers descended on wild pockets of British Columbia accessible only by air, and the charter outfits pushed their pilots hard, running hazardous back-country flights for as long as tourists swiped their credit cards. For the TSB, perfect summer weather meant accidents, and this year was no exception.

The flawless conditions hardly registered with Nathalie, who spent the three weeks in a personal fog. The Robinson R22 crash, which had happened on a day as calm and blue as any these past weeks had to offer, sat unsolved at the top of her list. From Monday to Friday she combed maintenance logs and researched service bulletins, desperate for a lead.

So far not a crumb. No developments for reporters, hungry for updates on James Stanhope III, and nothing for Tucker, to win back his trust. Please, Mémère, she said silently each morning while checking email, let me close this one soon. It was her first case as lead investigator since the Cessna 172 fiasco, and she needed to show Tucker, and anyone else who still doubted her, that she could still handle a high-profile accident — and could handle it alone.

Investigations weren't supposed to happen this way. Always the TSB assigned two people to a crash, more if the incident involved a large commercial plane or intense media scrutiny. When the R22 went down, Tucker had paired Nathalie with veteran investigator Vik Gill. A sixty-something former cargo pilot on the long, lazy countdown to retirement, Gill would have been Nathalie's last choice for a hard slog in the mountains. But having no desire to rile the boss, she shut her trap and went along with the assignment. The duo had spent only half a day at the crash site, a hot, sweaty spell of bushwhacking and precarious footing on the steep slopes, when Vik was called in for a long-awaited knee replacement. Within an hour of taking the call, he was on his way home. Nathalie imagined him fist-pumping all the way. And so now, with the other investigators scrambling to cover the summer's accidents, especially the headline-grabbing Tracker crash, Nathalie had to deal with the R22 on her own.

The Tracker. Oh, God.

Three weeks and the office still hummed with speculation. A routine drop, acceptable fire conditions and visibility, a high-time pilot with serious skills. What the hell happened out there?

Jesus, Rafe. What went wrong?

No. Tucker was right to order her off that crash. No way could she get involved. So she made herself leave the corridor or kitchen whenever talk turned to the air tanker and as a result had only the vaguest notion of how the case was shaping up.

Meanwhile, she didn't mind working the R22 alone — preferred it, truth be told. She could follow her own schedule, pursue her own hunches. If she hit a wall she could always confer with her colleagues, who were more than willing to abandon their own puzzles and reflect on someone else's for an hour.

Nathalie's puzzle was still a jumble of unmatched pieces. Goddamned helicopters. Equal parts sophisticated and simple, they were by far the most skittish aircraft to fly, intolerant of error, demanding instant action and utter precision to recover. Like balancing a unicycle on top of a beach ball—that's how pilots described being at the controls. Nathalie had never flown a helicopter, never piloted any aircraft apart from a few attempts on a fixed-wing in her early days at Howe Sound Air. That was enough. The experience had jangled her nerves. Too many variables to compute—controls, gauges, communications, navigation—all at the same time. She decided then and there to leave the flying to others and stick with her forte, the patching up.

It was no sacrifice. From the moment Nathalie picked up her first tool, she relished the thrill of finding airframe flaws and fixing them, of diagnosing a mechanical problem and being certain how to solve it. Aircraft maintenance engineer was the perfect job for a control freak, a label applied to her by more than a few ex-boyfriends. They said it like it was a bad thing. Why? Who, given the choice, wouldn't want to be in control?

Nathalie had loved her work as an AME. She drove herself relentlessly, taking few breaks, volunteering for the dirtiest tasks that no one wanted, staying without complaint into the wee hours to ready an aircraft for morning. Her single-mindedness stemmed in part from a natural work ethic but mainly from her need to show the men she could keep up with them. When midnight found you unkinking your limbs after an hour inside some tiny grease-coated compartment not designed for human entry, it shouldn't matter if you were man or woman as long as you held your own, logged your hours, and did good work. The work was the great leveller. And Nathalie worked. She worked harder than all of them and in the end was as skilled as any of them, especially with helicopters, which became her specialty once she transferred to Mainland Air.

You didn't need to fly aircraft to know them, and Nathalie understood helicopters inside and out, better than she understood her own body. In this case, given Stanhope's dead drop out of the sky, and the peculiarities of the R22, there was one thing she was reasonably sure of: the main rotor blade had stopped during flight. The R22, a popular and reliable chopper, came with an alarming handicap. If power to the rotor cut out, you didn't get the grace period granted by other models during which you could lower the pitch, wait for autorotation to kick in, and control the craft well enough to land it. The R22's low-inertia rotor gave you one second, maybe two, basically long enough to inhale and register that you were in deep shit. By then it was too late. In the space of a few wild heartbeats, your rotor RPMs slowed to where autorotation was impossible, your nimble aircraft became an unresponsive tank, and you were on your way to a rendezvous with the ground.

Power loss that stopped the rotor blade — she'd put money on that being a factor. But as always, the underlying question, the one she was hired to answer, was why. A rotor could stop for many reasons. Did an engine part malfunction? A transmission gear fail? A pitch link in the rotor break?

She needed to narrow down the options, and do it soon. All her hopes now rested on the engine teardown. Delayed twice to accommodate the observers from Robinson, the manufacturer, the event was finally on for next Tuesday. It meant a trip to Victoria, where Lycoming, maker of the R22 engine, would supply an authorized service centre and two mechanics to do the disassembly.

As much as Nathalie depended on the teardown and the evidence it would yield, she also dreaded an exercise that, if the Robinson reps employed their usual stall tactics, could spin out for days. Not that Robinson was unique in prolonging the process. All companies built in extra time so that if a teardown revealed some damning flaw in the aircraft's design or manufacture, they had time to concoct reasons why it couldn't possibly link back to them. Six years of accident investigation had introduced Nathalie to all the major players, and she knew how they worked, especially the helicopter companies.

So next week she would make the trip. She would cross the Strait of Georgia to Victoria, she would plan for an overnight stay, and she would play nice with the Robinson reps. As much as it chafed her to let them call the shots, she would do it. But she didn't have to like it.

∧ ∨ ∧

LACK OF MOVEMENT on the R22 crash was behind much of Nathalie's fogginess of late. So, too, was Jake Behrend.

Since the tingly encounter with her old classmate at BCIT on July 18, the day she got news of Rafe, Nathalie had scarcely given Jake another thought. Between the shock of the Tracker crash and the ongoing R22 file, her attention was fully absorbed.

Then came the email. It was a date she couldn't forget, July 26, the anniversary of Mémère's death. The email arrived that morning, tucked innocently among the couple of dozen others that had accumulated overnight. When Nathalie saw the name, and the sent time of 1:17 a.m., her stomach whooshed like an elevator.

Excited as she was, she waited. She diligently clicked through the work-related messages, most of them pointless and easy to delete. Finally Jake's was the only unread item. Her hand shook, actually trembled, as she opened it. For fuck's sake, she told herself, it's not what you think.

It was.

When they'd parted ways at BCIT, Jake heading off to his job interview there, he'd hinted that the chance encounter could turn into something more. Now the hints had grabbed a megaphone.

Hi Nat,

Its late where I am and I can't stop thinking about you. Seeing you at BCIT after all those yrs was a real surprise...it was exciting.

Like I told you your still as tough as nails. What I didn't tell you is your still the sexiest woman I ever met. I want to push your hair back and whisper it in your ear, then I want to do much more.

Please? You wont be sorry, I promise.

Jake

Her pulse raced as she reread the email, twice, astounded that it said the same thing each time. Jake Behrend wanted her. Holy shit. There was no doubt about it, no guessing required.

By the fourth read she had come to her senses. The wording was crude, not to mention badly spelled. It verged on arrogant. Hell, *he* was arrogant. In the busy foyer of BCIT she had told Jake clearly and unequivocally that she would not sleep with him, yet here he was again, presuming that a few cheap compliments and a sprinkling of innuendo could change her mind. The nerve of him, the self-centred bastard. The self-centred *married* bastard.

Yet the image of what he proposed would not leave her. Try as she might to forget the email, and she did try, she really did, she kept imagining his hands in her hair, his hockey-toned body against hers. She kept picturing that face — arrogant, yes, but still astonishing after fifteen years.

Breathe, she told herself, trying to loosen the vise on her solar plexus, which she recognized, grudgingly, as desire. Jake Behrend, the original stud. Holy shit.

On the matter of Jake's email, the voice of Mémère stayed silent. There came no warnings to steer clear of Jake because he worked in aviation, maybe because as an instructor he was barely in Nathalie's field. There was no whispered caution against tangling with a married man, maybe because on that front her grandmother held no opinion.

Bullshit. She had an opinion. Mémère had warned Nathalie before about getting involved with husbands. Maybe she'd gone silent this time because Nathalie never listened.

And so, at the end of the first bright week of August, Nathalie moved Jake's email to her Miscellaneous Crap folder, where it sat unanswered and on some days unremembered, and went back to sifting through the scanty R22 evidence, willing it to reveal something new. She went on logging the hours, counting down the time, trying to immerse herself in the distractions of the upcoming teardown and occasional images of Jake. Yet through it all, like a stream unable to remake its course, her thoughts kept returning to the Tracker, and to Rafe.

July 18 — she dated everything from that black day. The R22 went down three days before the Tracker. The email from Jake arrived eight days after.

The Tracker was not her crash, and Rafe was no longer her man, yet the scene played out repeatedly in her mind in a gruesome, full-colour loop. Six years on the job had schooled her in the many ways a downed aircraft can pulverize and incinerate a body. She had no need to view the wreckage, which filled a corner of the TSB warehouse, to know how Rafe had met his end. A dozen times a day his body lurched toward her, twisted, broken, and charred from the fire that engulfed his plane. Every time she checked email she saw him. Standing in line at Starbucks she saw him. When she sorted laundry or shopped at the farmers market or rode her bike in the evening, activities that bore no relationship to Rafe or the crash, she saw him. Rafe, his legs splayed at unnatural angles, the glint of bone winking through, waited on the front steps of her condo building. His head, cleaved open and spilling brains, lolled on the kitchen table as she sectioned grapefruit. In crowds she saw his leather bomber jacket slashed open across its broad back. On quiet evenings she saw his eyes, which had once swept her face and her body, alive with desire, now half-lidded by burned, lashless flesh.

Better to hit than be hit, Mémère always said. It was the piece of advice Nathalie heeded the most. She had ended it with Rafe. She'd folded him neatly and packed him away, another piece of memorabilia in the storage trunk of her past. She had protected herself. And what did she have to show for it? A haunting. Try as she might to scoff at the idea, that's what it was, this broken body of Rafe Mackie. The harder she tried to banish the disfigured ghost that trailed her everywhere, the more stubbornly it appeared.

FOURTEEN

Fourteen days after

IT'S OVER, that's the only good thing about it.

All week I've been dreading it, the thought putting me off food and sleep, not that I'm a poster boy in either area just now. Every day it's been crouching there in the background when I roll out of bed, do office errands for Jeff, or spool out the lunchtime confession hour. Today I had to face it. Since morning I've felt my guts coiled tight inside me, like springs that might let go and stick me full of holes, tiny and lethal.

The message had arrived on Monday, my first day back at work, while I was closeted away with The Counsellor: Roy Shields from the Transportation Safety Board needed to interview me about the accident. I knew from the brief questioning the day of the crash that the TSB would eventually haul me in for the full-meal deal, but still, I was pissed. Couldn't they give me one measly day to get my shit together before they pounced?

I waited until four thirty that afternoon to return the call, using Roy's office number instead of his cell in the belief that like every card-carrying government worker he'd have gone home for the day. He picked up on the first ring. It turned out the earliest he could meet me was today. At the time I thought I'd gotten a break, a few days to collect myself, but in hindsight the delay was no gift. What it gave me was three long days to worry, to run through what they'd ask me and think of ways to tell the story without losing it like a blubbering idiot, and without saying anything they could use against Rafe.

Because the fact is, and I keep replaying this in my head, he wasn't himself that morning. I knew it the minute his grin, predictable as the sunrise, didn't appear. He put it down to being tired, but I didn't buy it. He hadn't been himself all season, really — nothing major, just moody, a bit off.

What was up with him? I have no idea. He never said. So why the hell didn't I ask? That's the question that gnaws at me in the wee hours, when I lie awake replaying the crash day. Granted, that morning was hardly the ideal time for a heart-to-heart, seeing as the call to fly would come any minute, but that's not the real reason I didn't ask. The real reason, when I force myself to admit it, is simple and spectacularly selfish: I didn't want to go there. I was juiced up that morning, raring to go despite my short sleep. Maybe even because of my short sleep. The memory of Gracie was still fresh, I could smell her on my fingers, and I was hoping her long legs would wrap around me one more time before we left town. We had a hard day of flying ahead, but the conditions were good. That fire was ours, we had it in the bag. The truth is, I didn't want anything to bring me down.

Bring me down. There's a choice of words. My last chance to ask Rafe what the hell was going on with him before he was brought down — for fucking ever — and I let it go. I didn't ask him, and so I will never know.

None of that could I tell the TSB. I needed to stick to the facts of the flight and list all the things Rafe had done right: responded to our radio call, followed his pattern and drop instructions, flown the plane as accurately and confidently as ever. The TSB needed to know that whatever went wrong as he closed in over that fire, Rafe Mackie was not to blame.

I left home late this morning and drove straight to the TSB office. No point going to West Air first and pretending to work for forty-five minutes. I parked in a shady corner well away from the government building and peeled the gauze off my jaw where I'd nicked myself shaving. Good, the cut was barely visible. For some reason it seemed important to appear unscathed during this discussion of death and destruction.

So I'm at the rear-view mirror, dabbing my face with spit, when I catch a glimpse of leg and curly hair moving toward the front door. Of course I turn around and look. I mean, come on. The sure stride tells me it's someone who works there, and then it clicks. Nathalie Girard. I've never seen her in person, only heard about her, the lone woman in air investigation, the renowned babe. Last year I heard she landed in hot water over that Cessna crash up near Prince Rupert, blabbed to the media or something. I'd forgotten that she worked for the TSB and could be spotted around the premises.

I waited for her to go inside, then counted to a hundred, surely enough time for her to disappear into her office. Babe though she is, I was in no mood to meet anyone I didn't have to, to make small talk and pretend that I hadn't heard all about her and she hadn't heard all about me.

The person who greeted me when I pushed open the door was decidedly not Nathalie Girard. The front desk was commanded, and I use the term deliberately, by one who could be called the anti-Nathalie: a big-boned woman with thin yellow hair to her considerable shoulders, wearing glasses, a giant headset, a blouse buttoned up to her chin, and a scowl I was betting was permanent. *Luanne* said the nameplate on the desk. The woman herself said nothing.

"Hello?" I tried.

"Good morning can I help you," she fired off, eyes on the computer monitor. Her voice was as gravelled and deep as my father's.

"Yeah, I'm here to see Roy? Roy Shields?"

"Is that a question?" She looked up and pinned me with laser eyes.

"I — ah, no. It's a fact. I have an appointment."

"Fine then, I'll see if he's in." Her scowl intensified as she picked up the phone.

Great. Giving me the gears already. I scanned the employee board behind the desk, where the red marker beside "Shields, Roy" was one of five or six in the *In* column. Interestingly, "Girard, Nathalie" was still marked *Out*.

"He'll be here in a moment," Luanne snapped. She turned back to her computer.

Too fidgety to sit, I edged over to the wide front window. There, across the lot, was my black Tacoma TRD, truck of my dreams, resting in the shady spot I'd chosen. What I wouldn't give to retrace my steps, climb inside the cab, and drive — north or south, it didn't matter; my passport was always in the glove box — just drive until the sun set and the closest familiar face was hours away.

"Will?"

I turned to see a tall, fit man with a grey crewcut, hand extended. "I'm Roy. Good of you to make the time." His grip was mighty and he held on a fraction longer than necessary. "We appreciate it."

"Sure." Like I had a choice.

Roy led me past the front desk. "Luanne, I'll be in the boardroom. Lyndon too. No interruptions, okay?" If Luanne heard him there was no sign of it. She stabbed furiously at the keyboard, headset bobbing with every stroke. I pictured her shouting football plays into a mouthpiece, a field of oversized men quaking at her feet.

We turned the corner and entered a boardroom that was what you'd expect: beige walls, big flat-screen TV at one end, ceiling-mounted projector, no windows except a tall glass panel beside the door that gave a slivered glimpse of the equally beige hallway outside. Up the centre of the room ran a veneer conference table surrounded by a dozen chairs, few of which matched. In one of them sprawled a long-limbed man with a scrubbed face and thinning blond hair. He stood to shake my hand. "Good to see you again," he said from several inches above me. "We met two weeks ago at the crash site. Lyndon Johnson."

There must be some minimum height requirement for this job, I thought, forgetting for the moment Nathalie, roughly the size of an adolescent.

Lyndon waited a few beats before adding: "Like the American President."

I stared at him, lost.

"My name. Like the former US President, Lyndon Johnson."

"Oh, right. I'm Will. Like … Will Werner. Well, you know that."

Lyndon's smile flashed like a shark's bite. My cheeks flamed. I was what you might call ill at ease.

"Take a seat," said Roy, indicating the other side of the table. He settled in beside Lyndon and nudged a small voice recorder that sat on the table. "You don't mind if we record this."

It didn't sound like a question. "I guess not."

Roy switched the recorder on. "Standard procedure. If at any point you want it off, that's fine. It's your choice." He glanced down at a pad of yellow paper covered with writing. "I'm the IIC, the investigator in charge of this incident. Lyndon is the technical investigator. He'll ask you some questions on the mechanical side. I'm looking into the operational stuff, flight patterns, pilot decision-making, timing of the drops, that sort of thing. We may be here awhile, so if you need a break just say so. Washroom's down the hall to the left, water cooler's right behind you. Any questions before we start?"

"I can't think of any."

"All right. Please state your full name and position."

"William Joseph Werner. That's Werner with a *W*, not a *V* the way it sounds. Bird dog pilot with West Air Flight Services."

"How long have you been with West Air?"

"Ten years, since 2003. Though I did some part-time flying with them for two years before that."

"And your pilot experience before West Air?"

I walked them through it: first flying lesson at fourteen, a birthday gift from my dad; private pilot's licence at sixteen; commercial training once I dropped out of university; and once I qualified to fly commercially, four years in small planes around central and northern BC, spelling off regular pilots at any company that would have me.

"How'd you get on at West Air?" Roy asked.

"This floatplane pilot I'd worked with in Fort St. John got hired there. We'd stayed in touch, the odd phone call here and there, he invited me to his wedding, that sort of thing. He calls out of the blue to say they're looking for someone who can start right away. Two pilots bailed at the beginning of the season, health problems the way I understand it, and the company was in a panic. He put in a good word for me, said I was a fast learner. That's mainly what they needed under the circumstances."

"How long did you work with Rafe?"

"We started full-time at West Air the same year, so ten years."

"Were you usually the one to fly bird dog with him?"

"We were pretty much always a team. That's usually how it goes. If they get a bird dog and a tanker pilot who work in synch, they tend to keep them together. It's more efficient. Safer too. The more you fly together, the better you can read each other. You know how your partner operates, how he likes to do a drop, whether he's careful and picky or more fast and loose. You know, is he a Boy Scout or a cowboy. You get to the point where you practically know what he's going to do before he does it."

"Fascinating," said Lyndon. I'd been wondering when he would chime in. "Sounds not unlike a loved one, say a spouse."

What the hell was that supposed to mean? "Uh, more like someone you've known a long time, like an old friend or a family member." I shifted in the lumpy chair. It felt the way I imagine a camel's back would. "It's like a family at West Air. There's not a lot of turnover. Rafe ... God, it was the last thing anyone expected."

Roy nodded. Lyndon played with a silver pen, spinning it around on the table, so caught up in the action that I wondered if they'd finished, until Lyndon started in again.

"So tell us in your own words what happened that day."

My own words? Who else's would I use? I bit my lip and pulled myself back to the beginning. "I went up with Ernie Louis. He's an air attack officer with the BC ministry of forests, the one I fly with most of the time in the Interior. You're talking to him too, right?"

"Mmm," said Lyndon. "The Indian."

If this guy was trying to put me at ease, he was failing big time. The pen-spinning was bad enough. Now he was giving off serious asshole vibes.

I did my best to stay calm. "So we go up to assess the situation, do our dummy run. We overfly the area twice so Ernie can get a handle on the fire and the wind. We talk it over and decide how much of a load Rafe should drop and where. We come up with the circuit he should fly — basically drop retardant along the outer edges of the fire to box it in and keep it from spreading. The wind wasn't too bad. It was supposed to pick up later, but at that point it was only a breeze so we didn't have to adjust much for load drift. It also meant a simple drop, an equal release of retardant on all four sides, since the fire wasn't trending in any one direction."

"What about the terrain?" asked Roy.

"Straightforward. The ground rose a little on the west and east flanks of the fire, but it was gradual, maybe seven, eight percent. Not too steep. The plan was for Rafe to fly those parts of the circuit downhill so he wouldn't have to drop into rising terrain. It was an easy circuit to fly."

"What about the trees?" Roy asked. "How'd they look from the air?"

My tongue felt dry and sticky. I knew we'd get to the trees. "They were tall, mature. Eighty-five, a hundred feet? It was an even-age stand — you know, the trees all roughly the same height, no huge ones sticking out above the rest. We ordered up an even, steady flight, climbing after takeoff and then levelling off to come in parallel with the terrain on the south flank of the fire. And of course we did the dummy run first so he'd know what circuit to fly and where to drop." I looked at Roy, then Lyndon — looked them square in the face — and brought my fingers to my jaw where I'd nicked it. "There was nothing unusual about the run. The trees he clipped — well, I still don't get it. They were visible. The visibility was good up there over top of the fire."

Lyndon treated me to another predatory grin. It did not add to his appeal. His neat blond hair and shiny round cheeks suggested health and innocence with a strong vein of ugly underneath, like a televangelist or a pedophile. "Earlier you mentioned that when you fly with a pilot for a certain length of time, you learn whether he is more of a" — he consulted his notes — "more of a Boy Scout or a cowboy. How would you describe Rafe?"

Fuck. I saw instantly that I had set a trap and placed it right at my own feet. That's why I won't play chess, despite the hours my father spent trying to teach me. You need to think ahead more, he'd say. You've got the moves down, but you have to get inside your opponent's head and figure out how he's likely to react.

Once again I had proved that I'm not the tactician my dad hoped for but instead a bone-headed idiot. I licked my lips. "Rafe was a highly experienced pilot who was known for his accuracy."

"He had, what? Eighteen years as an aerial firefighter?" Roy asked, glancing at his yellow pad.

Lyndon spoke before I could. "You say he was known for his accuracy. Enlighten us further."

"He made a lot of bull's eyes, more than anyone." Lyndon's eyebrows drew together, so I explained. "A bull's eye is when you drop the load exactly where you're instructed to. You have to release it at the exact right second and pull up at the exact right spot. Rafe was very good at that."

"Presumably this bull's eye is a desirable accomplishment," Lyndon said.

"Right. It's like getting a hundred on a test. It's what the tanker pilots are always shooting for."

"But getting a hundred isn't always a good thing." Lyndon leaned back slightly and continued to play with his pen. "Sometimes getting a hundred has certain ... drawbacks."

My right knee began to jackhammer up and down. "I'm not following."

Lyndon gave the pen a few more spins. "Some people are so keen to score a hundred that they will go to any lengths to do so. They may act in ways that they know are wrong, like copying another student's answers or procuring the test beforehand. They are so badly in need of the perfect mark that they take risks which could put them in serious jeopardy."

There was a risk I wanted to take, and it was to grab the goddamned pen and plunge it into that asshole's smug round face. Roy must've sensed something because he leaned toward Lyndon and neatly smacked the silver pen, stopping it in mid-rotation. The thud of metal on table left the room resoundingly quiet.

"Time for a break," said Roy. He turned to me. "Can I get you a coffee?"

"I'm not in need of a break," Lyndon said. "Are you, Mr. Werner?"

"*I* need a break," Roy said. "Interview suspended." He shut off the recorder and I let out a long breath.

Which Lyndon heard, loud and clear. "Feeling better now?" he asked.

I touched my nicked jaw. "I'm feeling fine." You asshole, I wanted to say.

Lyndon pushed back his chair and angled his broad face, beaming nastily, toward mine. "Because you seem a little tense to me. It must be difficult trying to protect your friend. Your cowboy friend."

You bastard, I thought. You fucking desk jockey. You don't know the first thing about it.

His eyes glittered. "You feel better now? Think you turned a cowboy into a Boy Scout?"

I stood up so fast the chair rolled away behind me. "Shut up, okay? Just — stop." I fought to contain my voice. "We're talking about my partner. For ten years he's the person I work with and eat with and joke around with. Every single day, okay? And he's dead. He died right in front of me, do you get that? It happened in a second" — I snapped my fingers — "one fucking second and his life is done. Over. He's gone. So no, I don't feel fucking better. Not about any fucking thing."

"Okay, Will, okay. Take it easy." Roy touched my arm. "Don't let this one rile you up. He's not our most sensitive investigator."

Lyndon grunted. "I am sensitive to many things." He turned and strode out of the room.

∧ ∨ ∧

BY THE TIME ROY AND I had finished cups of strong, dark coffee in the TSB kitchen, the volcano inside me had subsided some. We returned to the boardroom. Lyndon was nowhere to be seen, but Roy switched on the recorder just the same. After a few more questions about the day of the accident – our alert status, weather, visibility, comms with the Cariboo Fire Centre – he asked about the weeks leading up to the crash, our working hours and rest days. That part was easy. West Air has strict ceilings on how long we can work. Skipping our days off is out of the question, no matter how busy we get.

"So from what you saw on the job," said Roy, "or from what Rafe told you, would you say that in the period leading up to the accident he was fatigued?"

"No, he was not."

The door opened and in walked Lyndon, looking more smug and superior than before the break.

"Was he unwell or sick? Complaining of a headache or any other physical problem?"

"No."

"Was he stressed?" Roy continued. "Acting different?"

I tried desperately to think like a chess player but at the same time wanted to be truthful. "Not stressed. I would say he was a bit quiet at one point. Not as talkative as usual."

"Distracted?" Lyndon said, settling himself in.

"No. Quiet."

"How long had he been that way?" Lyndon asked.

I touched my jaw. No way could I say a couple of months. They'd have a field day with that. But I couldn't lie either. "Hard to say. It's been a tough patch for all of us, not just Rafe. We've been on yellow and red alerts a good while. You almost forget what it's like to not be on call."

"So why was he not himself?" Lyndon asked.

"I never said he wasn't himself. I said he was quiet. I have no idea why. The busy season, I guess, like the rest of us." Lyndon was spinning his pen around again. Was it some interview technique for when the subject-matter got heavy? Was it supposed to make me think he was all nonchalant, barely listening, before he trapped me?

Lyndon kept his gaze on the twirling pen. "What about his marriage? Was that a factor?"

"What do you mean, a factor?"

"In his behaviour leading up to the crash. A factor in his being stressed."

"I keep telling you, he was *quiet*, not stressed. Why would it be?"

"I'm asking you."

Strategic thinking had abandoned me, and I honestly had no idea where he was headed. "I don't know. Seems pretty unlikely."

Lyndon gave his pen a couple more spins for good measure, then, thank God, stopped. He looked me straight in the eyes. "No need to pretend, Will. We are aware that Rafe's marriage was, shall we say, troubled. We have confirmed that two months before his death, he and his wife separated and he moved into a furnished studio apartment in New Westminster."

My mouth fell open. What the fuck? What kind of sick joke was this? "Yeah, right."

"We have plenty of proof. Paperwork, witnesses, not to mention confirmation from his wife."

Impossible. They were solid, those two. They loved each other for real, the way my mom and dad did. Besides, Rafe would've told me.

And yet ... As the idea sank in, I realized it explained a lot: Rafe's remoteness, his weight loss, his solemn face the morning that would be his last. I rubbed my jaw and noticed, when I removed my fingers, a faint smear of blood. Damn!

"Call me crazy," Lyndon continued, "but it seems more than a mere coincidence. Rafe rents his own apartment two months before the crash, he begins to act distracted around the same —"

"He wasn't distracted! I never said distracted. The recorder's still going. Do I need to play it back to you?"

"Calm down, Mr. Werner," Lyndon said. "Not distracted, perhaps, but you said different, out of sorts. It makes sense, don't you think? A long marriage ends, it takes a toll on a man. He becomes withdrawn, depressed, suicidal even —"

I slammed the table with my hand, fuck the blood, and stood up. "Quit putting words in my mouth, you asshole! I told you, Rafe was fine. He did everything right. He was an excellent pilot with a spotless record. He was one of the best air tanker pilots on the continent. He was reliable, he was well rested, he was himself, he was full of life —"

The sickening irony of what I'd just said landed like a sucker punch. The investigators looked at me, waiting for me to continue, maybe taking in my bleeding jaw, and they may have kept on looking, but I'll never know because I left the room, left the building, climbed into the shaded cab of my black Tacoma, and drove the fuck away.

∧ ∨ ∧

MY THOUGHTS REELED. How could Rafe and Sharon have split? And how could I not have known? Sure, Rafe barely mentioned Sharon this season, but as I told that sanctimonious American president prick, he was quiet about everything. And so what if he was quiet? When, during this summer of nonstop fires, have any of us had time to shoot the shit?

I peeled out of the TSB lot, corner of an old tissue stuck to my jaw, steaming. If only I'd had the balls to plant my fist in that bastard's corn-fed cheek.

I pointed the truck southwest, toward Steveston. I had to cool down before showing my face back at the office. Maybe half an hour of fishing boats and seagulls would do it.

As I sped down the highway, a classic Zeppelin mix cranked as loud as my ears could handle, I thought back to the last time I'd seen Rafe and Sharon together. It was the West Air Christmas party last year, a big do at the Rolling Acres Country Club. I went with Justine, a friend of Andy's I get together with sometimes, mainly for formal occasions. She always looks like she stepped out of a fashion spread, every hair in place, every nail perfectly painted, never the same outfit twice. She loves to dress up and she hates to be touched. Andy was clear about that before he ever introduced us. "She is strictly a gorgeous companion, all right? Try anything and I am no longer your friend."

Rafe and Sharon arrived late that night, I remember that. I'd been watching for them. My plan was to stick close to Rafe until the stand-up cocktails ended and the awkward business of musical chairs began. Justine was a looker but she was reserved – shy, I think, under all her perfection – and if the evening was going to be any fun for her, I'd have to snag seats beside Rafe, not get stuck at a table of bores.

You know how some people carry an energy field around them? Rafe was like that. Put him with Sharon and they had the wattage of a substation. I don't know if it was his vitality rubbing off on her or if she gave off her own sparks, but that night, when they entered the private dining room Jeff had rented, mine wasn't the only head to turn. They glided into the room like stars on the red carpet. They were dressed like stars too, certainly better than those of us who had that afternoon dusted off the only sports jacket and tie we owned. Rafe wore a real suit, which he filled prodigiously. Sharon was in some swishy dress that bared her back and offered regular flashes of leg. In heels she stood nearly as tall as Rafe, cementing the impression of a single stunning unit.

No question, they glowed. They chose chairs across from each other at the table we shared with Jeff and his wife, Hannah. The six of us made good company, laughing and drinking freely. At first Jeff looked like he always does, like he's got a broom up his ass, but one glass of wine and he quit playing boss and eased into the festivities. Justine, in the midst of so much chatter, relaxed too and seemed happy to listen.

Now, half a year later, I've gotta wonder – did I miss something? Were they truly a golden couple that night or did I just see what I expected to see? How could two people go from radiantly happy to living apart in such a short time?

Arriving in Steveston didn't answer my questions, but it did push the TSB inquisition to the back of my mind. The village swarmed with tourists, par for the course in midsummer, and it took fifteen minutes of circling before I could park. The sun shimmered as I strolled to the wharves. A short while later I sat with my face to the rays, a small cod and chips beside me, tossing the odd french fry to the gulls that wheeled in hope overhead. Around me was the steady hum of life: families eating fish and chips and ice cream, market workers slinging trays of fillets and prawns, toddlers from a day camp traipsing by in a roped-up line. I ate half the cod and a few fries before I realized what I was doing. *Sittin' on the dock of the bay* ... Like that, my appetite vanished.

The Christmas party. What did I miss?

I thought back to the point when dessert was finished, or toyed with and pushed aside in the case of Justine, who looked like a model for a reason. Sharon, too—her cake was untouched. We were ordering after-dinner drinks from our curvy ash-blond waitress, and Jeff's wife, Hannah, who had cleaned up her dessert along with the last of the wine, couldn't decide; she waffled between two choices, asked about a third, then settled on a fourth. When the server got to Rafe, he stroked his chin and pretended to think. "Be a sweetheart, would you?" he said. "Run through that drink list one more time so's I know what my options are." Like the pro she was, the waitress smiled dryly, holding pen and pad in front of but happily not blocking her well-displayed cleavage. She wasn't falling for it.

Sharon leaned across the table. "Rafe, there's no time for another drink. We have to leave."

"Leave?"

"We ordered a cab for eleven, remember? It's five to."

"A cab? We're just getting started." He beamed at the waitress. "Too friggin early to leave, wouldn't you say, sweetheart?"

The waitress, clearly schooled in the value of silence, waited.

"How about a bourbon to go?" Rafe said.

Sharon stood up and hung a tiny purse over her bare shoulder. "Goodnight, everyone. It was great fun." She headed for the exit.

Rafe watched her go, then stood. For once his smile didn't reach his eyes. "Guess we're off, then. Enjoy the evening, everyone. I'll settle the bar tab on the way out," he told our server.

Shannon, I should say. The blond server was named Shannon. A grad student at Simon Fraser University, psych major, I think, or maybe sociology. An hour and a half later, as the rest of the group cleared out, I went in for another view of her prodigious curves and we got to chatting. We hooked up a few times after that. Nothing serious, just a few late-night meet-ups when she had time between essays and work. Until today Shannon was what I remembered most about that party.

After today's bombshell at the TSB, what I'm remembering now is Rafe's failed smile. At the time I put it down to the obvious, that he wasn't ready to call it a night. A minor disappointment, hardly a big deal. Now I wonder: was his pasted-on grin covering a far bigger hurt, like his marriage falling apart? Was it a sign that I was too dumb — or let's face it, too busy ogling Shannon — to see?

The more I pick at the past, the more I find these glimpses into a less sunny side of Rafe, a side he was quick to cover up: his brother bailing him out when they were young, some shame he caused his mother, his fake smile at last year's Christmas party, and on the morning he died, his lonely sadness — because knowing what I know now, that he'd lost Sharon, that's obviously what it was. Were they all signals Rafe was broadcasting that I, partner, friend, and self-centred moron, failed to intercept?

A guy can torture himself thinking like this. That's probably what The Counsellor would say if I laid this memory in front of her. She'd tell me not to dwell on it or beat myself up, that I couldn't possibly know what was going on if Rafe chose not to tell me. Maybe she'd go all profound and say something like a secret well hidden, or a story withheld, is impossible to discover.

And I'd tell her to go fuck herself. He was my friend. I should have known.

FIFTEEN

October

THE FIRST THING THAT HITS HER is the smell. Last night, to force herself out of bed in the morning, she filled the coffee maker and set the timer for seven thirty. Now the aroma of French roast permeates the bedroom, tickles her awake, bids her throw off the covers and begin the day.

The next thing to come is the pain. She turns her head and buries her nose in the pillow.

Waking up: it's the most natural of human actions. One minute you're floating in a shadowy netherworld; the next you come to, the world takes shape, contours sharpen, and reality knifes you with its stealthy blade. Waking up has become a dreaded event, worse for being inevitable. She must endure it every day, the unbearable transition from not knowing to knowing.

It's a natural part of mourning, says Colleen, the desire to sleep and hold the world at bay. Her sister has become an expert on grief; she devoured piles of books on the subject while pulling Sharon through the interminable second half of summer.

Sharon never bothered to correct her — it seemed wrong when Colleen poured so much energy into caring for her — but the truth is, her reluctance to leave sleep started well before Rafe died. It's been years since she woke up gladly, re-entered life with anticipation or energy; years since morning was anything but a troubled time, a time of anxiety and suspension, of disappointment and lies.

∧ ∨ ∧

AN HOUR GOES BY. Or is it three? Rain is falling again, or still; she has lost track of when the beating against the windows last paused. Though it's late morning, the house is so dusky that she switches on the lamps. She eats a banana, too listless to make a meal, and picks up a cruise brochure. What to do about Christmas? She can't spend it alone, nor can she find the energy to make plans. Soon it will be November. She has to decide.

The haphazard pile of flyers and mail threatens to topple. She must go through it all, separate the items that need action from those that can be discarded. The same goes for Rafe's once precisely organized papers, now strewn around the spare room, no longer in chronological or indeed any kind of order. Each time she's had to locate some life insurance form, mortgage document, or piece of employment paperwork, she has upended his system a little more. Rafe, compulsive about neatness, he would abhor the chaos.

She often wondered where it came from, his need to arrange and tidy, to fix and put away. Was it a learned habit for pilots, with their endless procedures and checklists? Or was it in his makeup, perfectionism resident in his DNA? Did he learn it from his parents during the Cape Breton boyhood that remained a mystery to her? He had filed that part of his past away as neatly as any papers and locked the drawer of memory tight. "What's done is done," he mumbled darkly the March morning a decade ago when Sheldon phoned to say their mother had died. He refused to go to the funeral and refused to say why. Ignoring Sharon's incredulity, he spent the day replacing the hot water tank with Will, as if nothing had happened. The next day he stamped out of the house and installed himself at the pub. Then followed a long period when he drew in on himself, the blackness more lasting and impenetrable than any mood she had ever seen him in. His memory drawer stayed shut, and now she will never know what it contained, or concealed.

She sorts the neglected mail, a task that leaves her with a manageable pile of envelopes and an unaccustomed surge of energy. Best use it while she can.

The spare room, at the end of the short hallway on the second floor, is always over-warm and stuffy, boxed off from the rest of the townhouse and deprived of any cross-draft. Apart from housing their occasional out-of-town visitors, the room mainly stores items that have nowhere else to be. The desk contains personal files and correspondence, most of the drawers Rafe's, a couple her own; the closet is stuffed with Christmas wreaths, lights, and wrapping paper, and the glow-in-the-dark skeleton that adorns their door at Halloween; the bookcase holds old photo albums as well as videotapes they once imagined they'd transfer to DVD. A side table by the window is topped with an irregular mauve rectangle, her one attempt at knitting, its scruffy nap largely concealed by file folders and manila envelopes. Papers litter the carpet and the queen-size bed.

She sighs. The futility of it all. Several times she has vowed to put this room to rights and each time has slunk off in defeat. Maybe a smaller goal today: a single desk drawer.

Sitting in the swivel chair, a vintage oak piece salvaged from her father's insurance office, she opens the middle drawer on the left. Recipe clippings on top remind her that it's her drawer, not Rafe's. Idly she sifts through glossy cut-outs of layered salads, grilled salmon, stews, and coffee cake, all of which she once envisioned eating, none of which she has ever prepared. Beneath the recipes lies an untidy spill of notes and letters. A pink envelope stamped with Colleen's return address contains a curlicued card wishing Sharon and Rafe a happy life in their new Vancouver home. Dozens of notes, inked with Rafe's heavy printing, announce that he had gone to the drugstore or headed to the gym, x's and o's trailing the bottom of each paper. One note includes a lopsided drawing of lips and a promise to kiss her as soon as he gets home. There are anniversary cards, Valentine's cards, birthday cards. She pulls out one of the largest, sees the embossed balloons and champagne glasses, and drops it, scalded.

Many people have trouble with the big four-oh. Colleen took off on a cruise to the Black Sea, not to celebrate but to sidestep the whole affair. Rachel, thirty-nine, feigns nonchalance, but Sharon knows her friend is eking out every last week of her thirties. Rafe was unfazed when his time came, but it's different for men, at least the ones like Rafe who barely show their age. For the women she knows, turning forty means falling headlong into the wide ditch that separates youth from decrepitude. One day you will emerge on the other side, and it won't be pretty.

Sharon's fortieth was far more than the first step beyond youth; it was the cutoff they'd agreed to long ago: no children by then and they would stop trying. That was the deal. No more doctor's appointments, fertility treatments, or painstakingly timed intercourse. Adoption had been ruled out long ago, for Rafe was convinced they would inherit physical or psychological problems with someone else's child. His adamance made her wonder again about his own childhood, that stowed-away period he refused to share. "What happened to you back then?" she once asked. "Nothing worth talking about" was his curt reply. If that long-ago time was marked with trauma, Rafe had boxed it up for good.

For Sharon, who had yearned for a child since she first babysat her neighbours' kids, forty arrived like the thief of her life's last dream. And how did Rafe mark the occasion? With this bewilderingly cheerful card, and with gifts. Even now, four years later, her insides throb at the memory. How could he imagine that she wanted anything but sympathy that day, especially from him, the one person who knew the full extent of her anguish?

He was away at a fire base on the actual day she turned forty. It was wrong to blame him for that, July being the worst month for wildfires. Never before had she minded postponing her birthday until his time off, but that year was different. If he had wanted to, she was sure of it, he could have arranged the time off. He could have been there to hold her and console her, and together they could have blown out the wish to cradle their own tiny baby, to raise a romping, athletic girl or a smiling, sweet-natured boy.

Instead she spent the day alone, crying and then berating herself for her weakness. The minute it turned noon and alcohol could be justified, she filled a wineglass to the brim and climbed the stairs to this very room, where she hovered by the window, the brilliant sky and emerald lawns scouring her insides. She stood there, sipping and then gulping the wine, imagining all the fulfilled, unlonely lives behind the townhouse lawns. Finally she bent over her sewing basket and dug the creased magazine from its hiding place at the bottom. Years ago she had wedged it in there as a reminder of what lay ahead. The grinning baby on the cover, with his wide cheeks and merry brown eyes, looked strikingly like Rafe. The day she turned forty she longed for that baby, cried again, and drained the bottle of wine.

Later in the afternoon Colleen phoned. Sharon assured her sister that she was fine and couldn't wait for the evening out with Rachel and a few real estate friends. That night, after too many martinis and not enough tasting plates at an upscale Kitsilano bistro, Sharon lurched home, full-on drunk, to a message from Rafe wishing her the happiest of days. He might as well have punched her in the eye.

A week later he came home with the giant card that lies before her now, along with a pair of garnet drop earrings and a gift certificate for her favourite spa. He kissed her as he handed over the flowered bag that held it all. "You may be forty, but you're more beautiful than when we first met. Happy birthday, sweetheart."

She thanked him, scanned his face for sorrow, and saw none. Clearly he was saving the solemn talk for later. That night they lingered over a four-course dinner at Lagoon, then took a twilight stroll along the Seawall. Rafe described the latest fires, told stories about the other pilots, recounted the plot of some movie-of-the-week he'd watched in his motel room. How, she wondered as they passed the rows of pleasure craft moored in Coal Harbour, could he wait so long to broach the topic that truly mattered? How could he devote the entire day to small talk when the lodestone of their marriage had crumbled?

By the time they got home she was angry. If he was going to ignore the significance of this deadline, if their years of trying and hoping meant so little to him, then to hell with him. She would not be the one to mention it.

Later, in bed, Rafe slipped one last gift from his night-table drawer. He smiled shyly, his face hopeful. Would this somehow break the silence? she wondered.

She unwrapped the package and withdrew from the box inside a small string of balls.

"What's this?" It wasn't jewellery; the balls were too big, the string too short.

Rafe stroked her neck with one large hand. "They're Venus balls. We can put them, you know, inside you."

She stared at him.

"They make women crazy, or so I'm told." He leaned over and kissed her frozen lips. "What's wrong?"

The room spun. "I can't believe it."

"They're a treat, sweetheart. Just for you. Like the spa. To make you feel good."

She bowed her head.

"Sharon." He took her hand. "For years we've been going at it like minks for one reason and one reason only. We've been neglecting you, your needs. I don't want it to be like that anymore, just making sure I get off. You need to enjoy it too, you deserve that. That's what makes it good for me, knowing you're happy." He put his finger under her chin, tipped her face up. "I want to be a good lover to you, Sharon. Not just a good husband. This can be a fresh start for us."

She tried to understand, she really did. She thanked him for the gift and said they'd have to try it another night, when she was less full from dinner. But inside, her distaste grew, and with it her anger. By the next day the sight of the trinket beside the bed made her livid. What was the message? That the work was over and now sex could be fun? Meaning it wasn't fun before, that Rafe had only been going through the motions, plugging away dutifully as if nailing one more firefighting drop? How could he do such a thing, give her a sex toy — a *sex toy?* Their future had just died, a future they had counted on their entire marriage. Wasn't he sad too? How had they drifted so far apart that what for her was a time of mourning was for him an excuse for some tawdry pornographic gadget? No matter how she interpreted it, the gift leered at her, a shocking and insensitive rebuke.

That was when the relationship turned. Whenever Rafe reached for her she recoiled, his touch a sticky, unbearable intrusion. Instead of leaving her be, giving her space and time to grieve, he followed her everywhere, wanting to stroke her hair and hold her close, then inevitably wanting more than that. After three days he left for another month on the job, having uttered not a word about the true meaning of this stillborn birthday. To him it signified nothing. Sharon was shattered.

Once summer ended and Rafe came home from the fires, it was impossible to ignore the gulf between them. Mornings, always their favourite time to make love, Sharon slept later and later, or pretended to, ignoring the kiss on her shoulder that was Rafe's unspoken question. It was easier not to talk about it, not that he asked her to. At this point, what could she say? That her passion had flamed out months ago, along with her dreams? That she could not summon a spark of desire for a man who refused to share her loss? That it took all her energy to submit on the rare occasions when duty said she had to? Outside the bedroom she still had feelings for Rafe, she valued the tenderness and companionship that had always bound them, but he was a man, and for him tender feelings would never suffice.

Made of thick, heavy stock, the oversized card resists at first. Why didn't she do this ages ago, throw it into the trash along with the unused Venus balls? She tightens her grip, pulls for all she's worth, and at last the cardboard yields, tearing into long, stiff strips which she hurls onto the floor, on top of the papers scattered there.

To hell with it, she decides. It's my house and my mess. The voice that tells her every day, every hour, to smarten up and get a grip says nothing.

∧ ∨ ∧

IT'S NOT TILL EARLY EVENING that Sharon picks up the message.

Desperate for fresh air after quitting the spare room, she'd left the house for once without a list. At the library she returned a novel, a romance set in medieval times, and spent half an hour flipping through new books no one would hire her to shelve. She lingered at the farmers market, eyeing rows of Asian condiments and imported crackers, buying local granola and a bag of champagne grapes she didn't really want. She stopped at Arpeggio's for a latte, ordering a double in hopes of ripping through the shroud of memory that was suffocating her.

Now she's back home again, and the shroud is dissolved by the message that awaits her. There are two messages, actually. One is Rachel, saying how much she enjoyed lunch last week and could they do it again soon. The second hits Sharon like seawater. She cannot place the low, halting voice until he says his name, and then it washes over her — the voice, the man, the stinging connection.

"Hi, I was wondering ... could we talk sometime? There's some stuff ... Well, maybe we could have coffee. Anywhere you like. Or I can come over there? Only if that's easier, though. Oh, this is Will. You know, who worked with Rafe." He leaves his number, says to call anytime.

It's a short message. She plays it twice. She puts the groceries away, opens her new library book. Gets up and plays it again.

SIXTEEN

Fourteen days after

THE NEXT CHAPTER of this goddamned day, Thursday the first of August, the day that will never end, involved me putting in some face time at West Air. I drove there from Steveston after gifting the rest of my fish and chips to the gulls.

I'd no sooner closed the front door than Jeff asked for a briefing on the TSB interview. I've given Jeff so little lately that I could hardly deny him. Sitting in his office on the single wooden visitor's chair, installed I assume in the belief that because he never slumps others must not, I summarized the line of questioning and watched Jeff's face fold in on itself, the vertical lines that bracket his mouth deepening like crevasses in the spring.

"They're going for pilot error," he said. "It makes sense. They've got nothing mechanical or weather-related."

If you believe the TSB, the pilot's to blame for every crash, Rafe used to say. Not one pilot can properly fly his own plane.

"Did they ask anything" — Jeff flicked an invisible mote off his lapel — "about Rafe's state of mind?"

"They asked about his marriage, whether it had anything to do with him being quieter than usual."

"And you said?"

"I said no. Why would it?" I had decided in Steveston to keep Rafe and Sharon's separation to myself. If the investigators want Jeff to be apprised, they can tell him themselves. Obviously the state of his marriage was information Rafe didn't want to share with anyone. I've got to respect that.

"The last time I saw them together was at the Christmas party," Jeff said. "They seemed good, didn't they?"

"Far as I could tell."

"Do you think he made a mistake?"

I knew Jeff meant the crash, not the marriage. I hesitated, unsure how much to say. "Well, it was an easy drop, the easiest we ever get. He knew the pattern, he repeated it back to Ernie on the radio. He came into the circuit at the right height, from the right spot, and he started levelling out when he was supposed to. Then the plane just dipped. He knew to stay level, we were very clear about that, he repeated it back. But he went nose down, too far down, and clipped the trees. That's the part I don't get."

"So he misjudged when to level off?"

"No way. I mean, visibility wasn't perfect, it was a bit grey with all the smoke, but conditions were as good as they're ever gonna get over a fire. We could see the tree line, he could see the tree line, there was nothing to misjudge."

"Was he doing his big trick? That kissing the trees stunt?"

I'd asked myself that same question a thousand times. It's what Ernie and I thought he was up to when he came in lower than he had to. But the plane dipped so suddenly, went so obviously nose down — it wasn't a case of flying low and level and mistaking the height of the trees.

"No. That's not what happened."

"Could the retardant he was carrying shift, maybe alter his centre of gravity?"

Jeff, one of the smartest men I know, is a pinstriped, MBA-stamped businessman. This is a guy who in his twenties sold his car and bought a Hugo Boss suit with the proceeds. His collar is never more blindingly white than when he attempts to plumb the mechanics of flight. I went easy on him.

"Not possible. The holding tanks are separated by baffles, so there's never a big load sloshing around in the plane's belly." I ran my thumb back and forth in the groove that bordered Jeff's desk. "I've been racking my brain trying to figure out what could make him clip the trees like that. I keep coming back to a mechanical problem. That Tracker is ... *was* ancient. It's not a stretch to think something malfunctioned." I smiled faintly, remembering. "He was so attached to that stupid antique. Remember when you were selling off the other Trackers and he wouldn't let his go? Said he'd go on strike for the season before he'd switch to another plane."

Jeff smiled too, or as close as he gets to it these days. "He even got a petition going. Well, you know. You signed it."

As did most of the pilots. Rafe had invited us all to a pub downtown. It was late fall, too cold for pitchers on the patio but the perfect time to hear what everyone would get up to in the off-season. A couple of drinks in, after we'd all taken the edge off, Rafe whipped out the petition, printed in colour and official-looking. It stated that West Air would keep his Tracker until such time as it was deemed unrepairable. What could we do but sign? To us it was more of a joke than anything; we knew Jeff would cave with or without a piece of paper. He would never knowingly put Rafe's nose out of joint. It would be like scolding your guide dog when he's thumping his tail and staring at you with devotion. You couldn't do it.

"It could have been physical," Jeff said. "Some incapacitation that made him lose control. A heart attack?"

"Except he was on the radio with Ernie right before. He sounded fine."

"You hear about weightlifters whose hearts just give out. But you're right, it's unlikely. I can't share the details, but there was never an issue with his medicals, nothing glossed over. Not like with some of the guys."

I knew who he meant. We have a couple of tenacious lifers whose only retirement condo will be a coffin. They sneak pills with every meal even though twice a year, like clockwork, their medical exams come back saying no conditions, no medications. A staggering portion of Jeff's daily work involves dreaming up ways to keep those guys out of the sky.

"That mainly leaves mechanical." Jeff sighed. "It's still early days. The engine teardown is next week, and if anything goes to their lab it'll be months before the results come in. I just hope to God it's nothing maintenance related. The AMES are already in a lather worrying that they overlooked some detail. You know how they are. It's their lifelong terror. Twice now Wayne has sent me scans of the Tracker's maintenance logs from the days before the crash, and he's called I don't know how many times to say the crew is certain the plane was fine."

"I guess all we can do is wait." I scraped back my chair. That was it for me and this conversation. I was exhausted and could only think about sprawling in front of the TV in the soothing squalor of my apartment. "I gotta go. There's still two hours before quitting time but I'll make it up tomorrow, okay?"

"Not okay," Jeff said. "You don't owe me any time. Just go."

∧ ∨ ∧

THAT'S THE LONG, DEPRESSING TALE of this day, my fourth back at work, two weeks exactly after the Tracker went down and flipped my world on its ass.

Turns out I haven't spent one minute watching the tube. When I got home earlier I dumped everything onto the sofa — my gym bag, contents still pristine after I'd considered and then rejected the weight room; two weeks' worth of mail from my box downstairs; a bag of Doritos; and a jumbo container of chocolate milk now that the toxic table d'hôte is no longer an option. I flopped down beside the pile and ran through all that had happened since I set out this morning.

Despite what The Counsellor says, it doesn't make me feel better, all this thinking. Not remotely. It forces me to relive shit I'd rather not deal with, like Rafe going through a breakup and not saying a word about it. I can't wrap my head around that. During fire season we were together constantly and he told me everything, including a lot of stuff I didn't want to know, like how much nose hair he needed to trim and what kind of bowel movement he'd just had. The only negative I remember is that he hinted that the sex had slowed down. It came up a couple of times when I caught him giving some woman or another the once-over. But he was quick to make light of it. Put it down to being married forever and not getting any younger.

I remember something weird from farther back, too, a few years ago when we were on call in Prince George and he stepped out to buy earrings for Sharon's birthday. Why he asked me to tag along, I'll never know. Certainly not for my taste in jewellery. He was in a black mood that day. We were near the end of a big fire run, all of us down to fumes. It must've been taking a toll on him. He spent forever picking out those stupid earrings. When I finally asked him why, he gave me a strange answer: "The one gift she wants, I can't give her. So everything I give her from now on has to matter more. It's the only way I can fix it." He meant a baby, I'm sure of it. They'd pretty much given up trying by then. It's hardly a sign that they were on the outs, yet fast-forward a few years and Rafe's living alone – and keeping it a secret.

Somewhere along the line something went wrong. And I'll be honest: it's got me worried. That asshole Lyndon Johnson this morning, between spinning his fucking pen and fabricating ideas about Rafe being depressed or suicidal, he kept prodding me to say Rafe was distracted. What if he's right? A guy's happily married for more than twenty years and then it all goes south? You can't help but wonder if his head wasn't in the flying. Rafe of all people could normally clear his mind and do the job, but maybe this was too much for him. His moody spells all season, his remoteness – no, sadness – that last morning, did that add up to distraction in the cockpit? What if his attention wandered at the wrong second? Could it come down to one tiny miscalculation? Some random thought or decision that ends the man's life?

And me, dumb fuck that I am – if he was distracted, how much of the blame is on me? I knew something wasn't right. What kind of person shuts his eyes to his friend's problems? Answer: a fucking jerk. If my head hadn't been up my ass that morning, or if I hadn't been so busy thinking about ass, as in getting some with Gracie, and I'd bothered to ask him what was wrong, would it have made a difference? Could one well-timed question have turned around the whole goddamned day?

∧ ∨ ∧

TWO O'CLOCK IN THE MORNING. This day. This fucking day. Just when I think it'll end, there's something else.

An hour ago I gave in and tried the TV, but there's nothing on. Just sports, all of it shit, and stupid reality shows. I downed half the chocolate milk, desperate for something stronger. I opened the Doritos, opened the mail. A bunch of takeout menus for pizza and Thai. A couple of bills. A letter.

Who writes a letter anymore? That was my one profound thought before I slit the envelope with my forefinger, pulled out the sheet of paper, and read.

Now it's two in the morning. Dark, silent.

Fuck me. A *letter*?

There's a lot of mystifying shit happens in this world. Take the whole reality show thing. Like, what, real life doesn't dole out enough reality? Why would anyone watch a bunch of self-centred fame-whores acting out scenes that are scripted at someone else's desk so that they and the viewing audience can all pretend there is no script? Where's the reality in that?

It's lies. Horseshit and lies. It makes me want to fucking punch something.

You know the lies I hate the most? The ones people come up with when they're too chickenshit to say the truth. Fuck you, Rafe Mackie, I want to tell him. I hate lies. I am the worst possible person to do this. How can you ask me?

And why should I do it? Why lie for him when all he did was lie to me? Guy's supposed to be my friend and for two whole months he carries on this phoney act. Day after day, showing up at work, a bit quiet but nothing seriously out of joint, pretending like nothing's different. Pretending. When all the time – what? He's living in some shitty apartment none of us knew existed. And doing what? Counting off the hours?

Sitting and staring at some mouldy wall-to-wall carpet, figuring out what the fuck he's gonna to do and how the fuck he's gonna to do it?

All the time he was pretending — no, *lying* — what was he really thinking? What was he ever thinking?

Because now I know: he sure as fuck never told me.

SEVENTEEN

August

IT WAS FRIDAY, the sun was shining, and the teardown in Victoria was still days away. All good, as the guys at work would say.

To celebrate the week's end Nathalie treated herself to a sit-down lunch at the PanAm Grill: sliced tomato salad, spinach-and-feta-stuffed chicken breast, cappuccino. Adding a ten-dollar tip to the thirty-five-dollar bill, she reflected on how far she'd come to be able to splurge on a meal without cutting back in five other areas to compensate. Gone were the student days when dinner out was buck-a-slice pizza at the 7-Eleven. No more bulk buys of rice, beans, and chicken legs like in the early AME years, when every extra dollar went toward student loans and Mémère's monthly fee at the trailer park. These days Nathalie ate what she wanted, and if the service was excellent tipped big.

When she returned to the office at one thirty, it was to a pink message slip thrust at her by Luanne. The name stopped her in her tracks: Will Werner, Rafe's bird dog pilot. Quickly she composed herself and continued to her office. The less ammo you gave Luanne, the better. As for Will, she'd shut down any questions from him ASAP.

"I'm not on the Tracker case," she said the moment he answered — not his West Air phone, she noted from the number, but a private line. "You want to talk to Roy or Lyndon. I can transfer you."

"No. You're the one I want to talk to."

Tucker's warnings to stay off the case sounded in her mind but were drowned out by the clamour of curiosity. She could at least get a sense of what Will had to say before fobbing him off. "What's up?"

"I was wondering how things are going. With the investigation?"

"Like I just told you, I'm not working on it. You have to talk to Roy."

"I'm not talking to Roy, or Lyndon either. I did my time with those two last week and I'm not doing it again anytime soon. They're not exactly ... open-minded, you know?"

Nathalie had never met Will. Their professional paths had never crossed, something Will should be grateful for. A flying career with no accident investigators in it was a happy flying career. Nor did she see Will at Rafe's funeral. Word had it he was the only West Air pilot who didn't show. But his voice painted a picture for her: young (obviously) and laid-back judging from his drawn-out words and tendency to put question marks at the end of statements. He sounded more like a surfer than a pilot, though he was supposedly exceptional in the air, at least according to Rafe.

"I cannot help you on the Tracker. I know nothing about it. I'm busy with another crash."

"Oh. Which one?"

"The R22 that went down in the Coquihalla a few weeks ago. Killed the pilot and his new wife."

"Oh, yeah. Our safety director knew that guy, went to school with him in West Van. You know what happened?"

"Not yet," said Nathalie, carefully. The pilot grapevine was long and fertile, and she was not about to nourish it with unauthorized details. There was little she could tell him anyway. At this stage, pre-teardown, the cause of the crash was still a mystery.

"Well." He stopped. "I'm ... I've been thinking more about the Tracker crash."

Spit it out, kid, she thought. Don't waste my time.

"You knew Rafe, didn't you?"

She swallowed. "What do you mean?"

"You two had met, right? I'm pretty sure he told me that."

Watch it, she told herself. Your job is to gather everything and reveal nothing. "We'd met."

"I don't know how well you knew him, but probably enough to know he wasn't what you'd call a timid or tentative kind of guy."

"No, those are not words I'd use for him."

"Exactly. He was always sure of himself, decisive. That's what makes this odd."

"What?"

Will cleared his throat. "Well, the way Rafe was that morning, the morning of the crash. There was something bothering him. Something he was unsure of about his plane."

"Do I need to say it in another language? I'm not the one you should tell this to. Let me get Lyndon. He's the technical —"

"No!" The chill surfer dude was gone. "I told you, I will not talk to that asshole!"

"Okay, okay. Calm down." Whatever Lyndon had done, it had gotten under this guy's skin.

"It has to be someone who actually knew Rafe or I won't feel right about it."

She picked up her pen; instinct told her to take notes. "Have it your way. I'm listening."

Will took a deep breath. "So. There were four tanker pilots on standby that morning. We weren't sure how many would be called out, because a lot depended on the wind, right? And how fast the fire was spreading. Worst-case scenario, we'd need four. Since we didn't know who'd go up when, the tanker pilots all did their walkarounds early. That way they'd be ready to take off at a moment's notice. By the time I got out to the flight centre, Rafe had finished his walkaround and was standing over by the maintenance shed. I went over to talk to him. Hey, are you recording this?"

"No. Should I be?"

"I don't know. It's just … I think this could be important. Like maybe something to do with a mechanical problem?"

"Okay, take your time. I'm making notes."

"So we're shooting the shit same as any other day, talking about the fire, how we slept, our planes, and Rafe mentions that the day before when he was up flying, something felt … different. Just a sec, okay?" He stopped and took a drink of something. "So I ask him what he means, and he says the elevator trim felt a bit off."

"What do you mean, off?"

"He didn't get into the details. Just said that during his last flight, when he trimmed the plane nose down for landing, it stuck for a second. Like it continued to trim down when it shouldn't have. That morning during the walkaround, he'd climbed into the cockpit and checked out the trim switch, but he couldn't find anything wrong with it."

"Did he get it looked at? By an AME?"

"There was no time. We were gonna get called out any minute."

"Come on. There's no way he'd fly if he thought the trim adjustment wasn't working."

"I know. He was always careful about that sort of thing. But I don't think he took it seriously. He just mentioned it in passing, like it wasn't a big deal."

"It *is* a big deal," said Nathalie. "Runaway trim is bad news. Your trim goes and your plane can get stuck nose up or nose down. Before you know it you're in an uncontrolled climb or a dive and you can't do a thing about it. We've seen more than a few accidents because of runaway trim."

"He never said the trim ran away on him, okay? Just that he felt a lag, the one time, at the end of his last flight. He didn't even seem a hundred percent sure. He just mentioned it and then brushed it off."

"How much of this did you tell Roy and Lyndon?"

"Uh, none of it."

"*None?*"

"We … our conversation didn't get that far. That asshole Lyndon, he started putting words in my mouth, pushing my buttons. I left before we were done. I shouldn't have, but that's how it went. Anyway, I figure someone at the TSB should know what Rafe told me. Can you pass it along?"

"I can, but it'd be better coming directly from you. The guys may have follow-up questions."

"If they do, Roy can get hold of me. Roy, okay? Not Lyndon. And he can do it later. For now I just want to leave it at what I said."

Nathalie's mind raced. She knew there was more she should ask Will while she had him, but she was drawing a blank. A second later it was too late. He hung up.

She dated her page of notes, Friday, August 9, and reviewed what she had. Five lines of writing plus a doodled helicopter rotor. It looked like nothing special, yet it could make the case.

She stretched back in her chair, hands laced together behind her head, and savoured the moment. It was always a thrill to land a game-changing detail. It felt like winning a door prize or nailing a difficult news interview. But this feeling was something more. It was relief.

As much as she'd shut her ears and eyes to the Tracker crash, she couldn't help but glean that the leading contender for cause, at least for now, was pilot error. Other theories, some of them wild, like heart attack or a bird hitting the wing, had surfaced and then disappeared. In the absence of any mechanical cause, they were left with distraction, perhaps fleeting but enough to interfere with a routine drop. The possibility haunted Nathalie as doggedly as the ghost of Rafe's shattered body. Was he preoccupied, his thoughts focused on the recent turns his life had taken? Did his meticulousness desert him for a moment and he fumbled? A moment was all it would take, a moment of eyes not on the surroundings or mind not on the job, a single moment that meant nothing in isolation but that would launch all subsequent moments, in an unstoppable cascade to the end.

For the past three weeks, the more Nathalie had tried to shove these questions down, the more defiantly they bobbed to the surface.

Now: Will. His account pointed squarely to a mechanical issue beyond Rafe's control. If, as Rafe was flying into position, he had trimmed the plane down, and the trim jammed in the nose-down position, it would explain why he couldn't pull up from the trees. Runaway trim that close to the treetops was a problem no pilot could compensate for, no matter how talented or focused he was. If the trim was at fault, Rafe was not.

And neither was she.

She leaned farther back in her chair and felt the weight slide off.

I fucked it up, Rafe. But maybe I'm not to blame.

∧ ∨ ∧

IT'S UNCANNY HOW A SINGLE, sometimes microscopic, event can disrupt a much larger course of action. A phone call. A yes instead of a no. An email.

She knew before opening the Miscellaneous Crap folder that the message, though two weeks old, would appear on top. July 26. One year to the day since Mémère left this world. Another dislocation, another death, another phone call.

The news of her grandmother had come at the worst possible time, midway through last summer's agonizing wait for lab results on the Cessna 172. Nathalie knew Uncle Theo's smoke-roughened rasp as soon as he said *bonjour*, despite not meriting a word from him in sixteen years. In two gruff sentences he recounted the facts of Mémère's death, then hung up before Nathalie could respond. Typical. Words, for Uncle Theo, were a virus he felt dutybound not to spread.

The news was devastating but not surprising. Three weeks earlier another phone call had shattered Nathalie's sleep, this one from the trailer park manager, who reported that an ambulance was speeding Mémère to the emergency room. Nathalie stayed in regular contact with the hospital staff after that, waiting and hoping, convinced the old woman would rise from her stroke and get back in the ring, the way she'd dusted herself off and faced down every adversary in her ill-fated life. Nathalie considered booking time off for a visit just in case, but part of her rebelled, afraid that a surprise appearance after so long — it had been at least two years since she saw her grandmother — would spook the woman, maybe sound an early death knell.

Then came the call from Theo that said it was too late. Nathalie, who'd been killing time at her desk, dashed into the TSB washroom, called Theo's wife for details once she'd pulled herself together, and within twenty-four hours had landed at the Winnipeg airport. From there she steered a boat-sized rental forty kilometres southeast to Ste. Anne, mind lulled by the mechanical voice of the sedan's GPS, which guided her to the front door of the funeral home.

"I want to see her," she told the young undertaker on duty, who intoned with exaggerated slowness, as if Nathalie were hard of hearing, that the wake was not *this* evening but *tomorrow* evening. She leaned in, eyes wide, dark curls falling forward in a fragrant mass, and more firmly than necessary gripped the young man's shoulder. "I want to see her," she repeated softly, "and I am staying here until I do."

She settled on the edge of a brown suede sofa and eyed the abstract paintings in the foyer while the attendant placed a hasty, muffled call. "This way," he said a moment later, and ushered her down a flight of concrete stairs into a basement which, judging by the yellow fluorescent lights and scuffed grey walls, seldom welcomed the grieving. He led her to a small room, at the centre of which sat a simple pine casket on a raised bench, and lifted the lid.

Mémère's slack face was modestly rouged and contoured, framed by wavy grey tresses that fanned out on the satin pillow. "The makeup is good," she said. "Give us a moment."

Once the young man withdrew, she told her pulse to calm. Reaching into the casket, she gathered the long, heavy hair, hair she had not touched since she was ten. Carefully she fashioned it into two braids, securing them with the elastic bands she had tucked into her pocket. She laid the thick plaits across the dead woman's shoulders. "There you go," she whispered. She touched one powdered cheek with her forefinger. "*Tout est correct maintenant.*" It was something Theo would never think of, how the proud woman hated to be seen with her hair loose.

Time stopped whenever Nathalie relived this strange goodbye. The basement's chemical scent, the harsh overhead lights, her grandmother's coarse hair between her fingers — the details were as fixed in her mind as if they too had been embalmed, as if some part of her had been laid to rest in the casket alongside the old woman. The memory unsettled her, so she called it up seldom. Time is meant to march forward, after all, not stop, and life is too short to ache — and the ache, those times she allowed herself to remember, was unbearable. The ache contained grief, this she knew, but also gratitude, bittersweet, for a moment of closeness to a woman who, scraped bare by life, had mined her stony self and given what little she found. The ache also contained yearning. For the parents she never knew, or for the tenderness that might have been, or for the prospect of warmth and security ahead, Nathalie couldn't say, and because these were pointless wonderings, her investigator's instinct said to bury them.

All Nathalie knew was that as she stood over her grandmother that day, having touched Mémère's dead face and handled her dead hair, something shifted, like the hard top of her convertible opening to the sky. That shift, she realized now, explained so much of the tumultuous year that followed: her unshakeable sympathy for the family of the Cessna victims and the gross misjudgment that came of it; her entanglement with Rafe and the disaster it became. Everything could be traced back to that open casket and that unguarded moment of weakness.

Open yourself up and all the shit rushes in. Mémère never said that, but she could have.

∧ ∨ ∧

NATHALIE WAS OBLIGATED TO REPORT what she'd learned from Will's call, but as Friday afternoon wound down, she decided to wait. Just until Monday. Not because she took the obligation lightly, and certainly not because she felt vengeful toward her colleagues — Lyndon was her closest ally at work — but because she was in possession of a windfall and knew better than to squander it. *Knowledge is power*: not an original Mémère saying, but she did say it. Lived it too, ruling the family like a spy ring in which she was agent supreme. When you came into a valuable piece of knowledge, you didn't just hand it over. You assessed its worth, considered how you might exchange it or invest it, and estimated the returns it would yield.

So what did Nathalie need? Most urgently, a lead on the R22 crash, but that was nothing Roy and Lyndon could help with. They both specialized in fixed-wing aircraft, and besides, the Tracker was occupying all their hours and then some.

The Cessna 172. Everything circled back to that corrosive case, which had chewed through her credibility. Though by all appearances forgiven, and accepted back into the TSB fold by everyone but Tucker, she knew the investigation continued to taint her. Her peers, and worse yet reporters, would forever see her as that knee-jerk investigator — that knee-jerk *female* investigator, her gender in the view of many being the real reason for her stumble. But if she produced a trump card on the Tracker, a lead so smart and decisive it would redeem her in her co-workers' eyes, most of all Tucker's, it could put the Cessna debacle behind her for good.

The question was, how to make sure the lead came from her and not Lyndon or Roy? She wasn't sure, but she would figure it out and strike when the time was right. Her grandmother didn't call her Scrapper for nothing.

The memory of Rafe, could she put that behind her too? If she could prove that the Tracker crashed for mechanical reasons, not emotional ones, would his ghost quit shadowing her? Because Rafe was the other case she could not afford to leave open. She needed to close it as resolutely as she would put the top back up on her car.

She glanced at the clock. Four twenty, ten minutes to quitting time.

The Miscellaneous Crap folder was still open when she maximized the email window. She had never replied to Jake's note, hadn't even reread it since dragging it into the folder. She didn't need to. She knew the contents by heart, including the ending: "Please? You wont be sorry, I promise."

Pulse thumping, she hit reply and typed one word: "Maybe."

EIGHTEEN

October

THERE IS NO URGENCY in Will's voice. "Could we talk sometime?" Not "Can we talk?" or "I need to talk to you," but "Could we talk *sometime?*" Sharon knows the words by heart, having replayed the message several times in the past two days. Will has implied that she can take her time, and she will.

Taking her time is all she does these days. The strategy of stringing together an assortment of errands, classes, and low-risk encounters that she hopes through repeated association will coalesce into a routine has now, like the stretched grey cardigan she crawls into most mornings, worn thin, its weave too flimsy to hold together. She feels herself letting go: she is becoming untethered from time. Today, for instance, she spends half an hour trying to recall what she did yesterday morning. She got up, showered, had breakfast. Then ... She cannot think what she did between nine and noon, can only identify the many things she didn't do — go to the gym or yoga, buy anything, tackle the laundry, read her library book, talk to anyone.

By the third day after Will's message, her lethargy and feeble mental state are finally testing her patience. She calls. He picks up on the first ring. "Oh," she says, surprised.

"Sharon, is that you?"

Her number will be displayed. "Yes. Returning your call at last."

"That's okay. You must be pretty busy."

As if. "Yes, fairly."

"I won't take up much of your time. I just wondered, could we maybe talk at some point? You know, face to face?"

"You mentioned stopping by here for coffee. That would be fine."

"Great." He coughs slightly. His voice sounds rough. "How about tomorrow? Maybe three?"

She calculates: shopping, yoga if she can make herself go, then an interminable stretch of nothing. "Three is fine."

After putting down the phone, she considers the kitchen. Things look roughly okay. No startling changes, no unkempt corners if you overlook the pile of bills and brochures near the kitchen alcove (smaller now that she has sorted through them), no withered houseplants or dishes crusted with mould that might cast doubt on her ability to carry on.

When did she last lay eyes on Will? She doesn't recall him at the funeral, though that day, more than three months ago now, is heavily hazed with Xanax, the pills pressed on her by Colleen in the limo during another crying jag. Nasty, thieving drug, Sharon fumed afterwards, you stole the details of that last goodbye.

She tries to place Will at the chapel. Was he there, seated stiffly in a pew? Was he at the reception afterwards with the sombre blur of pilots clustered around the refreshments? She has no memory of seeing or talking to him since the crash, not even since the awful Christmas party last year, an eternity ago. What he might want from her, she cannot imagine.

∧ ∨ ∧

THE INTERVAL BEFORE last year's Christmas party, a formerly unmarketable period known as late autumn, was rebranded some time ago by the west coast tourism industry. Storm-watching season, as it is now called, has captured the imagination and dollars of the travelling public, throngs of whom surrounded Sharon and Rafe on Vancouver Island in late November last year.

Rafe's work had wound down two months earlier, and his return home did little to warm the coolness between them since Sharon's fortieth birthday. In an obvious attempt to close the rift, Rafe surprised her with a long weekend at an oceanside resort near Tofino. For three whole days they would walk the expanse of Long Beach, observe sleek black cormorants and wetsuited surfers, and explore the tiny streets of Tofino, where art galleries, craft shops, and tie-dyed twenty-somethings daubed spots of colour on the foggy landscape.

The first morning of their getaway Sharon woke early to the roar of surf outside their balcony door, which Rafe had cracked open before bed. It was still dark, morning barely under way. Propped up on one elbow, she took in the silhouetted trees that framed the ocean view. The room was quiet but for the pounding waves, and chilly. She burrowed back under the duvet.

"Cold?" Rafe whispered.

He was awake.

He inched over and took her in his arms. His heat seeped into her fingers and feet, and he blew a long, hot breath onto her cheek. "An extra shot for free," he said, as he always did when he warmed her this way.

She turned her back to him, fit her spine along his torso and her head beneath his chin. Faint daylight streaked the cloudy sky. "What time is it?" she asked.

"I don't know and I'm too lazy to turn around and look."

Rafe stroked her hair and they lay silent. Sharon resisted sleep, knowing all they had planned for the day, but the soft bed and the rhythmic waves exerted a narcotic pull. Her eyes grew heavy and her thoughts sailed free. The expensive sheets caressed her legs. It was so warm. The warmth spread around her right breast, encircled it with heat, then turned into a soft tug.

Rafe's hand.

Her eyes shot open.

Rafe's fingers touched her through her thin camisole, first rubbing the fleshy part of her breast, then closing in on the nipple.

"Mm. Not now." She made her voice slow and drowsy, though she was now wide awake. "I'm too sleepy."

"It's okay." His lips brushed her ear. "I'll be gentle." His hand continued its slow circles. The fabric of her camisole chafed under the movement.

"No, really." She shifted slightly so that her breast slipped away. "Later, when I'm more awake."

"You don't need to be awake. We'll have sleepy sex. I'll do all the work." His hand moved down and slipped beneath the waistband of her panties. He stroked her hip bone, his fingers thick and slightly calloused.

No. Tension snapped at her like an elastic. Sitting up abruptly, she trapped his big hand in the crease between her hip and leg, a slab of flesh pressing into fragile silk. She lifted the hand and dropped it onto the mattress, where it bounced slightly.

"Jesus, Sharon." Rafe rolled over on his back. "Leave a guy a little dignity."

In the dimness she saw that he was cradling his hand as if it were injured. For God's sake. Anger rose but she fought it. Don't make a scene, she told herself. Don't spoil the day. "I don't feel like it, okay? We can do it later."

"Later," he said, still holding his hand. "Always later. It's never now."

"Don't be so childish." The words spilled out. "I have a say in this too, don't I?"

"Childish!" He rolled over to face her, eyes narrowed. "How is it childish to want to make love with my own wife? How is that childish? You tell me."

She balled up a fistful of duvet. It was not a question she could answer.

"You always say later, like it's some kind of a ... a chore, something you want to put off as long as you can." He sat up, his massive shoulders pale in the weak light. "You know what? Later never comes. I wait and wait and it never comes. Then I can't stand it anymore so I touch you, or ask you flat out, and we're right back where we started. It's *now* all over again." He shook his head. "What's with you, Sharon? Aren't you ever gonna want to have sex with me again?"

It's not the time for this conversation. "Of course I will. But it's complicated."

He barked a short laugh. "The one thing it's not is complicated. You're my wife, I'm your husband, we're supposed to have sex. It's not complicated. What's complicated is that I'm a married man, in a supposedly happy marriage, who for some Jesus reason has to jerk himself off every few days because his wife, who supposedly loves him, can't stand to touch him anymore."

"I touch you! I touch you all the time." She could no longer keep the shrill out of her voice. Now they were in for a full-tilt fight. "I hug you and massage your shoulders. So what if it's not sex? Do you honestly think that's all marriage is about?"

"Try listening, why don't you. I never once said it's just about sex. But sex is part of it. A big part."

Sharon squeezed the duvet cover in her fist. "Not that big."

"I'm telling you it is!" Rafe pushed the covers down, his huge chest heaving. "It is! Why treat me like a freak or, or pervert for thinking that? It's natural, what I want. It's biology. Man, woman, bed — it's like the holy trinity. It's how we're engineered, for chrissakes."

"It's not that simple —"

"It *is*, woman!" He pounded the mattress. "It *is* that simple."

Her voice went icy. "So that's what you brought me here for. For this." She swept her hand over the bed. "You say it's a surprise for me, that I've been alone all summer and deserve a treat, but really it's an elaborate scheme to get yourself laid. You bring me to a fancy lodge on a secluded beach, pretend it's all romantic, that it's about *love*, just so you can feel entitled. So you can *fuck* me, whether I want to or not." She drew out the F-word, unfamiliar on her tongue. "You know what some people call that? Rape."

She could almost hear the air suck out of the room. Rafe's cheeks flushed maroon and his eyes glittered. Rage. She had never seen it in him before. She went still, suddenly afraid.

"You cunt." The words fell out of him, deadly boulders off a cliff. "You fucking cunt. Don't you *ever* say that to me."

She inhaled sharply. Never before had he called her that, or spoken to her with such ragged fury. She swung out of bed, pulled on her robe, and stumbled to the bathroom.

"That's right. Walk away like you always do, all superior. You fucking cocktease. Leave me here like I'm some kind of ... some kind of baby you can't be bothered to take seriously."

Sharon turned slowly and stared at the bulky shape that was her husband. Enough morning light crept through the balcony door to illuminate his face, twisted and ominous, a gross distortion of his handsome self.

"Yes, like a baby." She formed the words with care. "Not that I'd know anything about that." She stepped into the bathroom and slammed the door.

∧ ∨ ∧

THE FIGHT IN TOFINO was the bitterest they'd ever had, yet they made up, at least after a fashion. Practicality demanded it. There would always be somewhere to go or someone to see. It was their habit to patch the breaks so no tension could leak through.

In Tofino it was Rafe who made the first move. In truth, it was always Rafe. He was quicker to anger, but quicker to mend matters too.

He was gone by the time she emerged from the bathroom, showered and swathed in a towel. Relief coursed through her, and with it something like shame. The abandoned bed, covers in a tangle, stared at her in rebuke. I will not feel guilty, she told herself. I have a right to say no.

Nor was he in the breakfast area an hour later, when Sharon made herself leave their room. Head pounding and mind numb, as if gripped by a hangover, she carried a mug of coffee from the buffet to a small corner table from which she contemplated the ocean, wondering what to do next. He would be somewhere along the beach, she knew, walking off his anger. That was fine. He needed to cool down. Maybe they could still salvage the day.

She was on her third cup of coffee and had managed a bite

of croissant when the flat weight of his hand brushed her shoulder. Startled, she looked up.

"Can I sit down?"

His face had softened, his eyes no longer snapped. The fire had subsided.

"Go ahead."

He pulled his chair in to the small table, closing the space between them. He nodded at her plate. "Looks good."

"There's lots more at the buffet."

"It's okay. It's not like I'm hungry." He studied the striped sugar bowl on the table. "Sharon."

She waited. The words had to be his.

"I'm sorry I called you that. It was a terrible thing to say. All the things I said were terrible. I got carried away. I'm sorry." He looked up. "Really sorry."

Waves broke on the beach outside, their shushing just audible through the window glass. At one end of the cove, the sand that fronted the hotel gave way to craggy black rocks that shattered each swell into spray.

"Please, Sharon. The last thing I want is to ruin our weekend. I'm a big galoot that says stupid things. You know that." He smiled faintly at the old self-reproach.

He reached out his hand. The etched wedding band bit into the flesh of his finger. She knew she should soften, give way like the waves, but she was still smarting. Whenever this happened, it ended up feeling like her fault. She couldn't help it if she wasn't in the mood every time he was. And he couldn't expect her to want sex all the time now that they'd given up trying for a child. Since that cut-off birthday, she sometimes wondered if there was any point having sex at all. Except that Rafe was a man, and a man has needs.

She cradled her coffee mug, ignoring his hand. "I understand why you're upset. I do. But I've got a right to say no. You have to respect that, even if it's not what you want to hear. You have to not push me so much, okay?"

"I'll do better, Sharon. I promise." His brown eyes shone. "You're everything to me, girl. My whole life. It's just the two of us now, me and you. We gotta stick by each other. Let's forget the awful way today started. Just erase it and start again."

There was his hand on the table, the big hand that controlled airplanes and saved lives, the hand that stroked her hair and could fix anything broken.

She set down her mug and touched his fingertips with her own. "Okay, let's start again." They were the right words to say, whether she trusted them or not.

NINETEEN

August

DESPITE NATHALIE'S EVERY ATTEMPT to speed it up, the weekend following Will's surprise call to her office inched along. Cardio boot camp both mornings, a deep clean of the bathroom, Saturday afternoon shopping, dinner and a movie Saturday night with a Mainland Air friend, a long cycle through Stanley Park Sunday afternoon — no matter how full she crammed the hours, they defied her, lurching sluggishly, like her thoughts. *Knowledge is power.* This new knowledge about the Tracker — how could she leverage it? She examined from every angle Will's account of the sticky trim, but couldn't decide how to make it pay off. Nor, despite the weekend's diversions, could she stop daydreaming about Jake Behrend. Her heart hammered whenever she thought of her one-word reply to him and the new email that might be there on Monday.

When at long last Monday came, she arrived at the office at eight, half an hour early, and logged on to email first thing. Thirty-two new messages, none of them from Jake. There was, however, a note from Robinson Helicopters about tomorrow's R22 engine teardown in Victoria. As she'd predicted, the manufacturer, wanting to prolong the exercise, asked her in laborious prose to reserve Tuesday and Wednesday.

> It is in the interest of all of the involved parties, that the scheduled engine teardown proceed in as thorough, and methodical a manner as possible, in order that we may all assure ourselves, that the findings and outcomes are accurate, relevant, and, impartial.

It sounded admirable, if over-punctuated, but Nathalie knew a stall when she saw one. Reluctantly she asked Luanne to book her flights and hotel in Victoria, then informed Tucker she'd be away until Thursday.

"Try to come back with some answers" was all he said.

Sure, boss, no pressure. Good old Tucker the Fucker.

As for Lyndon and Roy, they were both out of the office, following up the Tracker crash, said Luanne. Excellent, Nathalie decided. The perfect reason to hold off telling them about Will's call.

With her travel arranged and her questions for the engine teardown finalized, there was little to do for the rest of the day. At two o'clock she checked email one last time, frustrated to see nothing from Jake and angry at herself for caring, then gathered her files and laptop. "I've got to run a few errands and pack for Victoria," she told Luanne, who frowned and muttered something about how nice it must be to leave early, not that she'd know anything about it. The woman was still in mid-sentence when Nathalie swung the door shut.

∧ ∨ ∧

PATIENCE HAD NEVER BEEN Nathalie's strong suit, and day one of the teardown was a gruelling test of how long she could hold out. All she wanted were explanations, or in their absence hints, for why James Stanhope's helicopter had in a matter of moments gone from sophisticated machine to scattered shards. Tucker had told her to come back with answers, and that's what she needed to do.

Hour upon hour she watched while the onsite mechanics dismantled the engine's outer components, set each part carefully in a rolling metal tray, and then bench-tested the magnetos, a process that by itself wasted two hours at the opposite end of the facility. By afternoon she had no more answers than when her floatplane lifted off from Vancouver Harbour that morning. The team had only confirmed what the wreckage and crash site had indicated all along: that the engine was producing power at the time of the crash. Now she could officially rule out engine failure as the cause, something she'd done inwardly weeks ago. But she remained convinced, based on the helicopter's straight-down plunge from the sky and the R22's low-inertia rotor, that the main rotor blades had stopped turning. Why? A helicopter rotor doesn't quit without another failure behind it.

Throughout the day the Robinson reps, two middle-aged desk types dispatched by California headquarters, remained as circumspect as any observers Nathalie had ever dealt with. Several times she questioned them about power loss to the rotor. What tended to cause that in the R22? What had they learned from past accidents? What could she look for in the wreckage to home in on a conclusion? Time and again the men folded their arms, changed the subject, and divulged nothing.

After work, determined to rack up some kind of accomplishment, Nathalie walked for an hour and a half along Victoria's Inner Harbour, past the rocky outcroppings, the bustling piers and waterfront booths, the stately Empress Hotel with its Edwardian wings and manicured grounds, the copper domes of the provincial legislature. The sky thrummed with floatplanes bearing the last commuters home to the mainland. Tiny water taxis scooted across the narrow harbour, laden with tourists in search of ersatz England — the double-decker buses, extravagant high teas, fish and chips, and British pubs for which the tidy capital was renowned. As Nathalie rounded Laurel Point, the salty breeze whipped her hair and propelled her into the nearest hotel for a quick dinner of *moules frites*.

That night in her modest quarters, in the terry robe she'd packed knowing that no government-rate room would offer one, she lounged on the bed and reviewed the scarce facts from the teardown. At least they had tomorrow, which they'd spend disassembling the engine's core parts. What should she focus on then? What magic words would persuade the Robinson reps to tell her something, anything, that might steer her in the right direction?

Except for the drone of the air exchange system, the Standard City View room was quiet. Her mind was anything but. To help settle it, she nursed a mini bottle of bourbon she'd stashed with her toiletries, experience in the form of Tucker having taught her that the feds did not smile upon a hotel bill that included liquor.

The rap on her door was so gentle that she thought she'd imagined it, until it came again. She slid off the bed, already annoyed at the room service mix-up or unrequested housekeeping.

Eye to the peephole, she caught her breath. Then opened the door.

"I thought I'd find you here, Nat."

Jake slipped inside and without another word kissed her full on the mouth.

Like that, it began. The ghost of Rafe Mackie did not visit Nathalie that night.

∧ ∨ ∧

AN HOUR LATER SHE GOT UP to use the bathroom, not bothering with the robe that lay where Jake had pushed it off her. As she crossed back to the bed, her visitor propped himself up on one elbow and the sheet fell away from his shoulders, revealing skin that was smooth, nut coloured, and nearly hairless. Not for the first time Nathalie wondered if Indigenous blood ran through the veins of this bold and gorgeous man.

"Stop right there," he said when she reached the side of the bed.

"Ordering me around already?"

He gazed straight ahead, at her crotch, and licked his lips.

"No one ever told you it's rude to stare?" She widened her stance slightly and thrust her hips forward.

"I like rude. I'm a big fan of it. Notice how I never said please once tonight?"

"You never said much of anything."

"Well, I've been busy." He reached for her left breast.

"Not as busy as you're going to be if you keep that up."

He gave her nipple a gentle squeeze. "We'll get around to it. I need a timeout." He lay back, hands behind his head. "I'm not nineteen any-more, you know. Back then I'd be ready to go again by the time you wiped yourself off."

She raised one eyebrow and hopped back into bed.

"You had your chance back then, Nat, and you blew me off. Okay, not the best choice of words since there was no blowing. Now you know what you missed out on."

"I need a reminder." She pushed the sheet the rest of the way off his compact, naked body and thanked the inventors of hockey for making men look the way Jake did. She took in the full length of him. "Looks to me like you're ready."

"The equipment is ready. The mind needs a little time."

She covered him partway up again, leaned over, and traced a circle on his chest. "So why don't you tell me what you're doing here? How did you even know I was in Victoria?"

"I didn't get your email till Monday afternoon. I was in classes all morning. When I called your office the receptionist said you were at an engine teardown until Thursday. So I said I had information on a crash you were investigating and asked how to get hold of you."

Nathalie tossed her head. "That's a load of crap. No way would Luanne tell you where I was. You think *I'm* tough as nails. She makes me look like tapioca."

"Tell me about it. I poured on the charm and I couldn't get a thing out of her. But I knew the teardown had to be for the R22 that went down last month. You mentioned it when we talked at BCIT. That helicopter has a Lycoming engine, and the nearest Lycoming-approved service centre is right here in Victoria."

"Not bad for a guy who's not a trained investigator. But that doesn't explain how you tracked down my hotel. Or what the hell you're actually doing here. Calgary's a long way away."

"The wife and kids are up in northern Quebec visiting her parents. I stayed behind to teach. That makes me a free man." He wound a length of her hair around his finger and gave it a playful tug. "I thought hey, no classes today, I'll fly down. Got a last-minute deal from one of my airline buddies. Soon as I landed I went straight to the service centre, but damned if I didn't just miss you. Lucky for me, two Robinson guys were there shooting the shit and one of them said you were staying here. You weren't in when I first came by, so I waited." He kissed the tip of her index finger. "I'm good at waiting."

"You're a piece of work. What if you got all the way here and couldn't find me?"

Jake reached for her breast again. "I would find you. All this time, Ms. Tough as Nails, and you finally say maybe? I'd find you anywhere."

∧ ∨ ∧

NATHALIE SHOWED UP for day two of the teardown with sore hips but a determined mind. She'd get answers today if it killed her, and she had a plan for how to extract them.

Near dawn she had turned Jake out of bed. He could shower with her, she said, but then he had to leave so she could pack and check out. As they soaped up, both of them groggy after only a few hours' sleep, she griped about the lack of progress at the teardown.

"Forget the Robinson reps," Jake said, squirting shampoo into his palm. "They make up their minds they're not gonna tell you anything, then they won't. Go for the mechanics. Think how many R22 engines those guys handle every year. Maybe they've run into something that'll help you out."

Nathalie watched as he rinsed his head and neck. Despite the lack of sleep, he moved like a fish under the streaming water, agile and sinuous. "That's a good idea."

"Don't sound so surprised. I'm not just a pretty face, you know."

"I know." She reached down and cupped his balls. "There's all this too."

Fifteen minutes later, hair wet and black, shirt wrinkled from spending the night in a heap, Jake leaned against the doorframe and kissed her nose. "You're a saucy thing, Nat. I like that."

"And you're a cocky bastard."

"Yes, I am. And I'll be cocky next time I see you too. I guarantee it."

"Who says there's going to be a next time?"

"I'll take my chances," he said, and headed off down the corridor.

Now, watching the Robinson reps stroll in, their California saunter not unlike her own bow-legged gait this morning, she mentally thanked Jake, for both the fuck and the plan.

The previous day the two mechanics had said little, doing all they were asked but speaking only to exchange instructions or answer direct questions. The older one, a small, leathery fellow in a Molson Canadian ball cap and the remains of a tee-shirt, judging by the frayed collar that peeped out from his overalls, hadn't been introduced as the lead mechanic but obviously he was. Every move and instruction to his younger helper telegraphed experience.

At eleven forty-five, when the group dispersed for lunch, the Robinson reps mumbling something about miso soup and gluten-free, she pulled the older mechanic aside. "Got a sec?"

He glanced around as if to check that she was really talking to him. "Sure."

Her hand lingered on his arm. "Look, you know and I know this teardown is turning into a giant waste of time. We're getting nowhere. It's not your fault," she added quickly, patting his sleeve. "It's these Robinson guys. You may have noticed they keep ducking my questions."

"Yup. You won't get a peep outta them. They been here a few times before. Last time was maybe a year, year and a half back. They had someone suing them or something. Same deal – they clammed right up."

"Company reps are all the same. They're interested in one thing and one thing only, covering their ass."

The mechanic reached under his ball cap and gave his head a good scratch. If he wasn't going to volunteer information, she'd take the direct approach. "What do *you* think happened? We all know the helicopter engine was working fine. The only damage to it is what occurred during the crash."

The mechanic nodded but said nothing.

"So why the accident?"

"Well." He contemplated the floor. "I'm mostly an engine man. I don't know much about rotors or airframes, and I don't know nothin' about being an investigator."

"Come on, you're being modest," Nathalie practically purred. "I bet you've got theories. Maybe from other R22 engines you've worked on?"

He scuffed the floor with one steel-toed boot. "I been in this business twenty-eight years and it's true, I worked on a good number of R22 engines. You hang around them Robinson guys long enough and you pick up a thing or two, whether they want you to or not. I can tell you it pretty near always comes down to the main rotor quitting. Your helicopter, it basically fell from the sky, right?"

"Right. My money's on the rotor stopping too. Problem is, I've got nothing to tell me what caused that."

"What happened to the pulley assembly? You know, that drives the main rotor? We never got it. We only got the engine. They take the pulley system off when they yarded the engine outta the wreck?"

Nathalie nodded. The pulley assembly was physically mounted on the helicopter engine and often had to be removed to get at the engine itself.

"You know the belts that drive the pulleys?" the mechanic said. "Well, think about it. Them belts come loose during flight and start flinging themselves around, you got a first-class shitstorm in the making. They loosen up enough, they'll come right off the pulleys. And then what?"

"The rotor stops turning."

"Yep. It just stops."

Nathalie considered this. "Okay, in theory that's what would happen. But how would the belts ever get that loose? I mean, if they loosen up even a little, the clutch kicks in and adjusts the tension —" She broke off as the idea dawned on her. "The clutch."

"Well now. I heard some Robinson fellas a few years back, not these two but a couple practically their twins, clean-cut cagey-type guys, talkin' about that very thing. Sounds like they seen it happen before. The clutch quits and one thing leads to another and you better say your prayers."

Excitement flared through her. Then just as quickly fizzled. "The thing is, I can't see the clutch going in this helicopter. It was so well maintained. Money was no object and the owner did everything above board. Hired a licensed AME to do all the work. The logbooks are spotless, the annual inspections all done. Now that I think of it, the engine got a major overhaul this spring. The belts you're talking about were all replaced." She shook her head. "And the clutch. No AME would miss a clutch that's due for replacement or that's worn."

"Not worn ..." The mechanic hesitated. "I'm talking no power."

"No power? To the clutch?"

He nodded, the Molson Canadian logo bobbing up and down.

"You mean the fuse? The clutch fuse could've blown?" Nathalie struggled to lower her voice, even though the others were long gone. Here was a possibility she hadn't considered, and it wasn't that far-fetched.

"Yep. I seen it happen. It's not the only explanation by any stretch, but if you're coming up empty, it could be worth a look-see."

Nathalie's mind raced. "I don't think anyone checked the fuses."

The mechanic removed his cap and scrutinized the logo. "I was you, I'd take a good close-up look. Them helicopter pilots — well, not the real ones, the commercial guys, but the rich pilots just fly for the hell of it — I can't figure it, but they can be the cheapest sons a bitches you ever wanna meet. Or maybe not cheap, maybe it's more lazy. One day they blow a fuse and there's no AME around so they just stick in whatever spare fuse they got laying around. Don't even check twice to make sure it's the right one. They'll put in a one or a one-point-two amp where they need a one-point-five. Even some old automotive fuse if that's all they got handy." He replaced his cap, giving the bill a sharp tug. "I can't figure it. They got all the money in the world. They own companies, houses, condos, boats, what have you. They got sports cars, motorbikes, they got their own gee-dee personal helicopter, and they won't spend two minutes and a coupla bucks on the right fuse. More money than brains, eh?"

Nathalie nodded, mostly to stay agreeable. It was unlikely that James Stanhope III would care enough about a minute or two, let alone a dollar or two, to take his chances on an improper fuse. But something else could have blown the fuse, maybe an overload. All in all, it was an intriguing theory.

"I really appreciate this." She touched the mechanic's arm again. "I'll look at the wreckage as soon as I'm back on the mainland."

"Okay. Now I got a sandwich waiting for me." The mechanic shot her a faint grin. "Can't say as it's gluten-free but at least the wife made it herself. That's something, eh?"

This was something, Nathalie thought as the skinny mechanic crossed the room. True, what she had now was little more than a chain of flimsy possibilities, but past investigations had taught her that every chain was worth examining, link by link. If you really probed an accident, if you looked behind the immediate cause — a failed engine or a stopped rotor — to what was behind that cause, and what was behind *that,* you'd find something extraordinary: if a series of circumstances aligns in just the right way, a single small failure is all it takes to bring the most powerful aircraft down. The Swiss cheese effect, investigators call it. Swiss cheese is full of random holes, and if you stack up slices of it the holes rarely line up. An aircraft, too, has its holes — its weaknesses and malfunctions — but it's designed so that other parts of the system will compensate. A single flaw or error almost never destroys the whole machine. Yet every once in a while, just as the holes in a pile of Swiss cheese slices will occasionally align, a series of problems will hit an aircraft at once, creating a single, profound gap that even the most prepared pilot can't plug.

In the world of aviation, Nathalie long ago learned, the alignment of holes spells catastrophe. Something as innocuous and minuscule as a fuse can wreck an entire aircraft and snuff out multiple lives. The trick is to find the fuse and trace back the series of consequences that lead from it, looking at all the layers affected. Only then, when you've gone all the way back to the beginning, can you fully grasp the end.

TWENTY

October

AT TWENTY PAST THREE Sharon opens the door to a stranger. She is expecting Will, but he has sent someone else in his place.

When the man murmurs hello and extends his hand, she is aghast: this gaunt, shaggy-haired, bearded apparition *is* Will. He looks at her sideways from sunken, bloodshot eyes. Good God, she wants to say, what happened to you? Without thinking, she clasps his hand with both of hers.

He stands there, staring at their joined hands, until she draws back. Her face burns. He has been here all of fifteen seconds and already she's gotten carried away. Get a grip, she admonishes herself, and gathers the shawl of reserve around her shoulders.

"Sorry I'm late." His voice is rusty, as if just out of storage.

"It's fine. Please, come in."

She sits at one end of the sofa and he settles down opposite her, in Rafe's chair. Will wouldn't know that. He has been here four or five times at most: once years ago to help replace the hot water tank, his first visit and the longest by far, and a few times since to collect Rafe for an evening at the pub. Mainly she has seen Will at West Air events: the annual Halloween barbecue, the Christmas party, a few milestone birthdays.

"Did you remember how to get here? It's been a while."

"Yeah, I just ... The drive took longer than I thought. Traffic this time of day."

Three o'clock, just before the afternoon rush, is one of the few times traffic is usually tolerable, but she lets it go. Clearly Will is not at his best. Scratch that — clearly he's in trouble. His legs, now that he is seated, look thin as sticks. One knee jitters and he cannot meet her eyes. Judging by his alarming appearance, punctuality is the least of his worries.

Her own appearance Sharon has taken pains to make normal. She lingered in the shower after yoga, shaving her underarms and legs so there can be no doubt she's keeping up with personal grooming. She applied makeup, a ritual she has abandoned except for meetings with Rachel, who scrutinizes her for any sign of slippage. She chose a vee-neck pullover in a flattering cornflower blue so she will appear rested and fresh, and her sandy hair is down so that it frames her face and softens its creases.

In all the time it has taken Sharon to ready herself for this visit, it never occurred to her that it might be Will who has slid. The young pilot seems utterly changed. In the past he exuded an easy energy, less intense than Rafe's but just as palpable. Like an athlete, she'd have said, which indeed he is, with his hiking and surfing expeditions, his skiing and snowboarding. This Will in her living room is no graceful athlete. A starved runner at the end of an ultra-endurance race, maybe. That is the best she can do to reconcile the ruin in front of her with the young man she has seen on and off for the past nine years.

"You're not well," she says, skipping over whole layers of niceties that would only, under the circumstances, come across as lies.

Will looks away, toward the big front window. Above his beard, light and shadow play on a cheek that is startlingly concave, skin stretched taut over bone. The house is hushed; Sharon hears nothing but her own breath, catching now in her throat. She watches Will collect himself, and waits.

When he turns back to her, his eyes are red-rimmed. He gazes beyond her, at the linen-coloured wall on which hangs a framed abstract of mountains, the paint colour and the print her own choosing, as are all things decorative in the house. Rafe declared when they moved in that she could have her way with the interior.

"It's been rough." He does not duck his head. She admires this.

"I know." And even though for months she has thought of Will Werner almost never, she does know. "You worked so closely together."

A small nod.

"He talked about you a lot," she says carefully. "He loved flying with you, Will. He said you were an excellent pilot, especially for a young man. He trusted you."

Will's jaw trembles. She recognizes the look in his eyes and understands, with sickening insight, how selfish she has been. How can she have imagined all this time that she was alone in mourning Rafe? The man in front of her spent nearly every day of fire season with her husband, putting in gruelling hours during extraordinary circumstances right alongside him. Of course he is grieving.

What Sharon has wanted from this visit is the chance to talk about Rafe with someone who knew him well. Ever since Will phoned, she has longed for the opportunity to remember her husband in detail, to bring him to life again. Now she understands the pain it will cause. She must not push.

"So you're off work now, finished for the season?"

"Yeah." He peers at her from a curtain of uncut hair. "The summer started so busy, but by September we were back to cool weather and rain. It was a quiet end."

They fall silent. Will rubs at a spot on his leg. He has many to choose from; his rumpled khakis are profusely stained.

"I'm glad you're here, Will," she says eventually. "But I can't help wondering. Is there something on your mind?"

He keeps rubbing at the spot, getting nowhere in spite of his diligence. "How're you holding out yourself?"

Sharon hugs her torso. It's chilly in here. She should have switched on the gas fireplace, but it feels wrong to get up and do it now. "Okay, I guess. Better than a couple of months ago."

"A couple of months ago." He appears puzzled, as if the time frame is incomprehensible. "For me it was easier then, I guess because of work. Something to concentrate on, you know? When the other guys were around we talked about him sometimes, told stories." He looks back out the front window to the street, where the wind scuttles leaves along the late-day sidewalk. Fall is here, Sharon thinks; the long summer has finally receded. "I miss that about work," he says, returning to the spot on his pants.

Sharon is freezing. "How about some tea? Or coffee — you mentioned coffee when you called."

"Tea's fine. Thanks."

She disappears into the kitchen, grateful for a few minutes alone. She is still puzzled as to why he's here, but maybe it doesn't matter. Maybe he simply needs to talk, even if that means talking around Rafe rather than about him.

"I miss that too," she says as she sets the tea tray on the coffee table. He looks at her blankly. "You were saying how it helps to talk about him, tell stories. I miss that too." She pours two cups and offers a plate of digestive biscuits. He holds up a hand but accepts the tea, adds two spoonfuls of sugar, and drinks greedily.

"Don't you talk about him?" he asks after a minute.

"The first couple of months I did, especially while my sister was here. I guess that's like you at work. Then she went home to Ontario. By that time everyone else had gone back to normal life, and when I did see friends it seemed like we should discuss other things. I even —" She stops, takes a sip.

"What?" Will's eyes are lighter than Rafe's, and his gaze is cool and steady rather than warm and dancing.

"I even —" She takes a deep breath. "I've never told anyone this, but I — I sometimes mention him to people who don't know he's gone. At the grocery store or the dry cleaner. I'll make an offhand comment about how my husband loves this cheese, or how my husband will be relieved they got the stain out of the blouse he gave me." Will smiles faintly and for a moment looks more like himself. "I'm aware of how pathetic that sounds," she says.

"I wouldn't say pathetic."

"Believe me, pathetic is what I'm an expert on. It's the new me."

"At least you're out doing errands. My dad invites me over to his place every week or two, but I don't go. He doesn't need to see me like this." He regards his stained pants. "I'm avoiding my next-door neighbour too. If she's home I keep the lights off and use headphones for the TV so she thinks I'm not around." Outside the light is fading, the cloud cover pressing lower. A muted softness steals over the living room. "I know a thing or two about pathetic is what I'm saying."

Sharon tries to picture Will hiding from the world. As much as she regrets his pain, she is also grateful that someone else deeply misses Rafe. Selfish, she berates herself again, and it is. But also consoling. The rest of the world has moved on; until now, she thought she was the only one lagging behind.

"Was he ...?" She doesn't know how to ask it. "At West Air, did they, did you get along okay without him? I mean, did they replace him or ...?"

One look at Will's face, emptied of colour, and she knows she has said the wrong thing. Completely, utterly. How has she been so oblivious? Will was not just Rafe's colleague at West Air; they were partners. For ten years, almost half the time she and Rafe were married, the two men worked side by side. They flew into infernos together; they saw things people shouldn't see; together they outran death. You don't replace your partner like you swap out a broken propeller. Will's stricken expression brings the realization home. They were partners at West Air, and they were partners the day of the crash.

"You were there." The enormity of it turns her stomach. "In the air with him. You saw it." She has not formed this thought until now and wonders how it could possibly have escaped her. Because she has thought only of herself, that's how.

For a moment he battles it. Then his jaw slackens, his shoulders slump. "Of course I saw it." The fingers of one hand dig into his thick, uncut hair. "I keep on seeing it."

"Oh, Will. I'm so sorry." She is at a loss for words. How can she have been so tactless?

When he finally speaks, she can barely hear him. "The rest of the summer, every time I went up there and watched a tanker come in for the drop, all I could think about was him. What was going through his head? What were his last thoughts?" Will's face is a ragged wreck. "You know? Was he panicky or did he feel in control? Did he want — Was he — Did he think even for a second that he could still pull out of it?"

They are questions Sharon asked herself repeatedly through the endless summer days. "Have you talked to anyone?" she asks. "A professional, I mean?"

"A few times at the beginning, but ... I had to get on with it, you know? It was a busy season. We were getting called out all the time. I couldn't keep an appointment if I tried."

"Maybe you should go back now that you're off work. It can be helpful."

He casts her a look. "Is that what you did?"

"No." She smiles wanly, caught. "I thought about it, and my sister desperately wants me to, but I haven't. Not yet anyway. I have seen a counsellor before, though, about other things. I know it can help."

He goes to the window, the street outside turned dusky and still. "It's gotten so cold." The last daylight outlines his scarecrow body, from which his clothes hang. No wonder he's cold. Sharon gets up and switches on the fireplace.

He turns at the sound. "That's not why I came here, you know. To dump all over you."

"Will —"

"Really, I'll be fine. Once I've had time to chill, some more time off work." He returns to the chair, perches on the edge.

She waits, sensing that he will come to the point. In a minute he does.

"You and Rafe, you weren't together when he died."

There it is, and it spears her every time. "No. We weren't living together." Why deny it? It's a fact, one she would do anything to erase.

"I didn't know. I mean, back then, at the time of the crash. He wasn't himself those last few weeks but none of us knew why. He didn't tell anyone you were separated."

"No one?" Rafe was not the type to announce the news far and wide, but she had assumed he would confide in someone. In particular Will. "Then how did you find out?"

"The TSB investigators. It really threw me for a loop. I mean, I had no idea." He pauses. "Was it ... was it really over? Or were you just taking a break?"

Again she hugs herself. "It's so chilly in here. That fireplace isn't doing a thing."

"Listen, I know it's none of my business. But you've got to believe me, it's important. I need to know what was going on with him at the end. I can't stop thinking about it, him living alone in some crappy apartment for two whole months and keeping it a secret. Why would he do that?"

"I don't know."

Her mind whirls. Why would Rafe not tell his partner about their split? It was the paradox of Rafe: open and gregarious about most things, fiercely guarded about a few. There were whole parcels of his life that her husband corralled off with barbed wire. His boyhood in Cape Breton, which he refused to speak of and which she guessed was harsh with poverty, maybe violence, possibly worse. Their failure to conceive, their fights, their sexual problems — he packed each difficulty away rather than acknowledging it head on. Whether from pride or natural meticulousness, he had to portray his world as shipshape even when it wasn't. Containing fires, the real outbreaks and the metaphorical ones, was a way of life with Rafe, so she can understand his not broadcasting their breakup. But why hide it from Will, his closest friend? Because it smacked of failure, the one thing Rafe Mackie could never tolerate?

"We did split up. But later, just before he died —" She shuts her eyes. Can she say it? "We decided to give it another try. Not long before the crash, about a week. He asked if he could move back in."

She feels Will waiting, feels a wall collapse inside her.

"He was going to keep the apartment for a while, just in case. But the plan was, he was coming back home on his next leave."

She opens her eyes. The same living room, the same tea tray on the same coffee table. The same gas fireplace, flickering. Outside, evening has fallen. Nothing has changed, and yet everything has. She has said it out loud, the deepest part of her grief: they were going to start over, and he died before they could.

Will looks at her, unblinking. "I don't get it."

"I can't—" She shakes her head. "I've never told anyone. My sister knew that we'd separated, but not that he was coming home again. I think that's why I mention him to people who don't know he's dead, the dry cleaner and people like that. I need to say he's my husband. Because he was, you see, even at the end."

"But that makes no sense." He gapes at her, as if she is speaking in tongues.

He is so young, more boy than man. What does he know of marriage? "We were together such a long time. You don't throw away twenty-three years without giving it every chance."

His leg is jumping again. "He was coming *back* to you? That is so — I mean, he never said that. He never said a word."

His distress tears at her. Does he feel overlooked, betrayed? "Will, you can't take it personally. He was like that sometimes, secretive. There were things he would never talk about. Maybe he didn't tell you because … I don't know, maybe he saw it as temporary. When he left, he made it sound like it was for good. But maybe in the back of his mind he sensed that we'd eventually be together again and life would go back to normal. Maybe that's why he hid it from you." She almost convinces herself, enough that her fingers tingle. Could there be some truth to it? Is it possible that despite all the crippling things he said, Rafe never intended to leave for good? The thought of it nudges the corner of a monumental burden.

Will's leg continues to hammer. "I don't know. This is so fu— None of this makes any sense." Abruptly he stands. "I've gotta go. I'm not even sure why I came here. It's not my business. I should just leave it alone."

He is so agitated. Is she missing something? All she knows is that she desperately wants him to stay. "You don't have to go, Will. It's good to talk."

"No." He heads for the door. "There's some stuff I gotta do."

She follows him. On the front step, his hand on the doorknob, he turns. "Thank you for the tea." The lifelong habit of good manners — she sees it around him, visible as an overcoat.

"Not at all. Thank you for coming. For the talk."

"I'm sorry." He looks at her with eyes once more red. "I am so sorry, Sharon. About Rafe, about everything that happened. I don't think I ever said that."

"I know. I know you are."

His hand is still glued to the knob.

"Come again sometime. You're always welcome here, Will. That hasn't changed."

"Maybe. Maybe one day."

As he closes the door, Sharon is certain she will never see Will Werner again.

TWENTY-ONE

August

NATHALIE SWUNG HER MIATA into the TSB parking lot, the August evening a cool coda to the sweltering day. The engine teardown was behind her, as was the short flight from Victoria Harbour, and she was itching to examine the R22 wreckage to see if the raisined old mechanic was indeed some kind of oracle. As she shouldered her laptop case and chewed the last cardboard bite of vending machine sandwich, she rejoiced at the empty expanse of asphalt. Everyone had gone home. She had the building to herself.

She made straight for the back warehouse, the cavernous hangar-like space that housed the TSB's tools, forklift, and other gear, plus a motley collection of debris, some of it huge sections recognizable as once-airworthy craft, some heaps of unidentifiable scrap. She donned her overalls and zipped them to the neck to protect her blouse. She loved this part. After six years as an investigator, putting on mechanic's clothes and assembling her tools still signalled the countdown to real work, physical work, unlike her desk duties, which felt a short step away from slacking off. Real work involved dirt and tools and checklists.

Job one: check the helicopter's pulley system, which connected the engine to the main drive shaft, which in turn made the rotor spin. If the mechanic's theory was right and the belts on the pulley system had come loose — maybe because the clutch designed to hold them tight had given out — it would explain why the rotor had stopped in midflight. The pulley system would have been incapable of turning it.

It took all of one minute to discover that the pulley system would tell her nothing, because the belts were no longer attached to it. Evidently, sometime between when the helicopter slammed into the mountainside and when its remnants bumped to their final resting place, the belts parted ways with the pulleys. Whether those belts had, at the time of the accident, been tightly cinched in to the pulleys the way they were supposed to be, or were loosely attached in a way that meant trouble, it would be impossible to tell. Disappointed, she prodded the belts, which lay in a pile of components that had just weeks ago been sprinkled around the debris field like confetti.

Job two: re-examine the clutch. There too she came up empty. The clutch had fared even worse than the belts; it was smashed beyond recognition. There was no way for her to know what condition the clutch was in before the accident, or whether it had power running to it or not.

It was what she'd feared in Victoria in the last hours with the tight-lipped Robinson boys. The parts told her nothing.

That left job three: look at the fuse. It was the one detail in the mechanic's story that she found improbable.

Luckily, the fuse panel had broken into just four pieces during the crash, and most of the fuses were still in place. Reassembling the panel was a snap. So was comparing it with the R22 schematic in her files. Three times she checked, and three times she saw the same thing. There on the warehouse floor, for the first time in months — in a year, actually, ever since the Cessna 172 albatross had settled round her neck — Nathalie got a break. The fuse that powered the clutch was still attached to the panel, and just as the mechanic had speculated, it was the wrong type, a one-amp instead of the one-point-five specified by the manufacturer. And the one-amp fuse, as any chump could see, had blown.

I could kiss that man, she thought, setting the broken fuse panel on a workbench. He's a wizened-up old coot but I could kiss him anyway. His trail of breadcrumbs had led not to a dead end but to an honest-to-God destination. At last, something to appease Tucker.

Yet soon her exhilaration fizzled. Notable as the discovery might be, it wasn't enough. She'd proven only two things. One, the wrong fuse had been installed. Two, that fuse had blown, disabling the clutch so it could no longer adjust the belt tension. But the clutch, she knew, would not suddenly quit gripping the belts just because the fuse had blown. It would continue to hold firm for some time. Only if the helicopter flew long enough, and the natural in-flight movement gradually loosened the belts, would the clutch be called upon to adjust the tension tighter. Only then would trouble set in. With no tension from the clutch, the belts would continue to slacken to the point where they no longer drove the pulleys and, by extension, the rotor.

During a short, simple flight like the one James Stanhope took with his *Sports Illustrated* bride, there was no reason for the belts to loosen. Stanhope's quick point-A-to-point-B hop involved no trick manoeuvres, placed no unusual demands on the helicopter. The existing clutch tension should have held the belts snug enough to deliver the couple safely home to the gym or the dock or the bedroom, wherever their happily married itinerary was supposed to take them.

Merde, Scrapper. She had hit a wall.

Think, she told herself. But it was no good. It was nearly eight o'clock. Her thinker was done.

What do the beautiful people do after the honeymoon's over? she wondered idly as she collected her unused tools. Do they return to ordinary life, whatever that means to those accustomed to the extraordinary? Why even bother with a honeymoon? From the snippets she'd heard from friends who jetted off after their ceremonies, the experience wasn't necessarily a bliss fest. In fact, nothing about marriage lived up to the hype from what she could tell. Passion shrivelled. People got bored. They strayed. Given that almost no one stayed together, how could you gaze into the eyes of a person you supposedly loved and vow that that would be different? The institution of marriage revolved around deceit. Look at Jake, running around on his wife and kids, albeit with some kind of marital understanding in place, albeit running around with *her*, for which she was thankful. Look at Rafe.

She glanced across the warehouse at the hulking Tracker wreck and steeled herself for the next appearance of his mutilated body. Each time he rose before her, broken and burnt, she relived what she longed to forget. How sweet it was at first. How tender. He was a huge man, he towered over her tiny frame. Beside him she looked like a child. It was almost obscene. She said that once, laughing, and he glowered and gathered in on himself like a thunderstorm. He was so strong and so gentle and she fell for it. She wanted it. Wanted everything, the clichés, the fairy tales, the happily ever after, all the goddamn lies.

Marriage was the biggest lie and an unstable machine, and it didn't take a mechanic to diagnose the flaws. A marriage might run fine for a while, but the minute one bit stopped working, the whole contraption ground to a halt. Not like an aircraft with its built-in redundancy, where if one part fails there are layers of protection that kick in: a warning light illuminates, a manual system is activated, a clutch automatically tightens loose belts so the pilot can safely land and repair the broken parts.

Unless, of course, the Swiss cheese theory kicks in. Like that, the pieces fell into place.

The R22 engine, as she had told the mechanic in Victoria, had been overhauled a few months before the crash. During the overhaul all the belts were replaced. And new belts, counterintuitive as it seems, loosen up faster in flight than belts that have been in service awhile.

"That's it," she breathed. New belts could go slack even on a short, routine flight. If the clutch didn't automatically tension them back the way it was supposed to, they'd keep loosening to the point where they quit turning the rotor.

A seemingly unconnected chain of events, but the holes in the cheese lined up. It all made sense. Nathalie felt the rightness of it in her gut, the investigative barometer she trusted most.

There was just one catch: she had no proof. The sequence of events was logical, and it offered a persuasive explanation for what had happened. But for her report she needed more. She needed evidence that the belts had come loose while the helicopter was flying. A plausible sequence of events plus a strong gut feeling did not equal evidence. She was right back where she started. Because the belts ended up strewn around the accident site, it was impossible to tell whether they'd come free before the crash or because of it.

There had to be something else, some clue, some indication, somewhere in the wreckage. It had to be there. All she had to do was find it.

Not tonight. She wiped her hands on her overalls, arched her back, stiff after the long day, and glanced at her watch. Eight fifteen. Over twelve hours on duty, on top of precious little sleep at the hotel the night before. Her eyes burned, her neck popped, and the walk-in shower in her condo, with the rain head she'd splurged on at Home Depot, was calling her name.

And yet. She glanced at the mound of scrap across the warehouse that was the Tracker. It had been a marathon day but also a lucky day — two days, if she counted Jake's visit last night. Maybe the streak wasn't over.

No. It was late, and the Tracker was strictly off limits.

It was late, yet curiosity beat its fists inside her. She was still the sole party to Will's account of a possible problem with the trim on the firefighting tanker. Now, tonight, she had a rare chance to examine the wreck while no one was around to catch her.

She shouldn't. But since when did she do only what she should? Not since she was a kid.

Not even then, Scrapper.

She crossed the floor.

∧ ∨ ∧

THE TRACKER — GOD, how Rafe loved that old plane. He told her so several times, eyes shining, body practically vibrating with devotion. *Love* was his word for it. She had taken note. As she learned for herself in time, it was not a word he employed lightly.

She first laid eyes on the ancient tanker one cold, damp morning in April. Four scant months ago. Rafe had offered her a tour of the plane during a conversation they'd struck up at the Flying Boat pub a few days earlier. She'd heard of Rafe Mackie. Who in the tight world of BC aviation hadn't? His skill as a firefighting pilot was legendary. But she'd never met him until he introduced himself in the pub. Intrigued by the chance to see a singular aircraft on the verge of obsolescence, she accepted.

Like a proud papa, Rafe led her slowly around the plane, pointing out its blunt, sturdy build and its aging yet reliable features, kicking the tires with scuffed cowboy boots, visibly delighted to talk to someone who appreciated the technicalities of design and operation. He followed her up the ladder to the overhead hatch that provided entry into the cockpit, and watched closely as she clambered in and lowered herself into the pilot's seat. "It's like something out of *Star Trek*," she said, taking in the 1950s instrument panel. She ran a hand lightly over the worn knobs and throttle levers, the latter mounted, unusually, above the main console. "This is seriously retro."

"She's a classic, all right," Rafe said from above. "Gets the job done every time."

Nathalie fingered the drop selector, a large rotary control that could have been lifted from a Motown sound studio. "You sure you don't want to trade up to an aircraft from this millennium? A fresher, younger model?" The aviation world was small enough that she'd heard about his petition.

"Not a chance." He rapped the top of the fuselage. "My old girl's as solid as they come and I know her inside out. Why would I give her up for some newfangled thing I'd have to learn to fly from scratch?"

"Because the new one might ... handle differently." Her heart pounded as she fell into the conversation's double meaning. "It might do things you wouldn't even know about until you tried."

"Well, you could have a point there." Rafe leaned in closer through the hatch. "Always tempting, the unknown."

It was mildly surprising that Rafe Mackie was flirting with her. He was by all accounts a family man, long and contentedly married. And it was mildly surprising that she was going along with it. This kind of banter revved her up, made her feel alive and desirable, and she took part in it freely with a few guys at the gym and in her condo building. But never anyone she worked with. Never anyone, she had promised herself, within her industry.

Yet the forcefield of desire around Rafe knocked her off balance. Eyes ahead, grateful for the distance and fuselage between them, she studied the altimeter with needless concentration. A silence grew, empty of sound but curiously full.

"Okay," she said at last, unable to sit under his gaze any longer. "I'm coming out." She boosted herself out of the seat and reached for the hatch frame. Rafe held out his hand and she grabbed it, practicality outweighing common sense for not the first time in her life. When their hands touched, the jolt astonished her.

"Not just tempting, the unknown. Dangerous too," Rafe said, waiting longer than necessary before letting go her hand.

"Oh?" She stepped down off the ladder and tugged at the bottom of her short zippered jacket, which had ridden up.

Rafe grinned. "You get a new plane and there's a learning curve. You don't know what you can and can't control. You're kind of at its mercy for the first little while." He shook his head. "Ach, listen to me. I'm an old fella now. Too old for new blood."

His eyes lingered on her, and her face pinked. This had to stop. Her whole career she'd resisted the many temptations aviation had to offer, and she wasn't letting up now. She needed the men she worked around to respect her, not want her.

"Show me the drop tanks," she said.

"Yes, ma'am." He snapped her a mock salute.

As they bent down to examine the plane's underbelly, and Rafe described how the tank doors were controlled and the retardant drops regulated, each tiny muscle in Nathalie's face, every fine hair on her arm, was attuned to the distance between herself and the big, handsome pilot. It was a distance she meticulously maintained, and the effort cost her. Barely a word of the conversation from that point on could she remember later.

When the tour was over Rafe walked her to the parking lot. "Nice car." He nodded at the gleaming blue Miata. He held the door as she got in, then leaned down, the scent of his leather bomber jacket everywhere. "You ever want a second look at anything, you just let me know." He handed her a business card.

Nathalie drove away fast, her palms sticky on the steering wheel. Rumour had it Rafe Mackie was a happily married man. It wasn't so much the married part that put her off; it was the happily. He had made her an offer back there, loud and clear. An offer of what, she wasn't entirely sure.

∧ ∨ ∧

RAFE WOULD BE DEVASTATED to see his beloved Tracker now. The front fuselage, including the pilot's side of the cockpit, the exact place she had sat the morning it all began, was a scarred, soot-smeared lump. It cowered in the corner as if ashamed of its ruin, one wing still attached, the engine and prop misshapen but still recognizable. The other wing was laid out on the floor in three pieces, the engine detached and beside it, the propeller in bits. The plane's rear section bore deep scrapes and dents, though the tail itself looked little altered. That's hopeful, Nathalie thought as she approached.

From what Will had said, there was a better-than-good chance that while Rafe was positioning himself for the drop, the Tracker's elevator trim had run away—had stuck in the down position and driven the plane into the trees. If that were true, the trim tabs at the rear of the aircraft might be set in the telltale nose-down position.

It was not the case. Not only were the trim tabs not nose down, they were loose and untethered, connected to nothing. She peered inside the tail through a wide gash that had clawed open the rear fuselage and shone her small flashlight on the electric motor, bellcrank, and rods that operated the trim tabs. The entire assembly hung loose like a smashed piñata. The rods were detached, and the jackscrew that connected everything to the motor had sheared in two.

That was that. With the trim assembly this badly damaged and the trim tabs loose, there was no way to determine what position the tabs had been in at the time of the accident. It made sense, she supposed. Had the tabs been nose down, Lyndon and Roy would have noticed early on and investigated the trim system from the get-go.

"Shit." She lightly rapped the fuselage with her knuckles. "Now what?"

"What are you muttering about?" The voice boomed all the way from the warehouse door. Not just any voice — Tucker's voice.

Fucking hell, she thought. What are you doing here?

"What are you doing here?" he called, flaunting his uncanny ability to tap her deepest thoughts. He crossed the warehouse in what seemed like five efficient strides and was at her side, impossibly, in seconds. Briefly, Nathalie considered the existence of superhuman life.

"Just back from Victoria." She kept her voice light. "The R22 teardown."

"I mean what are you doing *here*." He gestured at the Tracker wreck. "This look like a helicopter to you?"

"Ha ha." As always, Tucker's glare worked like a stun gun, freezing her brain and zapping her verbal abilities. She felt like a six-year-old caught in mama's underwear drawer.

"Well?"

"Well what? There was something I had to check on the R22 and then I just ... I just wandered over here. Speaking of the R22 —"

"Let us not speak of that," Tucker interrupted. "Let us speak of the Tracker, an accident you are not investigating, a wreck you have nothing to do with. Let us speak of why you are poking around over here when you should be all the way over there." He pointed at the far-off R22.

"I'm not poking around. I was walking around thinking about the helicopter and I just ended up here."

A tiny stream of air issued from Tucker's nostrils. "Nathalie, do not shit me, okay? You are on dangerous ground. You cannot, I repeat, cannot be involved with the Tracker."

"I know that. I told you, I'm not." She couldn't stand her own wheedling. "So here's where I'm at with the R22." She filled him in on the mechanic's tip and the blown clutch fuse she had just discovered. "It's promising. Not conclusive, but a lot more than I had two days ago."

"So what you're missing is proof that one, the belts actually loosened, and two, this hypothetical loosening was significant enough to make the rotor blade stop. What you are missing is, oh, let me see" – he looked skyward – "basically everything."

"Give me a break! Sure, there's some details to nail down, I just said so, but come on." She ticked off the points on her fingers. "We know beyond a doubt that the clutch fuse blew, which means for sure the clutch failed. We know the belts were new, so they were more prone to loosening than if they were older. We know that if they loosened during flight – and in this case, after an hour in the air, there's a good chance they did – there was nothing to tension them up. We know from the way the helicopter dropped out of the sky that the rotor wasn't turning. We know there's no engine problem behind it. The engine was producing power at the time of the crash, we confirmed that in Victoria. It all adds up."

A smirk barely lifted the corners of Tucker's mouth.

Nathalie fought to control her rising anger. "What, I'm supposed to think it's just a coincidence?"

"Be that as it may, you need *proof*." On the last word he smacked his palms together, and the sound echoed through the wreckage. "You know, proof, evidence, investigation one-oh-one. Talk to me again when you've got some."

With that, all of Nathalie's thought-out ideas and hours of work were discarded, yet more garbage for the wreckage heaps.

Tucker draped an arm over her shoulder and steered her away from the tanker. "Let's close up in here. You get out of those overalls and wash up, I'll get the USB stick I came in for, and we'll leave together, okay?"

No, not okay, although she had to admit, despite her annoyance with her boss, that she was exhausted after her long day and ready to go home, especially now that her optimism about both investigations had deflated.

"No arguments now," Tucker said. "You're exhausted. You've had a long day."

Mind-reading android freak, she fumed. But she let herself be propelled out of the warehouse. The thing about a downed aircraft is that it will be waiting for you, its devastation intact, the next day, and the day after, and the day after that.

TWENTY-TWO

October–November

FOR THE FIRST TIME IN MONTHS, Sharon is thinking of someone other than herself or Rafe. In the two weeks after Will's visit, whenever she enters the living room she pictures him in Rafe's chair — his hollow eyes, his unwashed clothes, his head unkempt and bowed low. When she boils the kettle, she recalls his desperate gulps of tea. When she comes home to voicemail, she wonders if it will be him, asking to meet again. She knows it will not be, and it never is.

She is beset by restlessness.

One gusty November afternoon when the wind fairly pushes her back inside the townhouse, the waiting message is from Rachel. She sounds as flustered as the weather.

"Oh, it's the … Oh, hi! Sharon. It's me. We're due for coffee soon, or lunch. Maybe next week? No, wait. I mean tomorrow. Just a sec." A complicated rustling ensues. "Yeah, tomorrow. The Starbucks on Georgia near Burrard, around three thirty. Can you make it? Call me."

The last time she saw Rachel was for lunch at the Left Coast Café in October, and their phone conversations since then have been brief. Between the Hong Kong investors Rachel has been squiring around and her own inwardness, they've gone longer than usual without a meet-up. She should be glad for the invitation, she tells herself. Late-afternoon coffee is hardly a major commitment. She can still be home by six or so.

Home for what?

No answer presents itself. Yet already she is counting down the time from when she will meet Rachel until she can sink back into the quiet invisibility of home.

She goes to the fridge and pours half a glass of white wine, then fills it to the top. She should eat something so the wine doesn't slam her. She surveys the fridge, pulls out a block of cheese, puts it back. Maybe later.

She carries the wine to the living room and takes her usual seat on the sofa, across from Rafe's chair. The chair where Will sat. Naturally she will tell Rachel about the strange encounter with Rafe's partner. She has omitted it from their quick calls, feeling the story deserves to be told in detail.

She sips her wine. It will be good for her to go downtown, get a shot of her friend's energy. Good to venture away from her usual haunts.

She adjusts the sofa cushions behind her back. The sofa is too firm. They bought it for the bed folded inside, not for comfort, and the cushions only help so much. Rafe's chair across from her is soft and wide, purchased to fit his large body. Why does she never take that seat? Will didn't hesitate to choose it.

Already the wine is making her sluggish. She should have sliced some cheese. She considers getting up to do it but doesn't.

She should return Rachel's call. An appointment will be restorative, will give her a goal. Get up and do it for God's sake, she tells herself.

Instead she drinks more wine. What is with her? She is so aimless and scattered. Her thoughts drift like fog, skimming the surface of life, never quite touching it. Does she even know what she wants?

For it not to have happened. Any of it.

Stop it, she tells herself.

For there to be a baby.

No. Stop thinking back. Think forward. That's what Colleen always says.

She wants to see Rachel, of course she does. She wants to talk.

Will talked to her. Two weeks ago he sat right there, in that big chair, and said things that mattered even though it hurt. Will loved

Rafe. *Love* doesn't seem too strong a word for it. He hung his head, he nearly cried.

She wants to see Rachel, but what she really wants is to see Will. Remembering Rafe with someone else who loved him feels like an indulgence, and the prospect of repeating it brings her pain and sharp pleasure, like an aching molar she has to bite down on.

She swallows the last of the wine. Decides to call him.

Then thinks: no. He was upset when he left here. He found it difficult to talk about Rafe. She is being selfish again.

She calls him.

Will answers immediately, the connection made just like that.

"It's Sharon." What should she say? She should have rehearsed. "I've been thinking about our talk. I'd like to do it again. If you're up for it."

A beat, then another. "I guess so."

He is so hesitant. "When?"

"Um ... whenever."

God, this was a bad idea. "I'm meeting a friend downtown tomorrow afternoon. I could drop by your place afterwards, say around —"

"No. Uh, I'm meeting a friend tomorrow too. We're going out for the evening. But the day after, I guess that'd be okay."

No question, she has made a mistake. But she can't backtrack now. "Late afternoon, like last time?"

"Okay. But look, it's better if you don't come here. It's ..."

She gets it. He doesn't want her in his space. "My place is fine. We can have tea again."

"Yeah, great. Tea."

"See you then," she says, and hangs up before she can mortify herself further.

∧ ∨ ∧

"SO LET ME GET THIS STRAIGHT. *He* comes looking for sympathy from *you*?" Rachel's brows arch up to her hairline. She does incredulous the way a mime would: huge and extravagant.

"Rachel, Rachel." Sharon invokes the old movie title that is a long-standing joke between them. "He wasn't looking for sympathy. It was more like ... an unburdening. He was so sad — miserable really. He needed to talk about Rafe and I could listen. I could help. It made me feel useful for once."

Rachel crosses her long legs, today clad in black tights set off by orange ballet flats. "Bullshit." She flips the end of her scarf, also orange, over one shoulder.

Sharon has tried to convey the significance of Will's visit, but her patience is wearing thin. "You know what? Just forget it. It's fine. There's no reason you should understand."

"Oh, I understand." Rachel hates nothing more than being accused of a failure to understand. In every personality test she has taken she has scored high in empathy; she prizes her ability to understand all people in all situations. "I understand that this guy's at the centre of his own drama and he wants someone there to watch."

Even for Rachel, such callousness is astonishing. Sharon stares at her so long that her friend must realize she has gone too far. She pushes back her chair. "I need another latte. Want one?"

Sharon shakes her head. As Rachel weaves purposefully through the disordered tables and chairs, half the patrons, including most of the men, eye the tall brunette, no doubt wondering who she is and what she is famous for. She is a goddess. Also, Sharon knows deep down, a true friend. Sharon owes her the chance to understand.

"I want to tell you something," she says once Rachel has returned, the leaf pattern on her latte still perfect. "About Rafe and me."

"Okay." Rachel shakes two sugar packets into her cup, licks a finger, stirs.

"At the end, when he died, we weren't living together. We had separated."

Rachel's goddess face crumples. "Oh, Sharon." She reaches across the table and grabs her friend's hand. "God, that is so ... I had no idea."

"I didn't tell anyone. Except Colleen." Sharon's sister knew the fact of it, that Rafe had moved out, but none of the circumstances.

For once Rachel has nothing to say.

"It happened a while before the crash. A couple of months." Sharon looks away as she says this. A couple of months is an eternity of silence in Rachel time.

"A couple of *months?*" Rachel withdraws her hand and cups her latte. "God, Sharon. How could you not tell me?"

"I ... It seemed better to keep it to myself. I thought – I guess I hoped it wouldn't stick."

"But you could've told me after. It's been so long now since he – since the accident," she finishes gently.

Sharon's eyes fill. Rachel is right, she should have come clean ages ago. Even knowing this, she cannot reveal the rest. Not here, in a Starbucks. She cannot tell Rachel about the day in the park, cannot admit the rush of hope it brought her, or how that hope had shattered along with Rafe's plane.

Get a grip, she thinks. She forces herself to hear the clatter and conversation, to wonder whether the pink-haired girl hunched over an iPad next to them, immense frozen coffee at her elbow, is mesmerized by her studies or YouTube. She wills herself to skim over the river of hurt inside her, which springs from more sources than she can divine.

The opening notes of Pachelbel's Canon escape Rachel's handbag. For the first time Sharon can remember, her friend ignores the phone.

"He loved you. You know that, right?"

Sharon nods, not trusting herself to speak.

"Whatever happened between you, that man adored you. He would move the earth for you. Anyone could see it." Rachel picks up her ceramic mug, then sets it carefully back down. "I always wished someone would love me that way."

It is an unlikely confession from one who samples men as if they were hors d'oeuvres, yet Sharon has guessed it all along. Her friend's cool exterior masks a deep capacity for emotion.

"It's complicated." Sharon casts for the right words. "Being loved like that, it's a powerful thing. But it's not always easy. It comes with ... expectations."

"How do you mean?" Rachel's handbag rings again, and again she ignores it.

"I mean if you are loved that much, you have to live up to it. Be worthy of it. All the time."

Rachel looks puzzled, but Sharon cannot articulate it any better.

"Are you saying you didn't feel worthy?"

"I'm not sure what I'm saying."

"Well." Rachel sips from the thick white cup. "Maybe the question is, did you love *him?*"

This is an essay question when Sharon is barely prepared for multiple choice. "Someday we can talk more about this," she says carefully. "Not today."

"I get it. Whenever you're ready." Rachel pauses. "You know, you don't have to keep everything inside all the time. It's okay to let stuff go. You don't have to hold on to it all."

∧ ∨ ∧

SHARON HAS TO HOLD ON to what happened that hot July day. It is a memory she cannot probe deeply, a wound that refuses to scab, but it is all hers.

When Rafe appeared on their doorstep that day he rang the bell, a visitor to his own home after two months of living elsewhere – where, she never knew. A college student offering lawn care was what she expected, or a pair of Walmart-wardrobed proselytisers. Instead her husband's bulk filled the doorway, his face as familiar as her own yet so unexpected that she flinched.

"I'm sorry. I should have called," he said.

She took in his altered appearance: hair shorter, buzzed close to the scalp; jaw stubbled with grey; shirt loose around his barrel chest; purple pouches beneath weary brown eyes. The time away had not been kind to him. She felt an ugly stab of satisfaction.

He shoved his hands in his pockets, uneasy as ever with close scrutiny. "I got the day off. Can we talk?"

You had your chance to talk, she wanted to say. Remember me pleading with you to talk? Asking you over and over why you were giving up on us? What she said was "Not here." Damned if she would let him back inside the home he had abandoned.

"In the park, then."

She hesitated. Every rational brain cell resisted, while every ungovernable hope pulled her to him.

"Come on. You can walk away anytime."

Why should she? It's over, he had said the day he disappeared with his duffel bag, and she'd had two long months to absorb the finality of his pronouncement. Twenty-three years she had stuck by Rafe Mackie, twenty-three years of long absences, sporadic moods, forced relocation, abandoned dreams. Nearly a quarter century of loyalty, snapped.

"If you come," he said gently, "bring your hat. It's a scorcher."

That was Rafe, looking after her in spite of everything, and it made her cave. She walked with him to the park down the street, to the talk that bridged their divide, to the promise that buoyed her heart only to smash it cruelly later, and as she walked she unconsciously fell into step with him, skin shielded by a broad straw brim.

TWENTY-THREE

Sixteen weeks after

ALMOST NOON AND I CAN'T DRAG my sorry ass out of bed. Even with the covers up to my chin, it's cold as a supermodel's stare in here because the cheapskate landlord won't turn the heat on until mid-November. My head's drumming like John Bonham, like it doesn't know I tossed back three Aspirin and three glasses of water before collapsing last night. My guaranteed stop-the-hangover technique, but this morning it's only affected my bladder. At least it woke me up. If I didn't need the bathroom, who knows what time I'd have come to. Maybe too late to make it to Sharon's.

Sharon. Jesus. If I had one ounce of self-respect I'd cancel rather than drag the shit heap that is me into her nice tidy house. Last night, for the first time since flying season ended, and with it my duty to live clean, Andy and I went on a tear. A lot of the specifics, the exact wheres and whos of it all, are blurry now, but some parts stand out sharp as glass. I am a waste of skin: that's the part I remember best.

We started around eleven at Shay's, a noisy martini bar behind an unmarked door on Seymour. There, we instantly radared in on three beauties arranged around a back table. I have no trouble remembering those whos. All three of them in their twenties, flawless, decked out in what Andy calls the classic low-high: low-cut dresses, sky-high heels. "A bowl of exotic fruits, my friend," he shouted in my ear. "I'd dirty the pink of any one of them."

We weaved our way to the back and leaned around a long time waiting for seats to empty near the trio. We'd almost given up when at twelve thirty the two earnest guys who'd been locked in discussion for over an hour, oblivious to the display at the table next to them (who goes to Shay's to have a conversation?), finally made a move to leave. I swear, Andy slipped into the one chair before the former occupant had time to recrease his khakis. The two altar boys hurled some righteous indignation his way and then hightailed it, to the relief of all concerned, including, it appeared, the ladies. With the table beside them purged of dweebs and five-syllable words, they shifted sideways, crossed their legs in unison, and checked us out.

Okay. In the interest of full disclosure, they checked out Andy. Here's a guy who like me hasn't seen the early side of thirty for years, but unlike me has divided his time between an investment bank that pays him astronomical sums, the best clothing stores in town, and the top nightclubs, where he has perfected the art of allure. As he said before we sat down, he knew in his bones, and in one bone in particular, that we'd be leaving with these three. He picks up girls effortlessly, even younger girls, ones with no twenty in their age, and when he parts ways with them after a night or a week, always amicably, they're too spoiled by his mature charm to ever fish again in the cesspool of youth.

I, to be clear, was not the target of the checking out. I've spent too long stewing in my juices, as Andy put it when he dropped by my place early for a few warm-up brews, fanning one hand under his nose to underscore the point. "Christ almighty, Will, you've gone all Downtown Eastside on me. So you're some kind of street person now? Dumpster diving for fun and profit?"

True, it was midsummer the last time I sat in a barber's chair, and what started as rugged stubble had bushed out into ragged-ass beard. And true, I haven't been all Martha Stewart in the laundry department. But I didn't think it was that bad.

Andy begged to differ. "No fucking way will I be seen with some rubbie-dub just got kicked out of the gospel mission. Either you clean up or I'm outta here."

Cleaning up, it soon emerged, did not entail a simple shower and change of clothes. This was Andy, after all; I had GQ standards to meet. Before my next swallow of Rickard's Red, he was on his phone. "Cam? It's me, Andy. Yeah, I'm great, man, it's all good. Listen, I got an emergency. Buddy of mine needs a cut and needs it now, before we can, you know, venture out in public." He stood tall, designer-denimed legs slightly apart, bench-pressed chest thrust out, a life-sized advertisement for himself. "Well of course you're not at the salon, that's why I'm calling your cell. I know it's, like, irregular, but could we meet you there in half an hour? There's something in it for you beyond just a big tip. Know what I'm sayin'?"

Apparently Cam knew, because the transaction concluded then and there. For the stated cost of sixty bucks plus twenty-dollar tip, which came out of my pocket, and the unstated cost of who knows how many pastel E pills, which came out of Andy's, I ended up at the only lighted hair station in a south Granville salon while Cam, a Type-A whippet with ferocious darting scissors, went into extreme makeover mode. An hour later I was done: short hair with some kind of flip at the front, like a reddish-brown whitecap, held in place with what Cam vaguely called "product"; face and neck stubble-free and smelling faintly of citrus; and neatly pressed shirt and artificially distressed jeans, both on loan from Andy, which hung off me like bedsheets but were fashionable, or so I was told.

Cam told me to stand up, whipped off the plastic cape, and eyed me top to bottom. "All good. Oh, except for the, um ..." Finding no adequate words, he flapped his hands at my feet.

My low-rise hikers, I grant you, have seen better days. Andy peered at them and, no exaggeration, winced. "Fuck me, Will. You think we've got a night of boggy trails ahead? Why the fuck are you wearing those shit-kickers?"

We quickly established that, one, I owned no other footwear except for an assortment of equally broken-in running shoes and one ancient pair of funeral-and-wedding wingtips; two, my size twelve feet could not cram into anything either of these two owned; and three, my certainty that no one would notice was a miscalculation of hysterics-inducing proportions. Cam and Andy fell silent.

"I don't know anyone in footwear," Cam said eventually. "There's a couple great shops down the block, but they're closed. I'm not sure breaking in is the way to go." I peered at him, then Andy. Was it possible Cam wasn't joking? "Women's shoes would be so much easier," he continued. "There's a few large drag queens owe me a favour."

"Okay, okay, hold it there," I broke in. "You did your best. This is as good as it's gonna get. I mean God, Andy, you've been out with me before when I'm wearing these shoes and it wasn't an issue."

"You have *never* worn those shoes when we've gone out." Andy glanced nervously in Cam's direction.

"Duh, I have. What other shoes would I wear?"

"I have no idea, bro, but it was not those. They are like the negativest footwear I've witnessed in my life to this point."

"They just stand out because I'm wearing these stupid things." The lower legs of Andy's skinny jeans were the only snug feature in the entire ensemble.

"Those are awesome jeans! They cost me over two hundred bucks and you better not —"

"Guys," Cam interjected. "Enough already. We have to accept that we are done here. The shoes will have to stay." He shrugged at Andy. "Maybe someone'll feel sorry for him. There's worse things than a pity fuck."

Long digression. The point is, by the time we sat down near the trio in the bar, I knew enough to plant my feet under the table so as not to ruin the spell Andy cast. It must've worked because after an hour or so of rapid drinking and heavy flirting, the girls invited us to a party in Kitsilano, at the house two of them shared with some guy.

By the time we spilled out of our taxis, the party house — the only one on that block of east Kits to have missed its half-a-million renovation — was shaking. Luckily it was cold enough that the windows were closed; otherwise the cops would've shut down the festivities by now. As it was, we opened the door to a blast of music and frat-boy yells that

I swear knocked me back a foot. When I stepped forward it was into a blowout the likes of which I haven't seen since high school.

People don't always know it, but pilots tend to be a sober bunch. We have to be. Our careers and our lives, and the lives of others, depend on it. Sure there's the odd alcoholic or speed freak in our midst, but by and large the aviators I know are light to moderate drinkers and they just say no to drugs. I'm the odd one out on that last score. If you're a Vancouver native you're born to it; you're basically at play in the land of weed. My parents were semi-regular partakers and could have laced my baby formula for all I know. Whatever the reason, the occasional strategically timed toke has been part of my life for as long as I can remember, *occasional* and *strategically timed* being the operative terms. Never when I'm flying, about to fly, or likely to fly, and never, ever during fire season. The exception being last summer's unplanned vacation from the sky.

This party was way beyond. Andy and I showed up most of the way drunk, and our new lady friends were even further along, but the lot of us were as straight as Mormon elders compared to the tripping, gyrating mass inside that house. The place was awash in pot and ecstasy and coke — at least, those were the substances offered to me within minutes of my arrival — and the air was thick with sex. Dozens of people were dancing — grinding, more like it — to a heavy bass mix of hip-hop and rap. More than one woman had experienced some degree of wardrobe malfunction, to use the old Super Bowl euphemism, but not one person seemed troubled by the sight of bare, jiggling breasts. In the corner of the living room a red leather armchair held two squirming women, one a pale pierced goth, the other a ripely rounded South Asian beauty with her arm up the goth's black skirt. A cluster of beer-swilling guys cheered and urged them to please, please take it off.

"Isn't that Speedman Steve?" Andy pointed at a pair of dancers. Sure enough I recognized the goateed deejay from bus ads for the Wolf, Vancouver's Home of Indie Rock. He was weaving beside a short-haired blonde who'd removed her sparkly top and was swinging it from her index finger, a narrow swatch of silver catching the light while she swayed, eyes shut. Speedman's eyes, in contrast, were wide open, fixed on the spectacular set of hard nipples in front of him.

"Willie baby, I admit it," Andy slurred, taking in the crowd, "I am one hundred percent pussified. In complete thrall to the pussy." Then he was off, in a slow slalom toward the armchair show, a snake lured by irresistible notes.

In my ear came a tickle of warm breath. It was Caitlin, the petite raven-haired member of the bar trio. "My girlfriends are so lucky to have this place, right? The parties are amazing." I smiled and grazed her bare elbow. She smiled back. Her teeth were brilliant, her eyes long-lashed and smoky. "So how come I haven't met you before?" she said. "You go to Shay's much?"

"Nope. I'm out of town a lot."

"How come?"

"Flying. I have to go where the forest fires are."

"Oh yeah, I forgot you're a firefighter." She looked around the room. "That's amazing."

It occurred to me as I watched her, so pretty and small and nicely decorated, that I was getting too old for the back-and-forth ritual of the hook-up.

She swung her attention back to me, offered a pink gloss smile. "So, Will. You like to party when you're not flying airplanes?"

Time to get on with it. "I do if you're around." I trailed two fingers up the bare skin of her arm.

She moved closer, butted her head against my neck like a lamb, ran her hand down my hip bone. "I got ways to make you fly, pilot boy. It'd be amazing."

The boldness of her and the shiny smoothness of her hair and skin finally kicked me into gear, and my heart thudded along with the bass-thumping speakers. She caught my fingers and pulled them to her warm mouth, giving the tips a tiny lick.

"I know where we can go." Gripping my fingers in her small but surprisingly strong hand, she guided me through the throng to a bedroom at the end of the hall.

I WAS DRUNK, IT'S TRUE, but not all the way to wasted, so it's no excuse for what happened.

Caitlin was stunning, sexy, and beyond proficient. She unstrapped her heels and peeled off her dress and push-up bra in a confident striptease. Is it something she practises? I wondered. I lay on the bed and tried to focus. If there were panties on that girl when the evening started, they'd gone missing, because the only thing between her legs was a dark, narrow runway of bush. Could she have lost them, like actually misplaced them? I watched her, my mind spinning wildly. Say she'd absent-mindedly left her panties in the bathroom at Shay's, would someone turn them in to lost and found? How long would the bar hang on to them? Would someone who'd lost underwear just call and say, hey, I might've left my thong in one of your stalls? Naked, she straddled me, unbuttoned my shirt and the fly of my jeans. No – Andy's shirt, Andy's jeans, that's why they're so loose, that's why there's a stupid button fly. I would never get a button fly. Plain old zipper, that's good enough for me. She planted kisses on each patch of skin as she bared it. She pulled my jeans down – no, Andy's jeans, two hundred bucks, who pays that much for *jeans*? – and kissed my thighs. Her breasts skimmed my knees and I felt a faint stirring. It was like the starter on my old Acura, a kind of half-hearted whir, but like that old starter motor, nothing engaged. I shut my eyes and concentrated on her skin, the touch of her lips and tongue on my legs, her nipples hard wherever they brushed me. I felt it all, but it felt like nothing. It was like being on a doctor's table or in Cam's salon chair. The circuit between body and brain was working, but the one connecting body to cock was busted.

Eventually I had to sit up and ask her to stop. She said not to worry, we were only getting started, there was lots of time. I cupped her shoulders and looked into her beautifully made-up eyes. "You're sweet, Caitlin. But it's not happening. Let's leave it." I pulled up my jeans – *Andy's* jeans – buttoned myself back up, and for the first time in my life turned away from a woman who wanted me.

I looked for Andy on the way out, and after pushing through the crush of dancers found him in the red leather armchair, where he'd somehow replaced the goth girl and was massaging the plump breasts of the South Asian woman through her tank top. He didn't look up when I said I was going, just muttered "Okay, man, whatever" and continued to fondle.

Outside the cold hit me, sharp fingers of sobriety jabbing through my clothes and into my brain. I didn't have a jacket — there was a limit to what Andy was willing to lend — so I jogged to keep warm, heading for the glimmer of Burrard Street where I could hail a cab. As I trotted past the multi-million-dollar houses, their driveway and porch lights the only signs of life in the early morning, my mind raced too — not, as you'd think, replaying the embarrassment of my first-ever failure to get it up, which faded the minute I hit the street, but instead tracking the same well-worn groove as always: Rafe.

He is never not there. Four months later, no matter what's going on around me, my thoughts circle the same old questions. Why'd you do it, Rafe? Why this, and why me? And my long-time favourite: Why didn't I ask you what was wrong?

It's been this way since summer, since the crash. Since the letter.

Rafe used to get on my case about all the women I hooked up with, said I was wasting my time and theirs with casual flings. He needled me about it that morning when I admitted to having company back at the motel — Gracie, who I haven't been in touch with since I left her in bed that morning, who I can't bear to lay eyes on again because of all she'll remind me of. When he first started giving me grief, I figured it was the envy of the married. You'd resent anyone who's getting taste tests if your jaw's wired shut. But as I got to know Rafe I realized that wasn't it at all. He truly believed in marriage, in committing yourself to a person you'd love and protect and lay down your life for if you had to. He was like my dad that way, an old-fashioned, true-blue romantic. The way he talked about Sharon, she was like a treasure he'd been entrusted with. He didn't just love her, he cherished her.

That's what I thought about as I jogged along the overpriced street, fighting for breath after weeks of avoiding the gym. It's what I've been obsessing about since summer, returning to each fact, asking the same questions over and over. No matter how I pull it apart, Rafe's death is still a mystery. Not one bit of it makes sense.

He adored Sharon, no question. He lost his way for a while – scratch that, he fucked it up royally – but he loved her just the same. And Sharon loved him. After seeing her two weeks ago, the way she wore his loss on her face, I know that beyond a doubt.

That might be the only thing I know. All this time I've been assuming it was the breakup that drove him to it. So I go to Sharon looking for confirmation, figuring it'll settle my mind, I can get some sleep again, get my life back. And then she tells me – pow! out of nowhere – that they made up before he died. He was moving back in with her, meaning he was happy, meaning … Now I'm back to square one, and it's more fucked up than ever.

I tried to make a good life, the letter said. *I spent decades trying to make it right. But no matter how careful you are, things can run away on you. I learned that long ago, how fast you can lose control. It's like flying. One minute you're level, the next you're going down.* He was never one for symbolism, Rafe. He wasn't a big reader like me or my dad. Except in that letter. There he's like some goddamned poet, his words working on two levels.

I've flown in terrifying conditions. Massive, voracious fires you'd never believe unless you saw them for yourself. An ocean of fire below my plane, waves and waves rolling over everything in their path. Animals fleeing in herds, entire forests vaporized, flames jumping over fireguards, leaping highways sometimes. It can scare you so bad that afterwards you shake, thinking how close you came, this time, to the end.

Well, those fires are a fucking cakewalk compared to this, because keeping that man's words to myself, knowing the truth of what happened and trying to live with my part in it, is the worst job I've ever had. I only have to look in the mirror to see how it's eating away at me. Guilt will do that. So will a secret, especially when it comes from the grave.

I talk to him sometimes, crazy as it sounds, on the lowest nights when my mind won't power down and I'm sure I'm going to lose it once and for all. I pull out the creased page and read, even though I know the words by heart, and it's like he's there again, only instead of being solid as a tree trunk the way he was when he was alive, he's all around me in a million tiny pieces I can't put back together. Rafe, I say to him, what the fuck? You loved Sharon and you were going back to her. So you hit a few bumps – so what? Your life was turning around. You had no reason to go. Why didn't you tell me what was happening with you? And why didn't I ask? Why this, why me?

TWENTY-FOUR

August

THE DAY AFTER THE R22 TEARDOWN in Victoria was a write-off, the way only a day in a government office can be. The morning, which Nathalie greeted half an hour late, bleary from the long day before, was blocked off for an orientation to OLMS, the new system for logging employees' vacation and sick leave. More than two hours into the session the heavily lipsticked, extravagantly highlighted facilitator, as she called herself, a buoyant but increasingly incoherent presenter, was waxing ecstatic about windows and tabs and fields as the investigators attempted to duplicate her disjointed instructions on their laptops, and Nathalie wondered who, in the wise hierarchy that was the federal government, had decided her time was best spent learning the intricacies of new software so that in future she could track administrative details that would be simultaneously tracked in Ottawa by an administrative clerk, someone who actually specialized in administration. By twelve ten her stomach was rumbling, her brain hurt, and she'd reached her limit.

"Excuse me," she said. "What are we doing here?"

The instructor had the pink megawatt smile of a former cheerleader. "We're updating the compensatory leave field. All you have to do is toggle the view pane."

"No, I mean what are we *doing* here?" Nathalie swept her hand to indicate the conference table, where her co-workers jabbed one-fingered at keyboards and peered hopefully at screens. Lyndon leaned back in his chair and smirked. He knew what was coming. "What are we learning all this computer stuff for?" she said. "We've got work to do, real work. You know, making aviation safer. This," she motioned at her laptop, "this is head-office secretarial work."

The woman smiled indulgently and shook her head, a schoolmarm gently correcting a toddler. "No, no, no. Not secretarial work. It's part of the job for all of us. Every employee at head office and in the regions has to track their own leave from now on. It will make everything easier, you'll really see that when we get to part two —"

"It'll make things easier for somebody," Nathalie said, "but not for us. We're investigators. We're hired to investigate." Roy caught her eye and gave his head a warning shake, which she pretended not to see. "We're not programmers or admin staff or, what d'you call them, HR people. With all due respect — not your fault — this is bullshit. It's a total waste of our time."

The instructor, smile destabilized, scanned the room for a knight to ride to her rescue. However, Tucker, instigator of the session and her most likely ally, had been excused from training by virtue of being a manager and had left the building the instant the boardroom door shut.

Roy glanced at his watch. "We've gone ten minutes over the end time. Our Nathalie gets a little testy when she hasn't had her lunch. Maybe we should call it a day and pick this up in part two next week." He frowned at Nathalie. "Okay by you?"

"Sure thing, *boss*," she tossed back.

The instructor made a moue but dismissed the group. As Nathalie piled up her handouts, Lyndon approached. "I am off to the ever-popular Bread Heaven. Would the testy lady care to accompany me? There's time before the videoconference at one thirty."

"Why not." Nathalie slammed her laptop shut. "It's not like I'm getting any work done today anyhow."

"Oh good, my favourite. A cheerful companion with whom to lunch."

"Fuck off. You want cheerful, take Sandra Dee over there." The instructor, at the front of the room, was packing up her giant fuchsia shoulder bag.

"At ease, mam'selle. The world will look better from the other side of a turkey panini."

∧ ∨ ∧

NATURALLY THE CAFÉ WAS SOLD OUT of turkey paninis, so Nathalie settled for grilled eggplant on focaccia. All the tables were occupied in the bustling dining area, so they sat outside, on a bench by the sidewalk.

"I *hate* eating when there's no table." Nathalie set her Diet Coke on the ground and peeled the wax paper from her sandwich. A roasted red pepper chunk dropped onto her lap. "Fuck!" She threw the offending bit onto the street, where a Lycra-wrapped cyclist promptly rode over it.

"What is up with you? You've been in a foul mood all day. Has the dreaded PMS made a visitation?"

"Oh, save it," she said through a mouthful of sandwich. "You're obsessed with PMS. There are times during the month when a woman is not on her period, you know, namely most of the time. If you ever had a girlfriend you'd be aware of that."

"There are very few times when you are not in a foul mood, so one is left to wonder." Lyndon took a long swig of iced tea. "And for your information, oh testy one, I've had girlfriends."

"Uh-huh. Not since maturing into an adult male you haven't. Of course that was like, what, a couple years back?"

"If you're trying to disprove the PMS theory, you are doing a shockingly poor job."

"If you're trying to convince me that you've dated anyone female *and* human in the years I've known you, you're the one doing a piss-poor job."

Lyndon bit into his sandwich, something meat-coloured on a puffy white kaiser bun. "I've dated," he said eventually, wiping mustard from his mouth. "I just don't issue a press release every time."

"Yeah, I bet you're on all the singles websites. I've probably swiped past your profile. Tall Caucasian man with steady income and bizarre passion for choir seeks petite — what's your favourite? — Vietnamese woman for good times and occasional singing, no strings attached. No, wait minute: G-strings attached."

"You are mocking me. The impudence of it."

"Yeah, well you are shitting me." Nathalie licked olive oil off her fingers. "If you were seeing someone, you'd tell me."

"Is that a fact?"

"It is. I'm your closest friend at work. I tell you when I'm seeing someone. Though admittedly, by the time I do it's usually over. And admittedly, it's been a while."

Lyndon opened his mouth, then closed it.

A stooped old man shuffled past on the sidewalk, on his head, pushed down tight to the ears, an aluminum saucepan. Just another day in Richmond, she thought, and nudged Lyndon as the man stopped by their bench to scan the clouds, whether for alien spacecraft or intestinally loose birds, she couldn't be sure.

"What's the update on your crashed helicopter?" Lyndon asked once the fellow had passed. "Was the teardown illuminating?"

Now was the time to come clean about Will Werner's phone call and to say that in the turmoil of preparing for the teardown she'd forgotten to pass along the Tracker lead. Instead she recapped her conversation with the mechanic in Victoria, her foray into the R22 wreckage last night, and her discovery that the clutch fuse had blown.

Lyndon nodded. "So the clutch wasn't working. No clutch, no tension on the belts. The belts could have loosened up so much that they stopped driving the main rotor."

"Right. It all adds up. Trouble is, I can't prove it. The belts were already off the pulley system at the crash site. We found them quite a distance away. There's no way of knowing if they came off during the flight and caused the accident, or if they were forced off by the impact of the crash."

Lyndon balled up his sandwich wrapper and tossed it straight up in the air, one, two, three, four, catching it every time though he continued to look straight ahead. Suddenly he snatched the wrapper in his fist. "I know."

"Know what?"

A satisfied smile stole over his face. "How you can prove it. We had something like this happen in another case, before you joined the TSB. Must have been twelve, thirteen years ago." He bounced the wrapper on his palm.

"What was it? What happened?" She tried in vain to hide her excitement.

"*Now* the lady is interested in the loser that is Lyndon." He grinned and collected his drink can. "Come on. I'll show you."

∧ ∨ ∧

BUT HE DIDN'T. They arrived at the office with only minutes to spare before the one-thirty videoconference, and for the second time that day Nathalie and her fellow investigators trooped into the boardroom, shut the door, and arranged themselves around the long table, where they spent the next two hours staring at and occasionally talking to the giant flat-screen TV. On it appeared the impassive faces of three managers in Ottawa, determined to pinpoint why the British Columbia office had already exceeded its budget only two-thirds of the way into the year. Tucker, present for this meeting, did little to conceal that he was attending under duress. As time dragged on and the managers' accusations mounted, Tucker's words dwindled and his face stiffened until he became a kind of projection himself, more the image of the man than the real thing. Eventually, whenever the region's turn came to answer, he repeated the same sentence, word for word, in a low monotone that his staff recognized as the smoke before an inferno: "We have more crashes than any other region yet we have exactly the same budget."

Repetition did not produce comprehension, so at three thirty (six thirty Ottawa time, Nathalie noted, with a grudging nod to the managers' uncharacteristic stamina) Tucker looked at his watch and declared the meeting over. Before the pixellated heads could disagree, he stood up, switched off the videoconferencing feed, and left.

"How does he get away with shit like that?" asked Joe, the newest hire.

"I'm not sure he does," said Roy. "He just does it, and let the chips fall where they may."

Lyndon stood up and stretched. "I predict the fall of chips." He glanced at his watch, then Nathalie. "I'm off. If I don't go now, the traffic will slay me. I'll show you that thing tomorrow."

Nathalie frowned.

"Lyndon's gonna show Nathalie his thing," Joe announced loudly. "Tomorrow, you all hear that? Tomorrow's the big day."

"Ha ha. Such a jester," said Lyndon, colouring slightly. "Let it be known that I am charging admission, and it's double for you, Joe." He was gone before Nathalie could persuade him to stay.

A waste of a goddamn day, she thought as she headed to her cubicle. Only one hour to go and nothing accomplished. No new R22 leads. Nothing on the Tracker since last night's discovery of the destroyed trim system. Yet she wasn't ready to hand over Will's tip. There had to be something to it, and something she could get for it. As with the R22 it was a matter of unearthing evidence, some fact that would convert conjecture into certainty. Then and only then could she remake her reputation, and with that regain Tucker's respect.

She opened email. Nothing of note, she quickly determined; everything deletable. No pink message slips from Luanne, no blinking light on her desk phone. But on her cell phone, which she'd left behind during the videoconference, a new text message:

Can't stop thinking about U and picturing U naked. Keep trying but its hard. Real hard. LY, Jake.

That was Jake Behrend, down to brass tacks in twenty words or less, and damned if it didn't work. Her body flooded as she remembered lifting the bedsheet and catching a full-frontal view of all his goods.

But LY? What was she supposed to do with that? What adult male would text "love you" to someone he'd slept with once (okay, twice)? Whether the sign-off was a breezy reminder that they were keeping it casual or a more deliberate, callous irony, she couldn't say, but the sex etiquette was undebatable: no using the L-word with a new partner in any circumstance, for any reason, especially when the liaison is one hundred percent lust and zero percent emotion.

WTF seemed like the only reasonable reply, but in the end she opted not to answer. Jake and his wife had an arrangement, which presumably meant he would fuck around but always go home afterwards. That suited Nathalie perfectly. No feelings, no commitments, and a thousand kilometres between their beds — that's what made Jake ideal. She had learned her lesson. No more being caught off guard, no more sentimental detours, no more foolish dreams. She wanted nothing more to do with love. Mémère's advice applied to feelings, not just actions: *better to hit than be hit.*

TWENTY-FIVE

November

OFF-KILTER, HAYWIRE, WONKY, WEIRD. Sharon weighs each word on her tongue, but none entirely captures her state. Not normal, is all she concludes when she hauls herself out of bed at ten thirty, hours later than usual, having tossed and turned and fretted until dawn finally lulled her to sleep.

Even the habitual motions of brewing French roast feel alien. She grinds the beans, inserts the filter basket, and lets the machine whir and groan until she notices she has forgotten to add water. She makes toast, more to absorb the coffee than to satisfy hunger since her keyed-up stomach feels none, and neglects to butter it. When the last dry bite is gone, it is eleven fifty. Somehow sixty minutes have passed in what feels like fifteen. No noon yoga class now, since no one may enter the studio after start time. Is it ironic that yoga rules are so inflexible? It is the first concrete thought to cross her mind all morning. The second is that there are hours to go before Will arrives. She checks the grey sky, today more soft than threatening, and decides on a walk.

November is no one's favourite month in this city, and Sharon, who can apply no superlatives to the west coast, understands why. It's the overcast, humid days like this one that push young fortune seekers and white-haired retirees back to their former homes in Edmonton or Ottawa or the sun-kissed prairies, where for the rest of their lives they proclaim that Vancouver is beautiful but unliveable.

Haywire, wonky, topsy-turvy. Outdoors, too, the world feels off. The damp air cools her skin and carries a bite, like chilled fruit, yet she moves through it like a sleepwalker. Three times she rounds the park at the end of her street, past the pond with its shooting fountain and the tall grasses that shush in the breeze. Three times she passes the secluded corner of the park where, under the spreading arms of a red oak, one week before he died, Rafe asked to come home. She dreams of this oak tree from time to time, on her worst nights. She dreamed of it during this morning's fitful sleep.

That July day was sweltering, even in the shade. The wind picked up enough to rustle the leaves but not enough to stir the air around them. It was humid, Toronto-hot; Sharon's hair hung limp under her straw hat, and rivulets of sweat trickled between her breasts. In the end Rafe begged her to take him back, his shoulders straining with effort. "I'll do anything," he said. "I'll give up firefighting, go back with the airlines so you're not alone so much. We can go back to Toronto, we can go home." Good. She wanted him to beg. After what he's done, he owes me, she thought. She was still furious that day — it is obvious to her now — furious that he had left her, furious at the how and the why. And yet. Twenty-three years she had spent married to this man, more than half her life. After that much time together, how can you just walk away? So much pleading under this oak tree, so many promises, and when she finally told Rafe yes, he wept.

Today, standing across from the shady oak, she is no longer flayed by the loss of a future that never came. The pangs have settled into a dull and steady throb. Today she tries out an idea that has formed since Will's visit, an idea that is simple but changes everything: Rafe intended to come back to her all along. It is the best and perhaps only explanation for why he kept their separation from Will. Not telling others at work she understands: they had agreed not to advertise the decision, besides which, Rafe would never willingly announce to his co-workers that he had failed. But to hide it from his partner? She has examined the facts every which way and she is certain of it. He would pretend with Will only if deep down he knew their split was temporary, if he meant from the outset to come home.

He meant to come home. The ramifications of it open her ears, at last, to what Rafe said over and over under the broad, leafy tree: that he loved her, had never stopped loving her. He had lost sight of his feelings, but they were always there. She was his one true love and she always would be. Her acceptance of his declarations, her belief in them, warms her on this chilly, wonky November day. Rafe never fully left her.

The realization is a gift from Will. He has, without knowing it, returned Rafe to her. So to Will, who also loved Rafe, Sharon will give the gift of omission. She will preserve for him the Rafe he knew, noble and loyal. She will never tell him everything.

∧ ∨ ∧

BY THREE O'CLOCK she has pulled herself together: showered, fixed her hair, done her face. Slipped on a pair of low-slung, slim-legged jeans, a rose-coloured cotton vee-neck, and a flared black cardigan. From a dresser drawer, where she stuffed them under the turtlenecks so useless here on the mild west coast, she unearths the garnet earrings Rafe gave her on her fortieth birthday. Looping around her neck a crimson scarf shot with silver, she rechecks the mirror. How would a stranger rate her? Acceptable, she decides. Not striking, never beautiful, but presentable.

By three o'clock she has also read a chapter of her library book, a thriller set in working-class Edinburgh that she cannot follow. She has boiled the kettle so it will reheat quickly later on; scrubbed the toilet in the main-floor powder room; synchronized her watch and all the clocks with the time on her cell phone; smoothed lotion onto her hands, frowning at freckles that suspiciously resemble age spots; and picked up and put down the cruise brochures, no closer to a decision about Christmas.

Even though she is waiting for it, the peal of the doorbell startles her. Get a grip, she tells herself. Her heart beats so rapidly that she worries the movement will show, like the twitching of a nervous bird.

"Hello," she says at the same moment Will says, "Hi." They laugh.

"Come in," she says.

"Thanks for inviting me," he says at the same time.

She steps aside to let him into the narrow vestibule, along with the crisp cologne of autumn that comes with him. As he passes, his arm brushes her shoulder. She feels it in her stomach.

He peels off his jacket as he enters the living room and sits again in Rafe's chair, the jacket on his lap. In the space of two weeks he has undergone another transformation. His reddish-brown hair is inches shorter and neatly combed. The scruffy beard is gone, a hint of stubble in its place. She notes an absence of stains on his jeans and red golf shirt, and although his clothes still fit loosely, his bare arms are ropy with muscle, the short sleeves riding up over rounded biceps. A faint smile eases the lines on his face and he looks almost handsome again. Heat flares inside her and she worries she is blushing.

"Can I hang that for you?" she asks, afraid that he will say no, he's not staying.

"Um, sure."

She carries his jacket to the front closet, grateful for a moment to steady herself. The fleece zip-up is charcoal-coloured, soft to the touch, the sleeves far longer than the arms of her coat next to it. She quickly closes the closet door to shush the message of the touching coats: she and Will are together.

Don't be ridiculous, she tells herself. He is Rafe's partner; that is the only connection. He's practically a boy, and she is a drifting widow with no desire, just empty hours and a head full of memories.

Back in the living room, she sits on the edge of the sofa and tries to think of one sensible thing to say. The coffee table is scattered with brochures. Will notices. "Taking a cruise?"

"No. I'm not a fan of cruises."

"That's a lot of literature for someone who's not a fan."

"I guess."

"You ever been on a cruise? I don't remember Rafe talking about one."

"No, never. He wasn't a big fan either. He was probably more of a not-fan than me. I mean, he was less interested than I was. Am."

She looks up to find Will's light hazel eyes on her and instantly drops her gaze. "Ready for some tea?"

"Sure. Let me help this time."

"No. Absolutely not." She hurries out before he can protest.

In the safety of the kitchen she switches on the kettle, gets down the cups and saucers, pours milk into a small pitcher. Her hand trembles and Will's cup makes a tinging sound against the saucer. For God's sake, she's as skittish as a schoolgirl. On tiptoes, she tries to extract the tray from the cupboard above the fridge.

"Here, let me get that," she hears behind her. She comes down off her toes, starts to twist toward him, and puts too much weight on one side. As her knees buckle, strong hands grasp her upper arms from behind. "Steady there. Were you into the strong stuff before I got here?"

Will's grip melts her last shred of composure. From her mouth comes a soft bleat, a sound she has never heard before this day and would give her left foot to take back. If it were a hundred years ago she could end her humiliation by collapsing in a faint, but being a modern woman and not prone to unconsciousness, she simply stands there, back turned, as his hands slide off her.

"Here." He reaches over her and takes the tray down, so close that his smell of soap and sweat and warm cloth tickles her nose. She prays that she might remain silent.

Will sets the tray down beside the kettle. "So were you?"

"Was I what?"

"Into the strong stuff. Before I got here."

"You got here at three o'clock. I'm not that far gone."

"What, it's against the rules to drink before three?" A dimple dents his cheek.

"A widow drinking alone in the afternoon, yes, I think some rules might be broken. There would certainly be cause for concern." She is aware of how prissy she sounds, the stereotypical finger-wagging librarian. "Why? Would you like a drink? Stronger than tea, I mean?"

"Only if you'll join me."

Her stomach flutters in a way it hasn't in years, maybe decades.

Maybe not since her first taste of something stronger at the grade nine winter carnival, gym awash in paper snowflakes, when Keegan Banks, the boy she liked most, tipped a pint of lemon gin in her direction. Several sips later, when the first slow song drifted across the gym's hardwood floor, he asked her to dance and she grew up by years. She could still taste the bitter citrus as he bent to kiss her later, in a dark corner by the lockers. Whatever happened to Keegan? They dated for a few months until his family moved to Wisconsin, and that was that. She hasn't thought of him in years. How can someone who was once at the centre of your life vanish? Someone whose lips touched yours, whose tongue traced your collarbone?

She accepts that her mouth has gone dry in a way no tea will rectify. "I don't have much to offer," she says. "Some white wine, maybe a little rum from Christmas." She bends down and rummages in a cupboard. "Oh. It seems there is scotch." She holds up a bottle of Glenlivet 15.

His eyes crinkle. "Quarter past three. Are we allowed now?"

It's good that he is teasing her. So much better than being scoured out with sadness like last time. She hands him the bottle. "It's the drinking alone part I'm concerned about. If you're here I'm not alone, am I?"

"There's one or two people might disagree with you. But technically, yeah, you're off the hook."

Sharon points to the cupboard that holds the glasses, and Will pours two astonishingly large drinks. "Good lord." She gets the ice tray from the freezer. "Better throw a few cubes in mine. Girls?"

"Sorry?"

"The people who might disagree with me, are they girls?"

Will smiles as he cracks ice into their drinks. "Well, women." He hands her a glass.

"Women, girls. At your age either one fits."

"What do you mean, at my age?"

"I mean ... at your age. I'm never sure what to call females under, say, twenty-five. *Girls* is too juvenile, like kids with dolls, not to mention demeaning to some. But *women* sounds too old."

He regards her quizzically, as if she were a not-too-bright pupil. "I'm not in my twenties. I was Rafe's partner for a decade and I had a career before that. It's not like I was flying as an infant."

Sharon tilts her glass. The scotch sears her throat, and she coughs and sputters and remembers why she never drinks the stuff.

"So *I'm* a kid? Who here can't handle the grown-up drink?"

"This is why I prefer tea. It's a nice, dignified beverage."

"Single malt is dignified. It's the drink of princes." As if to illustrate, he swirls the scotch before taking a long, slow, noiseless sip.

"*Tea* is the drink of princes. At least the British ones."

"Tea, scotch, Ovaltine, Dubonnet. They're not fussy. They drink whatever's lying around the palace." Will sets down his glass and leans against the counter. His legs are long, she notes, longer than Rafe's.

"Dubonnet? There's a strange choice."

"One of Her Majesty's favourite drinks. Dubonnet-and-gin cocktail."

"You're making that up." Sharon tries another taste, barely moistening her mouth. Her lips tingle.

"Google it. You figure a child like me wouldn't know anything about our sovereign lady?" His cheeks dimple again.

"Okay, I give up. I didn't mean that you're young like a child. Just young*er*."

"I'm thirty-six. Not much behind you. You're forty-three? Forty-four?"

"Forty-four. How do you know?"

"I was with Rafe when he bought those." He nods at the garnet earrings that dangle below her upswept hair. "In Prince George. He couldn't make it home for your fortieth so he wanted to get you something extra special. He looked at every pair in the store before he picked those. Guess it was a big deal, the big four-oh."

A very big deal. She says nothing.

Will misinterprets her silence. "Summer's a bad time for a birthday if you're married to someone in our line of work."

She lets out her breath, unaware that she was holding it. "He did his best. We celebrated whenever he got time off. It was fine." She picks up her glass. "Let's sit down."

She feels Will behind her as she heads back to the living room. The afternoon has dimmed the corners enough that she switches on a table lamp. They take the same seats as before, Will in Rafe's armchair, she on the sofa, but this time she chooses the end farthest away from him.

What is with her? Why is she sitting way over here? It will look ridiculous if she moves now, so she will have to stay put, even though it means practically yelling to be heard. Her body is behaving without input from her brain; she has no idea what she is doing. She readies herself for anything, an anthropologist observing an unknown tribe.

"That was Rafe's chair." She says it too loudly, misjudging the distance, and the comment hovers like an accusation.

Will scoots forward on the seat. "Sorry, I didn't know. Should I sit somewhere else?"

"No, no. Please don't. I didn't mean anything by it." He looks uncertain. "Really. Don't listen to me. Half of what comes out of my mouth these days makes no sense, not even to me."

He settles back tentatively and sips his scotch. With his other hand he feels the arm of the chair, the gold-coloured fabric smooth from use. "It's a comfortable seat. I can see why he'd like it."

"It fit him well. He wanted something that didn't make him feel like a giant on a toadstool. His words." She smiles, remembering the dozens of armchairs Rafe had sat on, leaned back in, and pronounced too puny. "That was a long time ago. Back in Toronto, when we bought our first house."

"So he was ... built up back then?"

"Oh, yes. He lifted weights before I ever came along." She remembers the shadow Rafe cast over her car the afternoon they met. "It was like a religion for him. He never missed a session. If he had early or late flights — this was when he was on a regular schedule with Canadian — he'd go to the gym either first thing in the morning or last thing at night. He even worked out when he had a cold, not that that happened often."

Will nods. "There's a gym at the Kamloops fire base. More like a storage closet and a few weights. That's where you'd find Rafe when we weren't in the air. Not like the rest of us, reading books, playing cards, shooting the shit, what have you. When we were away in the field, he always used the motel gym. He'd get so mad if we were in a place that didn't have a fitness room."

"Tell me about it. Wherever we travelled, we had to stay somewhere with a gym. If there wasn't one, say we were at some inn or B and B, he had a routine. As soon as we woke up he'd pile the bedcovers on the floor, like a mat, and he'd do a hundred push-ups, a hundred sit-ups, and a hundred leg lifts on each side. And he'd be cranky all day because he didn't get a proper workout."

Will chuckles. "He lifted people sometimes. There was this camp cook for the ground crew in the Kootenays, a French girl from Quebec. Every time we crossed paths with them Rafe would lift her right over his head. He'd do sets of ten and she'd count in French. God, we laughed at that." He gazes out the window, the dusky interlude before the street-lights blink on. "He used to cart me around too. Put me in a fireman's carry and jog up and down the runway. He was one strong guy." He tips his glass for the last amber drop.

Sharon stares at the warm pool beneath the table lamp, the only light in the room. Whether it's the scotch or the solace of reminiscing about Rafe, her restlessness has finally subsided.

"I miss him," Will says softly.

She curses the distance she has created by sitting at the far end of the sofa. "I know." Again she berates herself for having forgotten about Will all these months. "I should have been in touch long ago. You were such a good friend to him. I think … I was so busy missing him that I never thought about you. That's no excuse. I'm sorry, Will."

"God, don't be sorry. Not you. You're the one whose life totally changed. You were together so many years, half your lives. What I am —" He stops and massages the area between his eyes. "It's nothing compared to that."

"Will."

"I'm not looking for sympathy. That's not why I'm here."

"I know that. But you have every right —"

"No!" It comes out strangled. "I have no right. None at all." He rubs the arm of the chair again, back and forth, as if sanding rough wood.

Abandoning decorum, she moves down the sofa to sit nearer. "Why would you say that? He was your partner, your friend. Of course you have a right to miss him."

When he finally looks at her, she sees the toll of his attempt to stay in control. The cheerful mask is gone, the tormented man revealed. "You don't understand." He bites his lip, waits a beat. "That morning, when he came into sight, there I was in the cockpit, watching. Same routine we do every time, every day. He dipped a bit low, but he did that, you know? Just to show you he could. Then all of a sudden he nosed down. Just touched the trees, barely touched them, but that's all it took. It was over. Just … over. And what did I do?" He looks at his hands, clenched in a knot. "Nothing, that's what. It's like it was on TV or something and I was … in the audience. Through the whole thing, the whole goddamned thing, I just sat there and did nothing. I let it happen."

The lamplight picks up a wet line down his cheek. Sharon's heart creaks farther open, a door on old hinges. "There was nothing you could do. Think about it. Nothing."

He swipes at his eyes. "I should've known. He was my friend. We talked all the time. He talked to me that morning, before we went up. If I paid more attention, if I really listened to him. Fuck. I could have stopped him."

Now she understands. She leans closer, speaks urgently. "Will, they sent me the draft report last month. I know runaway trim was the likely cause, and I know Rafe talked to someone about the trim that morning. It was you, wasn't it? I had no idea."

Will stares at his lap.

"But listen to me."

Just do it, she tells herself. Connect.

She reaches for his wrist. "You have to listen to me. There was nothing you could do. It wasn't *up* to you. He was so experienced, he had years on you. If he didn't think it was worth checking out the trim, it wasn't." Will's wrist is burning hot; she feels him tremble.

"He made a mistake, Will. It's easy to see that in hindsight but that's what it was, a mistake, pure and simple. It can happen to any of us, no matter how competent we are or how cautious. You know Rafe. He loved the adrenaline but he wasn't sloppy, he never cut corners. It was a mistake."

His head stays down. "You don't understand. I can't ..."

"I do. I do understand. You're beating yourself up because he's dead and you're alive. That's what it comes down to, am I right? But it was his responsibility. His decision." She strokes his arm lightly with her fingers, wishing she could sweep away the guilt. "Not yours. Never yours."

He is crying for real now, fighting it but losing. The room darkens and shrinks around them, wrapping them in dusk. Eventually he takes Sharon's hand. "It's not about the trim." His voice is thick and he kneads her fingers. "It's just — it happened so fast, so fast. But I — as soon as I knew it wasn't a stunt and he was going down ... God, it makes me sick to say it. I closed my eyes." His voice breaks. "I closed my fucking eyes. I'm his partner, it's my job, my job to watch out for him, and I didn't. I didn't." He looks at her, broken. "I'm sorry. I'm so, so sorry."

She knows the heft of Will's burden because she has shouldered every pound of it herself: the weight of being the one left alive. She is ashamed every day the sun warms her skin. She tastes a strawberry and feels guilty for finding it sweet. When night comes, it corners her into admitting how natural and simple were Rafe's needs, and how destructive her power to deny them.

"Will." She frees her hand from his.

Do it, she tells herself. He needs this. So do you.

Her hand trails down his face, a slow glide from cheekbone to jawline during which she feels his slick skin and pall of guilt. She holds his chin, turns his head toward her. "Look at me. You have nothing, *nothing*, to be sorry for. Rafe loved you like a brother. Right from the start he said how easy it was to be with you, how he trusted everything you did. You were a huge part of his life, Will. You are allowed to miss him and you are allowed to feel sad. But you are not allowed to feel guilty." His eyes have broken away from hers, so she puts her other hand up to his face, cupping it and moving it in line with her gaze. She will not hold back. "Do you hear me? No guilt. You've got to let it go."

Will grasps her hands and puts them to his mouth, lips on her palms like the shimmer of silk. A shudder passes through her, a freezing bolt from hairline to ankles. His mouth moves from her wrists to her forearms; then he pulls her close and kisses her throat, the bare pulse point above the loop of her scarf. There the whisper of his breath and his fluttering kisses take fire. Her hands rake his hair, her lips find his, and the room and all its shadows combust.

^ ∨ ^

HOURS LATER SHE LIES AWAKE, listening to the furnace that the cold fall night has kicked into life. Their feet, which the fringed throw is too short to cover, glow in the light of the streetlamp outside. They never closed the drapes. The thought of people passing by, ordinary people out walking dogs or murmuring into phones or digesting dinner, people who might spy their naked lust, sets off a throbbing between her thighs.

Late as it is, she can't sleep. She is nowhere near tired. She shifts so she can see Will's face in the accidental light, smooth and sorrow-free at last. On the narrow sofa her breasts are inches from his mouth, and her nipples stiffen as she imagines brushing them secretly against his sleeping lips. In all the world there is only this sofa, damp and scratchy beneath them, and their bodies, long and pale, toes kissed with light.

She shifts again to release the pressure on her leg and Will stirs. In a minute he opens his eyes, then blinks, clearly baffled. She smiles. "Yes, you are actually here. It's not a dream."

He entwines his toes with hers, runs a hand along her upturned hip. "Good."

"Are you sure?" she asks, though she fears the answer. "This must be more than a little strange for you."

"What, it's not strange for you too?"

As she lay for hours watching Will sleep, strangeness was all she could think about. She recalled this morning, when the world felt so off-kilter. Not in a million years could she have imagined that by night-fall she would be naked on her living room sofa beside a man who is eight years but also a generation younger, after the most intense sex she has experienced in what suddenly seems a very sheltered life. "It's on the strange end of the spectrum. It's ... unexpected."

"I'll say."

"So you didn't come here with an elaborate plan to feed me scotch and seduce me as soon as my guard was down?" Sharon touches his earlobe, amazed at such downiness on a ropy man.

"You were the one who invited me. And produced the scotch. Seems to me I was the one who let my guard down." He looks away. "Big time."

A rush of sweet-tinged sadness compels Sharon to reach for him. "I didn't mean to tease. I guess it came as a surprise to both of us."

The furnace shuts off with a soft thunk. Will rests his head against her collarbone and she touches the short coarse hair at his nape, bewildered to have such intimate access to someone who hours ago was an acquaintance at best. She knows things she never dreamed she would know: how his skin smells under the waistband of his jeans, the butterfly of his ginger eyelashes on her shoulder, the rough wet of his tongue inside her, the way he arches his neck when he comes.

"What are you thinking?" he asks.

Her thoughts are many, her feelings too jumbled to convey: delicious and regretful, satisfied and guilty, excited and blue. She reaches into the tangle for the strongest strand. "I'm thinking that you ... you should ..." She is unable to say it.

"That I should —" His body tenses. "You need me to leave?"

"No." She moves her mouth to his ear. Her hand presses his chest and she takes courage from the pounding of his heart. "I'm thinking," she whispers, "that you should put it in me again." It electrifies her to say such words. Every inch of her wants this long, lean boy.

"Well then. Lucky for you, I was raised to do as I'm told." Will's lips trace a path down her belly, and Sharon believes she may never sleep again.

TWENTY-SIX

August

TRY AS SHE MIGHT, Nathalie could not get Lyndon alone. Yesterday he'd hinted at a lead that might revive the stalled R22 investigation, but today he was perpetually unavailable: on a drawn-out phone call with the Edmonton office, sequestered with Tucker over the lunch hour, then downtown at Transport Canada doing God knows what.

She despised waiting, always had, so she hunted for busywork to kill the time, starting with the R22 maintenance logs. There she found an entry dated July 2 of this year by James Stanhope, minus the pompous numerals that usually decorated his signature, confirming that he had changed a fuse. Whether it was the clutch fuse was not specified, but the timing was right: thirteen days before the crash. Next she typed up her findings since the engine teardown, saving them to her Mind Dump folder. In between she monitored email. A notice arrived from PAMEA about the upcoming annual conference, in theory a forum for Pacific-region AMEs to get updated on aviation developments but in practice their yearly chance to exchange industry gossip. She blocked off the two days in her calendar, and on a whim texted Jake:

PAMEA conference 3rd week Sep, Vancouver. I'm in. U?

It was the perfect excuse for him to come west again, and for two nights this time. Maybe she'd invite him to her condo. Then she thought of the LY that ended his last message. Maybe not. She'd have to think on it.

The afternoon wound down. Dammit, she thought. At this rate when Lyndon finally did reappear, he'd be itching to head home before the traffic snarled into lockwire as it did every Friday. No way could she last the whole weekend without knowing the tip he had for her – even though she was not yet ready to exchange it for her information on the Tracker. Will's statement about runaway trim was still hers, and she would guard it until she knew precisely how to convert the knowledge to power.

She knew Lyndon was back before she saw him. Emerging from the washroom, she heard a deep chuckle from the front desk – Luanne. Only one person could make that woman laugh. Nathalie raced to reception, grabbed Lyndon's elbow, and before anyone could protest dragged him out back to the wreckage warehouse.

"What is this, a hostage taking?" He freed his elbow but followed just the same.

"Look, you bastard. You say you've got something that'll help with the R22 and then you leave me high and dry. Show me before you go home for the weekend or I'm telling Luanne that you nurse a secret love for her and her feminine ways."

Lyndon snorted. "You would never –"

"I certainly would. You of all people know that under this sweet exterior, I am ruthless." Nathalie opened the heavy warehouse door, leaning into it with her small frame. "It'll be easier on the whole office if you just put me out of my misery."

"Fine. It was not my intention to put you *into* any misery. I just got busy."

"Bullshit. You get a sadistic kick from lording it over me. You always have. Whenever you've got something I need, you want me to beg for it."

His cheeks reddened, and a moment passed before he replied. "Mam'selle Girard, oh crazy one, paranoia does not become you."

Nathalie led him to the mangled remains of the R22. "See?" She pointed to four belts laid out on a workbench beside the fuselage. "Here they are. And here are the pulleys."

"The pulleys aren't attached. Did you take them off so you could haul the engine out for the teardown?"

She nodded.

Lyndon walked around the heap of metal that had once floated in the sky as effortlessly as dandelion fluff. Near where the engine should have been mounted, he stopped. "Got a flashlight?"

From a bin under the workbench she pulled out a pocket-sized light. "What're you looking for?"

"Just a sec." Lyndon trained the flashlight inside the fuselage, where the pulley system would ordinarily be, then edged in closer. "That's it. That's what we're looking for."

"For chrissakes, what?" Nathalie practically hopped with impatience.

He motioned her over. "Come look at this."

What she saw in the flashlight beam was unremarkable: two metal tabs fastened to the inside of fuselage. "The tabs beside the pulley system. So what?"

"Right here." He swept the light back and forth across one tab. "See that?"

The paint on the tab was abraded in several places. "A few wear marks in the metal. So?"

"So," Lyndon said, switching off the light, "in those marks lies your proof."

She stamped her foot. "What are you, Yoda? Quit being so fucking cryptic. Just tell me, in full sentences, what it means."

"It means the belts came loose during flight." He walked back around the wreck to the workbench where the belts lay. "If they loosen up enough, they'll come right off the pulleys. They basically fling themselves off."

"Duh. I'm a mechanic too, remember?"

"Think about what happens when the belts get loose enough to fly off. Think about where they go. The only direction they can move is outward, toward the sides of the fuselage. And what do they strike along the way?" He paused, enjoying his moment of drama. "The tabs."

Nathalie grinned as the explanation fell into place.

"The rub marks on that tab are from the belts hitting when they spun off. It's the only thing that can make marks like that. Nothing that happens during the crash, not impact with trees or breaking apart or whatever, can get at that tab. It's tucked too far inside the fuselage. There's no doubt about it. Those belts came off in flight."

"Hot damn! It's proof."

"Even better, it's proof we used once before. Maybe a dozen years ago, plus or minus. I'd only been here awhile myself. There was a crash up in northern BC, near Fort St. John, a Schweizer 300. A lot like your case here, the helicopter just fell out of the sky. It turned out the belts had come loose during flight, and fortunately for us they left their little calling card behind. The Schweizer reps knew what to look for. As soon as we ruled out an engine problem, they checked for rub marks. There they were, just like on your R22, and that was that. The report essentially wrote itself."

Visions of closing the case, of triumphantly announcing to Tucker the Fucker that she'd gathered all the threads, danced in Nathalie's head. "Lyndon, this is so excellent. I can't wait to tell Tucker. He's riding me for evidence on this one. Nothing I dig up is ever good enough for that man."

Lyndon gave her a long look. "If that's true, you know why."

Goddammit, would she ever be free of the Cessna 172? No matter what she did its odour dogged her, like persistent halitosis, fouling everything, even this sweet triumph. "Whatever," she muttered. "Look, thanks for this, I mean it. I owe you one."

"You owe me so many we have both lost count."

"Yeah, well fuck you too."

"Such poise, such eloquence. I know not what to say. Except that it's time to head homeward."

"Kiss Luanne for me on the way out, okay? Unless she's leaving with you."

"Oh, ho," said Lyndon. "I detect a faint note of jealousy."

"In your dreams, Mister L. In your *wet* dreams. Get outta here before you have to drive with other vehicles on the road. I know how traumatic that is for you."

The warehouse door creaked open and Luanne, as if summoned by their exchange, barrelled in, shoulders forward, a marine making for shore.

"Luanne, we were just talking about you," Nathalie said, glancing slyly at Lyndon.

The receptionist glared at Nathalie. "I've been looking for you everywhere."

"What's up?" It had to be important. Luanne was a non-migratory organism, seldom spotted beyond the front-desk environment.

"You have a visitor, says he has to see you."

"A visitor? Who?" Nathalie's mind raced. Jake?

"Some young guy. He was here before, a couple of weeks back." Luanne tossed her head impatiently. "I cannot be expected to wander around this facility tracking people down. There's nothing about that in my job description. I have to stay up front where I'm needed."

"Who's this, then?" Lyndon asked Nathalie.

A couple of weeks back? Oh, no. She knew exactly who it was.

"I have no idea. Must be about the R22. You better get out of here while the gettin's good. I'll see you Monday."

∧ ∨ ∧

THE VISITOR WAS PACING the reception area when Nathalie hurried in, Luanne lumbering after her, Lyndon thankfully down the hall getting ready to go home. Will looked much the way Nathalie had pictured him from their phone conversation: loose-limbed, athletic, sun-browned face with a dusting of freckles over the nose, thick reddish-brown hair. A good-looking guy, probably more so when he wasn't scowling.

Job number one: smuggle him in before Lyndon saw him.

"I'm Nathalie." She extended her hand. "How can I help you?"

"Will Werner." He pumped her hand once and dropped it. "We need to talk."

"Absolutely. Let's go to the boardroom." It was the first door down the hallway; they could easily scoot in before Lyndon emerged from his cubicle. She hustled Will inside. As she shut the door, she spied her co-worker at the end of the hall, hoisting his laptop case and glancing at his phone. He hadn't seen them.

"Sit down," she told Will. And hurry up about it, she added silently. Any minute Lyndon would pass the windows into the boardroom, the blinds of which, she realized, were fully open. "I assume you're here about the Tracker?"

"You assume right." He hesitated beside one chair and chose the one next to it, but not before Lyndon cruised by outside.

Shit. Did he see them?

Lyndon's pace never faltered, so probably not. Then again, the man had an insatiable need to know every event in the office. He'd be curious about who'd come calling. If he did glance in and see Will, she'd get an earful. But not until Monday. That gave her plenty of time to dream up an explanation for why she was closeted away with the chief witness in his case, the case she'd been warned repeatedly to avoid.

Will, meanwhile, was swivelling in his chair and drumming his fingers on the conference table. Someone had wound his key all the way.

"So where do things stand?" he asked.

"I told you before, I'm not on the Tracker investigation."

"You know what I'm talking about. What's up with the info I gave you? Did the others look into it? They find anything sketchy with the trim?"

Nathalie smiled wanly. "You obviously don't know the TSB. We operate at the speed of evolution around here."

"What's that supposed to mean? Did they find anything or not?"

"Nothing that I've heard. Not yet." She cursed herself for doing so little with the lead she'd been handed, and decided to offer a partial truth. "I do know that the trim motor, the rods, the whole damned assembly got trashed by the impact. There's no way to know what position the trim tabs were in when the plane went down. Without that, it'll be hard to say whether the trim had anything to do with it."

"Shit."

"Don't worry," she said quickly. "Your statement about what Rafe said that morning, about the plane not handling right, it still carries weight. It'd carry more if someone else had heard it too."

"Well, no one did." He frowned at the table. "It was just him talking to me."

"Lyndon and Roy will likely re-interview the AMEs on duty that day, the day before too, when Rafe first thought the trim was off. He could've mentioned it to someone else that you're not aware of."

"Doubtful."

"Why? If he had concerns, the logical thing would be to report them to an AME."

"Maybe. But I'm pretty sure he didn't tell anyone." Will looked around the boardroom, its beige decor uninterrupted apart from the TSB logo on one wall and the flat-screen TV at the front. It was the quintessential government space: clinical, drab, featureless. There were times, as Nathalie daydreamed through meetings, training, and videoconferences, when she imagined sneaking in one night and spray-painting the walls orange and pink, streaking them with graffiti, anything to relieve the stupefying blankness.

"Listen," Will said, "I accept that you guys are the experts. But I'm telling you, something was wrong with that plane and Rafe knew it. He should've listened to his gut. No one knew that old beater like he did. The sooner you get past pilot error and start looking for something mechanical, the better."

Pilot error: it always came back to that. It was the cause that no one who cared about, lived with, worked with, or respected a dead pilot would ever willingly accept. Nathalie could list a dozen recent crashes that stemmed from a misstep on the operator's part, yet those left behind refused to acknowledge it. No matter how iron-clad the evidence, their husband/son/brother/boyfriend/co-worker was always the best-trained, safest pilot in the skies; he could never make a mistake that would destroy an aircraft and end people's lives. Naturally Will, who had worked a long time with Rafe and by all accounts looked up to the man, wanted to absolve his partner of responsibility. Who could blame him? Nathalie wanted the same thing.

"What makes you think anyone's looking at pilot error?"

"Come on, everyone knows it's your main theory. The word's out, and not just at West Air. Some Conair pilots I talked to yesterday heard the same thing. They kept asking me was Rafe distracted, was he fatigued, that kind of horseshit." He shook his head, anticipating her question. "I didn't tell them jack about the trim. I said he was at the top of his game as far as I could tell and left it at that. But that's why I'm here. Why is everyone stuck on pilot error when there's a mechanical problem staring you in the face?"

A wave of fatigue washed over Nathalie. What was she doing? She had her hands full enough with the R22. Maybe she should cut her losses and send Will directly to Lyndon and company.

"Listen," she said, "I can go back to the guys and ask them to keep looking, but it'd be better if you talked to them yourself. You'll have to eventually. Whether or not they find any evidence to back what you've said, they'll want to take a proper statement and ask you questions of their own. Why put it off? You could move things along by talking to them now."

"No." Will folded his arms. "I told you, I'm not dealing with those callous bastards. At least you knew Rafe. I'm dealing with you."

She was sick of his pointless stubbornness. "Look, I've made it as clear as I can. You cannot deal with me on this investigation. I am not allowed to get involved."

"What do you mean, not allowed? I can see not wanting to trespass on each other's territory, but not allowed? That sounds harsh."

Nathalie exhaled slowly. As far as she was concerned, the meeting was over. She no longer wanted Will's story as a bargaining chip, especially when she had no idea what the chip was worth or how to play it. She'd come clean to Lyndon on Monday, tell him Will had contacted her but she'd been so immersed in the R22 that she'd been slow to forward the information. Honesty really was the best policy. Not one of her grandmother's sayings, but it had merit on occasion.

"Not allowed, as in out of my jurisdiction." She stood up. "It's good of you to take the time to come by, but —"

"You know, it was not remotely easy for me to come here today." Will stood up too. "I'm supposed to be on call with the rest of the crew in Kamloops, but I asked for a couple of days off, special consideration in light of the recent tragedy, yada, yada. I want this crash looked into properly, not swept under the carpet with a bunch of other so-called pilot error incidents just because it's easier that way." His eyes burned with something deeper than stubbornness.

"I assure you, the TSB is taking this crash very seriously. No one's looking for an easy way out. If there was a mechanical problem we want to find it, but it won't happen fast. You called me one week ago. That's a blink of an eye in TSB time."

"Fine. But you know, I'm interested in time too. I don't want a couple of know-it-all investigators wasting it looking in the wrong place. Rafe was an excellent pilot, one of the best in the country. He was flying a routine circuit when he went down. There is no way he messed up."

"I'll tell the others what you said. First thing Monday morning. Now let's call it a day."

Will took a few steps toward her. "I know you're humouring me. But I am sure of this. I'll stake my life on it. Rafe did not make any mistakes that day." He held her gaze, a final, unwavering plea.

Together they returned to the reception area, where the late-afternoon sunshine streamed through the plate glass window. It lit the low table with its fan of government publications. It lit the three armchairs, two of them empty, and in chair number three, Lyndon.

Nathalie flinched as he unfurled himself. The slanted sunlight cast half his face in shadow and accentuated his height.

"Hello, Will," he said.

"Oh. Hey."

"It's Lyndon, Lyndon Johnson. Remember? I interviewed you a couple of weeks back."

"I remember."

"So what's up?" Lyndon asked pleasantly. "Nathalie? What were you and Will discussing?"

In her peripheral vision Nathalie saw Luanne in front of her monitor, toiling over ... what? No computer-based task could command that woman's attention on a Friday afternoon, especially not while high drama unfolded on her private stage.

It was pointless to pretend. "Let's all have a chat," Nathalie said. "Not here. The warehouse. We need to look at the wreckage." She turned just as Luanne looked up from her screen, disappointment pinching her features. Nathalie had seldom liked this cantankerous woman less. "Luanne, we'll be out back if anyone's looking for us."

"It's Friday, for Pete's sake," Luanne stated loudly. "Everyone's gone home. And that's where I'm going too, thirteen minutes from now. If you take longer you'll have to lock up and alarm."

"You leave whenever you need to." Lyndon treated Luanne to a dazzling smile. "Nathalie and I are old hands. We'll close up. Now." He turned to the others, smile gone. "Let's go."

Bound in silence so tight it could snap, they made their way to the warehouse. Nathalie's mind raced. Lyndon's tirades were typically superficial and short-lived, the yapping of an irksome dog. Whenever he went cold and terse, he was ready to bite.

Will stopped inside the doorway. A hangar full of burned-out fuselage, blackened engine parts, and twisted metal was a sobering sight for any first-time visitor, but more so for a pilot. This aviation boneyard was a flyer's nightmare come true. Nathalie wondered: was it wise to bring Will face to face with his partner's coffin?

The Tracker hunkered in the far corner, sooted up from the fire that had engulfed the plane once it hit the ground. The distinctive orange and white of West Air showed in patches through the black, especially on the wing that had sheared off and lay to one side on the concrete floor. The largest chunk of fuselage contained what was left of the cockpit. The windshield was gone, as were both side windows. The space between the smashed instrument panel and the canted-over pilot's seat was little more than a crack, compressed by impact to a sliver-sized opening, no room for a child let alone a weightlifter. It was a story whose ending could not be glossed over.

"Jesus Christ," Will breathed.

"Not an uplifting sight. It never is." Lyndon chuckled drily. "It's always a closed casket with these guys. Just be glad it wasn't you."

Will whipped around. "You fucking asshole, I've had it with you! You may not give a shit about this crash or the person in it, but I do. He was my partner. He fucking died. Right there, right inside *there*." He jabbed a finger at the remains of the cockpit. "Show some respect, would you? Even if you don't mean it, just pretend for two minutes like he's a real person, not some statistic in your annual report. Otherwise I've got nothing to do with this investigation from now on."

"At ease, captain." Lyndon looked faintly amused. "No disrespect intended. I agree with you. It's no way for a man to end up."

"I wanna know what the fuck you're doing about it."

"We're looking at all the possibilities —"

"Fuck the possibilities. I wanna know what you're doing about the trim issue."

"Trim issue?" Lyndon's eyebrows tented up. "Perhaps you could elaborate."

"What I told her last week." Will nodded toward Nathalie. "Rafe saying the trim felt sticky when he adjusted it. What do you think I'm talking about?"

"Last week?" Lyndon turned to Nathalie. "I wouldn't know, would I? Ms. Girard ... well, she hasn't seen fit to share."

A moment of silence, an eternity. She glanced at Will's face, incredulous, and Lyndon's, frozen in fury. She prayed for inspiration. None came.

"I was going to tell you," she said finally. "But you know how busy I've been with the R22. There hasn't been time."

"Yes, of course. Let me think for a moment." Lyndon stroked his chin. "Did I not see you every day this week except for Tuesday and Wednesday, when you were in Victoria? Did we not have lunch together, oh, yesterday? Were we not standing together right there" — he pointed to the R22 wreckage in the opposite corner — "roughly one hour ago while I handed you the key to your own investigation? And there was no time for you to return the favour?" He addressed Will. "Tell me, captain. Does that sound right to you? No time to tell me? Does it sound believable?"

Will was slack-jawed, half a step behind.

Nathalie rushed to answer. "I know it's lame, but it's true. Whenever I thought of telling you, you weren't around. When you were around, we talked about other stuff and it slipped my mind."

"And those times when you thought of it, you didn't have access to, let us say, a telephone? Text messaging? Electronic mail? Ah, the modern-day modes of communication, so helpful yet so easy to overlook when one is busy." Again he spoke to Will, as if to enlist his support. "No access to a pen and paper even, to compose a brief note?"

She winced. The more enraged Lyndon got, the colder and more formal his speech. There was no way out now and she knew it. She cursed herself for holding on too long, for once again fucking up.

Lyndon smiled thinly. "Mr. Werner, why don't you just start from the beginning. Tell me word for word what you told Nathalie last week and I'll take it from there."

Frowning, the pilot recounted it all: Rafe's comments about the trim sticking slightly the day before; Rafe's walkaround the morning of the crash, which turned up nothing obvious; Will's belief that a trim malfunction or runaway trim might have led to the crash. As Lyndon listened, he grew fixed and still, a heron eyeing its prey.

When Will was done, Lyndon motioned him to the rear section of fuselage. "See this?" He pointed inside the tail. "This is the trim motor and what's called the actuator assembly, the bellcrank and rods and so forth that operate the trim tabs. It was all like this when we recovered the wreck, smashed to bits. We had a look at it ages ago, but it's useless to us. There's no way to tell what position the trim tabs were set to just before the crash, no way to determine if the system was functioning properly, nothing."

"I know." Will nodded. "She explained that to me before, in the boardroom. But it was such an old airplane, and the way he just clipped the trees, it makes no —"

"Nathalie told you about the trim system? Just now, in the board-room?"

"Yeah. I get that part —"

"Let me get this straight." He stared at Nathalie as he spoke. "She not only took down your statement and kept it to herself, but she also came in here, examined the wreckage, and discussed her findings with you? Do I have that right?" He didn't wait for an answer. "Why, Mr. Werner, do you think Ms. Girard would do that?"

"She's an investigator, she was investigating —"

"No, no, no." Lyndon wagged his forefinger as if chiding a schoolboy. "She is not investigating this particular crash. In fact, she was expressly ordered to stay out of it. So tell me, why do you think she would get involved anyway, and go to such lengths to keep this involvement a secret from the rest of us? Come on, captain. Any theories?"

"How the hell should I know? I guess because she knew Rafe? That's why I went to her. Unlike the rest of you, she might actually give a shit."

"Yes." Lyndon's eyebrows shot up. "Yes, indeed. She *knew* Rafe. She gave a shit about him, as you put it. Intriguing, yes? The interesting question is, how well did she know him?"

"I don't know. They'd met. That's all I know."

"They had met. That's one way of putting it."

Nathalie burst in. "What are you talking about? What does this have to do with —"

Lyndon whirled to face her. "You know very well what I'm talking about. In any of these ... these discussions you had with *my* witness about *my* investigation, did you tell him how well you knew the deceased pilot? How many times you had *met* him? Were you upfront about that particular detail? Because you've certainly not been upfront with the rest of us."

"Listen, you're overreacting. I get that you're angry —"

"Overreacting? No, I don't think so. What I think is that you would say anything, now that he's dead, to make it seem like you had nothing to do with it."

Will stared at her.

Breathe, Scrapper, she told herself. Just breathe.

"Come on, Lyndon. Have you lost it? Of course I had nothing to do with it."

In one quick move Lyndon had her, his hand like a vise on her arm. Hot rage rolled off him. "You had everything to do with it." Spittle flecked his lips. "You think I don't know, but I do. I know why Rafe made bad decisions that day. I know why his mind was not on his job. That man's marriage was falling apart because of you." He bent lower. "You thought you were so careful, didn't you? That no one would find out. Well, you were wrong."

He let go her arm and made to leave. Then he turned back. "It is typical of you, you know. You are so caught up in your self-centred world. You have no clue about the people around you. You think we're invisible, that we're not really here. You think we don't see. Well, I am here. And I do see."

His footsteps rang out as he crossed the warehouse and banged the door shut.

Nathalie sneaked a look at Will. He stood by the plane's tail, hands in his pockets, face unreadable.

"God, I don't know what that was all about. Obviously I should've told him a lot sooner about your call. My fault."

Will said nothing.

"He'll calm down. He just needs time. He'll look into your story. Just because the trim assembly is smashed, that doesn't mean it's the end of it."

Will slumped. He looks so young, she thought, like a sad little boy. "Is it true?" he asked.

"Of course it is. Lyndon will tell Roy everything you said and they'll work the scenario from a few different angles –"

"Don't jerk me around." The boyishness vanished. "You and Rafe, is it true?"

"Well, yeah. I knew him. We were … casual. You could say casual friends. We hung out sometimes after work."

"You were fucking him." Even in the glare of the fluorescent lights, he did not blink.

"No. God, no. It wasn't like that. It was complicated —"

Before she could finish he walked away, leaving her alone in the cave of a warehouse, ruined air tanker by her side, unforgiving lights burning overhead.

TWENTY-SEVEN

Eighteen weeks after

WHAT WAS IT LIKE WHEN movies and TV shows switched from black-and-white to colour? You'd be used to that flat pencil look because that's all you ever had, right? Then boom, the full spectrum of shades. One change and everything you see is rich and saturated and you realize how deprived you were before.

That's how it's been for me these past two weeks. It's not just colour — there are tastes and smells too. And feelings. If The Counsellor was still on the scene, I'd finally have something to tell her. The days up to now were like outlines of days, I'd say, and now they are filling in.

Sharon. I say her name and this sensation shoots through me, kind of like ownership, though not in a creepy "you belong to me" way. More like her name is mine to speak, like she is mine to think about. I'm allowed. And she *is* mine, at least for the moment. My unplanned, never would've thought it, deep dark secret.

Sharon Mackie. For ten years she's been on the sidelines, a face in a photo, hardly real, and suddenly she's the realest thing I know. Even when she's not with me I can taste her salty citrus flavour. I can feel her hips press into me. I can see her slip off her clothes, shy, like she's not used to showing her body, and at the same time daring; her eyes stay on mine, sure and on fire. Her face warms mine, her skin forces me to touch it, I hear her whisper, like she's afraid to say it, that I should go inside her. I think of her, I say her name, and she appears in all her beauty. Not a photo or a dream. Real, even when she's not there. A connection with life, my first in a long time. A step back from death.

It's kind of pathetic, all these feelings fermenting inside me and bubbling up whether I like it or not. I catch myself thinking stuff out of a schmaltzy Hallmark card and I can't believe it's me. The King of Flings, my dad has called me since my twenties. What the hell is going on? I don't know, except that it's deeply weird.

Two whole weeks we've been together. Time is doing some weird shit too. I've lost the ability to measure it. We say hello, we kiss, we have sex, we talk. We sleep, wake up, go at it again. We drink something, share an orange, go back to bed. The clock moves, the light through the bedroom window changes, showing and then hiding the clutter of papers and files, but the only thing that matters is me and her. When we're apart, like now, all I do is remember being with her, touching her skin, putting my nose in her hair.

Fifty bucks says The Counsellor, if I was still going to her, would tell me it's not healthy. How can it be? I can't focus. I can't get anything done. My apartment's filthy. My body aches from too much sex and too much lying in bed. When I'm vertical nothing works the way it should. I keep walking into furniture and tripping on stairs. In the basement this morning I lost two quarters under the washing machine trying to fit them into the coin slot. Thank God fire season's over. I'd be useless in the cockpit. Worse – dangerous.

You'd think I never got laid before. I mean, I'm no Andy, but there have been a lot. I lost count years ago. But none of them ... well, to roll out the old cliché, it never felt like this before.

It could be the sex, which is mind-blowing and addictive, in a category all its own. I can't remember when I wanted it this bad. We're in the middle of doing it, I'm in her and about to let go and already I'm thinking about the next time and how it can't happen soon enough. Sex is part of it, for sure, but if I listen to my gut – pull out my innards, strew them around, and read what they say – it always comes back to Sharon. The girls I've been with have been beautiful and sexy and usually sweet, but nearly all of them have been girls, even the ones the same age as me. Sharon is a woman. She's grown up. Complicated, sad, impossible to sum up. I want to be with her all day, to listen to every word she says and talk about stuff I never have. I keep waiting for the voice that tells me to take off for a while, be on my own turf with a book and a beer, maybe visit my dad, but that voice never speaks. I'm only home today because I've got no clean clothes and Sharon insisted on going to yoga and the grocery store.

I do things with her that are embarrassing. I hold her face in my hands, gently, like it's glass. After she falls asleep I pull the covers over her shoulders to make sure she's warm. I watch her dream sometimes, her eyes moving around under the lids, and I hope she's picturing something exciting or happy. Then I worry that she's not.

I think of all the tears she must've cried. Does she dream about Rafe? Does she remember him while she's kissing me? Does she feel guilty about what we're doing? The questions whirl in my mind and I'm afraid to ask them. Afraid of the answers, hers and mine.

We haven't talked about Rafe since our first night together, the night I lost it. We will eventually, we'll have to, just not now. And yet he's always with us. How can he not be? She was his, and he was hers, and he was my friend, though in death he's become much more than that.

The weight of what he asked me to do hits me hardest those times when Sharon turns melancholy and retreats into herself. Then it feels like my sole purpose in life is to rub out her grief and make her smile again, not just for her sake but for Rafe's. *Look after her,* he wrote. God knows, he didn't mean this. But now that it's happened, there's no going back. I will look after her. I'll do it any way I can.

No one knows about Sharon and me. Andy, if I told him, would wet his boxers laughing, then make a big deal about her being older and offer to set me up with some young hottie, maybe two, his answer to everything. He would completely miss the point. My dad would be the opposite. He'd go all doe-eyed and haul me out ring shopping before our coffee had time to cool. Two days later he'd have picked out names for the grandkids he's been hankering for since dawn broke on my thirtieth birthday. I don't get him, my dad. Love shattered him, yet he still believes in it.

So as wrong as it feels to hide it, almost like a lie, Sharon is my secret, at least for now. Even the photo she gave me after I admired it on her bookshelf is hidden away in my closet, in the fireproof box that holds a few school souvenirs and some belongings of my mom's.

And the letter. The biggest secret of all. The one I never asked for, the one that's mine for life.

∧ ∨ ∧

IT'S IRONIC FOR SOMEONE whose job is protection to have zero experience protecting an individual person. That's never been my role. I'm no one's parent or guardian, not a teacher or advisor or a leader of any kind. Yet here I am, keeping watch over Sharon, shielding her from the full story of Rafe's death and from the story of his affair.

Sharon has barely mentioned her marriage beyond a few comments the first time I was at her place, but it's obvious that she's in the dark about Nathalie Girard. There's been no sign of the anger or bitterness she'd feel if she knew Rafe had been cheating on her, so I'm guessing he kept the whole business to himself, the way he walled off the other upsetting parts of life. Somehow that bastard Lyndon knew, and shoved his knowledge in my face that day at the TSB, wreckage all around us. He'd have sniffed it out in some sleazy way, following them to motels or peeping through windows or whatever. Jeff knew too, as I eventually learned, and so did Tucker, but being the bosses they were obliged under the circumstances to keep the relationship quiet.

I will not be the one to tell her. What would I say, anyhow? That Rafe dumped her for some nymphette turned psychotic accuser? Hardly. I will not destroy Sharon's memory of the man she loved for half her life. He's dead and Nathalie has gone and taken her lies with her, and the whole episode is history. Better that Sharon remember Rafe as he really was, an adoring husband who got confused for a time but in the end was coming home to her.

Besides which, no one, certainly not me, knows what really went on between Rafe and Nathalie. How much of their so-called affair was fact, how much fiction? From the little I could squeeze out of Jeff, at least some of it was pure fabrication on the part of that scheming bitch. She was out for revenge and she lashed out like a cornered scorpion. Public sentiment these days has it that women never lie when it comes to how men treat them. Bullshit. Women are people. And people lie — all the time, about everything.

What was Rafe thinking, especially when he had a woman like Sharon? I still can't answer that. It's obvious he had no idea what he was getting into, who the real Nathalie Girard was under that tempting surface, but the bigger question is, why did he stray at all? Rafe was straight as an arrow and loved his wife fiercely. He looked around, I mean God, we all do if we've got functioning eyesight, but he never touched. The Rafe I knew would never intentionally hurt Sharon. I know that.

The Rafe I knew. No sooner do I think it than I realize what a joke it is. My firefighting partner, my mentor, my closest friend — that god-damned letter taught me that I didn't know the real Rafe any more than he knew the real Nathalie.

The Rafe I knew was ... what? At best an edited version of himself that accentuated the good parts, the parts he chose to reveal. At worst, some kind of tall tale that skipped over whole sections of his life.

I think of the letter, folded away in the box in the closet. My box of secrets.

The urge to tell is, like the memory of Rafe, always with me. Hiding the truth is the same as lying, no matter how much noble reasoning you dress it up in. My lie sits like a stone inside me, heavy and unnatural and begging to be passed. Occasionally if I'm sleep-deprived or under the influence, I imagine telling Melody. She may be an organic pain in the ass, but she's the most open-minded person I know. She would listen, she wouldn't judge, and she might, just might, understand, which is more than I've been able to do.

It's pure fantasy to imagine confessing like that. Just a way of venting the pressure. Because I can never tell. He underlined that in the letter, not that he needed to. Rafe had me pegged. In the air I was the bird dog; it was me who guided him. On the ground it was the other way around. He knew I would do whatever he asked, no matter what the cost.

So every time the urge to tell flares up, I fight it back. It's my duty to keep his secret. It's my job to guard the letter and the truths it contains: his love, his despair, his instructions. I failed Rafe Mackie in so many ways. I will not fail him in this.

TWENTY-EIGHT

August

MONDAY MORNING, SEVEN SHARP. Nathalie's clock radio clicked on to the all-news station. Gang-related shooting at a Surrey nightclub. International child porn ring with ties to Vancouver. High-school soccer coach convicted of sexual assault, the victim a female student he claimed to love. Indigenous man knifed by an unknown assailant outside an East Van ice cream shop.

Life beyond the condo is a series of hazards, Nathalie thought. Why voluntarily enter it? With weeks of unused sick leave coming to her — *merci encore* for the good genes, Mémère — she weighed the options. At home: a summer shower spattering the windows, the cocoon of sleep beckoning. At work: errors committed and consequences awaiting. However, calling in sick would mean speaking to Tucker, or at least leaving him a message, and he'd know she was faking it before her first sentence was formed.

Tucker the Fucker. There was no escaping him. Whenever she did show up at work, whether it was this morning or days later, there he'd be, tongue sharpened, waiting to eviscerate her for nosing around in the Tracker investigation. Because there wasn't the slightest chance Lyndon would keep Friday's revelations to himself.

She'd spent the weekend in a state of dread, expecting the boss's chilly call at any minute. She distracted herself as much as possible, shopping for clothes she didn't need and strolling aimlessly downtown, her cell phone on the entire time as per TSB policy. Sunday afternoon, when she found herself at a magazine stand flipping through a quinoa cookbook, she had to admit she was simply biding her time. Tucker was going to nail her and the whole sorry mess would spew out, the highly anticipated sequel to the Cessna 172 case, a fiasco starring her as the incompetent idiot. No one would care why Will took his information to her instead of Lyndon or Roy, namely their ham-fisted interrogation. No one would question why the two Tracker investigators had failed to identify and pursue the trim question themselves. It wasn't a stretch to call those two incompetent, but because they were the TSB's most senior staff — senior *male* staff — they were beyond rebuke. Tucker's hit list would continue to feature only one name: hers. She knew it and so did her stomach, which heaved and seethed as she showered, dressed, and entertained then rejected thoughts of breakfast.

On the way to work, out of habit more than appetite, she stopped at Starbucks for her usual tall non-fat latte. Two sips in, she tossed the battery-acid drink into the disposal bin at the counter. Beside her a lurching, booze-drenched woman set down an empty super-size cup, filled it to the brim with half-and-half from the communal thermos, and added a sprinkle of cinnamon. Nathalie marvelled at the open theft. People are shit, she thought.

At the TSB the early-morning contingent, namely every air investigator besides her, was present according to the in/out board. Luanne, enthroned at central command, barely grunted. Great, Nathalie thought. Let the fun begin.

She'd been at her desk ten minutes, long enough to boot up the computer and watch dozens of emails pour in — including one from Jake, she noted greedily — before Tucker materialized.

"In my office," he said, and was gone.

She took what might be her last controlled breath for a while, issued a quick plea for leniency, to whom she wasn't sure — God? Mémère? any benevolent spirit that might be listening — and smoothed the creases from her summer skirt before heading down the hall.

Tucker wasted no time. "This is a full-on, hundred percent snafu you've gotten us into. You're going to sit there and give me straight answers. Why don't we start with what the hell possessed you to contact the main witness in the Tracker crash."

"He contacted me."

Tucker waved one hand. "Semantics. Why have you been talking to him?"

"Like I said, *he* got in touch with *me*. He phoned me after his interview with Lyndon and Roy. They leaned on him so hard he decided he was done with them. He said he had information on a possible mechanical issue with the Tracker. I tried to explain that I wasn't involved and he needed to tell the others, but he wouldn't listen."

"You tried."

"Yeah, but he insisted. Said there was no way he'd talk to those two again. What was I supposed to do? Tell him thanks but no thanks, take your possibly critical information and eff off?"

"You could have come to me."

"How can I make this any clearer?" She paused, reminding herself to stay in control. "He was ready to talk right then and there. You know as well as I do you've gotta take advantage of that. You wait a day or two and they'll clam up."

"So you take the initial statement and then bring it to me. Or better yet, go to the investigators I have authorized to work on the case. There is no excuse for interviewing someone else's witness, and there is particularly no excuse for keeping critical details to yourself. Especially, *especially* when you've been ordered to stay out of it."

Nathalie said nothing. It was the least incriminating reply she could think of.

Tucker pushed back his chair and went to the window. Through the glass Nathalie glimpsed the hood of her blue Miata, in its usual corner spot where no one could park next to her and ding the paint. Such a long time she'd saved to buy that car with cash — no loan payments, no interest rates. *Don't pay no one for the privilege of spending money,* Mémère used to say.

How would she begin to pay the interest on this, her latest fuck-up?

"I don't know what to do with you," Tucker said, still facing the window.

In his uncertainty she sensed an opening. "You're doing it, aren't you? I know I deserve a lecture. I'm prepared to take flak over this. I've apologized to Lyndon, he knows about the trim now, and he and Roy will take it from there. So that's the end for me. No more contact with Will, no more involvement with the Tracker. My hands are full with the R22 anyway. Speaking of which, you'll be glad to know I'm ready to go on the report. I got the evidence you wanted. Found marks inside the fuselage that prove the belts came off during flight. That's why the main rotor stopped."

Tucker whirled around, his face distorted with rage. "I don't give a shit about the R22. You have no idea what's going on here, do you?"

"Look, I said I'm sorry. Knowing Lyndon, he came to you supremely pissed off. He has a right to be. But in the end there's no harm done."

"Lyndon did not come to me."

"For God's sake, did he get Roy to do it? Roy wasn't even there —"

"I did not hear about your involvement from Lyndon or from Roy. I did not hear about it from any of my own people. I was treated to a phone call Saturday afternoon while golfing with my brother-in-law. Tenth hole, to be exact. It was none other than Jeff Montrose, ops manager at West Air."

"West Air?" Nathalie let this sink in. "Will went to his boss?"

"So it would seem. And his boss came to me."

Her thoughts moved sluggishly. Why did she throw away that coffee? "So Lyndon didn't ... he hasn't talked to you?"

"Not in person. Of course I phoned him right away to deliver the little bomb that Jeff dropped." Tucker returned to his chair, folded his hands on the desk. "Now you see what's going on, don't you."

Nathalie licked her lips. "I guess."

"Thanks to your reckless, your thoughtless ... *stupidity*, I don't know what else to call it, West Air is now questioning our entire investigation. The day the Tracker crashed I gave Jeff Montrose my word that you would in no way be involved, that only impartial investigators would work the case. Now he thinks I am a liar or a fool, I'm not sure which." He adjusted a silver paperweight, an art deco Mustang fighter that held down no papers. "He also believes you are intentionally burying evidence because you're afraid the bigger story will come out. His assessment is one I am inclined to agree with. Finally, he has decided that the TSB has mishandled this case to the point where any findings we come up with will be tainted. He is taking his concern directly to our board, as any competent manager would. All of which means we are fucked. I repeat, fucked. Not just you, or me. The lot of us."

"But Tucker." She had to make him see. "We haven't mishandled the case. We're not burying anything. Lyndon and Roy will follow up on the trim issue. There's no reason to think they won't be thorough."

"That is not the point. It doesn't matter what any of us are doing, or will do. What matters is what you've already done and how it looks to anyone who scrutinizes our actions. Frankly, what it looks like is one giant cock-up."

"But we can explain —"

Tucker smashed his fist on the desk. "We can explain *nothing!*" His chair shot out behind him as he rose. "I am sick to death of you making excuses for your bone-headed judgment. You were involved with the dead pilot, for God's sake! Outside of work. To what degree I'm still not sure. Then the whole … entanglement turns sour, he is killed in a crash, and suddenly you're hiding vital details about what happened. How can we ever explain that? How can it look anything but suspicious?"

"But Tucker —"

"You have an axe to grind, Nathalie. You accused the man of sexual harassment. You of all people have a reason for wanting him to take the fall. If he can't be found guilty of treating you improperly, then by God he can be found responsible for destroying an aircraft and his own life in the process. You want this crash to look like pilot error and not some mechanical defect." He shook his head. "Believe me, I've had time to think it through. I've had two long days. So go ahead, tell me where I'm wrong."

This was happening too fast, she couldn't keep up. Stay in control, Scrapper. "God, where do I start? For one thing, no one outside your office knows about me and Rafe."

"Bing! Wrong. Lyndon knows. Will Werner knows. Jeff Montrose knows."

"Wait a minute! Lyndon doesn't know anything. He's only guessing. Same with Will, he's just repeating what he heard from Lyndon. As for Jeff, well, I imagine Will passed along Lyndon's version of events."

"Bing! Wrong again. Jeff Montrose has known for weeks."

Nathalie's stomach dropped. "What do you mean, weeks?"

"For weeks he has known about your fling or flirtation or abuse or inappropriate attention, whatever you're calling it today. And about your complaint."

"But I never made a complaint. Not officially."

"It doesn't matter. I had to let Jeff know."

"You *what*?" She gripped the arms of her chair. She must have misheard. Acid rose in her throat and she willed herself not to throw up. "You told Jeff at West Air? You told Rafe's boss?"

"I had to. You came to me with a serious accusation. I'm not allowed to sit on it. Government policy is clear. As a manager, I am responsible for ensuring that my staff work in an environment free from discrimination and harassment. If I learn that harassing behaviour is going on, or I suspect that it is, I am obligated to take action to stop it. Whether you like it or not." He sat back down behind his desk.

"Jesus Christ, Tucker!" The clenching in her stomach now grabbed her bladder. She desperately needed to pee. "I told you it was private. I didn't ask you to do anything, to take any so-called action. I was confused, I was scared. Rafe was pushing me to take our ... our relationship to the next level and I, well, I didn't want to. Then he started hounding me and threatening me. You know all this. But I never made an official complaint. Goddammit! I just needed someone to talk to." An innocent chat, that's all it was. To sow the seeds of her version.

"Nathalie Girard, don't you dare play innocent with me." Tucker stabbed his finger at her. "You knew precisely what you were doing.

You sat in that very chair and told me Rafe Mackie was sexually harassing you. Those are the exact words you used. They are the exact words I wrote in my notes after our meeting, and the exact words I used to tell Jeff Montrose that one of my employees had a complaint about his pilot."

"I can't believe it! You had no business telling him. I spoke to you in confidence and I have a right to privacy. Your precious policy is clear about that."

"The policy says that once I'm aware of a complaint, I am required to pursue it. But you're right. Because your complaint wasn't in writing yet, I couldn't tell Jeff which of my staff had raised the red flag. I didn't name you."

"Oh, that's big of you. For chrissakes, I'm the only woman here. Who else would accuse Rafe of sexual harassment? You as good as identified me."

"I did not. I was very careful not to specify the gender of the complainant. It could've been a man for all Jeff knew. Or Luanne. You like to think you're the only woman here, it comes in extremely handy whenever you think you're getting a raw deal, but you are not the only one."

"Luanne, right." She snorted. "Of course Jeff knew it was me. He'd know it in a heartbeat."

"When or how he determined it was you, I cannot say. But as Rafe's manager he had to be informed that a complaint was in the works. It's policy. Jeff had a chat with Rafe, told him what was brewing, told him to quit doing whatever it was that made you feel ... what did you call it? *Uncomfortable*." Tucker's upper lip curled.

Nathalie's fear switched to anger. "Don't you get snide with me." She pressed her legs together, fighting the urge to urinate. "He did make me uncomfortable. Like I told you, as soon as I ended it he started following me around and phoning me every couple of hours and sending me all these emails." Rafe knew?

"Oh, right, the emails. What happened to them, by the way? You were going to give me copies."

"I changed my mind. Like I just told you, I decided not to put in an official complaint. But that doesn't mean it didn't happen. Don't you go painting this as something I made up now that it's convenient for me to look bad. He was stalking me, he was threatening me. He was ..." She searched. "He was engaging in predatory behaviour. Jesus, he followed me to the gym and tried to make me leave with him. He shouted at me, grabbed me. There were witnesses." He *knew*?

"Right. I'm sure there were." Tucker leaned across his desk, hands knotted together so tightly the knuckles shone. "My point is, you have an indisputable reason for wanting Rafe Mackie to be blamed for this crash. You want to nail him, and Jeff knows it. At the moment he's the only one who knows it, but that won't be the case for long."

Her mind spun, a carousel of fears, not one of which she could properly grasp. Something was deeply, frighteningly wrong. Her brain didn't know it yet but her gut did. "What about Will and Lyndon?"

"As far as I'm aware, they know nothing about the complaint. They only know that you and Rafe were having an affair —"

"It was not an affair!" The need to pee was a desperate ache now. "How many times do I have to tell you? I put a stop to it before it got to that point, which is why he started coming after me. There was no consensual ... you know, no consummation."

"Okay then, they *believe* you and Rafe were having an affair. Be that as it may, they know there was something between you two that went, shall we say, beyond a work-related association. That in itself is enough to convince anyone that you've deliberately tampered with this investigation."

She stood up, ready to burst. "I will say it one last time. I haven't tampered with anything, and I'll tell that to Jeff Montrose and the board and anyone else who wants to know." She turned to go.

"Listen to me, Nathalie." Tucker's voice dropped. "You utter one word to Jeff or anyone else from West Air and I will slap a disciplinary action on you so fast you won't know what direction it came from. I mean it. You make any more trouble and I will throw the book at you. You will rue the day you ever got the brilliant idea to join the Transportation Safety Board."

Her back to Tucker, fighting to keep her posture straight, she left.

Fled to the washroom, pushed into the nearest stall, and without bothering to bolt the door, sank to the toilet and let go. As the torrent of urine left her body, her insides gave way.

How in God's name had it come to this? A private matter between Rafe and her now a sideshow of policies and publicity?

Four simple words, that's how. *I love you, Rafe.*

She said it to him, words she'd never spoken out loud before, words she would give anything to unsay. They were lying together, sweaty, on her bedroom floor. They hadn't even made it to the bed. He trained those gentle brown eyes on her as if the rest of the world didn't exist, and she knew that he saw her in a way she had never been seen before. He saw her all the way through, even the bad parts, and there were many, and he didn't even blink. Just looked and smiled.

I love you, Rafe. She said it without thinking. They were the truest words she'd ever spoken. They changed her life. Maybe changed the course of history.

In the silent stall she sat, head in hands, the white tiles gleaming beneath her feet. Rafe knew. He knew. It played on an endless loop as the implications sank in. He knew about the complaint, he went up in the air, and he crashed.

Two deep breaths, then three.

It was the trim. She spooled toilet paper off the roll. *Not my fault.* She had to believe that. It was mechanics that brought him down, not feelings.

Not my fault.

She would get through this. She always did.

She wiped herself and for a single delicious moment pretended the outcome had been different, that Rafe had wanted her as much as she'd wanted him, that he'd been willing to go all the way and choose her over his wife. That he'd gone public, made their relationship legitimate, declared to all who would listen that she was his. She imagined him waiting for her in the small, stylish condo she'd worked so hard to buy, waiting with a smile that said how proud he was of her, waiting with those penetrating eyes.

She shivered. She had wanted it all with Rafe, all the conventions she said she never cared about: love, marriage, a home. She had let herself go, goddammit. She knew better than that, she was Mémère's granddaughter after all, and she did it anyway. Now what was she left with? A disfigured, bloody spectre that appeared when she least expected it, and another colossal fuck-up she had no idea how to repair.

As the toilet flushed she looked down. The swirling water was light yellow, the discarded tissue unmarked.

A bloody spectre.

There was no blood.

Her dream of happiness ripped the rest of the way apart. No blood. How — ? When the hell did she last see blood?

Her stomach roiled as she worked to remember. She'd been expecting her period when she travelled to the R22 crash in mid-July and was glad it didn't come there, out in the field. It crossed her mind again in Victoria a month later, when she spent the night with Jake. And just last week she'd joked with Lyndon about PMS.

How could it not have occurred to her until now?

No, no, no!

Mémère, she pleaded silently. *Dis-moi* — what do I do now?

TWENTY-NINE

November

"**MY WORST FEAR IS THAT** I turn into that humming woman," Rachel says as she pulls on a lime-green cashmere sweater. "You know the type. She's always older, kind of precise and fussy. Always grey-haired, like she never clued in to what the hairdresser's for. She walks into a quiet public place like the ladies' room or a waiting area and she starts to hum. Not a song or anything, just this tuneless humming. This random string of notes."

Sharon plunks down on the wooden bench to zip up her leather boots. "I haven't the faintest idea what you're talking about."

Rachel gathers her glorious long hair to one side and rubs vigorously with a towel, a deity in the land of lockers. "Come on, you've heard them. They hum, all nervous and old-lady-like. To break the quiet or, I don't know, fill up the space. Maybe they're calming themselves down because they're suddenly at the centre of things." She finger-combs her hair into place.

Sharon stands up and adjusts the stretchy black skirt that hugs her thighs. "You think this is too short?"

"Hell, no. It's good to see you in something that doesn't look like it once held bulk vegetables." Rachel fastens a large pendant and shoves half a dozen silver bangles onto her wrist. "They're depressing, those women. It's like they're apologizing for being who they are. Saying sorry for being alone."

Sharon twists before the mirror in an attempt to check the back of her skirt, which ends many inches above her boot tops. "So that's what this is about. You're afraid of ending up alone."

"No!" Rachel says, affronted. "That's not it at all. I don't care if I'm alone. In fact, it's better if I am. I can do my own thing, on my own schedule. I like someone to keep me company now and again and not worry that he'll leave his shirt in my closet or rearrange my cutlery." She takes a grey-and-black cape from the locker, drapes it artfully over her shoulders. "It's just that if I do end up alone, I don't want to feel like I have to apologize for it."

"Oh, you think *I'm* afraid of being alone and that's why I'm doing this." Sharon should have recognized the elaborately veiled criticism. It's Rachel's specialty.

"No, you goof. It was just some random observation. Forget it."

Sharon knows that in Rachel's world very little is random. Twenty minutes ago, in the shower after Pump and Jump class, she told Rachel about Will. Not the lurid details, just the broad strokes, that they were spending time together in a more than platonic way. Trust Rachel to take your tender young confession and wring its neck. As they push through the double doors of the community centre into the cold November breeze, she tries again. "That's not what this is about, you know, this … thing between me and Will. It's not because I'm afraid of being alone."

"Girl, I never said that. Here, it's open." Rachel jabs the electronic key fob at her black Audi sedan. "Left Coast Café?"

Sharon sinks into the low-slung passenger seat, her skirt riding up under her butt — barely under — and wonders if her creaky hips are due to the pelvic lifts just inflicted on them or Will's vigorous thrusting last night. Over the past two weeks nearly every room in her house has been the site of some act or another of spontaneous, frenetic, achingly intimate sex. They have done it everywhere, it seems, on every surface and against most walls, roughly, tenderly, fiercely, lazily. Never in the master bedroom, though. And seldom in Will's apartment. He seems embarrassed by his untidy student-like quarters, despite her insistence that she doesn't mind. "It's like camping out," she declared one night as they lay sprawled on his mattress, his unzipped sleeping bag rucked down around their feet. Will's grimace told her how unreassuring the comment was. Since then they've been exclusively at her place. They sit on the sofa and talk, with intervals of what in school they called heavy petting, order in sushi or Greek, drink too much wine. They laugh and flirt, drawing out the inevitable until one of them can't bear it any longer, and then they finally, thoroughly, succumb.

Never before has she been so inhabited by lust. She wants Will from the moment he crosses her threshold until at last they start up, pulling at each other's clothes, pressing their bodies and faces together, speeding toward the prolonged, aching sweetness of satisfaction, after which, in no time, she wants him all over again.

Who is this insatiable woman, with her dirty talk and take-me ways? And where was this wantonness in recent years when it was needed, begged for, by her husband? She can't begin to understand, nor does she care. All she knows is that one look at Will, one sniff, one touch, awakens a gnawing hunger that grows with every feeding.

Now it is lunch she's hungry for. "I'm sick of the Left Coast. Let's go someplace different."

Rachel tries to exit the parking lot and gets stuck behind a left-turning SUV unwilling to venture into traffic no matter how lengthy the gaps. "Baby on Board" proclaims a yellow sticker on the vehicle's rear window.

"Moron on board is more like it," Rachel mutters as she lays on the horn. The SUV rolls forward half a foot, then jolts to a stop. Approaching them is a single car more than half a block away. Rachel honks again and the SUV leaps forward, then slows to a creep as it makes a wide left-hand turn, nearly cutting off the oncoming car. They glimpse a ponytailed blonde, vacant and slack-jawed, clutching the steering wheel.

"Lady, grow a brain!" Rachel yells. "Honestly. What is it about motherhood turns these women catatonic? Like Stepford wives." She peels onto the street ahead of a slow-moving contractor's van, then floors it and shoots up the hill. The back of Sharon's head is pinned to the headrest.

"Where're we going?" Rachel asks.

"Let's try a food truck downtown. I read about one by the art gallery that does soft tacos."

Rachel looks at her sideways. "O-*kay*. If you say so."

"What? You don't want to?"

"Sure I want to. But you have never, in all the years I've known you, wanted to eat outside. I can't talk you into the patio when it's mid-July and twenty-five degrees out."

"Don't be ridiculous. I like eating outside."

"Uh-huh. Name one time we've done it."

"Come on. We have."

"Name it."

"Well ... nothing comes to mind this second, but we must have. If not, it's just a coincidence. I don't have issues with eating outside."

"Okay, whatever." Rachel swings onto the Burrard Street Bridge and makes for downtown, the gunmetal grey of False Creek slipping by beneath. Ahead, green-glass highrises stretch like bar graphs from the city centre, forming a kind of maquette of the Coast Mountains, which line the horizon beyond. In the bike lane beside them cyclists in colourful jerseys whiz along, their helmeted heads like a line of advancing beetles. Sharon questions why so many require racing gear to pedal to the office or the park.

"This guy's getting to you."

"God!" She should have known Rachel wouldn't let it go. "Just because I want to have lunch at a food truck. They're all over the place. It's time we tried one."

"You never decide where we go to lunch. You always let me decide. I'm telling you, he's getting to you. The young ones have a way of doing that."

Sharon stifles her impatience. Why can't her friend simply be happy for her? "He's not that young. Just a few years' difference. Not like one of your barely legal boys."

"Hey, I've seen him and he is more boy than man."

"What do you mean, you've seen him? When?"

"I googled him while you were finishing in the shower. Saw his photo on the West Air site."

"Rachel, what is *with* you? I don't need you to check up on me."

Coming off the bridge, Rachel pulls out to pass a motorbike already doing well over the speed limit. When she replies it's as if Sharon hasn't spoken. "He's attractive enough if you like that polar-fleece, rock-climbing dude type of guy. But there's no getting around that there's a thirty in his age. For you, that's young."

Sharon's temper flares. There's a thirty in Rachel's age too, at least for a few more months, yet she's never commented on the five scant years that separate them, has always treated Sharon like a contemporary. Why the sudden emphasis on age? She scrutinizes her friend, who is impatiently eyeing the traffic which has come to a halt at Davie. Pairs of men cross the street, some holding hands. An idea dawns.

"Rachel Zarya, you're jealous. That's why you're acting all high and mighty."

"Okay, now you're making shit up. It's only ..." Rachel inches up and up to the bumper of the car ahead of her even though the light is still red. "You just ..." Sharon waits. A professional communicator, Rachel is unable to leave a thought unfinished. Finally, as the cars crawl forward, she spits it out. "I just hope you're being careful, that's all. Taking it easy. This is happening really fast. It's only been a few months since Rafe, and I know you. You're still hurting. I'm not sure you're ready for this."

Rachel's unshakeable righteousness makes her both a lively friend and a supercilious pain in the ass. Sharon tries to check her annoyance. "I do know what I'm doing. As you pointed out, I'm so much *older*. One perk of which is being wiser."

"I'm serious." They stop at another red light, abreast a rumbling sports car that hugs the street even lower than the Audi. With a practised glance out the side window, Rachel assesses the driver, a smooth-skinned, crewcut guy in his twenties. "Not bad." Once she has his attention she smiles, arches her eyebrows. The light changes and she takes off half a beat before he does, then cuts into the lane in front of him. "Right where I can see you, baby." She adjusts the rear-view mirror.

Sharon is not finished. "You don't have a monopoly on this stuff, you know. You're not the only one who gets to have sex with no strings." Rachel has really gotten to her. "It's not like we're moving in together. It's just physical. He's fun to spend time with. It's just fun."

"Fun." Rachel looks dubious. "Fun is seeing whether Ahmed here follows us in his Ferrari all the way to the food truck. Fun is finding out whether he can say anything intelligent or unpredictable enough to earn my phone number." Rachel turns right on Georgia, the low-slung sports car close behind. "Fun is seducing him, screwing him in enough ways to give him a whole new outlook on the older woman, and moving on."

Sharon gazes at the teeming sidewalk. "Catch and release."

"That's what I'm talking about. You, on the other hand, are a loyal, monogamous woman who has just lost her husband of many years. You don't know how to fish for fun. Or if you did at one point, you don't remember how. You don't even know how to pull on the hip waders." She turns right onto Howe and zips into a miraculously available parking spot. The Ferrari roars on ahead, but not before the driver shoots Rachel a two-fingered salute and a dimpled smile. "Well, shit." Rachel gathers her bag and gloves. "The one that got away."

Sharon is reaching for the door when Rachel lays a hand on her arm. "Don't get hurt, okay? That's all I'm worried about. You don't need more hurt in your life." Her brown eyes shine, and Sharon knows she is sincere.

"Quit worrying about me. I'm a consenting adult. It's fine, it's all fine. Except I'm starving."

"Good. Me too."

"Fish tacos for the lady?" Sharon grins.

Rachel lets go the long, throaty laugh that has lassoed herds of unsuspecting men and that convinces Sharon, at least for now, that this story of casual fun she has told her friend is true.

THIRTY

Nineteen weeks after

NOVEMBER 29, A FRIDAY, a date to red-circle if I owned the kind of calendar you write on. It was yesterday but it feels like forever ago. Time's still moving in weird ways.

The morning stormed like a sonofabitch, gusts pitching rain against the building, huge spigots gushing off the balcony railings outside. I spent the day fall cleaning, if that's what you call it when you forget to do it in spring. I bagged up the trash and recycling. I scrubbed every dirty dish, even my toothbrush holder from the bathroom. I emptied the fridge, stacked magazines and books, ran the dirty clothes through the laundry, folded – sort of – the clean ones, and stowed the lot of them away. It felt good to get reacquainted with the coffee-table top, to see towels in squares instead of heaps, to sort the valuable crap from the junk.

Around noon came a sharp knock that had to be Melody – anyone else would buzz from downstairs – but the bowed, sniffling girl at the door, her slight frame wrapped in plaid pyjamas, bore no resemblance to my neighbour. Only the mop of hair springing from her twine-tied ponytail gave her away.

"Christ almighty, you look like shit. What's wrong with you?"

"Thanks. Nice to see you too." Melody did look miserable, nose red and eyes streaming, and she smelled funny, like a Chinese stir-fry. "It's just a cold."

I stepped back. "Well, don't give it to me."

"Fine, whatever. It's just been a while and I was wondering how you're doing. But never mind." She turned to leave, swabbing her nose with a balled-up tissue, and I noticed she was wearing puffy Bart Simpson slippers. Something in me melted.

"Okay, you can come in. But just for a minute. Sit over there." I indicated a camp chair in the farthest corner of the living room. "Wait. Go wash your hands first. Then you can sit down."

She shot me a look, all astounded, as if I'd asked her to fling snot onto the carpet. "What are you, some kind of public health Nazi?"

"I'm serious. I am *not* getting sick." I waited on the sofa while she busied herself in the bathroom. The water ran for a suspiciously short time, and she came out drying her hands on the legs of her wrinkled PJs, undoing any small good that had come from soap and water.

"Okay, Herr Hygiene. Now I can sit down?" She plunked into the camp chair, legs apart, yellow-and-brown Bart Simpsons thrust out. Despite the soap, the funny smell was still there. She sized up the living room, nodded at the mound of green and blue plastic bags destined for downstairs. "You're taking this cleaning thing kinda seriously. I never saw your place so neat." She ran her hands along the canvas arms of the camp chair. Fuck, I thought. Just sneeze in my face and get it over with.

"So you're off today," I said. "Fridays you usually work days, don't you?"

"Duh. I work retail, dude. No one wants to buy essential oils from a germ bag." She snuffled wetly. "I'm supposed to stay home until my nose stops running. This is, like, day two of mainlining garlic and ginseng and drinking ginger tea, and I am bored out of my freakin' skull. Two life lessons so far. One, daytime TV sucks. Two, even Instagram gets old." Picking at a loose thread on her flannel sleeve, she looked like an eight-year-old up past bedtime. "I keep thinking, what about the people who don't have a job? What do they do all day? Or people who are just, like, old?"

I spent two seconds pondering how to even begin to answer, then changed the subject. "I'd make you some tea or something, but I've gotta go out for groceries."

"Groceries? As in uncooked food supplies? Not takeout?"

"Well done. Excellent vocabulary for a girl who works retail."

She ignored the jibe and sat forward, eager for intel. "What's the occasion?"

"No occasion, just daily life. You know, a human being equals breakfast, lunch, and dinner, which equals groceries. A normal equation."

"Wow, it has been a while." Melody's eyes had gone big, intensifying the little-girl look. "Last time I was here you were licking the crumbs out of Doritos bags and scrounging old pizza crusts." She eased one foot out of Bart Simpson's face. "You back to your old self, then?"

This was it, my chance to tell someone about Sharon. I was dying to say her name out loud, to admit that I was actually involved for once, not just going out or hooking up. Yet some instinct told me to keep it to myself a little longer.

"Yeah, things are better. I'm trying to get out there, socialize more. Guess it's working."

"I'll say." She studied me. "You look like a guy with a fixed address again. That marginalized person thing you had going on wasn't doing you any favours. Your income must be taking a hit, though. No one offering you spare change anymore."

"Wait. Stop. I'm, like, hurting from the laughter. Inside, where you can't see it."

"Jerk." Melody grinned. "Seriously, it's good to see you doing better. You had me worried for a while there. I didn't know if I should stage an intervention or what. Now you're just a regular asshole. I guess my work is done and I can go home." She headed to the door, slippers slapping the floor, then stopped. "Will?"

Tell her, I thought. There's nothing to be embarrassed about.

"Pick me up a pint of Chunky Monkey at the store?"

"Sure." I couldn't do it, didn't know how to say it.

"And Will?"

"Yeah?"

"She's pretty. You look good together."

"Huh?"

"The woman you've been seeing." She sniffled. "C'mon, I've got eyes. And ears. I know what all this" — she waved at the neat apartment — "is about."

My face went hot. "She's ... she's a friend."

"Not a friend."

"She is!"

"Nope. You're in love with her."

"What are you talking about? What would you know about it?"

She smiled. Melody has a pretty smile. I never noticed before. "I just know." She tapped her temple.

My throat was dry, probably the onset of Melody's cold. I swallowed hard. "Sharon," I said. "Her name is Sharon."

∧ ∨ ∧

LATER, WHEN I GOT BACK from shopping and tapped on Melody's door, there was no answer. Sleeping, I guessed, or earbuds in. The ice cream would keep, especially now that my freezer was cleared of unidentified frost-burned lumps.

I unpacked the groceries, lined up two bottles of red wine and a baguette on the shiny kitchen counter, and arranged bananas, oranges, and two ripe avocados in a glass bowl I'd found at the back of a cupboard. I was pleased with the effect. A neat kitchen with real food in it looked pretty damn fine.

I took the biggest shopping bag into the bedroom and pulled out a thick burgundy duvet, which settled on the bed like a cloud. My old green sleeping bag, lumpy and stained as a dog's blanket, had gone out with the trash, along with the foam slabs that for seven or eight years had propped up my head. On top of the duvet I arranged the two puffiest down pillows the bedding store had in stock, so fat they barely fit inside the just-washed cases. Then the finishing touch: a low yellow candle on a pewter base that was in the store's front window. The woman was reluctant to sell it — it was the only one they had — but channelling Andy I leaned in and told her, my voice all seductive, that it was for a very special occasion with a very special lady. She nodded, unfazed by the cheesiness, and added the items to the already sizeable bill.

Taking in the transformed room, I concluded it was the best five hundred bucks I'd ever spent.

Sharon thought so too when she stepped into the bedroom hours later. This was after the homemade guacamole and margaritas, and the baked chicken and vegetables. Sharon was dumbfounded I could cook. It was also after the half game of Scrabble we played while putting away a second bottle of wine, and after the flirting and touching that took over when neither of us could figure out a good word to play.

"Oh, Will. It's lovely." I'd made her stay in the living room while I lit the candle beside the bed, wanting everything perfect. The flickering light shrank the room to a warm, safe hideout on a blustery night. "Really lovely," she repeated as she kissed her way down my neck.

I lightly traced her breast through her blouse. "I wanted to surprise you. You deserve better than Sally Ann castoffs."

"You're sweet." She pushed one hand inside the waistband of my jeans and ran the other down my bare chest. She'd unbuttoned my shirt in the other room, making a joke about strip Scrabble. I shivered at her touch. "Am I tickling you?" She tongued my earlobe. "That's very bad of me, teasing you like that."

"I'm a big boy. I can take it." My voice came out strangled, perhaps in sympathy with my cock, which strained mightily to escape the denim.

"You certainly *are* a big boy." She rubbed her hand up and down. "Very big. Big enough to take this." Before I knew it I was on the bed, pushed onto my stomach. Sharon lay on top of me and worked her hand underneath to stroke the bulge that now pressed painfully against my jeans and into the bed. She wriggled, grinding into me. It was delicious and frustrating all at once.

"God, Sharon. Take my pants off."

"No."

Somehow she had worked her hand way down my jeans and was brushing the head of my cock, which had popped out the top of my underwear. It was making me crazy and I pushed my hips into the bed, bearing down on her hand. "C'mon. Take them off."

"No."

She palmed the back of my head and held me down, my face buried in the mattress. I moaned, most of the sound swallowed by the duvet. "Then let me get inside you."

She bent down over my ear, her hair fanning across the back of my neck. "No."

I tried to flip onto my back, but she was surprisingly strong and kept me pinned. The new duvet pressed into my nostrils. It smelled of plastic packaging.

My patience for this game was over. I didn't like it, I wanted free, yet my hips, with an agenda of their own, kept writhing. "For fuck's sake. I can't hold out much longer."

"Then don't." Her lips were feathers on my ear, and her fingers — Christ, her fingers were playing with me lightly but gripping me hard at the same time, driving me wild, driving me to the edge.

And then over.

I groaned and my hips bucked hard. I must have crushed her hand, but I didn't give a shit. She had orchestrated this and she could fucking well take the consequences.

Half a minute passed. My heart thudded, my mind reeled. "Goddamn," I said finally, my voice husky. "You made me come in my pants."

"Don't go blaming me," she said in a little-girl voice. "It's not my fault you can't control yourself."

A jerk of my torso and I flipped onto my back at last. Sharon slid off me and stretched out on the bed. A pool of slime greased my belly, and with it came a surge of shame — the same shame I'd felt as a boy waking up from my first wet dream, the same guilt that stabbed me at fourteen when in the closet at a friend's party Sheila Hauser felt me up and I exploded, my jeans blooming with a stain that made her tease me for peeing myself. Now I'm a grown man. Such degradations should be way behind me.

I turned away from Sharon and curled up on my side, a mood settling over me. When she touched my hair, I flinched.

"Will. What is it?"

I didn't answer.

"Come on. I was only playing with you." A soft laugh. "Literally."

There was no reason to feel ashamed and yet I did, like I'd been caught naked in public, performing some dirty, perverted act. Why? I've never been embarrassed about anything we said or did together. Sharon has only been kind and accepting of me, and God knows she's seen me at my worst. What's with the boundaries now? If I can't show her everything, what's the point?

As if acute embarrassment wasn't enough, my eyes watered up.

"Will, talk to me. What's going on?" Her voice, soft and consoling, undid me. My shoulders trembled and soon my whole body. I couldn't make it stop. She pulled in close, spooning me from behind. "Will, I'm sorry. I thought — you seemed like you were enjoying it. Did I hurt you?"

I shook my head.

"Then what?"

There was nothing to say. Still, a day later, I can't explain why I was so upset. I only know that losing control like that, being so completely in her hands, did something to me. I felt pulled open, exposed in a way I never have before. It was like being in freefall.

Gradually, with Sharon curled against me, her arm loosely around my waist, I relaxed. The new duvet cushioned my cheek. The candle burned on the night table, hot and steady, and I let the flame hypnotize me. After a time I turned onto my back and ventured a sidelong look. Her face was puckered with worry. "Will, I feel terrible. What I was doing, I didn't realize you didn't like it." She stroked my arm. "I shouldn't have."

My index finger on her lips shushed her. "No. It's not what we did." I moved my finger across her mouth, feeling her breath. "Not that."

"Then what?"

I drank her in, this woman like no other. This woman who turned me inside out and accepted, unflinching, all the slop that came out.

She terrified me.

I traced the lines of her brows. "I think I'm in love with you."

She didn't look away.

As I touched her face, I understood both the steel and the gentleness of her, braided into the strongest of lifelines. And when she kissed me, I knew that if I went under, she would pull me back up.

THIRTY-ONE

August

BAD CAN ALWAYS GET WORSE, Mémère used to say. She said it when the Manitoba storms robbed them of power and reduced their world to six feet of warmth around the woodstove. She said it when Nathalie came home in fifth grade sobbing because she got only four Valentines, including the two that every child received from the teacher and the principal. She said it repeatedly when the bank took away her home, the four-room bungalow on three acres of wind-blasted prairie complete with dirt driveway, tarped woodpile, and caved-in doghouse that held no dog, not since the puppy Nathalie got on her tenth birthday was run over.

Nathalie was sixteen when they lost the house, mortgaged years earlier by her grandmother in a last-ditch attempt to amalgamate the small but pressing debts that had mounted since she took the girl in a decade earlier. Nathalie's carefree parents, married just seven years, believing in a long life of children and earning ahead, had left no insurance policy when they died, no T-bills squirrelled away, not even a shoebox of tens and twenties under the bed. Mémère had searched everywhere for capital to fund the unexpected acquisition of a child, but there was none to be had. The girl arrived without assets or prospects, and with few natural attributes, as her grandmother reminded her when some forgotten chore or lacklustre report card tugged the old woman's jowls into a frown.

Bad can always get worse. Uncle Theo took them then, installing them in the two basement rooms his sons had vacated for the Alberta oilfields. Theo's wife was none too keen on her mother-in-law and teen-aged niece crowding in under her roof, but imperious Theo, his mother's son through and through, collected every ounce of will that he could not exert over Mémère and poured it onto his wife. She had no choice but to swallow her resentment, which she did, burping the noxious gas into Nathalie's face until the girl finished high school and retraced her cousins' escape from the dank Manitoba basement to the open skies of Alberta. Mémère, with no future but the one she was in, lived off her son's charity until Nathalie got her first aviation job and bought her the mobile home. In the kingdom of the trailer park the old woman lived out her days surrounded by snot-nosed kids and welfare bums, as she liked to remind her granddaughter. It was one dig in a rich litany of complaints: too cold in winter, too hot in summer, no such thing as privacy, ever short on space. But at least Mémère lived independently, no more answering to Theo or appeasing his wife. It was the best home Nathalie could make for the woman who had housed her.

Bad can always get worse. Tucking a tailored white blouse into her slim grey skirt, adding a violet-and-green scarf to suggest cheer, Nathalie told herself that even though she was on Tucker's shit list, not to mention Lyndon's and no doubt Roy's, she was dressing in her own one-bedroom condo, bought and paid for (or at least mortgaged) by herself, an apartment outfitted with tasteful furniture and a designer bathroom. She would shortly depart for a secure government job which offered superior pay and benefits, which she was fully qualified for, and which, when she wasn't fucking up, she adored. As for the other business, the waistband of her skirt felt no tighter and her figure in the full-length mirror looked trim as ever. That was the least of her worries, the easiest fuck-up to correct.

Again this morning she'd debated calling in sick, but skipping work after the big blowup would be pointless. Tucker would see through her in a second. Better to show up on time, unruffled by yesterday's fireworks – though unruffled would take some doing, said her raccoon eyes and mottled complexion. Last night she fretted for hours, finding no comfort in her Egyptian cotton sheets or pillow-top mattress. He knew. No sooner did her mind empty than the words re-echoed: He knew. As the night wore on it settled, cold earth over a grave. He knew, and then he flew.

It was true, what she told Tucker: she never intended to lodge an official complaint against Rafe. Had she realized how quickly matters would escalate, she'd never have involved her boss in the first place. In the blistering days of early July, all she knew was that the situation with Rafe had come to a head and pre-emptive action was needed. *Better to hit than be hit:* Nathalie had lived by her grandmother's code ever since school made her into a scrapper. Whenever word of the affair leaked into the narrow world of aviation, so clean-cut and decent and starving for scandal, it had to portray Nathalie as the wronged party. Her public record contained enough fuck-ups. One more and her reputation would be beyond rescue.

Pre-emptive action meant shaping the story before it broke. It wouldn't take much. The broad narrative could remain. That she had flirted with Rafe, she would admit freely. What red-blooded straight woman wouldn't banter with a charming, attractive man? That she'd slept with him, she would vehemently deny. It was a lapse she deeply regretted, breaking her own rule about no affairs with men in her field. Better to pretend it never happened. It was better for Rafe, too, if nobody knew his desperation. She'd sensed his hunger when they first met at the Flying Boat, then confirmed it during the flirtatious tour of the Tracker. When she called him several days after that, accepting the invitation implicit in the business card he'd handed her, there was no denying his eagerness. One encounter led to another, a few supercharged coffees turned into an after-work beer at the Flying Boat, upgraded to cocktails in her living room, and at last, when his old-fashioned resolve finally cracked, the intense culmination in the Egyptian cotton.

That was the first plot twist: for a light-hearted man Rafe was deeply serious in bed. She should have guessed – he wavered so long before doing the deed – but his intensity caught her off guard. She was used to sex being sex, and if it came with a few laughs and the occasional compliment or gift, that was fine too. With Rafe there was more. A forcefield grew around what they did together; she aroused passions in a man renowned for self-control. It was unexpected. It was intoxicating.

Then came the second twist: she let herself go. For a few heady weeks she eased into the riptide and let it carry her toward a future in which she belonged to Rafe – chosen, adored, coveted, looked after. No more checking out guys at the gym. No more hours wasted on online dating. No more managing every detail – home, work, leisure, money – alone. The luxury of being cared for exerted a dangerous, irresistible pull. When Rafe left his wife, the future drew near. She envisioned them together, felt the texture of a shared life, heard whispered promises that no one had ever made to her. It was happening, the dream she had long disdained but now craved more than anything.

The third twist smashed them down. *I love you, Rafe.* One fragile moment and four simple words – a tiny slip that tore down the entire facade. Rafe's brown eyes no longer peered inside her; now they skittered away. His wedding ring remained on his finger, encircled by flesh too stubborn to budge, and he made it clear when pressed that it would stay. She reeled. All the intensity, the tenderness, the chivalry – was it only an act? Was he playing her, the arrogant bastard, just to prove he could land a bull's eye? Well, good luck with that. Nathalie was no one's runner-up, no matter how beguiling the dream. Life was short, and second-best was not her style.

Better to hit than be hit. She remembered, at age ten, reaching for Mémère's heavy braids and having her hand slapped. You're a big girl now, the woman said, too old for foolish fondling. Nathalie was no one's fool. She was tough. Tough as nails, as Jake teasingly reminded her. No one was going to hit her.

She ended it.

Rafe played dumb, his voice low yet determined in the bustle of the downtown brewpub. She'd chosen the place knowing he couldn't make a scene there, especially not that Friday, the onset of the July first long weekend, when pitchers of draft flew fast and laughter spilled from every table. It helped that Rafe couldn't drink now that fire season had him regularly on call. There would be no sloppy pleading, or so she hoped.

"Jesus, girl," he said when she was done. "Where did that come from? It's not over. I left my wife to be with you."

"You left the house. You didn't really leave her. As you've made clear." Nathalie tossed back half her martini. "Your living arrangements seem to be for your own convenience, so you can fuck me every night and skip the guilty crawl home to the little woman."

Rafe flushed deeply and dropped his head, a bull prepared to charge. How unappealing, she thought, and how typical. How had she gotten so carried away? What possessed her to encourage this man, then bed him, then allow herself to be overcome by fantasies of him, when there were so many others out there, just as good-looking, just as randy, but effortless and uncomplicated? There were half a dozen prospects in this pub alone: young, unaccompanied, studly guys eyeballing every female under forty.

Rafe seized her wrist. "Look at me."

She looked and what she saw was a Neanderthal hunched over the table, brow furrowed, mouth angry, tangle of hairs climbing out his shirt neck. Like that it was gone. All she had felt for him. *Fini.*

His eyes bored into hers. "It is *not* over." He squeezed her wrist for emphasis.

"You're hurting me." She pulled her hand from his instantly loosened grip.

"Nathalie, you're going to have to explain this real slow, because I don't understand a word of what you're saying. Yesterday – hell, this morning – everything was fine. We laughed, we had great sex, I made you cinnamon toast for breakfast. And now, what" – he glanced at his watch – "ten hours later and it's over? That's foolish."

"I'm not a fool, and I don't have to explain myself to you. I've thought about it and I want out. Simple as that."

"Jumpin' Jesus, girl. What're you talking about? We got something good here."

"I told you, I don't need to explain. There's no future in this, so I want out."

Rafe looked at the ceiling. "Ah, Christ. So that's what this is about. You ask me this morning if I'm going to divorce my wife and I say it's not in the cards right now, and that's it? I mean, patience isn't your biggest virtue, no big secret there, but come on."

"I am not impatient. I'm done."

"All I said was it's too soon. It's only a couple of months since we got together and now it's fire season and I won't be around. It's the worst time to make big decisions, ones that'll change our lives." His giant head pushed closer. "You can understand that."

Nathalie leaned back. At the table kitty-corner to theirs, two guys in shirt sleeves and loosened ties were swigging beer and sliding their gaze her way.

Rafe's excuses could not have interested her less, yet he persisted. "I care about you, Nathalie. This isn't some friggin game. I've got feelings for you. And you do for me. I know you do. You told me."

I love you, Rafe. Whatever ungovernable impulse had made her say those words, she had squashed it flat. She sat still and said nothing, her response of choice when there was nothing left to say.

"This can't be your decision alone. We need to talk about it." He reached his hand across the table. "You woke me up, girl, made me feel alive again. Don't throw that away." His neediness was sickening. "Come on now, don't be like this. Just relax and be with me. Let me take care of you."

Take care of her? The one thing he'd made crystal clear he would not do? Her blood rose and she pushed back her chair, the legs scraping the adobe floor tiles. "You're wrong. It *is* my decision. I don't want to see you anymore and that's final." She grabbed her purse and stood up. All she wanted was out: out of this conversation, out of this pub, out of the sticky, dreamy web she'd let him spin around her. Take care of her? What was she, a child? Nathalie Girard took care of herself.

"Don't try to change my mind," she said. "And don't come around again. My time is precious and you're wasting it."

As she threaded her way between tables, bumping a chair in her hurry to reach the wide front doors, she felt all the eyes on her, sweeping her smooth legs, appraising her narrow waist and sleeveless dress, fantasizing about the shiny dark curls that cascaded over her bare shoulders. Behind her, the great Rafe Mackie grew smaller and smaller, fading into the crowd, no one's legend, no one's dream. Just another man.

∧ ∨ ∧

NATHALIE STOPPED FOR her usual latte on the way to work, upsizing to a grande and drinking every drop. She had to stay sharp today, and she'd need to avoid the kitchen coffee maker because she might run into Tucker. Job number one today was to steer clear of the boss. His anger was like Rafe's wildfires: it would burn bright, die down, then flare up again in unpredictable pockets before finally guttering out. Her only hope was to starve the flames by making herself scarce.

Job two was to mend fences with Lyndon and make sure he and Roy were looking into trim failure on the Tracker. Her sleepless night had pushed her to one certainty: the sooner they concluded that the Tracker crashed for mechanical reasons, the better. The alternative, that Rafe was upset to the point of bungling a routine manoeuvre, was unthinkable.

He knew, and then he flew.

It was unthinkable and so she would not think it. For the sake of all involved, including Rafe, whose memory merited some respect, she'd make sure no one else thought it either.

She ran into Lyndon immediately, and almost literally, pulling her Miata into the TSB lot just as he approached the front door. With a sneer, he leapt extravagantly to one side. Totally unnecessary, she thought, forgoing her usual faraway spot for the first space available. She girded herself for the treacherous mission of eating dirt that lay ahead and jumped out of the car.

"Lyndon! Wait up. I need to talk to you."

He turned partway, granting her his bulbous profile. Even from this distance she could see the put-upon expression that signalled full grievance mode.

She trotted over. "Got a minute?"

"No."

"C'mon, just a minute."

"I have no minutes for you at this time. I have things to do."

She put her hand on his arm, aware that her touch would keep him there. "I know you're mad at me. This won't take long, I promise. Just give me a second before you go in." She pulled at his sleeve, and after a moment's resistance he followed her to the cherry trees that separated the TSB lot from the industrial complex next door. The leaves filtered out the baking August sun that would land this summer in the record books.

"I know I am completely in the wrong," she began. "You should be pissed at me. But what matters is the investigation, getting to the bottom of why the Tracker would dip like that. You know as well as I do, an experienced pilot, routine flying, excellent conditions – it doesn't add up unless there's a mechanical issue. Will's information could be game-changing. Don't sit on it just because of, you know, the way it came to you."

For a long, unblinking moment Lyndon stared her down. "Are you done?"

"Don't be like that. Please." She reached again for his sleeve, but he stepped aside. She waited for a word or a look to suggest he was softening. None came. She nodded tiredly. "That's all."

Hands stiffly at his sides, Lyndon marched to their building and disappeared inside.

A light breeze rustled the leaves over Nathalie's head. *Bad can always get worse.* Worse than this? For the life of her she couldn't think how.

THIRTY-TWO

December

SHE JERKS AWAKE. What? What now?

The weight of Will's arm flung across her breasts. The dark of the spare room. Then the shrill ring that must have woken her. Will rustles, removes his arm, moans softly at the intrusion.

The readout of the clock radio hurts her eyes. Six ten. Panic flares as she picks up the land line, though not enough to chase the bleariness from her hello.

Silence on the other end, then: "Ah, shit. I always forget the time difference. You asleep?"

"Mm-hmm." She switches on the lamp and falls back onto her pillow, pulling up the covers against the early-morning cold. Her mouth feels sand-dry, too much wine consumed too late. Will props himself on one elbow, no doubt wondering who it is.

"Sorry, Sharon. I'm a stupid arse. Want me to call back later?"

"No, no. It's fine, Sheldon. I'm awake." Will lies back on his pillow, laces his hands behind his head. His spicy scent drifts over and from the corner of her eye she can see the hair of his underarm, the triangle of muscles around it, pulled taught. Desire knifes her, sudden and sharp. It doesn't care that she's barely awake and Rafe's brother is on the phone.

"I won't keep you," says Sheldon. "It's just the boys got themselves invited up to Quebec for Christmas. A friend of theirs from university days, family's got some kinda ski chalet up at Mont Tremblant if you can believe that. You know the boys. They're all fired up to go."

"Mmm. Sounds great." Sleep and lust take turns pulling at her.

"So Nancy and me, we're thinking, we don't wanna be on our own for Christmas. We got a whole whacka air miles saved up and if you can't come out here, then why don't we come out there?"

Her mind rushes, as much as it can in the pre-dawn. "Oh, well … sure. Okay."

"You wouldn't have to lift a finger, Share. We'll book a hotel, rent a car. Nancy'll take care of cooking the bird." There's mumbling in the background. "Yeah, or we can go out for dinner, whatever. Just it's been a long time and we'd sure like to see you. It's been some long."

Has it really been that long? The funeral was in late July — Sharon struggles to count — just over four months ago. Not long given that it's usually a year, even two, between visits with her in-laws. Yet she knows what Sheldon means. The past four months have stretched well beyond their calendar time.

Nancy's voice comes on the line. "Oh God, Sharon, our bad! We're morons to call so early. I keep forgetting it's four hours now that you're out on the coast. The math's not that hard, eh? Subtract four. You'd think we could do that. How's it going, anyhow?"

Sharon loves her sister-in-law but wonders if there is ever a time of day when she is not peppy. "Okay. Sleepy."

"I know, I know. Sorry. It's just that we're online right now looking at flights. There's not many we can get on points this late, but there's a couple. What do you think? Can we come?"

"Give her some time, woman. This isn't supposed to be some early-morning ambush. We'll call you back, Share. How's that?"

Later this morning she and Will leave for Whistler, a two-hour drive north that will transport them from coastal rain to winter wonderland. They've discussed it all week, how they'll wander around the snowy village, check out the high-end shops, stop for hot chocolate, maybe fondue. She doesn't want to spend the day deliberating over whether she's up for a family visit. "It's fine," she says, sounding certain. "Please come. It'll be wonderful to see you."

"Atta girl," Sheldon says. "We'll have a grand time."

"We can get there on the twenty-second," Nancy says. "Or else the night of the twenty-fourth. Not too many wanting to fly Christmas Eve, eh?"

"Any time is fine. Whenever you like."

"Let's go with the twenty-second. I'm booking it now, Sheldon."

Frenetic tapping begins on the other end. Now that it's done and she's committed, Sharon sinks further into the pillow. "For heaven's sake, don't book a hotel. There's plenty of room here."

"No, no, no," says Sheldon. "We don't want you going to any trouble. You don't need to be getting the place ready or having a bunch of people underfoot. Not this year."

There is silence on the line. The ways in which this Christmas will be unlike any other — it's been on Sharon's mind all fall. In October, when Sheldon and Nancy first invited her to spend the holidays with them, she'd dismissed the idea: Halifax would feel too foreign, too far outside her comfort zone. For the same reason she'd ruled out a cruise. It was bizarre to think of sailing away for Christmas, even though Colleen had offered to accompany her, horrified that her sister might spend the season alone on the high seas and unpersuaded by the argument that no one is alone on a cruise. Sharon knows that piling one alien experience on top of another at this time of year will only topple the precarious life she's constructed since summer. A visit from Sheldon and Nancy will be familiar, a glimmer of life as it used to be.

"I mean it," she says. "It's no trouble. I'd like it if you stayed here."

"If you're sure then," Sheldon says. "But you change your mind, just say the word. We'll do this whatever way's easiest for you."

Nancy pipes up. "And ... we're booked. Evening of the twenty-second. Be there in time for dinner."

"You go back to sleep now," says Sheldon. "We'll see you in a few weeks."

After saying goodbye she lies still a moment, eyes shut. His voice is not as deep as Rafe's and his Nova Scotia accent is thicker, but the cadence of Sheldon's speech is identical to his brother's. "You go back to sleep now." Rafe always said that when he had to work early. Then he'd lean over and kiss her forehead. "I'll love you all the day long." His own special farewell to her.

She misses him still, in spite of everything. It is a complicated ache.

The mattress shifts as Will leans over to take the phone from her and place it in its charger. He hovers but she's no longer ready. He must know: he returns to his side without touching her.

Eyes closed, she lets her mind drift. The last time she heard Sheldon's voice was over six weeks ago, mid-October, after the Transportation Safety Board released the draft report on the Tracker. As next of kin she'd received an early copy. Three times she read it and three times got the same message: the elevator trim may have malfunctioned and forced the plane down. Rafe's long experience was noted, as was his accident-free record. The report ruled out many factors – fatigue, alcohol, drugs, medical issues – and described the flight circuit as routine. There was no evidence to suggest that Rafe had done anything wrong. Pilot error was never mentioned.

At the end of her third read, the fear she had quietly nursed for months fell away. He was exonerated. He'd made no mistakes that fatal morning. No matter what his state of mind, he went up and performed his perilous job flawlessly, same as always. She stared at the slim report, which had arrived by courier, "Protected" stamped across the cover page. It wasn't me, she thought. I didn't kill him.

She went out to the side yard that October day, desperate for air, and steadied herself against the rough bark of the witch hazel. It was a fear she was barely conscious of harbouring, the fear that their separation and the upheaval it caused might have contributed to the crash. Even though they'd reconciled that day in the park, and a new start awaited them, she had made him work for it. She had made him beg. What does that do to a man's confidence? The question had lurked unasked at the back of her mind. Now, thank God, she had an answer.

One question the report did not address, however, at least not directly, was what precisely caused the crash. Her careful readings could not tease out an answer. The elevator trim *may have* malfunctioned. Did it or didn't it? If a trim problem didn't cause the crash, what did?

Doubt gnawed at her long enough that she finally emailed a scan of the report to Sheldon. She'd been cautioned not to share the draft, but he was family, she reasoned, and had as much right to the truth as she did — maybe more, having shared his younger brother's life from beginning to end.

He called the next day. "I see where you're coming from. It's a shifty bit of writing. The finessing that must've went into it. That's the feds for ya."

"What do you make of it?"

"Seems like they think the trim got stuck and forced his plane down."

"But they don't come out and say that was the cause."

"Well, they can't, now. At least that's how it looks to me. They only got the say-so of that witness, whoever it was Rafe talked to before takeoff, and that wouldn't be enough. They'd need some proper evidence to go further."

"So they haven't really come to a conclusion."

"You could say that. Or you could say there's lots of conclusions. There's lots of things they *haven't* named as the cause. They can't find anything wrong with the engines. They rule out the weather. They rule out visibility, seeing as how the fire wasn't massive and most of the smoke was underneath them, not around them. He had the right amount of fuel and retardant, so the weight and balance wasn't an issue. Doesn't seem he went against orders or made a bad decision, or did anything wrong at all. Way I see it, that says a lot right there. Those're all conclusions about what's not the cause."

"I take your point. But still ..."

"You wanna know for sure."

"Well, yes. Don't you?" In the background metallic clanging rang out, like cars smashing in a derby. "Everything all right there?"

"Oh, it's fine, it's all fine. That's just Aaron having conniptions in the kitchen. Him and his brother are supposed to be cooking dinner. At least I think that's what they're up to. For our anniversary."

"Sheldon! I completely forgot."

"No, no, no, don't you worry about that. It's not till next week anyways. Just this is the only time they can come over. They're like friggin CEOs or something, the two of them, between the jobs and the sports and the girlfriends and the gym and the I don't know what, they're booked up months ahead. I want a hand stacking firewood or putting up the storm windows, I gotta make an appointment for chrissakes."

"Dad! Quit exaggerating!" It was a rich baritone that boomed out, a man's voice. How long had it been since she'd talked to the boys? They flew out for the funeral, but did she speak to them? She must have, can't imagine ignoring them. Yet the memory was lost, like so much of that dreadful day.

Now she will make new memories by spending Christmas with Rafe's brother, in the rain, in her cramped townhouse, no rowdy boys underfoot to lighten the mood. She comes to. Glances over at Will, hands behind his head, eyes closed. Maybe asleep.

There will be one boy.

The realization lands slow and hard: Will. How does he fit into this holiday reunion? How can she explain that there is a man in her life, in her bed, mere months after the death of Sheldon's beloved brother? And not just any man — Rafe's flying partner. She cannot fathom it herself. How can she expect them to? She has made a mistake, a terrible mistake. Now it's too late. The flights are booked, the plans made. How could she have been so thoughtless? She flings one arm over her eyes as if to block out the morning's developments.

Will isn't asleep. He rolls over and taps her bent elbow. "Hey. Look at me."

She presses her arm tighter.

"You doing that hungover actress thing?" He pokes her side, trying to rouse her. "Should I bring you your diamond eye mask? No? Your little dog then? Poochie always makes you laugh."

She doesn't move, will not smile.

"A crust of toast? Dry toast, of course, never butter. Scotch on the rocks? No? How about that big blond gardener who's always raking out back with his shirt off?"

She can't help it; her mouth twitches.

"I saw that."

She shakes her head, keeping her arm in place.

"You smiled." He plucks her arm away and kisses her eyelids. "You can't help yourself. I am too hilarious to withstand."

She purses her lips and blows a jet of air into his face.

"What?"

"You said *withstand*."

"So?" His mouth grazes her jawline.

"So who ever says that? No one actually speaks that word out loud."

"Says who?"

"I've worked in libraries. I know these things."

"Mmm, the sexy librarian." He is kissing her neck now. "All quiet and bookish, then off come the glasses, down goes the hair, and boom, she's a hottie. She winks at you, then waves, and before you know it you're in." His tongue touches her earlobe.

"That's pretty fast. You sure you didn't skip a step or two in the whole seduction process?" She guides his head down to her breasts, still baffled by her unflagging desire and her new brazenness.

"Nah." He kisses one nipple, then the other. "Librarians are always ready to go."

He rolls on top of her and she feels his hardness pressing her. She parts her knees and in he slides, easy, effortless. He knows the way. Deep inside, in a place both intimate and foreign to her, a place she has never touched or seen, she feels every thrust, each one going farther than the last until she is sure he will push up through her throat, and she wants him to, wants some invisible part of her to rip open and let him, impossibly, all the way in. Never, ever, has she felt like this.

"Will," she breathes. "Spend Christmas here with me."

PART THREE
FLIGHT

THIRTY-THREE

Twenty-one weeks after

I'VE ALWAYS THOUGHT CHRISTMAS was overrated. Only now that it's fashionable to scoff at all the hype, the canned music, the dollar-store decorations, to disapprove of the excess packaging and the consumerism, I find myself kind of wishing I didn't. Who wants to be part of a trend?

The aversion goes way back. When I was a kid and my mom was still alive, it seemed that Christmas wound you up only to let you down. Mom always went big. She put aside her translation work for two weeks and dove right in, shopping, baking, sending cards, putting up lights, making wreaths, wrapping way too many presents, inviting people over for cider, taking gifts to neighbours and random people like her hairdresser. There was no such thing as too much. The closer we got to the big day, the more she stressed about getting it all done, and doing it all perfectly. Every detail had to be just so, like a translation, I guess. By the time Christmas Eve arrived, the three of us were worn out. It's like those store-bought birthday cakes you think you want, neon icing and candy sprinkles and your name on it, but then you get one and from the first bite it's too much, so sweet it's sickening.

After mom died, we didn't have the heart to do anything special. We had some pretty bleak Decembers, my dad and I. Mostly they involved ignoring the calendar as long as possible, usually until Christmas Eve, at which point my dad would mumble some apology for forgetting to put up a tree and I would say I didn't care. On Christmas Day we went to my aunt's, my dad's sister's, for turkey. Sitting at her table with a bunch of cousins and the occasional stray neighbour, we'd act like the people we used to be, warm, laughing people who loved our family and enjoyed trading stories over eggnog and shortbread, when what we really were were shells, the living matter sucked out of us, our casing still intact but so brittle that it would take one person, with one careless step, to crush us into powder.

Last night's West Air Christmas party took me back to those dismal years when the joy was fake and the smiles were forced, and the person who mattered most was the one who wasn't there.

This year Jeff chose the North Shore Lodge, a 1920s ski chalet turned conference centre in a wooded area at the base of the North Shore mountains. The place was decked out: pine boughs framing the windows, wreaths on every door, red candles and mistletoe and logs blazing in the eight-foot-high fireplace. Before dinner I wandered the dining room, mulled wine in hand, saying hi to guys I hadn't seen since September, hearing tales of scuba diving in Mexico, skiing in Banff, kitchen and bathroom renos, and, in the case of our youngest and newest pilot, a knifepoint mugging on a beach outside Cartagena. Over it all hung a thick sheet of artifice because of what we didn't talk about. Not one person mentioned Rafe.

I get it. It's a party, the wives and girlfriends are there, you want to keep it light. But for such a central person to be missing, a dynamic, attention-stealing person – well, his absence rang loud. To me, the crater he left behind far surpassed the physical space he'd occupied.

So I was relieved when at fifteen minutes to prime rib Ernie stumbled in, cheeks red from outside, black hair standing up like the bristles of a boot scraper. Every year Jeff invites the provincial air attack officers and every year they send their regrets, scattered around the province and a marginal part of our flying world as they tend to be. Ernie's the exception. Most years he uses the gathering to escape from Vernon, where his extended family goes a little nuts in the lead-up to the holidays, getting on each other's nerves and taking sides and breathing life into old resentments that lie dormant the rest of the year. Judging by his worn-out eyes, I figured this year was no different.

"Hey man, good to see you." I pointed at his hair. "Your new look?"

"Heh. Shit." He ran a hand over his head to smooth down the brush, which instantly returned to vertical. "Pain in the ass hair. One day I'm gonna give up and shave it all off." He beamed at me. "Good to see you, bro. Lookin' good."

"Doing what I can." I was more pulled together than usual, in a pale blue shirt and slim-fitting sports jacket that Sharon had helped me buy.

"Who you with?" It was the question I always got, and Ernie asked it the same way every guy did, looking not at me but all around, curious about the leggy beauty who should've been a few steps away awaiting an introduction.

This year I had no one to show. There was never any question of bringing Sharon. When the invitation came in mid-November, right after we got together, I considered not telling her but then realized how stupid that would be. She went to the West Air bash every Christmas; of course she knew there'd be one this year. So I gave her the when and where, but before I could frame the question she smiled and said, "You go and enjoy it." And that was the end of it.

"I'm on my own."

"Seriously?" Ernie went all wide-eyed, as if I'd said I brought a pony.

"What's with everyone? I'm not allowed to enjoy my own company once in a while?"

He shook his head slowly, his gaze somewhere in the region of my knees. Not much of an eye-contact man, our Ernie. "Oh-kay." He drew it out. "If you say so. But it'd be a first. Heh. Definitely a first."

"Screw you." I downed the last of the mulled wine, my third cup.

"Just sayin', you always get the ladies." He chuckled as he surveyed the festive decor. "Not like me, eh?"

"Christ almighty, not this again. I keep telling you, you'd get ladies if you ever talked to them. There's no accounting for the women who walk this earth, but they have a weird preference for men who say actual words to them, like, out loud. Silent guys who stand there staring at the floor, not so much."

"Heh, heh. You're a card." His smile split his wide face. "You should be dealt with."

"Come on, Leno. Let's get some seats." I steered him to a table where the new pilot, the one who'd been mugged, was settling himself and his shimmering girlfriend onto two of the six chairs. I figured the Colombian exploits of a guy who barely knew Rafe beat an evening of bullshit small talk with a bunch who did. Evidently no one else agreed, because the last two chairs at our table stayed empty.

The evening played out as these things do. We discussed the weather, then Colombia, then backpacking in South America, then surfing in Tofino (my meagre contribution). We ate salad, beef, Yorkshire pudding, mashed potatoes, peas. Slices of frozen Yule log topped with smashed raspberries. Ernie smiled a lot and offered the occasional schoolyard joke, every one of which collapsed the new pilot's girlfriend into giggles that brought tears to her sparkle-lidded eyes. I had to hand it to Ernie — he was *almost* talking to a woman. Granted, she wasn't an available woman, and he never spoke to her directly, but as the evening wore on and her laughter met with increasingly forced smiles from her boyfriend and me, it became clear the humour was for her benefit.

"Oh, God," she said, breathless after an especially energetic burst. "You are *too* funny. I have to visit the ladies' room before I pee myself."

She sauntered off, unsteady on her high heels, and her boyfriend quickly fled to the bar, where the server was cracking open the hard stuff. Ernie toyed with his unused wineglass while I beckoned the waitress over to top up mine. She obliged, throwing in a sweetly lopsided smile for good measure. I drank off a third of the glass, which, I might add, had been refilled an untold number of times. I briefly wondered how I'd get home now that driving was no longer an option.

"Thirsty, eh?" Ernie coughed up a brief version of his trademark cackle, but his eyes weren't laughing.

"What the hell. 'Tis the season."

The party's clamour closed around us. A peal of female laughter soared, then fell back into the general din. At least the women were having a fine time. Ernie twirled his wineglass some more and addressed the tablecloth. "So, how you doing?"

Another sip of tart red slid down my throat. "Pretty good, man, pretty good. Feeling no pain."

"No. I mean ... you know. Since summer."

I motioned for the waitress. Whether she'd been checking me out or had me pegged as the bottomless drinker in the crowd, I can't say, but she arrived instantly with the bottle. I got her hundred-watt smile before she resumed her post at the side of the room.

Ernie nodded at my full glass. "You're not driving tonight." It wasn't a question.

"No way, bro. I haven't completely lost it."

"Heh. Well, it's hard to tell. The end of the summer there, you had your moments, eh? Is it ... You good now?"

I drew a breath and hoped courage would tag along. Where to start? In the end it was easier to drink, so I did.

And there we sat, me and Ernie, side by side with the table as our cockpit. To the casual observer we'd have looked like two guys not talking. Two guys comfortable enough with each other to sit quietly, each in his own world, thinking about hockey or trucks or getting laid, or just taking in the surroundings. The casual observer would be wrong. There was an exchange happening between Ernie and me, just not out loud. I knew from the way he kept playing with that stupid wineglass and the way he wouldn't look up from the table that he was more keyed up than he was letting on, and that his questions about how I was doing were inquiries directed back at himself. I'm not Ernie's best buddy or anything, but it's not hard to tell when a guy's torn up inside and trying not to show it.

I drained the last of my wine, sour now. The hawk-eyed waitress caught my attention and held up the bottle, but I shook my head.

"How's things in Vernon? Your family spinning out because it's Christmas?"

Ernie's mouth pushed into a half-smile. "Same old same old. My ma, every year she gets out the credit cards, right? Blows way too much on presents. I keep telling her, you don't have to go all out like that. It takes her half the next year to pay the bills, you know? Then she takes a cab all the way down to Kelowna. A cab. Won't let me drive her, won't ride with our neighbour who's going anyhow. Spends the whole day shopping for stuff nobody needs, drops a bundle at the Costco, buys a shitload of fancy groceries from some deli when we'd rather eat her cooking anyway. It's too much. Good money gone, just like that." He shakes his head wearily.

"My mom was the same. Christmas was like ... there was no such thing as too much. Maybe it's a mom thing."

Ernie shrugged.

"What about you?" I ask. "Anything new?"

"Naw. Work's the same. Wintertime, it's pretty quiet for us. Lots of paperwork, too many bullshit meetings. Government, eh?" He shifted his bulk on the chair. Ernie's a big fellow, a serious gut on him for a forty-something, but every inch is solid. I never understand how some bellies are soft fat and others are hard. Ernie's is the second type. You could belay off that thing.

"Sleeping, that's not going so great," he said after a bit. "I fall asleep okay, but then I get up to take a leak and I'm wide awake. Just lay there, mind won't shut off. You know?"

The new pilot from our table was still at the bar, in a knot of others who looked relieved to be on their feet.

"What if you don't drink anything before bed? If you didn't have to piss, maybe you'd stay asleep."

"Heh. I tried that. Gave up the evening tea. I still wake up, three, three thirty. Fall back asleep around six, just in time for the alarm at seven." He smiled faintly. "Sucks, eh?"

I'd put Ernie's strained appearance down to the pressures of the holiday season in Vernon, but now the circles under his eyes took on a different meaning.

"What do you think about?" My leg started jumping. I knew the answer.

"Lotsa stuff. But, you know. A lot about the summer." His expression didn't change. Still the faint outline of a smile. It hurt my throat to look at him.

"I hear you."

"Then do you … like, do you think about it?"

It floored me that he'd have to ask. "Hell yeah. Every day. Every fucking day."

"Do you, like, *see* it? Me, I always see it." He was back at the wine-glass, running one finger around the rim. "I see him coming in, you know? He's low but I figure he's just doing that stunt of his. But then the trees, he's so close. Too close. And he just — he just falls." He ran one flat palm back and forth over the mouth of the glass. "And there we are, just sitting there watching. Doing nothing."

My stomach lurched, because Ernie's words could have been my own. He saw exactly what I saw, except that now I had no choice but to see it through the overlay of the letter.

"I think …" He dropped his head lower. "I keep seeing it, over and over, and it's like I'm waiting for the one time we can do something. Like, we can stop it. Just … It's dumb, because it happened and it's over. But I keep thinking we can do something different this time and stop it."

The new pilot turned away from the bar, girlfriend now on his arm, tumbler of thick amber in his hand. Ernie sat frozen, a rueful smile on his face.

I'm going down, Rafe wrote. *I can't say why. But it has to be that way.*

"Ernie." I leaned toward him. I wanted to make some kind of physical contact, but the pilot and his girlfriend were headed our way. "You and me, we're never gonna forget that morning, ever. But I've thought a lot about it. It was fate, what happened up there. It was bigger than us. Much as we hate it, there's nothing we could've done to stop that crash. Not one thing."

Don't you worry, young William, he wrote. *It's going to be fine. It's how I always wanted to go.*

Ernie's head hung lower and I touched his knee anyway, fuck the pilot, let him think what he wants. All I wanted was for Ernie to let it go, to accept how powerless he'd been to alter any part of what unfolded that scorching July morning.

There was nothing we could've done. I told Ernie that, and in telling him, I came closer to believing it myself.

∧ ∨ ∧

I WENT TO SHARON'S AFTER THAT. It wasn't the plan. I was supposed to go home after the party and meet her the next morning for brunch, but I had to see her. I paid the cab driver and let myself in with the spare key she hides under the side mat. She didn't stir as I stood outside her bedroom door, debating. Her bedroom, not the spare room. Then I entered and shed my clothes. Only when I pulled back the covers and crawled in, my skin cold and craving hers, did she wake.

"Will?"

I pressed into her warm side and kissed her shoulder. "I couldn't stay away."

She barely moved. In the dim light of the clock radio I could see that her eyes were still closed. "You have a good time?" she mumbled.

I held her close. There are times I can't hold her tight enough, can't get near enough. "It was weird."

"How do you mean?"

Back at the party, when I stood to leave, Ernie got up too. He hugged me, a real hug where I could feel his solid gut and his big arms. And I hugged him back. It felt good. It felt ... I don't know, *real*. Then he whispered in my ear: "Fate's a motherfucker."

I kissed Sharon's forehead. "It was weird not having you and Rafe there."

His name rarely comes up between us, but after an evening of mostly pretending he never existed, I'd had enough.

"I guess it would be. We never missed the Christmas party. Rafe loved dressing up and he got along so well with all of you. It was a good combination for him."

"And you?"

"Me?"

"You make it sound like he was the one who enjoyed it. Didn't you?"

She rolled onto her back. It was a while before she spoke. "Last year we arrived late. I don't know if you remember. We got there just before the meal. We sat with you."

"I remember." It was my most vivid image of Sharon from her days with Rafe, the two of them sailing into the room like Hollywood stars, radiating energy, beautiful and alive.

"We had this awful fight beforehand. It's why we were late. I'd been crying and had ruined my makeup and I told him to go without me. He wouldn't."

"A fight?" I thought about how tight they'd seemed as a couple that night. Like two parts of a single unit. "It didn't seem that way."

"Oh God, one of so many fights. Really they were all the same fight."

I couldn't imagine them arguing. "What happened?"

She sighed enough to make the covers move. "You don't want to hear about all that."

"Of course I do. I love you, Sharon. I want to hear everything."

She went quiet. I wonder sometimes if she's uncomfortable when I say I love her. It's not like I do it all the time. Only when I can't help it.

"Our fights were always about … the physical side of things. It always came back to that. The night of the Christmas party I was here, in our bedroom, putting on my dress. It was this long satin gown, slits up the side." I needed no reminder. "Rafe came over and zipped me up. Then he got down on his knees and started running his hands up under the slits, stroking my thighs. I … I was not in the mood for that. The timing was all wrong. We had to go and my dress was getting wrinkled and I just —" Her voice broke.

"It's okay. You don't have to tell me."

"No, I want to. I'm sick of keeping it all in. And look where we are. Our bedroom, his and mine. You and I have stayed out of here until now. Maybe it's time." She rolled onto her side and faced me. "We had a terrible marriage in the end, Will. Terrible. Things only looked normal because he wanted it that way." She paused. "That's not fair. Because *we* wanted it that way. That night at the Christmas party we were in public and it was a celebration, so we had to look happy. We threw ourselves into the part, the loving couple, but all I could think was that I didn't want to be there and I didn't want to be with him."

"God, you seemed more than in love. You seemed smitten. It's hard to believe you could fake that."

"Love." She sighed. "I suppose we always loved each other. I never thought I didn't love him. But loving someone and wanting them, those are two different things. Well, for Rafe they were the same, but not for me. I loved him, but ..."

"But what?"

She plucked at the sheet. "I didn't want him. At all. It got so I couldn't stand being touched. Every time he'd hold me or kiss me, I knew he wanted more. And the harder he tried, the more I pulled away." I heard her swallow. "It was different at first. As you can imagine. It was all new then, I'd never slept with anyone before him. Then for years it was about getting pregnant. We had sex all the time, on a schedule, and it was fine. It felt like ... like something we were doing together, like building something. I don't know, a project. Oh, that sounds stupid." I reached for her hair, hesitant to touch her but unable to resist. "After we gave up on kids, everything changed. There was no more project, I guess, so there didn't seem to be any point. I tried to keep him satisfied, but in the end I couldn't pretend."

My ears were listening but my brain was stuck. This is the woman who wants me every day, who gives herself to me night after night. The woman who takes me. She takes me.

"The night of that party, after I told him no for the umpteenth time, he really lost it. He yelled, called me names. Frigid bitch, I remember that one." She let out a single short laugh. "He was right, I was. And that night he threatened me. No —" She must have felt me tense up. "I don't mean physically. Never that. It was something he said. He said if he wasn't getting fed at home, no one could blame him for eating out. That's the part that hurt so much. He'd always been faithful to me, no matter how bad things were. He was loyal and I was sure he'd stay that way, but that night he was telling me all bets were off."

I reached over and took her in my arms, and she let me hold her awhile. I kept replaying last year's party, adjusting the footage so that the energy and sparks I'd taken for attraction changed into thinly concealed bolts of anger.

"I don't know why it's so different with you, Will. It was never like this with him. Not remotely. You know what I'm talking about."

"I know."

"What we have, it's ... I don't know, it feels necessary. And addictive."

"Maybe you're making up for lost time."

"Could be." She half-smiled. "Maybe it's because you're such a young thing." She scratched my chest lightly with one fingernail. "Or maybe ... it's because I chose you. For once I didn't just let things happen to me. My life feels like this series of things that have happened to me. This, with you, was something I wanted. I made it happen."

Before I could respond she gave me a quick kiss. "Enough with the true confessions. Let's go to sleep."

∧ ∨ ∧

TODAY THE AFTER-EFFECTS of last night, especially all the wine I put away, are messing with my head, but another piece of the puzzle has fallen into place. Until now I couldn't even begin to see how Rafe could leave a woman he loved for one he hardly knew. It made no sense, and I was angry at him. The Rafe I knew was a better man than that, more noble. But now, maybe, I'm starting to understand.

Last night I watched Sharon as she slept, her hair fanned out on the pillow, and wondered if what she described could ever happen to us. If it did, how long would I last, asking for her and being rejected, wanting her and not being wanted back? Who's to say I'd behave any better than Rafe on a steady diet of no? We're animals, after all; we're governed by nature. It's a rare man can wrestle nature to the mat without getting pinned in the end.

There's one thing I would do different, though. No amount of rejection would ever drive me into the arms of Nathalie Girard. Maybe after years of being beaten down, not to mention backed up, you're more easily blindsided by a tangle of curly hair and a come-hither look, but how he didn't see through her selfishness and her lies, I'll never know.

What I do know, and what I'd stake my life on, is that Rafe never harassed that woman or molested her or whatever it was she accused him of. She made it up, simple as that. Maybe because he dumped her or wouldn't commit or agree to her terms. Maybe because he looked at her funny one morning. Whatever her account was, it was skewed. Rafe Mackie was a straight-up, old-fashioned, trust-your-life-to-him good guy. A cowboy in the air but a Boy Scout on the ground. He respected women — hell, he respected all people. It was coded in his DNA. That's why I can't think about that two-faced manipulator and her *supposed* complaint about Rafe's *supposed* behaviour without wanting to put my fist through a wall.

This made-up complaint, I wasn't supposed to know about it. Jeff let it slip. It was the third week in August, the day I'd gone to see Nathalie at the TSB and ended up talking to that fuckwad Lyndon and finding out about the affair. I stopped in at West Air afterwards, still steaming, and Jeff was ready for me. Hauled me into his office and lit right in, asking what the fuck I knew about Rafe having fucking trouble with the fucking trim adjustment the day before the fucking accident. For the usually regal Jeff, a lot of *fuck*s were uttered. His outrage made sense. Even in the moment, in the hailstorm of swear words, I got it. The trim problem, which he'd just had a call about from — who else? — Lyndon "the Pres" Johnson, was news to him, shocking news. Why hadn't I told anyone, namely him, about this trivial little fact a month earlier, say at the time of the crash? Had it somehow slipped my mind? Had I lost my mind? Was I out of my mind? Besides which, the story stank to high heaven. The Tracker logs were impeccable and the AMEs backed them up: the trim system on that aircraft worked perfectly, which made my so-called recollection all the more bogus.

You get the picture. Jeff was supremely pissed, to say the least. Though I believe his posture was unaffected.

For my part I said little, by which I mean nothing. I let him rant. I remember thinking this must be what a politician's job is like, to sit there ignoring the sniper fire. Once he wound down and accepted that I wasn't going to explain, he offered theories of his own. The one he settled on was that I'd fabricated the trim story because I didn't want to see Rafe, my partner and friend, impugned — Jeff's word — by the taint of pilot error. To this, the account closest to the truth, I still said nothing. What could I say? Jeff, you're getting warm? Actually Rafe handed me the trim story in a letter mailed the morning of his death and asked me to relay it to the TSB to cover for him? I don't think so.

It's while I was mulling this over that Jeff, I suppose to fill the void, mentioned that Nathalie had lodged a complaint which he'd notified Rafe about a few days before the accident. At that point Jeff lost it in a way I'd never seen before — blaming himself for the crash, saying he should've known the complaint would hit Rafe hard, he should've pulled Rafe off duty, that Rafe was in no condition to fly, and so on and so on.

In the end we agreed, Jeff out loud and me silently, to leave it all be. My statement to the TSB would stand, Jeff would quit asking where it came from, and we'd both hope for a report that was kind to our pilot.

After that I drove straight to the gym and let loose on the heavy bag, Nathalie's smug face at the end of every jab. For a week my knuckles were purple and the other pilots kept asking who I'd tangled with. I laughed it off but continued to seethe. I know how wrong it was to want to hurt her. I know how much of a monster it makes me. But since when do feelings know right from wrong? She killed him, that's what I thought with every punch. She as good as grabbed the controls and pointed his plane at the ground. She will never be arrested or tried or even questioned for taking his life. She wakes up every morning, same as ever, gets dolled up and goes to her job, same as ever, flounces around and charms everyone and basically goes about her business. Meanwhile Rafe not only died a meaningless and horrific death, crushed and burned beyond recognition, but he was tormented beforehand in a way that doesn't bear thinking about. The anguish that must have clawed at that man in the days before he did it, that's the part that kept me hitting and hitting, as if my pain could somehow cancel his.

Rafe's murderer: that's how I thought of Nathalie for months, convinced that she and her fake complaint were what pushed him over the edge. Then this fall Sharon told me she and Rafe had reconciled, and it undid every conclusion I had reached. If Rafe was going home to Sharon, he should have been ecstatic. No way would some trumped-up harassment charge overshadow the joy of returning to the woman he loved – the same woman who slept beside me last night, her face serene, safe for once in her world of dreams.

I didn't follow Sharon to dreamland, not till dawn. I thought of Ernie and his insomnia as I lay awake, tormented by helplessness and bewilderment. Why'd you do it, Rafe? What the fuck? The same old question loop that's been plaguing me since the letter. It doesn't add up. An affair, a breakup, an accusation, a reconciliation. I shuffle them around like Scrabble tiles, but no matter what order I put them in, they don't spell suicide.

Before that goddamned letter I'd have sworn on my mother's grave that Rafe Mackie, jovial weightlifter, unrivalled pilot, loyal friend, fixer of broken things, could ride out any misfortune that came his way, could deal with any sadness.

He could not.

He took his own life, and the hardest thing for me to accept is that I will never know why. His letter gave the how. The why went down with him.

THIRTY-FOUR

December

FOR SHEER FESTIVE FERVOUR, little rivals an airport in late December. People wait in a way they don't at other times of year, not sullen, stressed, or bored, but alight with anticipation. In the arrivals hall people shout and laugh, kids scoot around unscolded, lovers bestow bouquets of flowers and balloons, relatives hopefully scan each knot of travellers on the escalator. Families hug and kiss openly, friends clap each other's backs and brush much-missed cheeks and smile with their eyes. Men relieve women of their carry-on bags and feel joyously useful.

Sharon waits alone, taking in the others' excitement, her attention drawn repeatedly to three unclaimed suitcases circling on the nearest carousel. She's as eager as anyone to greet her visitors, but she's also jittery. More precisely, afraid. Since asking Will to stay with her for the holidays, an invitation he accepted with the caveat that he'd spend Christmas Day at his father's, she has failed to devise any strategy, effective or flimsy, that might clarify for Rafe's brother and sister-in-law how she has come to have a man in her house – and, more to the point, in her bed – and how that man was once the closest friend and partner of Rafe himself. In the end she gave up, hoping an approach would materialize at the appointed time. Now here she is, minutes away from her own round of hearty hugs and laughs, with nary a clue.

Again she tears her gaze away from the revolving luggage. Off to one side, near the bottom of the escalator, a man and woman cling to each other as if life must never divide them. The woman, a fall of blond hair down her back, presses into the man; his arms circle her waist and his chin rests on her head; and they sway as if to the slowest of songs. They telegraph love, pure and solid. Sharon thinks of this morning, dropping Will off at his apartment. She knows how it feels to be held that way, as if she were the tenderest, dearest prize.

Then she sees Sheldon, and her thoughts bloom with guilt.

He steps off the escalator, Nancy close behind. Together they weave through the crowd, waving wildly. The big man who barrels toward her, wide and powerful as a polar bear, face creased with happiness, looks so much like Rafe that time wrinkles backward. She has forgotten — how could she? — how alike the two brothers are, despite different lifestyles and a continent between them.

Sheldon drops his sports bag and folds her in an enormous embrace. His thick arms and broad back feel so different from Will's. And so familiar. The imprint of Rafe's body will be on her forever.

Sheldon lifts her off her feet as if twirling a child. "Lord thunderin', Sharon! It's good to lay eyes on you. Don't you look lovely."

Nancy takes her turn, giving Sharon a lingering hug and a kiss on the cheek. "Oh, sweetie. It's so good to see you." The sympathy is unmistakeable.

"I'm so glad you could come." Sharon is relieved to discover that she means it. "You're already dressed for Vancouver." Both wear Gore-Tex rain jackets, navy blue for Nancy, slicker yellow for Sheldon.

"Halifax was minus ten and snowing like a bastard. They weren't sure we'd get off the ground, eh Nance? The locals were givin' us the eye, wondering who are these half-dressed nitwits." Sheldon flings one arm around his wife's shoulder. "Must've thought we were from away. From Tarrana." He glances at Sharon to see if the jibe has hit, Toronto-bashing a well-worn joke between them.

She smiles. "You've got nothing to worry about. They'd have you pegged right away as a crazy Cape Bretoner who wouldn't listen to sense if it was shouting in his face."

"Oh, the claws are out, eh Nance? Where's the Christmas spirit? Where's the love and respect I flew all this way for?"

Nancy's smile is one part affection, three parts forbearance. "You flew all this way for the booze and the food. And the booze."

"Anyhow, Tarrana girl," he says, squeezing Sharon's shoulder with his other arm, "one look at me and everyone knows I'm a godforsaken mainlander now. After all these years the Cape Breton's beat right outta me."

Nancy laughs. "Except for every summer when we drive back for a visit. This one cries like a baby the minute he sees the causeway. By the time we're back in Halifax a week later, he's a Caper all over again, the accent, the foul mouth, the sweets, the binge drinking. The whole shebang."

"You're a sauce-box," Sheldon tells his wife. "The pair a youse. It's hardly fair. You got me outnumbered, not an ally in sight."

The memory of Rafe looms suddenly and achingly. Sheldon shifts from one foot to the other, searching the busy arrivals area for the one who will never arrive.

He gives Sharon another squeeze. "It's not gonna be easy, girl. We know that, eh Nance?" Nancy nods and reaches for Sharon's hand. "You know," he says, "people ask me now, you got brothers and sisters? And I say sure, a brother. Then I remember."

Sharon's fingertips are numb despite Nancy's warm grip. The baggage area has grown cold.

Soon the three unclaimed suitcases are joined by two more, then four, as the luggage from the Halifax flight topples onto the conveyor belt. Sharon breaks away from her visitors. "Come on," she says over her shoulder. "Let's get your bags and go home."

∧ ∨ ∧

THE MOMENT OF TRUTH, when it comes, is both more and less momentous than Sharon imagined.

After forty-five minutes of nudging through traffic stalled by holiday shoppers and early-evening rain, the streets a technicolour blur of taillights and Christmas bulbs, they pile into the townhouse, stretching their cramped legs. Sheldon and Nancy unpack in the spare room and wash up. Sharon frets. She has to tell them before five tomorrow, when Will is due for drinks and dinner. She's given herself a whole day, but now it seems unfair to wait that long. Her in-laws will need time to process the news before Will appears. So she decides: tonight they'll order in, and before the food arrives she will tell them. The certainty of a plan lightens her mood, and she smiles when Sheldon and Nancy emerge. "Drinks?"

"Lord, yes." Sheldon settles himself in Rafe's chair. "As many as you got."

Minutes later Sharon brings in a tray: three cold beers and an assortment of takeout menus. "There's plenty of home cooking in our future, so let's order in tonight. It's too miserable to go out."

"Sounds good to me," says Nancy, sitting cross-legged on the sofa. "All day long we've been going somewhere. It's nice to just *be* somewhere for a while."

Sheldon picks up a beer, still in the bottle, the way he likes it. The women follow suit. "A toast," he says. "To being with family at Christmas."

"I'll drink to that." Nancy tips her bottle.

"Cheers," says Sharon, taking a long swig for courage. She offers the menus to Nancy. "Here, you pick something."

"We're not fussy. Order your favourite and we'll be happy to have it." Nancy yawns and arches her back like a cat. A phys-ed teacher her whole life, she is as lithe and athletic as a girl.

"You must be tired," says Sharon. "It's four hours later for you."

"All the more reason to stay in." Sheldon studies his beer bottle. "Some kinda local brew, eh? Not too shabby. For the west coast."

"On behalf of the west coast, thank you." Sharon smiles, the competition between oceans another long-standing joke.

She phones the local Szechuan place and returns to the living room to find Sheldon wandering, eyeing the furniture, the table of photos beside the sofa, the gas fireplace, the Christmas tree framed by the wide front window. "You like it out here any better now?" he asks.

She hesitates. Toronto will always be home, with its big-city hustle and culture, its brick houses and lakeshore and distinct seasons. Yet there are aspects of Vancouver that she's growing used to. The sea, the soft cloud that buffs the harshest lines, the year-round green — they have their muted appeal. And now, of course, there is Will.

She has to tell them. The food will be here in half an hour. "I'm staying put for the moment. That's all I know."

"You ever get the urge to head east and live by the *real* ocean" — Sheldon winks — "we'd love to have you. Halifax is a great town, the finest kind. The past decade or two she's really come along."

"I'd love to see more of you, the boys too, but I think there's enough going on now without throwing a move into the equation."

Nancy shoots her husband a look so pointed Sharon practically sees it arc through the air. Don't go there, it says.

Sheldon inspects the Christmas tree. Its boughs give off the heady scent of fir; tiny blue lights reflect off the ornaments Will helped her hang yesterday. "Decent-size tree you got here. You put it up yourself?"

Sharon's pulse speeds. "I had some help."

"You must've. It's what, seven feet?"

"About that."

He circles the tree slowly, admiring the decorations. He touches one with his forefinger, a pink glass ball, concave on one side, a tiny crèche painted inside the hollow. "By God, would you look at that. That's one of Ma's old ornaments. We used to put that one up when we were boys. She'd always yell at us to make sure it was hanging right. 'The baby Jesus has got to face out,' she'd say. 'Don't hang him with the arse-end of him to the world.' Huh. I didn't know Rafe had this."

"Sheldon —" Sharon stops.

He turns, waiting for the rest.

"Ready for another beer?"

"I was born ready."

In the kitchen she takes three more bottles from the fridge. Get a grip, she tells herself. What's the worst they can do? Accuse you of being unfair to Rafe? Call you an unfaithful slut? Storm out, vowing to never see you again?

Less than reassured, she re-enters the living room, where Sheldon has returned to his chair. Rafe's chair. She places the tray on the coffee table and sits on the sofa beside Nancy. They all reach for the dewy bottles. "The Christmas tree," she begins. "Like I said, I got some help with it." She clears her throat. "It was Will Werner who gave me a hand. You remember Will? He flew with Rafe."

"Sure I remember," Sheldon says. "Bird dog pilot. Damned good one from what Rafe said. Helped with your hot water tank a few years back too, right around the time Ma died." He takes a long pull of his beer. "Sounds like a helpful kinda guy."

"Yes, he is. Helpful."

"You sure went all out with that tree," says Nancy. "I hope it wasn't just for us."

"He's more than helpful." How to say it? "He —" Why didn't she practise this beforehand? "Will has become a friend, a close friend. Over the past month or so. He, I mean we …" She looks at Nancy, hoping comprehension will dawn, but her sister-in-law's face shows nothing but mild curiosity. Sharon plunges ahead, her stomach falling. "We've started seeing each other."

Sheldon leans back in his chair. His beer bottle clunks down on the side table.

Here we go, Sharon thinks. She braces herself. In the distance a dog yips, the high pitch of a townhouse-sized animal.

It's Nancy who breaks the silence, Nancy who has absorbed the confidences of a generation of wholesome girls who play sports and also battle misfortune, heartache, family conflict, pregnancy, addiction, and abuse. Nancy, who meets all crises with equanimity, says the last thing Sharon could have predicted. "So that's why you look so different. We were talking about it in the bedroom. Your hair, clothes, everything.

You perked right up. We haven't seen you that way since ... well, for a long time. Right, Sheldon?"

He scowls.

"You better tell us about it," Nancy says mildly. "How did it happen?"

Sharon focuses on Nancy, hoping to expel her anxiety. "He came here about a month ago, in rough shape. Really rough. He needed to talk to someone about what happened, about Rafe." She glances at Sheldon. "He saw the crash. He was guiding Rafe that day, watching him come in for the drop."

"I know that," he says.

"We just — we talked a couple of times. One thing led to another."

A noise comes from Sheldon, something between a grunt and a cough.

"Sheldon," Nancy says.

"No, he has every right to be upset. You both do. I don't ... I can't explain it myself."

Another snort from Sheldon. He chugs the rest of his beer.

"You know," Sharon says, "all summer, for weeks and weeks, I'd wake up every morning and think, he's dead. What do I do with this day? How do I fill the time until I can go to bed again? I'd visit all these different stores to use up the hours, get produce in one place, bread somewhere else, cheese at this special deli. I'd go to exercise class, see my friend Rachel sometimes, wander around the library. Try to read. But it wasn't enough. There were still so many hours with — nothing." She pauses. "Then Will showed up and it just seemed ... He needed help. Helping him started to fill the time."

"Help," Sheldon mutters. "That's one way to describe it."

Sharon clasps her hands tight in her lap. She hasn't known whether to tell them everything. She decides she will.

"Sheldon, I still love your brother and I still miss him, every single day. But things were not good between us at the end. They hadn't been good for years."

"We know a little about that, don't we, Sheldon?" says Nancy. Her husband looks off at the tree. "He didn't tell us much. You know Rafe, always putting on a happy face no matter what. But he did say you'd hit a rough patch."

"Rough, yes. You could call it that. He ..." Sharon's throat is so dry it catches, yet she can't drink her beer, not now. "We were both to blame. We'd fight and make up, but every time, the fights got worse and the making up got harder. Finally he left me. He moved out two months before the crash."

Sheldon turns back to her, surprise all over his face. "Ah, no. Don't say that."

"We didn't tell anyone. Rafe, well you know, he was private about things like that. And me, I just wanted to pretend it hadn't happened." She grips her hands, which are somehow sweating and freezing at the same time. "I'm not telling you this to make excuses. I know it's too soon for me to be with someone, and it's worse because that someone is his friend. But you need to know. The truth is, I lost Rafe a long time before he died."

Sheldon's great head droops and her heart goes out to him. She knows this is a version of his brother that's hard to accept.

"Jesus, Jesus." Sheldon stands up and starts to pace. "I can't believe he'd leave. Was there nothing you could do to stop him?"

"Sheldon, don't —" Nancy begins.

"No, it's okay. At that point, when he left, I don't think either of us knew how to fix it." Sharon allows herself a sip of beer.

"But couldn't you see a counsellor or something? Nancy and I did that once, back when the boys were in diapers and I was working extra shifts all the time. It saved us, it really did."

"There wasn't much to save." Sharon looks away. "You see, he'd found somebody else." She has never said it out loud before, and the words detonate inside her.

"Jesus Murphy."

"There's no way," Nancy says at the same time. "That man loved you like he loved his own life."

Sharon picks at the label of her beer bottle, fighting to stay calm. "I suspected it for a while. You live with someone that long and you know.

He'd come home late and not say where he'd been. He'd go out for long walks and take his cell phone, when he always used to leave it at home. Finally I confronted him and he admitted it right away. You know him, he never liked to lie." She looks at Sheldon. "That's when he left. As soon as it wasn't a secret anymore."

"But who?" Nancy says. "Do you know?"

"I didn't at first. I never asked him. It was easier not to think about it, not to think about … *them*. But I found out later. At the funeral."

"What?" Sheldon is incredulous. "We were there with you, the whole day. You mean someone came up to you and —"

"It wasn't quite like that."

The doorbell startles them.

"Jumpin' Jesus," says Sheldon, running a hand over his forehead.

Sharon carries the bags of food into the kitchen. She wonders, as she returns to the living room with cartons spread out on a tray, if any of them will be able to eat.

"Let me give you some money for that." Nancy stands up.

"Not now, woman!" Sheldon thunders. "What the fuck happened at the funeral?"

Sharon sits down. No one knows this, not even Colleen. "There was a group from the Transportation Safety Board there, at the back of the chapel."

"I remember," Sheldon says. "They all came up together when we had the reception line."

"All but one." It surprises her how clearly she recollects this part of the funeral when the rest of the day is indistinct. The TSB investigators, all dark suits and grave faces, moved as a single platoon. The men were so tall, not one of them under six feet. It occurred to her that they must keep company with tragedy every day of their lives.

"When I saw them coming, I knew who they were," she says. "I'd met one of them before, a fellow named Roy. He was at a banquet Rafe and I attended a few years back. There was a woman with them, dark curly hair, in a grey suit, tiny. She stood out next to all those tall men. At the last minute, just as they came up to the reception line, she broke away.

She headed for the exit, but I watched and she didn't leave. She turned around to make sure the other investigators weren't looking and she doubled back to the front of the chapel. Remember that big picture of Rafe that was up there on a stand? The photo from the West Air website that you got enlarged?"

Sheldon and Nancy both nod.

"She stayed there for the longest time staring at it. I kept shaking people's hands but I watched her. There was something about the way she stood, like she was mesmerized. Then she reached out." Sharon extends her own hand. "She touched his face. It was only for a second or two, but I saw it. I knew it was her."

Time has not diminished the revulsion that crawls over her when she recalls the intimate gesture. Rafe's face. Her husband's face. On that day of public goodbyes, what right did that woman have to such a private farewell? With the disgust comes a feeling Sharon has always been swift to dispel, an emotion that now, having pushed the scene out in the open and thereby made it real, she is dumbfounded to identify as anger. It is an alien sensation, almost forbidden, a low fire glowing in her belly. Why didn't she feel it that day? She imagines a different Sharon, confident and strong, not drugged up, striding toward the photo to confront her — Nathalie, for she has learned the woman's name — and say ... what? Leave this place at once? You have no right? I understood him in ways you never could? He always loved me? He was mine and never yours?

She is forty-four years old. How has she made it this far without being able to name her own feelings? Desire and need, love and anger — she has distanced herself from all these red-hot embers. Acknowledged or not, they've been burning inside her just the same; and in the case of the anger, growing.

"There's one more thing," she says. "Will doesn't know. About the affair, I mean. He knows Rafe and I had separated, but he doesn't know there was another woman." She holds Sheldon's eyes, so like the ones she knew for decades. "I don't want him to find out. He looked up to Rafe like a mentor, like the brother he never had. He loved Rafe, he did.

And he's going to be around over the next few days. You mustn't tell him. It's been hard enough for him to come to terms with the crash without this."

She can't help it. She is furious and determined, yet tears roll down her cheeks.

Faster than you'd think a big man could move, Sheldon is beside her. He folds her hands into his. "It's all right, now," he tells her. "Don't you worry, Share. It's gonna be all right."

Maybe it will, she thinks. Maybe if she can bury the old Sharon alongside Rafe.

THIRTY-FIVE

September

UNLIKE THE HARSH AND HECTIC SUMMER, September spooled out at a glacial pace. It crept more slowly than even the last year of high school, when Nathalie longed to flee her small, mean life under Uncle Theo's roof. More slowly than the final weeks of AME apprenticeship, which she ground out shift by shift, unsure she'd ever earn a licence or rise above beginner rank. More slowly even than the worst stretch of the Cessna 172 case, when she wondered daily if Tucker would fire her and she'd have to crawl back to her old mechanic's job, feign gratitude for oil-stained overalls and cheerless night shifts, her limbs contorted inside the tight spaces of grounded aircraft.

At least now she understood the federal public service more intimately than she did during the Cessna screw-up. A few discreet inquiries plus a review of her collective agreement confirmed how close to impossible it was for Tucker to fire her. The Cessna 172 case didn't provide sufficient grounds, nor did her interference in the Tracker crash. Nor did the fact that after submitting the R22 report, she missed three days of work suspiciously wrapped around a weekend. She had plenty of sick leave banked, after all, and three days for what she termed stomach flu was not excessive, just enough to right the final error in a relationship that had proved one giant miscalculation from beginning to end. No, Tucker would need considerably more than that to let her go. Such was the beauty of a unionized government job.

Reassuring as it was, the security of Nathalie's livelihood did little to ease the strain of recent weeks. As soon as Labour Day passed, the skies opened and dumped months' worth of precipitation on Vancouver, and residents, lulled into complacency by the longest, driest summer on record, felt cheated in ways they could not express. At Starbucks, where Nathalie stopped for her morning latte, the baristas sulked and the patrons groused. At noon, when she straggled in to Bread Heaven or the sushi bar, rain sheeting off her after a short sprint from the car, she joined queues beaten down by the elements. It was the wrong season to be lonely. Yet as quickly as summer was sluiced away, like hopscotch on a sidewalk, so too was the camaraderie of Nathalie's fellow investigators. No one ignored her outright or refused to answer her questions, but neither did anyone seek her out or prolong a conversation. The office bustled with all the staff back from summer holidays and immersed in two new crashes, yet Nathalie passed her days alone and, once the R22 report had wrapped up, unoccupied.

What had led to the office-wide chill? Try as she might, she couldn't pinpoint the cause.

Did everyone know that she'd sat on Will's tip about the trim? Ordinarily she'd bet that Lyndon, with his infamous lack of compassion, had complained loudly. Except Lyndon, as far as she could tell, had stayed quiet about her role in Will's lead. It wasn't Lyndon who told Tucker that she'd withheld information on the Tracker; it was Jeff Montrose from West Air. And Jeff would have learned it from his own employee, Will, who'd stormed out of the TSB after Lyndon spilled the beans about her and Rafe and likely went straight to his boss.

Was there more, then? Did anyone at work, besides Lyndon and Tucker, know about her entanglement with Rafe? Had Lyndon sniggeringly told other investigators? Had Tucker leaked word about her complaint, as he insisted on calling it? Doubtful. Tucker's lips were sealed by privacy policies, and Lyndon, occasional work resentments aside, was her friend. Her close friend, she'd have called him, though now she wasn't sure. The lattes she brought him skimmed over on his desk. Her attempts at small talk reminded him that he had pressing tasks to attend to. While drafting the R22 report, she'd asked him to help her describe the clutch mechanism, the kind of task he usually relished. He didn't refuse, but he delayed so long that she churned out the section herself, counting on head office to smooth the garbled prose.

It was a mess, that's all she knew, another fuck-up she'd have to atone for, though the exact nature of the fuck-up remained a mystery. Unwilling to quiz her colleagues or re-inflame her boss, she crawled through each workday, puzzled, isolated, and lonely.

Finally, on a Wednesday afternoon in the third week of September, while the rain took an hour's recess to shore up its energy, Lyndon came to see her. She'd been reading other regions' accident reports now that her work was caught up, not to mention daydreaming about the PAMEA conference tomorrow, in particular the two nights she'd spend with Jake at a nearby Marriott. Visions of bare limbs and Jake's stunning face played in her mind until a rustling of papers brought her back. Lyndon leaned against her cubicle divider, arms folded, the way he had for years. One look at his sardonic expression and his uniform of worn blue jeans and white button-down shirt and it hit Nathalie how much she missed him — his odd turns of phrase, his mocking wit.

He unfolded his arms and offered her a sheaf of paper.

"What's that?"

"Read it."

The date and aircraft model on the cover told her: it was the draft report on the Tracker crash.

She glanced up. "You sure this is a good idea?"

"The work's all done. As soon as head office and the board review it, it's going off to the employer and the family, hopefully in a week or two."

The report weighed almost nothing. "This is it? It's pretty short."

Lyndon's mouth compressed into a straight line. "We did our job." He turned, and as quickly as he had appeared was gone.

Nathalie laid the report flat on her desk. It was merely a collection of words: headings, with phrases and sentences underneath, a one-paragraph synopsis of when and how the incident had unfolded.

An accident report. She'd seen hundreds and had written her fair share. A familiar template populated with information. Flat, factual, neutral.

She did not feel neutral.

Bypassing the first few pages, she went straight to the analysis section and began to read.

The evidence shows that the drop circuit being flown at the time of the occurrence was routine and uncomplicated, in particular for a pilot with the subject's years of experience and documented proficiency. Duty logs, the pilot's medical examinations, and toxicology reports confirm that the pilot was rested and fit to fly. The autopsy report indicates that the pilot did not experience a medical event that resulted in loss of control. Witnesses state that the flight instructions were clearly delivered by radio and were confirmed by the pilot. Furthermore, visibility and weather conditions were within satisfactory ranges for the flight as undertaken.

Overall, there is no evidence to suggest that pilot decision-making, operational, or environmental factors contributed to this occurrence. This analysis will therefore focus on the issue of whether an aircraft system malfunction was responsible.

Inspections of the airframe, engines, and systems following the crash yielded no physical evidence of a system malfunction. However, as noted in Factual Information, one witness stated that approximately 30 minutes before the occurrence flight, the pilot indicated that the previous day the elevator trim controls had not responded normally during flight. According to the witness, the pilot stated that while trimming the aircraft nose down for landing, the trim mechanism briefly became lodged in place. This witness statement introduces the possibility that the trim adjustment malfunctioned during the occurrence flight, forcing the aircraft into a nose-down attitude which the pilot was unable to correct.

During the crash, the trim actuator assembly sustained significant damage in all its parts, and the trim tabs disconnected. It is therefore impossible to determine, from the post-crash condition of either the actuator assembly or the trim tabs, whether the elevator trim system was functional at the time of the occurrence.

The markings left on trees and terrain, as well as statements from witnesses, confirm that the aircraft was in a nose-down attitude when it contacted trees. This attitude was inconsistent with the circuit the pilot had been instructed to fly. It was also inconsistent with any circuit the pilot would have chosen to fly, leading as it did directly into treetops. It is evident from both the rate of descent prior to impact with terrain, and the impact signature on the terrain, that the aircraft travelled consistently nose down and the pilot did not successfully alter the aircraft's path.

The most probable explanation for this series of events is that the elevator trim controls may have malfunctioned as hypothesized above. However, in the absence of physical evidence to support this hypothesis, it is impossible to conclude with full certainty what led to the aircraft's uncontrolled flight into terrain.

Nathalie read it twice and reviewed the first two paragraphs a third time. No evidence to suggest that pilot decision-making contributed to this occurrence. Not a single reference to Rafe's state of mind or personal circumstances, no suggestion that he'd been distracted or careless. Such a statement would be pure speculation and would have no place in the report, but she had feared the blow of culpability just the same.

It was the outcome she had prayed for: full absolution of Rafe and, by extension, her. So what if the exact cause of the crash remained uncertain? Certainty didn't matter as long as it was obvious to Tucker and Lyndon, to Will and Jeff at West Air, and to anyone else who'd wormed their way into her personal life that her liaison with Rafe had nothing to do with his death.

Not her fault. She was off the hook. Her conscience was clear.

The phone rang. Best leave it for voicemail or she'd never make her hair appointment. Her stylist had squeezed her in for highlights just in time for the conference and, of course, for Jake.

Another ring, and another. Two days she'd be out of the office and the message would languish unreturned. Better to just deal with it. She sighed and picked up.

"Nat. My lucky day. I was hoping you'd still be there."

"What the hell? I told you not to call me at work."

"Guess what? If you put the pedal to the metal, I'm a ten-minute drive away."

"Ten minutes? Your flight's not until tomorrow."

"Change of plans, babe. I'm at the Marriott, room 414, showered, buck naked, and — hold on, let me check — yup, one hundred percent cocky. So get that pretty little ass of yours over here. Now."

Grinning ear to ear, Nathalie slammed down the phone, grabbed the essentials, and obeyed. Hair appointment forgotten, Lyndon forgotten, Tracker report a shadow in the past.

∧ ∨ ∧

"THEY'RE LINED UP FROM HERE to the US border, for God's sake. I knew we should've stopped at Starbucks on the way in."

Nathalie, deprived of both sleep and caffeine, scanned the crowd of AMEs and other delegates, who en masse surged toward the coffee and mini-muffins set out for breakfast at the PAMEA conference kick-off. The lineup snaked through the cavernous BCIT lobby — the scene of the crime, Jake said when they entered, recalling their chance meeting here in July. The space rang with voices, mostly male, many of them familiar to Nathalie. Pacific AMEs were a tight clan: most of them graduates of the same handful of institutions, all of them united in collective disdain for white-collar managers and pilots. Briefly she wondered if it was wise to stand so close to Jake, him being a married man and all, but his smell and heat glued her to his side. Damned if she didn't want him right here, right now, even though they'd just done it, mostly dressed, fast and frantic, minutes before leaving the hotel.

"Wait here, Nat," he said. "I'll get you a coffee. Seeing as I'm the reason you're so groggy this morning." He gave her hand a surreptitious squeeze and ventured off. Nathalie watched him snake through the crowd as if on hockey skates, as tasty going as coming. How would they make it through the next seven hours without the entire AME community finding out they were an item? More to the point, how would they go that long without fucking again? She'd have to scout the lobby later to see if there was a single-stall washroom.

"Jake Behrend, I believe?"

She started at the familiar voice and turned to see blue jeans, crisp white shirt, tidy blond hair, shiny cheeks. Jesus Christ, how long had he been standing there?

"Jake, yeah." Her mind reached for an explanation. "We were at AME school together back in the day."

"SAIT, right?" said Lyndon. "He's still based in Calgary if I'm not mistaken."

"I think so."

"Odd to find him here, then. Alberta AMEs usually attend the western conference, not the Pacific one." He squinted at her. "Must be something here he is particularly keen to see."

Merde! Had he overheard what Jake said to her, maybe seen him grab her hand? Time for a curveball. "Your Tracker report's good. Thorough."

"Oh, you read it? It didn't make its way back to my desk, so I assumed you were still perusing it."

"I read it. I just forgot to return it. It's good."

"Mm-hmm." His eyes swept the crowd. "It's open-ended."

"The whole trim question, sure, but you handled it great. Even without hard evidence, readers will come to the right conclusion. They'll know the cause."

Something, or someone, had captured Lyndon's attention. He replied absently. "Will they?"

"Sure. The pilot complains about the trim sticking right before the flight, then the plane unexpectedly goes nose down. It all adds up, even if you can't say so conclusively in the report."

"There is a great deal we couldn't say conclusively in the report. There is a great deal we couldn't say at all."

"What do you mean?"

He locked her in a cold stare. "You know precisely what I mean."

Unable to hold his drilling gaze, she scanned the coffee lineup. It was moving, but Jake was still far from the front. She decided to try the soft touch. "Lyndon, let's not play games. We know each other better than that. If you've got something to say, say it."

"Believe me, I have things to say to you. But it is a conversation you do not want to have. Especially not here."

Quick as lightning her anger flashed. "You arrogant shit. Don't tell me what I do and do not want to talk about."

"Fine. You want to do this? We can do it. I'm trying to save you some humiliation, but if you want straight talk, fine. I'll give it to you." He grabbed her shoulder and yanked her over to the wall, away from the crowd. "That stuff about the trim, it's bogus. I know it, you know it, and Roy is pretty near convinced too. Every instinct in me, every bleep on my horseshit radar, says the whole story stinks."

"What's that supposed to mean? You think Will made it up?"

"Sometimes I think that. Other times I think you put him up to it."

"Me?"

His lip curled. "Don't give me that wide-eyed innocent act. I've had a lifetime of that. I can't believe I ever fell for it."

"Why would I – *How* could I do that? I don't know Will from Adam. How am I supposed to convince him to go along with some … some fabricated story about a dead pilot who happens to be his partner? You think he'd do it just because I asked him, because I said pretty please? What the fuck?" Where was Jake? She craned to see. Near the front of the line now. Shit! No way could he hear any of this.

"I'm not saying I have it all figured out," Lyndon hissed. "But there is something seriously off about this supposed trim story. A, Will is the one who introduced it, *after* Roy and I interviewed him, I might add, and B, it only came out after I caught him meeting with you."

She laughed, a single humourless sound. "You've lost it, man. You're getting paranoid."

"No, I don't think so. What I think is you had every reason to plant this story."

A couple of men drifted closer. Did she know them? She dropped her voice, willing Lyndon to follow suit. "And what is that supposed to mean?"

He watched her steadily but said nothing.

"Jesus, would you quit it? All this superior, inscrutable bullshit, it's driving me nuts. Just be a man, grow some balls, and say it." The two men glanced at them, then went back to talking.

"Fine, I'll say it." An ugly smile twisted his face. "That airplane crashed, and that pilot died, because of you. Because you were fucking him." The men glanced their way again. Lyndon lowered his voice. "And then, when that wasn't enough of a thrill, enough of a, a conquest, you started fucking *with* him. You took away his marriage and you took away his self-respect, and then to top it all off you took away his concentration. Rafe Mackie crashed that plane because he wasn't thinking straight. He went up to fight a fire, something he did day in, day out, for years. But that day, because you had fucked with his head, he didn't know which end was up. And you don't want anyone to find that out."

Unbelievable. She thought she knew Lyndon, but the man in front of her was completely unhinged, a stranger. And where was Jake? Not in the coffee lineup. Nowhere to be seen. She had to make it stop.

He wasn't finished. "You think so highly of yourself. A plucky little lady in a man's world, gutting it out with the guys, showing us you can do it, you can take it — all the injustice, the discrimination, the *harassment* you supposedly experience every goddamned day of your life. You put on this act, this poor struggling little-girl act, and the whole time you're just lording it over us. Your long hair and your high heels and your tight skirts, sashaying all over the fucking place. You've got every one of us wrapped around your finger."

The two men had stopped talking and inched closer. For sure they were listening. Nathalie flushed and searched the crowd for Jake.

Lyndon must have seen the men because he bent in closer. His voice was low and glacial. "Every day since you joined the TSB, I have watched you. Not that you've noticed. Oh, you pretended like we were friends, it was useful for you, but you never really gave a shit about me. And to think that for years, I wondered if maybe one day we would —" He stopped, shook his head. "None of that matters now. What matters is I've learned a lot about you. For one thing, you are not that bright.

As an investigator, I mean. You're — what's the word Tucker likes to use? Second-rate. But he can't say that to you because you're a woman and that would be discrimination."

Was Jake nearby? Desperately she tried to look, but Lyndon was blocking her view.

"Also, you are not particularly observant. You don't, for instance, notice a fellow investigator sitting three tables away in the Flying Boat when you are there cavorting with a married man. Your drinking companion is a pilot, so it could be a work-related rendezvous, until he puts a big paw on your leg, under the table, very secretive. And you? You giggle. Like a bimbo. It's fake, like everything you do, but he doesn't notice. Every person there, including your fellow investigator, is watching the two of you, and every person knows precisely what's happening. You might as well be going at it on the table, him ramming you right there between the beer bottles and the nachos."

Lyndon's voice was so low now that he was almost talking to himself. The two men had finally left. Nathalie stood stiff with fear, unable to absorb what he was saying, unable to leave.

"And you don't notice how obvious it is to anyone who is watching you, anyone with eyes, when this *thing* that's going on comes to an end. No more leaving work early. No more whispering into the phone. You go back to proper work clothes instead of the tiny little slutty tank tops and stiletto heels you've been prancing around in. But you, you're not depressed or sad. Not at all. In fact, you seem more lively, more — what's the word? — more *open* to your co-workers than you've been in a long time. So it's clear that you were the one to end it, not him."

She tried to leave, but Lyndon grabbed her arm. "Still that's not enough. You haven't ground him down enough, convincing him to leave his wife and then throwing him out on his ass. No, you can do more. You can concoct a phoney complaint, say he's harassing you. All you are is a victim, an innocent little victim. Oh yes, Tucker told me all about that. So your jilted pilot lover is now humiliated on top of everything else. He goes up in a plane he knows like the back of his hand and in one second, when he's wasting a valuable thought on *you*, he makes a rookie move, goes nose down instead of nose up. One second of distraction, that's all it takes. Maybe it's not even distraction. Maybe he's so beat up, so ashamed at how he's been disposed of like a used tampon, that for one crazy second he wants to do it, just so it will all stop. Either way, before he can correct himself, it's too late. He's clipped the trees. Game over. That," he hissed, "*that* is what should have been in our report."

His head dipped closer and she drew back, horrified that his lips might touch her.

"Now," he purred. "Here's what you are going to do. Transport Canada is starting a big audit at the Vancouver airport and they need someone in System Safety ASAP. They're open to a transfer and they're willing to train someone with the right experience. I told them all about you, Nathalie, and they have Tucker's enthusiastic endorsement. If you know what's good for you, if you ever want to work in any sort of pleasant surroundings again where people will, say, talk to you and take you seriously, you will apply today, as soon as the presentations are over."

This couldn't be happening. This was Lyndon, her champion, her biggest supporter. Lyndon, who'd made her want to become an investigator in the first place, who'd always been a little sweet on her. Now he was turning against her too, trying to get rid of her, blackmail her?

"Lyndon, I—"

He squeezed her arm tighter, his face pinched with contempt. "Nathalie Girard. You are such a liar. You make out like you're some poor brave girl who's battling her way in a world full of powerful men. That's the story you tell, and it's a lie. It's you who has all the power."

Toward them came Jake, coffee cup in each hand. Seeing him, Lyndon hissed in Nathalie's ear. "I've seen the photos. Rafe Mackie didn't even look human when they found him. That's what all your power did."

He released her, pivoted, and greeted Jake with a radiant smile. "Jake Behrend. We've met a time or two." He stuck out one hand, then withdrew it. "How thoughtless of me. Your hands are full. Is one of those for the lady?"

Jake nodded, smiled awkwardly.

"Good, good. Well, I have to be going." Lyndon clapped Jake's shoulder, buddy to buddy, splashing one of the coffees. "Hey, Jake. Take it from me. She's a decent piece of ass, but she's not worth it. She's a liar and a troublemaker, and everything she touches — it dies." Still smiling, he strode off, head high, into the crowd.

THIRTY-SIX

Twenty-three weeks after

IT'S LATE, SO LATE, but I'm too wound up to sleep.

There was no question of staying at Sharon's tonight. We talked about it while we were clearing away the Boxing Day leftovers, but she said no, not while Sheldon and Nancy are there. Even though she invited me to spend Christmas with her, meaning at her place, meaning all the time — or so I thought — I guess I understand. It's hard enough for them to accept that she's seeing another guy, especially when that guy is me, without them running into said guy in the bathroom the next morning.

At least the first awkward hellos are behind us. I went over for dinner three nights ago to break the proverbial ice. It broke. We scraped against a cold, jagged edge here and there but overall managed to converse politely, even laughed a bit, and no one got punched. That's a success in my books.

The weirdest moment by far was seeing Sheldon for the first time, packed into his brother's armchair, beer in hand, like Rafe come back from the dead. Their similar build I had noticed from photos — it's hard to miss a person built like a Humvee — but no photo prepared me for the brown eyes and wide smile, for Rafe's booming voice and joking ways. "Finest kind," Sheldon declared, waving the bottle of local brew in my direction. The remark struck a chord in me; it was something Rafe had once said. Over dinner Sheldon told stories of Halifax, the two young brothers working construction, hitting the bars, getting into

316

mischief. He told us about first meeting Nancy, at a laundromat there. She had scolded him, something to do with his folding. I kept losing track because I'd fix on Sheldon's grin or the crinkle around his eyes, the way he conducted the story with his broad hands, the Maritime accent, a thick gumbo compared to his brother's thinned-out broth, and I'd miss whole sentences. It threw me but also lulled me. It made me miss Rafe all over again.

One thing I was ready for, lines memorized and all, was the moment when Sheldon, assuming he hadn't turfed me out by then, would pull me aside for a man-to-man about how I better treat the lady right, not mess with her or break her heart or he would maim me in a variety of excruciating ways. Strangely that moment never came. Maybe he'd decided to tread softly our first evening and save it for later, or maybe he recognized what to me seems painfully obvious – that I'm a lovesick hound around Sharon, and I'd bite off my own tail before doing anything to hurt her.

As for Sharon, she remained gracious and unruffled. Poise is a trait that was never on my radar before, but now I understand its value. The first evening wore on her, though. By the end her eyes had lost their shimmer and her smile seemed forced. Who could blame her? Guess what? Your brother's dead and I'm sleeping with his best friend. An announcement like that doesn't go down without a hiccup or two. I'm just glad she's not hiding my existence from Sheldon and Nancy, quite possibly the cowardly route I'd have taken.

Tomorrow we'll all meet for coffee in the late afternoon and cross to the North Shore to see the lights at the Capilano Suspension Bridge. It's supposed to be spectacular, multicoloured strands in the mammoth trees and beside the walkways and along the swinging bridge itself. It'll be dark by the time we get there, so I'm hoping to hold Sharon's hand for a minute or steal a kiss. How I can play the chaste suitor until New Year's Day, when Sheldon and Nancy fly home, I'm not sure. Every minute I'm with Sharon I want to touch her. Some of it is regular lust but some is desire of another kind: the urge to remind her that she is beautiful and cared for, and that I need her.

∧ ∨ ∧

THAT FIRST EVENING with Sheldon and Nancy was a milestone in more ways than one. It was the first time Sharon and I had been together in someone else's presence. We were out of the closet, so to speak. I got to thinking afterwards about how I haven't told anyone about Sharon — apart from Melody, that is, and I didn't exactly offer it up to her.

I've got my reasons. One is that I'm worried it won't last. I keep waiting for Sharon to wake up some morning and realize there's this lightweight moron in her bed. And I'm embarrassed about being in so deep. I mean, love? I never planned on that. Top of the heap, I'm queasy about the ethics of sliding into the romantic vacancy left by your dead partner. It happened so naturally, so inevitably, for both of us, but that doesn't mean it's right.

Those reasons aside, I admit it: it's strange to be involved with someone for a month and a half and to completely fall for her and keep the whole thing to yourself. Now that Sheldon and Nancy know and are more or less okay with me — at least that's my impression — it feels ridiculous to keep the relationship under wraps. So yesterday I sucked it up and told Dad.

It was Christmas Day, that morose day he and I would both rather skip but always spend together. Weather-wise it was ideal, frost sparkling on the roads and roofs in the morning, low sun in the late afternoon. As much as I missed Sharon, who I'm with nearly all the time, it was good to spend a day with Dad in his little rancher in Burnaby, his retirement fixer-upper as he calls it, watching his annual foray into the farthest corners of the kitchen where he has stored but can never find once-a-year implements like the roasting pan, meat thermometer, china platter, and gravy boat. Christmas dinner at his place involves a lot of banging and swearing, copious alcoholic beverages, precious few vegetables, and in the end a surprisingly tasty meal. He's never been one to skimp, my dad, especially when it comes to the few rituals we've kept up in a life devoid of a woman's touch. It's not the spread my aunt used to put out for us, but it's not the crazy circus her table was either. We both prefer it this way. It's quiet and civil. A little sloppy. Very male.

I waited until dessert. Dad had plated thick slices of mince pie topped with sharp cheddar, the only part of the meal that wasn't homemade, and we were mellow the way you get when your stomach is layered with booze, meat, and gravy. Dad had plunged the Bodum, his last task as cook, and the aroma of dark coffee rounded out the holiday table.

Telling him, it turned out, was easy. I always forget how much age has mellowed the old man. He hurled no barbs about why I'd kept Sharon to myself all this time. There was nothing about my future intentions, none of the wedding fever or need-to-breed pep talks I'd been dreading. Mainly he asked if I was happy and if I'd bring her around sometime. I said yes to both.

He did make one peculiar comment, one that has stuck with me. It was after I'd talked his ear off about how wonderful Sharon is and how good we are together. "Remember that he can't see you," he said.

I said I didn't follow.

"Rafe. He's gone. He can't see you or your life anymore."

He cut another sliver of pie. I shook my head so he slid it onto his own plate and took a bite. I knew he wasn't done. My dad's a slow thinker, which I blame on a lifetime of chess. "I know you're as good an atheist as the rest of us," he said eventually, "but sometimes people get funny ideas. They worry that when someone dies, that person can look down from the clouds and see what the living are up to. And judge them. I'm saying, don't fall for that fairy-tale crap. He's nothing but ashes now. You and Sharon are alive. You're allowed to be together and enjoy carnal knowledge" – I rolled my eyes at the very dad-like expression – "without feeling like you're wronging someone who no longer exists."

I wonder about my dad when he comes up with stuff like this. He spends a lot of time alone, and a lot of time in fictional worlds. "Duh," I said eloquently. "Why would you even say that?"

"It happened to me after your mother died." He pushed his plate away, the pie unfinished. "For a long time, if I looked at a woman and thought golly, she's attractive, I wonder if she'd pay any attention to me, there was your mother right behind the woman's shoulder. She'd give me this wounded look, like I was cheating on her and she couldn't believe it. So I'd walk away. For years that went on. I knew it was silly, that there's no afterlife or soul or any of that made-up crap. But still. Then one day in the Bay — I was in there to buy underwear, of all things — I saw this reflection in a mirror and thought, who is that old guy? Well, it was me. This grey-faced, dried-up old geezer. I was gobsmacked. When did I start looking like that? That day I told myself that if I was ever going to enjoy the pleasure of female company again, I'd better get over the idea that I was a cheater and get on with life. Now don't get me wrong, Will. I knew she was never really there looking over any woman's shoulder, not in spirit, not in any way. It's not like I was hallucinating. I was seeing her because I desperately wanted — no, I *needed* her to be here. But she was gone. She had always been gone. The only place she still existed was here" — he tapped his chest — "and here" — his head — "and none of that was real." He stared at the silver pie fork in his hand. "It might sound pretty obvious to you, but it wasn't to me, not until that particular experience. What dawned on me was that the person keeping me from enjoying the company of other women was not your mother. It was me."

It was without question the longest speech my dad, the classic strong, silent type, had ever made in my presence. It was also, by an enormous factor, the most personal. That he had summoned up such words for me, flexing emotional muscles in some unused part of himself, moved me more than I can say.

What he wanted, I know, was to take away the guilt that fathers can probably smell coming off their sons. What he couldn't know, and what I can never tell him, is that the guilt I'm carrying around is not because of what I'm doing now that Rafe is dead. It's because of what I failed to do when he was alive.

THIRTY-SEVEN

December

SHE WAS A PILOT'S WIFE. For more than two decades she lived on aviation time, the months divided into when her husband worked and when he didn't, into fire season and off-season. She does not love flying but does not hate it either, is neutral about takeoffs and landings. She does not particularly care for aircraft, cannot explain how they stay aloft, has never kept the terminology straight: piston, turbine, turboprop, single, twin. She knows the words but not their meanings.

Will she ever live outside the world of flight? As she enters the lobby of the office compound, Sharon wonders. No sooner did she receive the Tracker report in October, which severed her connection with the Transportation Safety Board, than she fell into the arms of another pilot who in several months will resume the gone-again rhythm of the aerial firefighter. To top it off, here she is at Transport Canada's civil aviation office in Richmond, scanning the building directory for the regional System Safety Office, a bureau unknown to her until yesterday.

It's the morning of December 28 and the Boxing Day sales are still going strong. Will and Sheldon, whom she dropped off fifteen minutes ago, believe she is among the hordes at Richmond Centre picking through discount bins. Nancy, thank goodness, begged off the drive to the southern suburbs, preferring a leisurely morning at home followed by a bus ride downtown to check out the Lululemon and New Balance stores. "Once a jock, always a jock," she said, pouring a second cup of coffee as Sharon, Will, and Sheldon donned their jackets.

Will and Sheldon are at the TSB, where they have an appointment to view the Tracker wreckage. Sharon finds it hard to believe that the remains of Rafe's plane are still there, but the investigator who spoke with Will confirmed that they would go nowhere until it was determined who would pay for their removal, there being no insurance claim because of the plane's age. Sheldon wants to see the tanker, for closure as he put it. She cannot begin to understand — she hasn't laid eyes on what's left of her husband's aircraft and she never will — but it plainly matters to his brother. Will, who is doing all he can to please her in-laws, offered to book a viewing and to accompany Sheldon there.

Once their appointment was set, Sharon got down to business: did some googling, placed a few phone calls, and within half an hour had arranged a viewing of her own. Not an appointment per se, it will be more spontaneous than that, but a meeting of sorts.

The list inside the glass-fronted directory includes at least a dozen Transport Canada divisions. It's a vast government department, and this isn't even the region's main office, which is housed in a downtown highrise near the athletic stores Nancy plans to raid. But Sharon has done her research: this is the building, a generic office tower, the lobby wide and high and mostly empty apart from a few low benches and potted plants that do little to soften the lines of glass and steel. She touches a leaf of the ficus beside the directory. Fake.

She scans the listings. There it is, in the third column: System Safety, suite 501.

The agitation she's been trying to quell all morning quickens her pulse. The office is real, and she is really here. To do what? She is still unsure. Just getting here, not only thinking about it but actually doing it, is an accomplishment, and she indulges in a moment of congratulation. The next step is to get herself to the fifth floor.

She crosses the lobby, sees the corridor that contains the bank of elevators. Sees the back of a woman, a petite woman with thick brown hair swept into a twist, a pert and fidgety woman in heels, holding a black laptop case, and her resolve crumbles like a sandcastle. Impossible, she thinks. I'm not ready. I need more time.

She considers leaving. The woman's back is to her; she hasn't been seen. She can do this another time. It doesn't have to be today.

The woman shifts from one high-heeled foot to the other, hips twitching beneath her belted trench coat. Twice she stabs at the already-lit elevator button. You fool, Sharon thinks. She hates it when people do that.

The woman pushes the button a third time, and her impatience is the elbow that prods Sharon into action. In five steps she looms beside the shorter woman. She still has no idea what to say, but pride and wonder — she is really here, she is really doing this — straighten her spine. She takes a deep breath.

Nathalie beats her to it. "I know who you are." She looks Sharon up and down.

"I'm sure you do." Sharon's voice is icy.

"Okay, fine. Let's skip the small talk." Nathalie jabs the elevator button yet again.

"That doesn't make any difference, you know."

"Huh?"

"Hitting the button again and again. It doesn't make the elevator come any faster." Anger and superiority make for a high-proof cocktail, and Sharon savours the taste. "You're not that smart, are you?"

Nathalie whirls to face Sharon head on, her cheeks red, her eyes sparking. "And you're a dried-up old cunt, aren't you?"

Sharon's gasp coincides with the ding of the elevator, which opens to reveal two business-suited men. "Hey," the younger, good-looking one says to Nathalie as the elevator doors close behind them.

"Tate." She bites off the name like a gingersnap.

"I emailed you that file you were looking for, the one from Ottawa with the SMS updates. Should be waiting for you when you get up there." He smiles, a bright boy eager for his reward.

"Right."

The other man heads off, but Tate lingers. "We're going to Starbucks. Wanna come?"

"No."

"Can I bring you anything? A latte?"

Give it up, Sharon thinks.

"No. Look, I'll talk to you later."

"Sure. Maybe we'll do lunch, okay? Or a drink after work?"

"Mmm."

"It looks like rain." He jerks his head toward the front door. "You got the top up on your Miata?"

"It's fine. Later, okay?"

Tate flashes another bright smile and sprints outside to catch his companion. The lobby rings with emptiness. Nathalie pushes the elevator button again.

"I have very little to say to you," Sharon says. "I just want you to know that I know all about you. You are not a secret to me, and you were never, ever a threat. Rafe had a thing with you, but in the grand scheme it was nothing. He was coming back to me. We made up before he died and he was moving back in."

Nathalie tilts her head to one side. "So?" Her nose is faintly freckled. Sharon wants to smash it.

"He always loved me and he never loved you. That's all I want to say." Sharon turns to go.

"Do you know why he was coming back to you?" Sharon stops and Nathalie continues, her voice gritty. "Because I was done with him. We had a good time. He was a great fuck, by the way, like any man who hasn't had a decent lay for, like, years. But it ran its course and I sent him packing. It was so sad at the end. He begged me not to leave him. So touching." She purses her neatly glossed lips and jabs twice at the elevator button. "He died before I could tell him the rest."

Keep quiet, Sharon tells herself. Don't ask, don't give this creature the satisfaction.

The elevator dings and the doors glide open. Nathalie holds them ajar. "It's amazing," she says. "Only one time we did it without a condom.

The box was empty and he was too worked up to go buy more. One time, that's all it took. Bingo, knocked up." She steps into the elevator. "Don't worry, I took care of it. There won't be some little Mackie bastard out there to ruin anyone's reputation."

She smiles triumphantly, tosses her head, and is whisked away.

∧ ∨ ∧

SHE WAS A PILOT'S WIFE, yet she has never flown an airplane. Once in the early years, when they had reached cruising altitude in the little Cessna he sometimes took her up in, Rafe offered to hand over the controls. Piece of cake, he told her. She could do it no problem, and besides, he was there to guide her. She refused. She didn't want to take charge of such a powerful machine. She was afraid she couldn't keep it level, afraid of what might happen.

Afraid.

Fear has ruled so much of her life. Fear of change, fear of anything new and unpredictable. Fear of not getting what she wants, fear of losing what she has. Fear of being loved too much, of not being loved enough.

She crosses the empty lobby, her low-heeled boots ringing loud on the polished tiles. The glass door pushes open easily. Outside she surveys the cars lined up side by side, like so many sleeping cows. She was married to a man who loved sports cars. She knows what a Miata looks like.

It takes less than five minutes to find it. For a moment she is fooled by the shiny roof; she has expected the usual soft-top convertible. But this is it, a gleaming blue Miata, so clean and unmarked it could have come off the showroom floor yesterday. The final proof is the personalized plate: NAT AME.

She scans the parking lot. No one. She is alone. She reaches into her purse. The heft in her palm is reassuring. The square-topped Yale that unlocks her front door is the largest key on the ring, and she digs it into the pristine blue, experimenting.

Piece of cake, she tells herself. No problem.

It starts to rain, fat sweet drops. She wants to do this, and she can. She can make it happen.

She starts the circuit slow, then picks up speed, and her fears fall away, and Sharon takes off.

THIRTY-EIGHT

Twenty-three weeks after

IT WAS UNSETTLING, at first, being alone with Sheldon. Ever since the first nervous evening I met him at Sharon's I've been doing a sales job, trying to convince him that I'm a decent guy and not some fickle fly-by-nighter, hoping he'll see that Sharon made a good choice, one that's helped her to heal. Practically speaking, this has involved a lot of hovering in the background, waiting to be useful, listening and only occasionally interjecting while the stories fly, and noting, not without a trace of jealousy, the exceptional bond created by family ties. All the while I've felt appraised, the way you do when you're hawking your wares. There have been no failed tests, no grievous errors, but there hasn't been absolute acceptance either. Sheldon swaps stories with me and laughs a lot, but he hasn't let go the reins. For days I've felt him holding back.

Now, at the offices of the TSB, I sense a change.

It's something to do with the place. Push open the heavy door between the standard-issue government cubicles and the wreckage warehouse and you're in another world. Blown-apart aircraft shells. High-performance engines now blasted piles of scrap. Stench of aviation fuel and charcoal that coats your nose hairs so that hours later it's still with you. Tools everywhere, the wrenches, sockets, drills, and pry bars that let investigators deep inside a wreck to probe the whys of what brought it down. Wherever you look it's a war zone, each piece of shrapnel a reminder that simple acts align to produce horrific consequences, and we're fools if we think we're in charge.

We are shepherded into the back warehouse by Luanne, the TSB receptionist. She's one of the few people here during the furlough between Christmas and New Year's, and judging by her lemon-puckered look when we arrive, on time and as arranged, she's none too happy about it. Our path takes us past the TSB conference room where I was interrogated by Lyndon and his partner, and where I later met with Nathalie. It takes us past Nathalie's bare cubicle, stripped of papers and personal effects now that she has gone to Transport Canada. That sick feeling when I handed her the trim information, afraid I would mess up the mission Rafe gave me, washes over me. So does the bewildered rage I felt when Lyndon spilled the truth about Nathalie and Rafe.

Luanne delivers us inside the cavernous space. She points out the Tracker in the far corner — not that I need a reminder; the image has visited me for months — and says the lone on-duty air investigator will join us as soon as he's back from coffee. Then she declares that we must not, even though the file is closed and the wreckage due to be removed, touch so much as a rivet on what's left of the aircraft.

When we reach the ruined tanker, Sheldon, a born talker, falls quiet. What sort of person can view the heap of debris that sopped up the blood and brains of their only brother and chatter on about it? Not Sheldon.

He circles the wreck a couple of times, stopping to take in the singe marks that blacken the fuselage as well as the broken wing and propeller that lie off to one side. He peers through the glassless side window into the cockpit, takes in the wires hanging loose from the ceiling, and the pilot's seat rammed up against the smashed instrument panel.

"This where they found him, then?" He nods at the cockpit, voice gruff.

"Yeah. He had his seatbelt on, goes without saying, so he wasn't thrown clear."

"I always wondered, but Jesus. I never wanted to ask. Sharon had enough on her mind."

"I don't think Sharon knows. She hasn't seen this and who the hell would want to tell her?"

Sheldon grips the bottom of the side window, once a bubble of plexiglass. Evidently the Word of Luanne has struck less terror into his heart than mine.

"It's good he didn't get thrown clear," he says. "I hate to think of him smashing into the ground. At least this way he was ... protected." He blows a breath through pursed lips. "Foolish thing to say. I mean he was ... Ah, who the fuck knows what I mean? Not me."

He lets go of the window and wipes his hand on his jeans, his brow drawn in like someone told him a joke he doesn't get. I know that look. It was my reaction for the first two weeks after the crash. How could it have happened?

"Your brother was the best tanker pilot West Air had," I say. "It took him a year or two to get the feel of mountain flying, to learn his plane inside out and when to punch off and everything, but after that no one could touch him. If we had a tough circuit to fly, say a tricky wind to work with or bad terrain, Rafe was our guy." I can still picture him in that cockpit, headset barely fitting over his wide helmet of a head, shit-eating grin on his face. He was never happier than when he was inside that plane.

"He was a natural, his first instructor said." Sheldon smiles faintly. "He was twenty, twenty-one, and he was coming off such a terrible ... well, he needed to take his mind offa things. He takes his first flying lesson and like that he's a new man."

"This was in Cape Breton?"

"No, Halifax. We'd moved to the mainland by then."

"Your parents too?"

"No, no. They stayed where they were." He runs his eyes over the cockpit. "He didn't tell you all that? How the two of us ended up in Halifax?"

"Never. He told a lot of stories, but mostly about Ontario, flying the big planes for Canadian Airlines, fighting fires up north. Once in a while a little about Halifax. He never talked about anything before that, in Cape Breton. Well, he did say once that he'd caused your mother some trouble. This was after she passed away, we were toasting her." I pause, a moment of silence for dead mothers. "And he once said you bailed him out in those days."

"I might've." Sheldon brushes a small smear of soot off the fuselage. "Tell me more about his flying."

That's when my uneasiness with Sheldon evaporates. It's surreal but also deeply satisfying to discuss Rafe with someone who could be his fraternal twin, who understands him through and through. Sheldon listens with his whole body, like a stray mutt starved for attention, as I describe what it was like to fly with his brother: the precision and fearlessness of his moves, the daredevil flourishes when he'd swoop and turn and coax that relic of a plane right up to the edge of aerobatics. As I conjure up Rafe while looking into eyes that could have been his own, I almost trick myself into thinking he never left.

Then Sheldon asks about the crash. He's quick to add that I don't have to tell him, but I want to. I want to bring him inside. I want him to understand what happened above the fire that day, how whole lives flipped in the blink of an eye, how my guts plunged as suddenly as the Tracker hit the ground. This is the moment, as I'm reliving the terror of that morning, when a tectonic plate inside me shifts and the need to tell comes on hard. To hide the truth from this man, Rafe's near double, his only brother, feels deeply wrong.

"The part I can't wrap my thick head around," Sheldon is saying, "is why he didn't get the trim looked at. I mean, he was a crazy fella but he was always safe. Verged on obsessive when it came to checking, once, twice, three times. Everything had to be just so with him, no shortcuts. Not just with flying, he was the same when we worked construction. It wasn't like him to let something just ..."

"Just slide?" I finish for him. "I know."

He goes to the tail of the plane, where I'd pointed out the trim tabs earlier. "I read the report a couple of times," he says. "First the draft, Sharon wanted me to look at that, then the final, which was more or less the same thing, and it keeps nagging at me. You know yourself, he was particular about the details. He wouldn't blow off a snag like that."

Sheldon smells the lie as if it's a bucket of sewage at our feet. No way in this world would Rafe feel the trim stick and not report it. It's the weakest link in the story he wrote for me and it feels inevitable that his brother would spot it. It's bullshit, I want to say. It never happened.

I imagine it, the pure release of honesty.

"He was no dummy," Sheldon continues. "Not like his brother. He could've gone to university if things were ... if he had the chance." His brown eyes, so much like Rafe's, sweep the wreckage. "I can't believe he fucked up like that. It's the one thing I just don't get."

The need to come clean washes over me. I want it more than I've wanted anything, flying, women, anything. So many months of pretending and battling my conscience – I am exhausted.

He stares at the trim tabs, lost in thought.

"Sheldon." I step closer. He looks up at me. "He didn't fuck up."

"Ach," he says impatiently. "I know the report didn't come out and say so. It let him off the hook. But jumpin' Jesus, if he had a mechanical problem and didn't take care of it, that makes him responsible."

I stare at the painted concrete floor, scratched and pitted from years of wrecks, the Tracker just one more in a long line of disasters. It should put things in perspective, but it doesn't.

"There's not one of us wants to admit it," Sheldon says. "We all love the guy and think he was the world's best pilot and all that, but who're we kidding? He was a man, not some kind of a god. He made a bad call. He fucked up."

It comes on me, unstoppable, and I let it come. "He didn't."

You can't tell, a voice booms, like a foghorn warning me. I hear it, I swear. But washing over it, like the surf of the most dazzling wave I'll ever ride, comes the promise of sweet relief.

"There's something I know." I look up, meet his eyes square on. "The truth. I know the truth."

He waits. That man talks as much as Rafe ever did, long, rambling sentences, frequently funny, spilling out one after the other. But like his brother, when it matters, he knows how to shut it.

My eyes blur as I make up my mind, and the face across from me becomes Rafe's — open and eager when we nursed our ale or talked about cars, steady and focused when we trained and flew, deadpan when he was about to deliver another stupid joke, and lit-up happy every damned time I came into his line of sight. That's when it hits me: all these months of being at war with guilt and grief, and truth and loyalty, all I've wanted is to talk to him again. Just once. To tell him how hard it's been to pretend for him, and how angry I am that he forced me into a pact I never agreed to and then left, giving me no chance to try and talk him down. I look at that face, so much like Rafe's, and think: you bastard, you knew. You knew I would tell your lies, that I'd stand up for you no matter what. You knew me and you played me like the loyal coward I am.

"There was never any trim defect." My voice is so low that Sheldon has to step closer. "It was a lie. It was a story Rafe told me to tell the TSB. I was supposed to say that he mentioned trim problems to me. But he never did."

"What do you mean, he told you to tell the TSB? What, like he came back from the dead? Came to you in a friggin dream or something?"

If I say it there's no going back, but I am bone-tired of being alone with the truth. I want Sheldon with me.

"He told me before he died. In a letter. Who sends a letter anymore, right? Going by the postmark, he mailed it the day before the crash." My voice cracks. "I didn't get it until two weeks later, two weeks exactly. I'd been back at work a few days and was just getting my bearings. I hadn't checked my mailbox since the crash, there was too much going on. I never get anything except takeout menus anyhow."

I pause, remembering the night I opened the letter, the end of the endless day when I got grilled at the TSB, found out Rafe's marriage was on the rocks, took off to Steveston, and then briefed Jeff at West Air. The envelope was at the bottom of a pile I'd picked up in the lobby when I got home that evening. My name and address were in block letters; that told me nothing. It was only when I unfolded the page and saw the dark, pressed-down handwriting, so familiar from logbooks and reminder notes around West Air, that I had any clue what I was holding. When I glanced at the bottom and saw the scrawl of his signature, the guessing was over. It was a boot to the gut, getting a letter from a dead man.

I hesitate to say more to Sheldon, this has been a secret for so long, but then I say fuck that. He is Rafe's flesh and blood. He should know. "If I tell you this, Sheldon, you have to swear you won't tell anyone. Not Nancy, and definitely not Sharon. Not ever. Swear it on your mother."

He lets some time go by. I like a guy who doesn't promise things easily. Finally he nods. "Okay. I swear." His voice is sure. I believe him.

"This letter, he told me never to show it to anyone, never to tell anyone. It was ... like a deathbed promise." I grope for the right words.

Don't explain, a voice says. *Just say it.*

"There was no trim problem. No mechanical problem at all." I place a palm on the ruined fuselage. "This plane was old when Rafe got it ten years ago, and the last couple seasons it's been flying on fumes, but that had nothing to do with the crash."

Rafe's face still hovers there inside Sheldon's, and I make myself look him in the eyes.

"He did it on purpose. So he would die. In the letter he asked me to cover for him, to tell the TSB this bogus story about a trim problem. I did talk to him the morning of the crash, anyone at the fire centre would've seen it, but it was routine stuff. Nothing about the trim. Nothing, not one fucking word, about ... his plans."

I take a moment to steady my voice, then continue. "He'd been acting different for weeks, we all noticed it. Kind of quiet, preoccupied. But nothing so serious you'd think ..." I comb my memory for the millionth time for any sign in the days before the crash that Rafe had come to a final crossroads. As always, I find nothing. "I knew him as much as anyone did, besides you and Sharon. I could read his moods. There were times I knew what he was thinking before he said it. He talked to me, you know? Or he used to. But not about this. About this, I had no fucking clue."

I am losing it, blinking hard. "That morning I was the last person to talk to him at any length on the ground. He seemed normal. He didn't smile at me the way he usually would, and he was a bit … lost in his thoughts, but it didn't seem like a big deal. Only it was. It was a huge deal, and I didn't see it. I keep asking myself every goddamned day, how did I not realize the state he was in? How could I not know? I was so caught up in my own stupid life that it's like I lost track of him. I could have stopped him, Sheldon. I should have stopped him. But I didn't."

I turn away to hide the tears. Every joint and muscle in me, every inch of skin, pulses with fresh guilt. The warehouse is silent; Sheldon is silent.

I backhand my eyes. "That's the whole story. Part of me still can't believe it. I have the proof, for God's sake, I have his suicide note, and still it won't sink in."

Sheldon doesn't move. Through everything I say he stays still as a post, I guess trying to absorb the shock. It's taken me weeks — God, months — to absorb it and I was just Rafe's friend, not his brother.

His brother.

For fuck's sake, what was I thinking? I look at Sheldon, standing frozen and blank beside the wrecked plane. How could I bring him here, all unsuspecting, where he can see and smell the fact of his brother's violent death, and then bring a fucking avalanche down on him? Plus break my vow to Rafe, ignore his dying wish? All for what — to ease my own load?

You self-centred moron. So that's what it all comes to. Sessions with The Counsellor and a bunch of sleepless nights and fifteen, twenty pounds lost and a giant fucking obligation and pretending like I'm Sharon's shining knight and I haven't learned a goddamned thing. I'm the same selfish, chickenshit bastard I was that morning I let Rafe climb into his plane.

I hang my head, ashamed to the core.

When Sheldon finally speaks, his words take me by surprise. "The affair. The goddamn affair."

I blink. "What?"

"He was screwing around with some TSB investigator, I don't know her name. That's why he moved out. That'll have something to do with … his decision."

"Jesus. He told you about her?"

"Not a word. Sharon did."

Just when I think the truth has crawled all the way into the open, it turns out its hindquarters are still in the shadows. All this time I've been protecting Sharon from the truth about Rafe and Nathalie, and she's known about it?

Sheldon unfolds the whole story: how Sharon told him and Nancy about Nathalie their first night in Vancouver, and also told them that she and Rafe had reconciled. "That's the part I don't get," he says. "So he feels guilty about cheating on Sharon. Running around on his wife, that was way outside his personal code. But if they were getting back together, why would he ...? Ah Jesus, Will, I can't even say it. Kill himself. You must've read that letter wrong. You must've misunderstood."

Time is running out — our investigator escort will show up any minute and Sharon is picking us up soon — but Sheldon has to hear the rest. I tell him about the complaint Nathalie lodged just before the crash.

He says exactly what I would say. "A complaint? That makes no sense at all. Rafe and Nathalie were together, they were a couple. Rafe left his wife for her, for Jesus sake. How could that be harassment?"

"Jeff, my boss, Rafe's boss too, was convinced there was nothing to it. When he talked to Tucker here at the TSB, Tucker agreed. They figured it was an empty threat, something she cooked up to get back at Rafe for breaking off with her. She wasn't going without a fight."

"Jesus Murphy. Sounds like a piece of work. But you know, you listen to the news these days and they're always saying ... Well, in this kind of a situation it's always down to he said, she said. You know Rafe. He was a big galoot but he was gentle as a lamb. He'd never force himself on anyone. I'd lay every cent I have on that, I'd lay my life on it. But other people —"

The warehouse door screeches open and we wheel around. I'm expecting the air investigator who's supposed to keep an eye on us, but it's Luanne, heaving toward us, looking decidedly unhappy.

"My air guy is MIA and now your ride is here." She glares at us, these developments clearly no one's fault but our own.

We freeze like startled grouse, hoping that our stillness will camouflage us.

"Snap out of it, boys. You coming?"

"Two minutes," I say. "We'll be out in two minutes."

You'd think I just promised to make the wreckage fly again from the dubious look she shoots me, but she doesn't argue. Just lumbers off and bangs the door behind her.

Sheldon reaches into the cockpit, snaps the knob off the smashed gyrocompass, and hides it in his jacket pocket. "Better make a break for it, buddy." He gives me a sad smile. "Before Osama bin Laden out there takes prisoners."

I feel foolishly grateful to him for lightening the mood. "You're a braver man than I."

"I still don't see the connection," Sheldon says as we cross the warehouse. "This lady made up some complaint that no one ever knew about. So what?"

"Well, the two bosses knew. And Rafe, of course."

He stops in his tracks. "Rafe?"

"Yeah, Jeff told him right away. Figured he had a right to know."

"Ah fuck, no." It comes out as a whisper. "This was right before the crash?"

"A day or two. That's what I think —"

"Wait, let me get this straight." He is wound up. "Rafe makes up with Sharon, then finds out there's a bullshit harassment complaint against him? Was there anything ... did something else come to light?"

"No, that's it. I don't even know which came first, making up with Sharon or the complaint. Not that it matters. Either way, the complaint was bogus and he was putting his life back together. Believe me, I've had a long time to think about it, and there's not one bit of what happened that makes sense to me." I glance at my watch. "Our two minutes are up. We better not poke the bear."

THIRTY-NINE

December

THE NUMBER'S HERE SOMEWHERE. Goddammit, where? Not in her cell phone log. Will's call to her that one time came to her TSB phone. She must've written it down, then. Where the fuck ...?

Nathalie rifles through her file drawer. She is shaking, her arms and shoulders, her chin.

Not from frustration, although she is beyond annoyed by how she can't find one fucking thing in this stupid fucking place. The regional System Safety Office, despite its name, contains no offices. There's a surprise, she thought when she first glimpsed the grey-carpeted field of laminate desks over two months ago. Instead of offices there are stations, docks, and pods. "Like a goddamn space station," she muttered to no one at the end of her bounding tour of the fifth-floor area – a tour led not by her boss, who waited two full days before granting Nathalie a face-to-face meeting, but by the gazelle-like office manager who went by the name, and this was apparently not a joke, of Peppi. Nathalie was accustomed to a no-walls layout from the TSB, but there they at least had shoulder-high dividers that gave the illusion of personal space, plus a few enclosed offices for the most senior investigators. Here at Transport Canada the officers of the SS (her private name for the SSO group) don't merit dividers. Just a seat, monitor, and docking station at one of the long communal tables, with a single rolling file drawer per person underneath.

Which is where the goddamn Tracker file should be. Why can't she find it? It's a slim file because she wasn't supposed to have one in the first place. The investigation wasn't hers, as she'd been warned repeatedly by every smarmy jackass at the TSB. *Not mine to resolve,* she wishes she'd said, *but mine in ways you morons will never understand.*

Rafe's wife, goddammit! An ambush. Shit, piss, and *tabernacle*. The woman's name is a poisoned dart that Nathalie dodges by never speaking it, out loud or to herself. A nameless person is easier to erase. Dried-up old cunt, Nathalie just called her. Colourful, but not accurate. The wife is no longer the pasty-faced shadow who slumped through the funeral. She is forceful and striking.

No wonder he picked her.

Shut it, okay? *Pas maintenant.*

Nathalie is shaking not from frustration but from fury. Did that really just happen? As the elevator whisked her from the lobby horror show to the all-too-real fifth floor, she had dug her nails into her palm, hard. She actually has nails now that she's a soft office worker, and sure enough they've left red marks on her skin. Proof aside, the exchange feels surreal, like a trippy dream or a daytime soap scene: wronged wife versus mistress, hero facing off against villain.

Which makes you the villain.

No! Not now.

When Will phoned that time, she was out of the office, so Luanne must have jotted his number on one of her famous pink slips. Who knew pink slips existed outside of the movies? Nathalie certainly didn't until she joined the TSB. Thank God for federal agencies, landfill sites for the junk that other offices toss: paper notes, an in/out board, an actual water cooler, even Luanne for that matter. Who has a receptionist anymore?

That pink slip has to be in the goddamn file. But where is it? The drawer is crammed full of folders, nearly all of them from her current work. "System Safety, what do they even do?" she'd asked Tucker the Fucker while signing the papers that sealed her transfer. He'd launched into a garbled explanation that the ensuing two and a half months have done little to untangle. To the best of her knowledge, officers of the SS devote their talent and energy to getting other people to do their jobs. Airline managers, safety advisors, maintenance operators, consulting firms, you name it – if safety tasks and audits can be offloaded onto them, the SS will cheerfully do it, then spool out the rest of their seven-point-five-hour day plotting how to further divert and delay workflows while (ideally) earning overtime in the process.

She hates it here. Hates the gigantic high-school cafeteria that passes for an office; resents the paper-pushing they call work; detests Peppi, whose name she can't say out loud without smirking; loathes her boss, whose eyes slide off her as if she's another article of hand-me-down furniture; despises the other SS officers except for maybe Tate, but only because he's easy on the eyes and goes out of his way to please her. She has applied for three other jobs since landing here in October, two of them at a lower level and pay scale. It'll be a worthwhile sacrifice if it comes to that. At this point she's in pure countdown mode, marking the days until she can get the fuck out.

Goddamn Tracker crash! She had pegged last year's Cessna 172 disaster as the deepest pit she'd ever have to climb out of. What a joke. The Tracker case is an undersea mine shaft by comparison. Why won't it leave her alone?

At least she has a plan. She will use the rage unleashed by the wife to do something she should've done months ago. Will Werner, the asshole narc, went straight to his boss, Jeff Montrose at West Air, and ratted her out, told Jeff that she, Nathalie, had buried his precious lead about the Tracker's trim malfunction. Bad enough that Lyndon discovered her stall; at least he had enough loyalty to shut his trap. No, the shit rained down on her once the news hit Tucker. And Tucker got wind of it from Jeff at West Air, who could have heard it only from Will. Will Werner, the weasel who brought her the information in the first place, is at the bottom of everything. He's the reason she is serving a sentence in this hellhole.

Bad can always get worse.

Shut up, Mémère!

How hard can it be to find one tiny goddamn file? It's not like she got to keep much from her glory days at the TSB. Her move to Transport Canada was hurried, and she was ordered to leave all work material behind. Following the PAMEA conference, Lyndon, her buddy turned bastard, proved himself to be as efficient as he was furious. True to his word, he had lined up her application to System Safety, gotten Tucker the Fucker on board, even put in a good reference with her new boss, someone he knew through choir channels, and in a scant couple of weeks Nathalie's name was wiped off the TSB's in/out board. Why didn't he go ahead and box up her personal effects while he was at it? Maybe cut her phone line? Plant one shined-up loafer in her back as she exited the building?

What hurt most was the pleasure he took in ending her career as an investigator, a career he had inspired in the first place. Lyndon was never her best friend but he was a kind of friend, there for her most days, good for a laugh and a latte. Now he is nowhere, their association severed as cleanly as any wing sheared off an airplane.

Gone. Just like the rest of them.

All her adult life Nathalie has heard her grandmother's voice in her head, the woman's homespun, accented advice both a prod and a reminder of life's priorities. More guidance has come Nathalie's way from this disembodied voice than ever did from the woman in the flesh. Except nowadays Mémère plays tricks. She is no longer content to repeat the pearls of wisdom she dropped when Nathalie was a girl. *Only a nutting does nutting. Don't speak ill of the dead. Better to hit than be hit.* Now she utters new and unpredictable phrases, ones Nathalie does not want to hear.

The TSB files had to stay behind, the paper documents and digital records alike. Her archive of crash photos was no longer hers to peruse. Her laptop went … where? Back to government stores, maybe, purged of its contents. Or to some charity desperate enough to take ten-year-old equipment. Only a few personal items came with her: framed certificates from workshops; a shot someone took of her in overalls, beside a Sikorsky s-76, at Mainland Air; the graduation photo from

AME school, which now sits on her desk — correction, her allotment of the shared table — Jake Behrend at one end of the front row. Jake, so young and delectable in the photo, is as much in the past as the TSB and Lyndon.

Bad can always get worse. It's all going for shit.

It was partly a matter of convenience. How could she possibly explain to Jake why she was being shuffled to Transport Canada? He would know in an instant that it wasn't her choice, and telling him the truth was not an option. Easier to ditch him before the transfer took place. She ended it fast and without regret — without *much* regret, she thinks, glancing at his magnificent face — the decision made easier because after two days and nights together during the PAMEA conference he was starting to go puppy-eyed. The morning he was due at the airport, as they recovered in bed from their farewell fuck, he started in on how his marriage had been dying ever since the kids came, how his wife hardly noticed him, was caught up in the house and the children, the romance was gone, their relationship was a dead thing it was time to bury, yada yada yada, moan moan moan.

"I'm still young," he said, predictably. "It's time for something new." Another teaching job had opened up at BCIT and this time he was a shoo-in. "What if I moved here?" He flashed his blinding smile. "These two days have been amazing, Nat. What do you think?"

She put her finger to his lips. *"Assez,"* she said. "We need to get up. No missing your flight." There was not time, and there were not the words, to say how unthinkable was the life he'd proposed. Move here? A future together? It was preposterous.

She broke it off by email, two lines sent later that day, a fitting end to a liaison Jake had launched by email in the first place.

Jake, we've had some great times but it's over. Time for me to move on. You know me, tough as nails. Your friend (with benefits), Nat

He is gone. We are all gone.

Good riddance, Mémère.

Aha! There it is. The thin Tracker file is lodged inside a bigger folder from her new job, and the pink slip is right in front, Will's phone number in Luanne's fierce scrawl.

She is going to blast Will Werner, but first she needs to calm down. Angry and composed is better than angry and explosive, as the wife's cool ambush in the lobby just proved.

It's all going for shit.

Enough!

Mémère is getting to her. Often when Nathalie talks back to her grandmother she can silence her. Not today.

One of the best features of the SSO layout is the pods, Peppi enthused the day she showed Nathalie around. However, the sound-proof booths at either end of the open space are transparent, so when Nathalie needs a real refuge, the women's washroom is her best bet. Luckily the SS officers, like the TSB investigators, are all men so she typically has the space to herself.

She heads for the end stall, sits down, breathes deep.

Better to hit than be hit.

No question, the lobby confrontation hit her, and she was in no way prepared to strike first. How could she be, after so many months? Her affair with Rafe is ancient news, for God's sake. At least she got her two cents' worth in. The wife was shocked, especially at the C-word, which she probably never heard before in real life. Nathalie chuckles. What do you expect if you're going to attack someone out of the blue?

Like you attacked him.

Mémère never says his name. She doesn't have to.

Not an attack, she tells Mémère. I ended it. That's all. What came later, Tucker turning it into an official complaint, Rafe finding out, that wasn't me. Not my fault.

He knew, and then he flew. And then he died.

Mechanical. It was mechanical.

They've gone over it many times, she and her dead grandmother, the same accusations, the same defences. Call and response is the name for it in music. Lyndon, who sings in a soul choir, once told her that. Lyndon, who *used* to sing in a soul choir. Who knows what he does now.

All of us, gone. What is wrong with you?

With me?

The barrage of personal jibes is getting to her. Mémère was never what you'd call soft, but at least she was on Nathalie's side. Now there's a harping edge to her remarks. The only good thing about all the needling is that it has chased Rafe's mutilated body from Nathalie's kitchen and her dreams. The voice of her dead grandmother, it would seem, has expelled the ghost of her dead lover.

Not lover. There was no love.

There was, Mémère! There was.

Loud pounding rattles the washroom door. "Nathalie? You in there?"

What the fuck? It's Tate. "Yes, I'm in here! What do you think? I'm busy."

"Nathalie." He must have opened the main door because his voice is louder, closer. "You better come out. There's something … Well, you need to see something. In the parking lot."

"Look, I'm occupied. I'll come out later."

"Okay, but trust me. You're gonna want to see this."

Whatever. So there's some fancy car he wants to show her. Big hairy deal. It can wait.

She hugs her middle and stares at the spotty tiles beneath her feet. What does it say about you when so many of your emotional moments take place near a toilet? She fled to a TSB stall when Uncle Theo gruffly informed her that Mémère had died. In the same washroom she gave herself daily pep talks during the Cessna 172 fallout, when her colleagues shunned her and Tucker simmered. She was on a toilet, or hovering over one, that catastrophic day when she learned her complaint had gone forward and she was pregnant.

Her stomach, toned and flat now under her crossed arms, never got so far as a bulge. No one guessed there was a baby, and Nathalie never told. Even Mémère is strangely silent on the topic. So what the hell possessed Nathalie to fast-pitch the information in the lobby just now, and at the *wife* of all people? It was by far the worst part of the ambush, and it's the reason she is shaking again. Until today that baby was her secret, her one private scrap of the wreckage that was Rafe. That they'd so effortlessly made a child, in one single unprotected act, a bull's eye if there ever was one, is a miracle that has rooted in the deepest part of her, where it has accumulated layers of meaning. It proves there was love, not just hers, his too. Rafe Mackie saw inside her like no one else. His body was made for her, and hers for him. They were fated to be together – that had to be true; otherwise no seed would have taken hold. Their future was assured, except Rafe died before he knew it, before she and the baby could show him.

See, she tells Mémère, there was love.

No love. All the love is gone.

Is her grandmother testing her? Well, she is no crier. Tough as nails – Jake called her that for a reason. Mémère can say what she wants and so can the wife. It won't change a thing. There was love.

Except a niggling part of her knows there is more to it. The evidence, which she has been too busy –

Afraid.

– to compile tells a different story. She has done everything right. She has made her own way, heeded Mémère, hardened her heart, taken no shit, buckled down, and done it all herself. Where has it gotten her? Her inner investigator, which no job change can silence, kicks in and she follows the chain.

Evidence – parents: gone, leaving behind an orphan. Result: Mémère, who made the orphan into a tough loner. Mémère: gone, leaving behind her voice. Result 1: Cessna 172 fiasco (*Only a nutting does nutting*). Consequences: professional humiliation, alienation. Result 2: Tracker disaster (*Knowledge is power*). Consequences: professional humiliation, alienation, TSB job gone, Lyndon gone, Jake gone. Result 3: Rafe affair (*Better to hit than be hit*). Consequences: personal humiliation, Rafe gone, baby gone, love gone.

Conclusions – humiliation, alienation, loneliness, loss.

The facts are there, as indisputable as if they're written on the bathroom floor. How can they be true? How can her life have come to this when she has done everything right?

Yet the report holds up. It is damning but also solid, evidence-based.

In a flash she understands: it's the Swiss cheese theory. She has stacked every circumstance, or slice of cheese, from when she was a girl up to this moment in the locked bathroom stall, and the result is a pile in which the holes align. They align and create: a hole.

A nothing. An absence.

Everything she touches dies — Lyndon had flung that nugget of a conclusion at Jake at the PAMEA conference. Lyndon was livid that day, and maybe jealous. She used to wonder if his feelings for her went beyond platonic. But he is also the best accident investigator she knows.

Everything she touches. Mémère in her casket, dead to her granddaughter's affection since the day she slapped the little girl's hand away. Rafe in his cockpit, as crushed and lifeless as her heart. The baby in her womb, a spark extinguished before it could flare.

Around each dead creature a shell.

Around her, too, a casing that hardens and thickens with every hit. A shell, designed to protect. To protect what, exactly? She hugs her middle tighter. What is in there that's still alive?

FORTY

December

SHARON WAITS OUTSIDE THE TSB, fingers drumming the steering wheel in time to the radio, which she has switched from the news to a dance music station. When the buildup of energy is too much to bear, she leaves the car, rain be damned, and paces the nearly empty parking lot.

Keying the Miata, trailing her jagged signature from one end of the immaculate hard-top to the other, thrilled her to the core, but why didn't she do more? Nathalie Girard is monstrous, viler than she could have imagined. Sharon should have slapped her repugnant little face or gouged her taunting eyes. She should have kicked her in the stomach, the empty space where briefly there was life. A life made by Rafe.

Impossible, unimaginable. She can't bear to imagine it. She can't bear not to.

It's not the abortion — she doesn't care about that. In fact, thank God no baby will come from that woman. It's not even the woman's hideousness or vulgarity. Plainly Rafe was with her for sex, nothing more.

Sharon comes to a halt beside her car, oblivious to the puddle she has stepped in. All the visits to fertility clinics, all the calendars carefully marked with the ebb and flow of her cycle. All the days she urged Rafe to change his flight schedule or come home from the gym or interrupt a project in the garage so they could go to bed, right now, when the conditions were right. All the times they did it for the schedule, Rafe performing as reliably as he delivered drops from his plane, but with little of the passion that gripped him when conditions were wrong. All the years it never happened, when every month she held her breath, hoping this would be the one. How could he have made that smug little tramp pregnant, just like that?

The answer is so obvious that in her jangled state, for one golden moment, she almost misses it. The answer is: it was her. She was the defective one. Doctors and their normal tests be damned, the truth of their decades-long roller coaster of trying to conceive and failing was right there, staring her in the face, hurling insults at her in the echoing lobby. It was her fault all along.

Will and Sheldon jog into sight, their shoulders hunched in a vain attempt to escape the rain. She is soaked, she realizes, water streaming from the tip of her nose and the ends of her hair.

"What are you doing out in this?" yells Will. When he's at her side, while Sheldon is climbing into the backseat, he brushes her neck with his lips.

"Sorry you had to wait," Sheldon says once they are all inside.

Her wet pants are already sticking to the upholstery. She starts the car. "Don't worry about it. I was early." She backs out of the space.

"The sales no good?" asks Will, pushing wet hair off his forehead.

For a second is she confused. The she remembers: she was supposed to be shopping. "No. There was nothing there for me."

∧ ∨ ∧

AN HOUR LATER they push burgers around during an early, desultory lunch back in the city. Sharon offers Will her dill pickle, forgetting that he'd already declined it when their plates arrived. Will rearranges his fries and folds napkins into paper airplanes. Sheldon pushes aside his half-eaten cheeseburger and stares out the window, where the only signs of life are raincoats dragging reluctant dogs through the downpour.

We're lost in our own worlds, Sharon thinks. When Will says he has things to do at home and will meet up with them again tomorrow, she is relieved. Some time apart will be good. But the minute she drops him at his building, she knows that being away from him is the last thing she wants. Her heart sinks as his lanky frame disappears into the lobby.

Sheldon moves up to the front seat, and as if reading her mind takes her hand, which lies limply on the gearshift. "He's a good guy."

"You think so?"

"I do." He squeezes her fingers. "I can see why you're with him. There's something, I don't know, open about him. Like you could trust him. Like you could tell him anything."

She nods, her eyes on the door of the shabby building. That's Will.

"I don't hold it against you, Sharon." Sheldon's voice is kind. "Neither does Nancy. Neither" — a gruff sound as he clears his throat — "neither would Rafe."

The name floats between them, a delicate balloon.

She covers Sheldon's big hand with her other one. "How can you know that?"

"Because he wouldn't. Believe me. He of all people would understand."

∧ ∨ ∧

THREE HOURS LATER she is back, in the very same spot, watching the very same door. Don't do it, she told herself sternly when Sheldon and Nancy retreated to the guest room for a nap. Go to the bank, buy wine for dinner. She unstacked the dishwasher and flipped through the cruise brochures, but nothing reined in her galloping mind. In the end, distracted and twitchy, she pulled on her rain jacket and drove to Will's.

Where is he? She peers at the building's dingy front door. If only her longing could summon him home. She had buzzed his apartment when she arrived but got no answer, and opted not to interrupt his errands with a text. He won't have gone far. His usual haunts line Commercial Drive, close to home.

She wonders, as rain hammers the car roof, how she will explain the unannounced visit. She has no intention of telling Will where she really was this morning, and she will certainly not share Nathalie's shocking revelation. She simply wants to be with him. The physical need leaks from her skin, fingers, lips. She wants him to hold her and say that things will be fine without getting into what those things are. Sheldon is right — Will is a soothing balm that she is desperate for after this morning. She still can't believe it. She had prepared herself to say harsh words to Rafe's woman. Never did she imagine that the woman had a far more damaging message for her.

A baby. There was a baby.

The red oak they had sat under that sweltering July afternoon in the park had cast welcome shade, but Sharon kept her straw hat on just the same, the wide brim affording some protection from Rafe's intensity. None of their bitter fights, and the past year had featured many, had ever left Rafe in such a state of remorse. Pleading, apologies, and promises flowed from him in a torrent. "Leaving you was the worst mistake of my life. I know how much I've hurt you. I will never make you feel that way again." He gripped her hands as if to press his words into her. "I was selfish, Sharon. I've always been selfish, thinking about my own needs. Please." He reached over, removed her hat, and smoothed her hair. "Please take me back and I swear, I'll spend the rest of my life making you happy. I'll do anything. I'll give up the firefighting if you want me to, get back with an airline so you're not alone so much. We can go back to Toronto, we can go home."

A sharp knock breaks her reverie. At the car window stands a pierced girl holding a blue, orange, and green umbrella that looks for all the world like a patchwork quilt, as does the girl herself, in a long multicoloured coat, purple fingerless gloves, and green knitted toque. Sharon doesn't move, is unsure what to do. Will this person ask for spare change?

The girl motions her to roll down her window. "You're Sharon, right?"

How does she know? "Yes."

"Then you're waiting for Will." The girl leans in, her thick hair wafting the scent of patchouli into the car. "He'll be here eventually. I ran into him at the market down the street. He has to go to the liquor store, then the deli, and then one more place, I think, but then he'll be home."

It's Will's neighbour, Sharon realizes, the hippie girl he's mentioned.

"Melody," the girl says, offering one green-nailed hand through the window.

Sharon gives the hand a half-hearted shake. "Pleased to meet you."

The girl giggles. Has Sharon said something funny? "He's coming over to my place for a beer when he gets back. Why don't you wait for him there?"

Sharon draws back slightly. The last thing she's in the mood for is forced small talk with a stranger.

"Really, it's no trouble." The girl holds up a canvas carry bag. "I have ginseng tea."

There has to be a polite way to decline, but there is no denying reality: Sharon is in a cold car, in the rain, being offered shelter by a good Samaritan.

Minutes later she is installed in a beanbag chair, a species of furniture she had presumed to be extinct, in the middle of a tiny studio apartment. The girl has switched on the kettle in the built-in kitchenette. The one-room apartment is a riot of colour, from the braided rugs strewn across the floor to the iridescent glass mobiles suspended from the ceiling. A series of African masks lines one wall, narrow cheekbones smudged with bold hues. A mirror-spangled purple-and-pink blanket is tacked up on the other. The only unadorned surface is the sliding glass door to the balcony, outside which the end-of-December dusk is falling.

"How did you know it was me out there?" Sharon asks.

"Well, duh. I've seen you with Will a bunch of times." The kettle whistles and Melody pours water into a mug. "Don't get me wrong, I'm not spying on you. But it's, what, a month or two now that you guys have been, like, a thing? You're hardly a stranger around here." She approaches Sharon with a steaming mug in one hand and a red shellacked saucer in the other, and sets both on a low table beside the beanbag. "To put the tea ball in after," she says, indicating the saucer.

"Aren't you having any?" Sharon asks, unable to summon up a thank-you for something she so profoundly does not want.

"No, I'll hold out for beer when Will shows up. But you've gotta be cold from waiting. It's gross out there." The girl goes to the balcony door and checks outside for confirmation.

She's only being kind. Sharon berates herself for her churlishness, removes the tea ball, and wets her lips with the dirt-flavoured liquid. "You've known Will a long time, I guess?" As the taste hits her she grimaces, then tries to convert the expression into a smile.

"Three and a half years. Since I first moved in." Melody nods toward the balcony. "I met him out there. His balcony's on the other side of mine. I'd see him now and then, in the lobby, the laundry room, that sort of thing, until all the ... you know, the trouble last summer. We've been tighter since then. He still thinks I'm kinda flaky, but I don't mind. That's Will for you. He's still learning."

She turns on a batik-shrouded floor lamp beside the sliding door, then settles cross-legged on a cushion, revealing purple-and-green striped tights under her long skirt. She sits very straight, like a person schooled in posture. "He's in love with you, you know."

"Uh ..." Sharon flounders. "I don't know what to say to that."

"You don't have to say anything. *He* never has, but he doesn't have to. I can tell. I've seen him with a lot of women over the years, a *lot* of women. He's no shy guy, our Will. But he's never been like this before. He's in L-O-V-E." She sits straighter, her deductive powers seemingly a source of pride.

At a loss for words, Sharon unthinkingly raises the tea again. The smell, not far off rotting leaves, brings her to her senses and she sets the mug on the far edge of the table.

"Do you have a boyfriend?" A change of subject is in order.

"Sometimes." Melody smiles wanly. "Mainly Friday and Saturday nights, after he's been out drinking with his friends. The rest of the week, not so much."

"That doesn't sound ... ideal."

"Ha. No. It's temporary, just for, you know, sex. Until I find someone real. It's nothing like what you and Will have."

What do Will and I have? Sharon tries not to ask herself that, choosing pleasure in the present over anxiety about an unknowable future.

"What you and Will have is beautiful. The way you light him up, that's the real thing."

"Is that what you're looking for, the real thing?"

Sharon hopes reciprocal nosiness will shut Melody down, but the girl is not remotely flustered. "I've had it, actually. More than once. It used to be easy for me to fall in love. I could do it like that." She snaps her fingers. "But I was too young to appreciate what I had. I let them go."

"But you're still young. You're just a girl."

"No, I'm the same age as Will. Well, almost. Two years younger."

Every cradle-robbing worry Sharon has entertained surfaces at once.

"Thirty-four and my clock is ticking. Tick-tock, tick-tock." Melody wags one finger. "I *so* want a little one. I never thought I would. For sure not in my twenties. Back then I was worried it'd tie me down, keep me from experiencing life, all that negative stuff you think when you're that age. Of course that's when I hooked up with the two guys who would've had kids with me if I wanted. They said so, both of them, but I was so not ready. Not like now. God. Now I'm this giant egg just waiting for someone to come along and fertilize me. Honestly, I'm not even that picky about who it is. Except that he has to be into me more than two days a week."

In Sharon's ears a low roar, like inside a conch shell. Forty-four, ten years older. Her time is up.

Melody shifts on her cushion. "I'm rambling. My bad. So do you have kids from earlier, like before Will?"

Sharon gazes at her lap, shakes her head. No kids. No baby.

"You never wanted them? I get that, I really do. It's great to live in this era, isn't it? Where women don't have to have kids. Not like when my mom got married. She tells me all the time how if she was my age now? Knowing what she knows and having a choice and all? She'd never have kids. She tells my brother too. She's not what you'd call a tactful sort of person." In one motion she pushes up from the cushion, uncrossing her legs as she stands. "More tea?"

Sharon's head is still bowed. The low roar builds, becomes wind in the leaves, the leaves of the red oak. "I'll do anything," he told her.

"Hey, you okay?" Melody stands over her.

The wind picked up his words that July day as they sat under the tree, and now Sharon lets herself hear every one of them. "I'll do anything. We can go back to Toronto, we can go home. We can adopt." The promise he had steadfastly refused to make, the words she had given up on hearing.

The girl squats beside Sharon. "What happened? Did I say something?"

Sharon shakes her head but is betrayed by her body, which begins to tremble.

"I've given it a lot of thought," he said. "It doesn't matter about the baby's past. I've been stupid about that. Sometimes you got to pack away the past so you can go on with the rest of your life. Let's sign up and start the wait. Come on, Sharon. Think of it."

She did think of it that day, she thought of it and her throat tightened and hope rose in her breast and she saw a baby, a tiny child, in her arms, in their home. Their child, hers and Rafe's; a new start with a new family. She was giddy with hope. No more ache at the smile of another's toddler, no more hiding baby books around the house like a closet drinker, no more concealing from Rafe her bitter, bitter sorrow. Together they would make space for a child, and in doing so make space for each other. She saw the long span of their future, their baby growing up, their family of three.

"Oh, God, I did say something." The girl's voice drops. "Shit. I'm such a moron. I'm sorry." She places a hand on Sharon's wrist, dainty green fingertips resting there lightly. "Really sorry."

Sharon begins to weep, a shaking, shuddering, absolute surrender that she has never permitted herself, not alone, not in front of another person, not ever.

Melody doesn't hesitate. She slides one hip onto the beanbag chair, enfolds the woman in patchouli-scented arms, and rocks her.

As Sharon sobs she hears Nathalie by the elevator: *One time, that's all it took.* She hears Rachel in the café: *Maybe the question is, did you love him?* She hears Rafe in the mornings: *I'll love you all the day long.* She hears herself beside Will: *Maybe it's because I chose you.*

Hears herself tell Melody: "It was me." Her voice tear-scratched and stricken. "I blamed him, I held so much against him, I thought he didn't care enough. And the whole time it was me."

FORTY-ONE

Twenty-four weeks after

^ ⌄ ^

JANUARY 2. A new year, a new start. A time for resolutions, bright hope, a new you. All that pop psychology bullshit. And it is bullshit. Fragrant, steaming turds of bull.

I can't think about beginnings today. Only endings.

^ ⌄ ^

BEGIN AT THE BEGINNING, they always say. Sounds easy, but it assumes that you know what the story actually is and where it really starts.

I thought the story of Rafe began last summer, when he crashed his plane and died. Except his story is woven into Sharon's story, and that began much earlier. Two months earlier, when her husband moved out? Or years before that, when her hopes for a baby died? Or even longer ago, when she let a charismatic giant whisk her away? On top of those stories lies another, the story of Nathalie Girard, in which (I now know) disappointed love got way out of hand. And there's my own story, too, touching them all.

Now I know that the origin story, the real beginning, involves none of these. The real beginning goes back to a time before me, before Nathalie, before Sharon even, to a time that Rafe erased. A time when two overgrown, boisterous brothers came of age on Cape Breton Island, a place as remote and wild as they were, cut off in spite of the causeway that tethered it to the mainland. The real beginning was, like the new year is for me, an ending.

But I'm getting ahead of myself.

Begin at the beginning.

∧ ∨ ∧

I COULD BEGIN WITH how I haven't felt this wrung out since the darkest weeks after I got Rafe's letter. Some of the emptiness is the lingering hangover brought on by too many drinks over too short a time on New Year's Eve. Most of it is the story that came out during those drinks.

I could begin by saying I haven't laid eyes on Sharon since then. Technically it was into New Year's Day when she and Nancy begged off, around one thirty in the morning. We'd reduced the buffet in Sharon's kitchen to a few shrivelled shrimp, and we'd emptied the champagne and moved on to freezer-chilled vodka. Like the sensible women they are, they said they'd drunk enough and danced enough and would leave us be until brunch the next day, before Sheldon and Nancy went to the airport. It was a brunch I didn't stick around for and a goodbye I didn't say. By the time Sheldon and I were through, hours after our women went to bed, I had to escape that house and be alone with my pounding head and reeling thoughts. Since then the only thing I've been sure about is that I can't go back. Not yet.

I could begin with the morning Sheldon and I went to the TSB and how everything changed after that. Of course it did. I spilled a secret that had been eating me like a tumour, and turned the truth into a burden for two.

I could begin with how that day not only shifted things between me and Sheldon, a hush and a closeness sprung up between us, but how it altered Sharon too. When I showed up at Melody's apartment that afternoon and found Sharon there, red-eyed and pale, I knew I'd interrupted something beyond the small talk you'd expect between strangers. After that some part of Sharon seemed walled off. She was loving and sweet and said all the right things, but her mind was in two places at once.

I could begin with the phone call I got the same afternoon while I was shopping, before I walked in on Melody and Sharon. Nathalie Girard is a name I never expected to come up on my phone, and I'd never have guessed that I would willingly pick up. But the element of surprise won out, that and curiosity. I hadn't finished the word *hello* when she lit into me for telling Jeff that she'd buried my lead on the trim problem with the Tracker. Once she wound down some, I told her it wasn't me who told Jeff, it was her TSB buddy, Lyndon. That obviously took the wind out of her because there was this long pause. Next thing you know she goes ballistic, yelling that it wasn't her fault, she did everything right, she had feelings for Rafe, real feelings, it wasn't supposed to be a complaint, it wasn't her fault, it wasn't her fault, it wasn't her fault.

See what I mean? Who's to say where a story begins?

∧ ∨ ∧

TO HELL WITH COMMON WISDOM. I'm starting in the middle.

Two thirty, New Year's morning. Picture two guys, one half again the size of the other, slouched in their seats in a townhouse living room. The room is dim, down to one lamp and the blue Christmas tree lights. Everything about the men screams drunk: their splayed limbs, their wobbly necks, the way they stare with fierce concentration at the coffee table or their own sock feet. Listen closely and you'll hear soft jazz, the livelier R&B and disco gone out with the old year, the volume so low that the quietest notes vanish. Inhale and you'll detect the skunky tang of marijuana that the men enjoyed on the patio as soon as their mildly disapproving women were tucked away.

It is a cozy scene. Warm, intimate, inviting. You might wish you were there, in the low light, enjoying the buzz of intoxicants and music and conversation. But because this is the middle of things, be grateful you are somewhere else. These drunk men are not happy. They are discussing matters no man wants to discuss, and they are unravelling.

At first our guy time, as Sharon called it when she kissed me good night, consisted largely of shooting the shit. Sheldon, despite living only an hour from Nova Scotia's South Shore, has never stood on a surfboard, and he requested a few tales of the waves. We talked about airplanes – turns out he learned to fly with Rafe back in the day but never kept up his licence. I chose some of the more colourful Andy stories from my vast repertoire, and he countered with exploits of his motorcycle club, a group of middle-aged Harley lovers who meet for pancakes Sunday morning before tearing along back roads where the cops never show. But once the pot kicked in, draping its languid sheet over our drunkenness, we turned quieter, more nostalgic, and inevitably circled back to Rafe.

"You've had a couple of days," I said. "What do you think?"

"About?"

"About your brother. About any of it." Ever since I'd broken my silence on Rafe's suicide, I'd felt a pressing need to talk it through. It was time to release the brakes. "Does it make sense to you? Would that sexual harassment complaint have sent him over the edge?"

Vodka and cranberry juice was our late-night drink of choice. Sheldon took a large slug of his and thunked the glass down. He didn't answer.

"For me it didn't add up at first," I said. "Then it dawned on me that the whole thing would go public, the complaint, the affair, everything. Not public in the sense of media coverage, but public in aviation circles. Everyone we worked with would hear about it. Everyone on the wildfire side too, the ground crews, the ministry of forests guys, all the ops and communications people. Rafe ... well, he had this stellar reputation – as a pilot, absolutely, but as a man too. A husband, a friend." I thought of how often I'd walked into a fire centre beside that force of nature or laughed with him at the pub or kept him company over breakfast. Times like that, I felt his shine rub off on me. This pilot's pilot and all-round good guy, universally welcomed and admired, was my friend. "It would destroy his reputation," I said. "The affair, the complaint, all the sordid details. Doesn't matter that the complaint was fake. You know how it goes. There's no presumed innocent with this type of thing. He'd be smeared forever."

Even to my ears this explanation sounded feeble. I'd had ample time to sift through Rafe's final months, and although Nathalie's accusations would unearth some dirt, it wasn't the kind of dirt that would lead a man to take his life. It was a harassment complaint. She wasn't accusing him of sexual assault or, God forbid, rape. Sheldon and I were probably the only people on the planet who knew how baseless the whole thing was, seeing as I'd told Sheldon about Nathalie's surprise call to me and her insistence that she had never lodged a complaint. But others would be skeptical too, especially if they knew or suspected that Nathalie and Rafe were an item. They would see the complaint for what it was, a retelling born from Nathalie's anger and humiliation.

I staggered over to the Christmas tree, hoping its cobalt lights might relieve my troubled thoughts. It felt like a violation to be in Rafe's house discussing his darkest secret, the one he asked me never to tell. That was before I knew it was not his darkest secret.

When Sheldon finally spoke, his words came slow and slurred, buttered with his thick east-coast accent. "That's not why he did it, my son." He stared at the last inch of his drink. "At least, that's not the whole of it." His head flopped forward onto his chest. Had he fallen asleep?

"Ah, Christ," he said a minute later. "I'm wasted. This brain a mine, she's none too good at the best a times and she sure as shit's not working now. And that Jesus BC bud. That's hardly helping now, is it?" He polished off his drink. "What a world, eh? Who'd've thought a year ago that I'd be sitting here in Vancouver, New Year's Eve, talking about why my only brother offed himself? It's a batshit crazy world, I'm tellin' you."

A noise from the hallway stopped us dead. There, hair mussed, squinting, robe hanging off her, stood Sharon. We were like statues, the three of us. No one said a word.

Fuck, fuck, fuck. I prayed to a God I only believe in at times like this: please don't let her have heard. Please. Sheldon's ashen face told me he was requesting something similar.

"What are you two doing up? It's so late."

She sounded sleepy but ordinary, and relief flooded through me. "Just talking. Drinking too much and talking."

"Okay." She stayed there, swaying slightly. Never had a woman looked so vulnerable.

Unsteadily I made my way to her. "Were we too loud?"

"No." She nestled her head into my chest.

"We can call it a night anytime."

"You didn't wake me up. I just had to pee."

Her body felt limp under the padded robe. I told Sheldon I'd be right back and did my best to steer her down the hall and back into the bedroom. My heart pounded. That was close, too close. What was I thinking? Discussing a secret I'd vowed never to share as if it was the hockey playoffs? Saying things Sharon must never hear when she is literally feet away? Rarely has my judgment been worse.

Sharon peeled off her robe and rolled into bed. I bent close. "We won't be much longer. Maybe one more drink."

"Will? I'm going on a cruise. A New Year's resolution type of thing. I booked it yesterday." Her eyes were closed; she was more asleep than awake. "Don't be mad. It's just something for me."

I leaned over and planted a kiss on her cheek. "Of course I'm not mad. Go back to sleep."

"Will? Stay here tonight. They won't mind. It's so late."

"All right, I will." I kissed her again, breathed the apple scent of her hair, and closed the door tight behind me. I didn't know I had just made a promise I couldn't keep.

Sheldon's chair was empty, but bright light spilled from the kitchen. I found him there cracking ice into two fresh glasses of vodka.

"Did she hear?"

"I don't think so. She was mostly asleep."

"Mix?" He held up the nearly empty bottle of cranberry juice.

"Don't bother."

"Jumpin' Jesus, she gave me a start. You too." He returned the juice to the fridge without pouring any for himself. "We shouldn't be talking about this here."

"We shouldn't be talking about this, period." The first sip of vodka was like an icicle, and I shivered as it broke trail down my throat.

"Yes, we should." Sheldon swirled his ice cubes. "You did the right thing telling me. It might not feel that way, but you did." He looked up. "You really knew all this time and never told a soul?"

I nodded, took another numbing sip.

He picked up his glass. "Come with me."

He led me into the tiny laundry room off the kitchen, through the side door, and into the narrow attached garage. "Here?" I asked.

"Why not? It's private." He went to the driver's side of the Honda S2000, which gleamed lavishly in the fluorescent light. "Don't get your knickers in a twist, now. It's not like we're taking her on the road." He opened the door and wedged himself behind the wheel. I took the passenger's seat. "This here's one beautiful fucking car."

He's right, it's a stellar piece of engineering. Sharon keeps saying she's going to sell it on Craigslist, but so far it's only talk. Meanwhile the convertible marks time in the garage, a pro athlete waiting to compete.

Sheldon fit his drink into the centre console and adjusted his position. "Jesus Murphy, I'm like a vacuum-packed halibut in here. How'd Rafe ever get into this fuckin' thing?"

I'd often wondered that, the low-slung car designed more for a slender Japanese than a burly Nova Scotian. Rafe had a technique, though. He would pivot into the seat and ease himself under the steering wheel, then scoot his ass forward so the top of his head barely brushed the roof. "Hugs me like a condom," he'd say. Which was true, barring unforeseen potholes or speed bumps.

Once Sheldon was settled, he took a slug of vodka. "Some night this turned out to be, eh? Jesus Murphy. If I'd a shot glass worth of sense I'd be sleeping it off beside the little woman instead of hiding out here like a common criminal, ready to confess."

So he did have something to say. I was relieved. Any theory he could offer, I wanted to hear. I had brooded over Rafe's death long enough on my own.

I waited while he dealt with his drink, missing the console by an inch before fumbling the glass into place. He wasn't kidding — he was well and truly hammered. Whole minutes went by while he squirmed and contorted in the seat, trying to fish something out of his pants pocket. Finally he had it: the gyrocompass knob he'd swiped from Rafe's airplane. He stared at it so long, holding it lightly in one hand, that I wondered if we were done.

I considered downing my vodka, but it held no appeal anymore. I'd hit the worst part of wasted half an hour ago. Now my only hope was to claw back up the other side.

Eventually I prompted him. "You said the harassment complaint wasn't the whole reason."

Still he sat there, almost catatonic. He was starting to creep me out and I wondered if he was simply too drunk to hold up his end of the conversation. I studied him, wrestler's torso spilling over the compact bucket seat, legs wedged like timbers under the steering wheel, wide face waxy. The sheer mass of him brought to mind the last time I stood next to Rafe, that hot morning on the tarmac outside Quesnel, the last hour of his life already ticking away.

Sheldon never did snap out of his trance, but from somewhere inside it, a place only he could enter, he did what I had done three days earlier in the TSB warehouse. He told a story that no one else had ever heard, at least no one else alive.

I will try for the sake of accuracy, and for the sake of closure, to recount it in full as Sheldon told it to me. It is, after all, the story that sets off all the others.

∧ ∨ ∧

CAPE BRETON ISLAND in the seventies, Sheldon tells me, is a remote and insular world. The digital age has not yet happened, and the mass media have not yet flung their nets over the island and declared it a fine catch for tourists. It is a rough, unsophisticated place to grow up, especially the scrubby patch where Sheldon and Rafe live with their ma and da.

Not a town, not truly rural either, Braelorn is a smattering of houses grouped around a potholed road and a general store at one end of Bras d'Or Lake, the sprawling inland sea that pokes into Cape Breton's centre like an oversized navel. Besides the tiny farmhouses and aluminum-sided bungalows that sit atop scrubby lots an acre or three apart, there's a regional fire hall, its clapboard always thin on paint; a line of summer cottages on the lake side of the road, the land side occupied by the year-rounders, who prefer shelter; and an assortment of dilapidated sheds and barns from which spill dented dirt bikes, leaky rowboats, and rusted equipment from failed attempts at farming. In the yard next door to theirs, a broken-down school bus that old man Ferguson never did convert into a camper is being absorbed by a spreading hayfield.

Galloping through this landscape is a gang of boys, aged ten to seventeen, bored and undisciplined, well versed in strong language, cigarettes, and the shrewdest methods of entry into whatever shuttered cottage has something to offer, which is most of them.

There are girls in Braelorn too, though not many in the boys' age range. For proper sightings of girls – girls with long shiny hair, bracelets, and dresses, girls who gather in chattering groups and ignore the boys with such diligence that it is clear they are scrutinizing every word and movement – for these beguiling girls, the older boys rely on the consolidated junior high plus high school to which another, functioning school bus carries them each morning.

Sheldon Mackie and his younger brother, Rafe, are central members of the gang and among the most ardent admirers of the girls. From their early teens on, they are big, strapping boys, quick to laugh, nearly as quick to fight. They land themselves in trouble every week or two, but their ma and da, who after all bequeathed them the gifts of energy and spontaneity, brush it off as boyish pranks.

Cape Breton in the seventies is a difficult place to find work. If you're on the coast it might be you can fish; this is still years before the cod stocks disappear. If you're in the industrial area you can work at the steel plant in Sydney or the coal mine near Glace Bay, though fewer men go underground each year. If you are in Braelorn or anywhere in the Bras d'Or Lake area, you're shit out of luck. That is how the Mackie brothers come to be living with their parents after both have finished high school and should by all accounts be on their own. It's not like today, when kids don't leave their childhood bedrooms until their twenties, even thirties some of them. Back then there is shame associated with being stuck in the family home once your schooling has finished and your manhood begun.

Sheldon makes it out of grade twelve, barely, in 1975 and lands the occasional shift at the Braelorn general store, filling in a few hours a week while the regulars take summer holidays. He pisses off no one, makes change quicker than most customers can calculate, and turns in a balanced float every time, so he is offered more hours and soon has a bona fide part-time job, pulling down twenty, twenty-five hours a week.

Rafe, younger by two years, finishes school in 1977 and is less lucky in the employment department. He picks up odd jobs at a couple of nearby farms, haying, painting outbuildings, fixing fences. He babysits days for a single mother in a neighbouring village if her usual sitter is off at the bingo. He applies for all the road work, graveyard maintenance, and provincial park jobs, but they consistently go to married men with kids to feed. He understands but nonetheless succumbs to black periods of feeling useless and undervalued. He knows he is capable of more, if only he had the right outlet.

The outlet arrives, though he won't know it until much later, in the spring of 1978, in the form of new neighbours. Old man Ferguson next door, now in his eighties, goes off to live with his sister, who will boil his cod, roll his cigarettes, and wipe his arse through the long, dismal slide into decrepitude. Into his small two-storey farmhouse moves a family of three: Judge J.D. MacInnis, his wife, Joan, and their thirteen-year-old daughter, Amber.

Why a county court judge from Sydney, one of the highest-paid men on the island, would choose Braelorn as home, and then purchase Ferguson's mouldering homestead, are matters of endless conjecture in the Mackie household and, from what Sheldon overhears at the store, throughout the tiny community. The rumours are florid and varied. The judge is a raging alcoholic whose escapades forced him to flee the city and sober up. A murderer he sent up to Dorchester Penitentiary, now out on parole, has threatened revenge. His heavily lipsticked wife is a nymphomaniac who had to be snatched from the temptations of a populated area (this tops the rumour list among the boys). The judge has gambled away their fortune on the horses and the lotteries.

Whatever the reason, the neighbourhood boys agree on one thing: the arrival of a new girl is long overdue, especially a girl as entrancing as young Amber MacInnis. The straw-coloured hair that brushes her slender shoulders, the freckles that dot her high cheeks, the legs as long as a full-grown woman's, the round, peach-like ass held high by tight designer jeans, and the plump and, sweet Jesus, pert breasts whose nipples are forever – and the boys will swear to this – erect, in all temperatures, behind all brassieres, under all items of clothing. The combination is more than the gang of boys ever dreamed might exist on their home turf. That she is scary-smart and a year young for her grade because of skipping ahead, normally grounds for ridicule and rejection, are matters easy to overlook in a package so fine.

The matter of Amber's hard nipples absorbs the gang's attention and crowds their conversations in the weeks after the MacInnises move in. It comes up whenever the boys gather to smoke cigarettes or exchange dirty magazines or discuss how to break into the next summer home. Theories are offered and rejected. One boy attempts to research the phenomenon at the library in Sydney – the local book-mobile, staffed by stocky Miss Cann, offering scant anonymity – but he turns up nothing of consequence. In the end no one can deduce how a girl, barely a teenager, can possess such breasts, engorged with desire and visibly ready at all times. She must be like her mother, snicker the older boys, who crave finality and logic – a nympho. It must be something you can pass down to your kids, like red hair or a cleft palate.

By this time Sheldon and Rafe, twenty-one and nineteen respectively, are no longer members of the gang. Once you graduate high school, or drop out as some boys do, you quit hanging out with the group, in part because you're working, if you're lucky, but mainly because you're beyond all that. As a young man you do, however, retain an emeritus status that permits you to join the boys on occasion, especially at parties and in the parking lot outside school dances, where you enlighten and mentor the younger ones, dispensing liquor, dope, adjustments, and advice.

Sheldon and Rafe are therefore doubly aware of Amber MacInnis. Not only do they glimpse her across the yard that separates their houses, watch her board the bus each morning and ride off on her bike after school, but they hear lurid speculation about her and her eye-popping attributes from half a dozen horny boys. None of those boys will speak to her — that goes without saying; she is from the city and she is beautiful — and even Sheldon has failed to progress beyond "That'll be a dollar twenty-eight, please." It is Rafe who actually meets the girl.

It happens by accident. On a tender green afternoon in May, Rafe is on his way home from a rare job at the Lewis farm, tilling the field that will be sown with seed potatoes. He is driving their da's pickup, which the old man seldom uses these days, the occasional spins to Baddeck for tobacco or rum his only ventures out of Braelorn. The sun shines and the lake, when Rafe sights it from a rise on the road, is deep blue and crowned with whitecaps in the afternoon breeze. He is thinking of supper and the long evening light as he closes in on a girl wheeling a bicycle. It is Amber, her after-school ride curtailed by a flat.

Rafe tells her to hop in. Effortlessly he hoists her red five-speed into the back of the truck — effortlessly because he is strong, forearms ropy with tendons and tanned from the spring sun, wide shoulders barely contained by his blue chambray work shirt. He is rated, in the view of the scarce neighbourhood girls and most mothers under fifty, as a specimen, one that none have sampled and that none, even the few who are happily wedded, would refuse. Yet the opportunity never arises, for as long as anyone can remember, Rafe Mackie has been off the market. From the age of thirteen, the same age as young Amber MacInnis, now safely belted into the cab of his truck, he has loved Gretchen Kramer, a redheaded town girl from Baddeck, volunteer in the small local hospital, Winter Carnival Queen two years running, valedictorian their graduating year. He has never spoken to his love other than to say "hello" or "nice day" and once, stammeringly and unsuccessfully, to ask her to dance. She barely knows he exists, yet he remains faithful to her, unable to transfer his ardour to another, even during the occasional heavy petting initiated by the single mother whose toddler he babysits. Sheldon questions this pointless devotion; Rafe replies that when someone more loveable comes along, he will love that person instead. He makes it sound simple.

Love is not what Rafe finds with Amber. She is a kid with a flat tire, and he drives her home with a minimum of conversation and, he tells Sheldon much later, hardly an impure thought. His mind strays only once, when they hit a rough patch that makes her breasts jiggle. The movement is barely detectible in his peripheral vision, but it reminds him of the boys' talk, and when the truck levels out he cannot help but steal a glance to see for himself whether the pointy-nipple syndrome is true or the product of feverish imaginations. It takes two glimpses to ascertain that yes, there's a nip in the air, and several more to confirm the staying power and full, bursting quality of the spectacle.

"Are you really only thirteen?" he hears himself ask. Recounting the ride later to Sheldon, he berates himself for the blunt inquiry.

"And a half," she says, then goes back to contemplating the fields, barns, and abandoned houses that speed by. Amber MacInnis, it would seem, is a girl of few words.

After that the new girl can be spotted in her yard more frequently, digging with a trowel in the kitchen garden or crouched on the steps with a book. One unusually warm afternoon she lies on a blanket in an orange bikini, possibly a size too small, for maximum exposure to the sun. It gets to where Rafe sees her nearly every time he goes outside, whether he is unloading groceries for his ma or mowing the scrubby clover that passes for lawn.

One warm afternoon in early June, he is tuning up the truck when the school bus deposits Amber at her driveway. Under the hood, mind on his work, he doesn't notice the bus, doesn't notice the girl either until later, when the scent of strawberry gloss straightens him up.

There she stands, beside the truck, golden hair in a ponytail, school-books clutched to her flower-sprigged white sundress. He notices that her eyes are as blue as the lake and, as she lowers the books, that her dress is so thin he can see not only nipples but areolas.

His breath catches.

You went to school like that? he wants to ask. Your parents let you outside like that? When he sees the white cardigan tied around her waist, he thinks he understands, but soon the questions resume. Why would she go around without her sweater on? How can she be only thirteen, the same age as little Sally MacDonald who he babysat until last year? Why in God's name is the girl not wearing a bra?

He is flustered, no denying it, but it is nothing compared to how he feels when Amber takes his hand and leads him into her yard. He looks around to see who is there — no one, the judge's car gone, the nympho mother's car gone — but regardless of whether they are being observed, he knows it is wrong for this child to be holding his hand. He slows down and she tugs him forward. She knows where she is going.

The abandoned school bus has stood in old man Ferguson's yard since Rafe was small. He and Sheldon nurse an ongoing argument over its true colour. Yellow, says Sheldon, all school buses are yellow. Orange, says Rafe, the colour of flame.

Hay grows up to the bus windows. All four tires are flat. The ground beneath is uneven, and the long vehicle sways slightly as she leads him up the steps and down the aisle. The smell of earth and mildew and old forgotten cars tickles his nostrils, overpowering the girl's delicate scent of strawberries.

He stops in his tracks. "Listen, I've gotta go. I've got an appointment in town."

She turns and smiles. Not a full toothy smile, but a Mona Lisa version. "No, you don't."

He looks at her stupidly. "How would you know?"

"You're working on your truck. There are pieces of it in the driveway. You're wearing a dirty undershirt and you need a shower. There is no appointment."

Jumpin' Jesus, who is this girl? he thinks wildly.

She walks all the way to the end of the bus, to the backseat that spans the vehicle's width, then turns around. "Why don't you come here." It is not a question.

He is frozen to the spot. Every rational brain cell tells him to leave, that he does not need this, that it spells trouble. Only six years separate them, nothing like the thirteen years between his ma and da, but at her age six years makes her a child and casts his desire in the blackest of shadows.

Then she pulls off her dress, and with it goes his power to choose.

She is naked, completely naked. He can see everything, the brown circles around her straining nipples, the sparse blond thatch between her legs. Everything a nineteen-year-old man could want, dewy flesh, parted strawberry lips, stands there in front of him.

"Where ... where ...?" he stammers.

"They're both out till supper."

"No, where are your ... undergarments?" Where did that come from, a word straight out of the ancient novels they had to read in English class?

Her smile widens, and then she does something extraordinary: with her right thumb and forefinger she pinches first one nipple, then the other. She does not look away; on the contrary, her eyes are like headlights trained on his. The pain between his legs makes him want to howl.

"I took them off," she says, circling one nipple lazily. "When I got home from school. I didn't think you'd mind." She sits on the backseat, over a rip in the upholstery, leans back, parts her legs. Now he can truly see it all.

"This is ... You don't know what you're doing. You're a girl. A kid. You ... How do you know about anything like this?" He stands motionless in the aisle, holding on for all he's worth.

"My father has the world's biggest *Penthouse* collection in his night table. I've always been a reader." She squirms slightly, pushing her bottom into the torn seat. "Could we skip the big discussion? I'm tired of doing it alone, I want to know what it's like with an actual person. You're good-looking and quiet, not like those gross boys on the bus. I just want you to play with my tits and I'll do the rest. Nothing more. Okay?"

Later, when summer is over and Rafe tells Sheldon everything, he takes care to explain that when the girl led him onto the bus, he wanted to say no. When he stopped in the middle of the aisle, he wanted to say no. But from the moment she peeled off her dress and began fondling herself, no was not in his vocabulary. He walked toward Amber with yes echoing in his brain and vibrating in his cock and did exactly what she told him.

Their experimentation, as she takes to calling it, carries on through the summer. They meet at unpredictable times, most often in the old school bus but sometimes when he is babysitting and the toddler has gone down for a nap, or in his da's pickup, which transports them far from prying eyes. They never appear together in public, both of them silently but keenly aware that their liaison is socially unacceptable. There is no talk of romance or dating – in fact, there is almost no talk at all. They meet for sex, secret and illicit, and they get down to it as soon as possible.

They progress from trying everything they can think of without technically doing it to finally, one morning in late June, on a blanket in the woods, doing it. Rafe worries about taking the girl's virginity, he tells Sheldon later, even though he himself is a virgin, but there comes a point when he cannot hold back and she doesn't refuse. Once they cross that threshold, the serious learning begins. Sometimes Amber sneaks a magazine from the judge's pile and wants to copy an act she has read about. Sometimes, if schedules allow, they do it several times in a row. Rafe comes to understand that he can do anything to her, ask for anything in return, and she will not deny him. Often he doesn't need to ask. Her intuition is eerie; she always seems to know what will push him over the edge.

In this part of Cape Breton in July and August, when the summer people take over the lake, and the campgrounds fill with families from

Sydney who want to sleep closer to strangers than they do in the city, it is surprisingly easy for careful lovers to hide. And they are careful. No one sees them. Sheldon suspects Rafe is up to something but knows better than to pry. His brother will fess up in his own good time.

When September comes and Amber begins grade nine, opportunities are harder to find. He manages to meet her some days after school, on the farm road where she punctured her tire. She cycles there and he picks her up, tosses her bike in the back, and drives them to one of their secret places.

One afternoon late in the month, after he parks the truck in a grove of birch, she does not lean over to kiss him. Instead she talks. From that day forward, life as Rafe knows it is over.

It's an old story, Sheldon tells me, especially in Cape Breton three decades ago. The pill is not widely available, condoms are unreliable, and young lovers, then as now, are not renowned for meticulousness. The twist in this story is that the girl is thirteen, the boy is nineteen, and the girl's father is a judge. What they have been doing all summer is in other jurisdictions called statutory rape; where they live it goes by a milder name, sex with a minor. Either way, it is an indictable offence of which Rafe is the depraved perpetrator and Amber the innocent victim. Another twist is that Rafe is arrested and held in the Sydney jail for six days, long enough for the story to decorate the front page of the *Cape Breton Post* and the *Baddeck Bugle* and to be featured on CBC radio and the suppertime TV news. For six days Rafe and his family cower behind the curtain of shame that encloses those who go wrong in the unforgiving hamlets on Canada's east coast, places where priests hold sway and money is king and you can perform certain deeds with impunity, like shooting your neighbour's dog or pummelling your wife's face, but God help you if you fuck the judge's daughter.

On the seventh day of the ordeal, Sheldon tells me, a bitter smile on his lips, they rested. The judge, worn down by his daughter's pleas, her delusional insistence that she had consented to and indeed instigated the entire perversion, drops the charges in exchange for a promise, the public version of which is: Rafe will never set foot on his property or speak to his daughter again. Rafe comes home, Ma and Da hug him and weep, and Rafe tells Sheldon that he is getting the hell out of Dodge.

"What're you on about?" Sheldon asks. "It's over. The charges are dropped, you got no record."

"I leave in the morning. I bought the bus ticket before I left Sydney. I'll send for my stuff once I find a place in Halifax."

"I don't get it." In their brief lives so far, the one immutable rule is that Sheldon is the older brother, and when it comes to serious matters he has the say. Yet at that moment he looks like a confused child. "You don't know a soul on the mainland, and Jesus, Halifax? It's huge. People are after getting lost in that place."

"I know. I'll have to figure it out as I go."

"But what about home? Ma and Da and the rest of us?"

Rafe answers wearily. He has aged a decade in a week. "Believe me, I got no choice."

Rafe packs a duffel bag and so, that evening, does his brother. "You'll never manage alone, you friggin dimwit," Sheldon says. "I'm coming with you and that's final." He draws himself up to full height, reasserting his older-brother seniority. This time Ma and Da hold them both and weep. "Don't go," their ma cries. "You don't have to go." But they do.

Three days later, after a bus trip that bounces them through dozens of tiny villages, after a disorienting day navigating the maze that is Halifax, after the brothers have installed themselves in a low-ceilinged basement suite complete with one bed, one sofa, one table, and a hotplate, Rafe explains: it was the only way the judge would drop the charges. Even though the tainted orange school bus (yellow, says Sheldon) has been towed to Buddy's salvage yard, and Amber is grounded until they whisk her off to the nuns, the judge will rest easy under only one condition: the degenerate next door must go.

It is also, Rafe says, because of their parents that he must leave. As long as he stays in Braelorn people will point at him, the sexual deviant who raped that little girl and wormed his way out of a conviction, and will jeer at their ma and da, the soft-headed parents who raised him, and not a one of them in the family will ever buy bread at the general store or visit a bank teller in Baddeck without hanging their heads in humiliation. But if the deviant disappears, the scandal may subside, people may forget, and Mr. and Mrs. Mackie may have a hope of melting back into the landscape.

The brothers settle in the big city of Halifax, which for months remains baffling and friendless. They eke out a living thanks to their cheap, leaky suite and diet of marked-down baked goods from Ben's Thrift Store. In time they land steady jobs in construction, and are eventually persuaded by a foreman with his private pilot's licence to sign up for flight lessons. Rafe, determined to put his transgressions behind him, works longer and harder than anyone. Never misses a shift. Logs all the overtime he can. Saves money, takes more flying lessons, decides to become a pilot. Seldom dates, and when he does it's to accompany Sheldon and Nancy, the sporty girl Sheldon meets at the laundromat down the way. Joins a gym and begins a lifelong regimen of controlling his body the only way he can. Becomes a man of discipline, a man of good behaviour and iron will. Becomes a man who could be great.

"When he left the island," Sheldon told me at ten past four on New Year's morning, "he left for good. He never went back, not once, not even for our parents' funerals. He was scared shitless someone would recognize him and stir up the past, and Sharon would find out. When I started going back for old time's sake, even though I always stayed in Sydney or out on the Mira, never at Braelorn, he wouldn't hear of coming with me. Wouldn't hear of it."

As if the past were a road ahead of him, Sheldon stared through the windshield of the powerful car his brother had loved. Little by little, he'd talked himself sober. Now he was winding down.

"After we left Cape Breton he remade himself, turned into the upstanding citizen you knew him to be. But his whole life he was petrified of being found out. No one knew. *No* one. Of course not Sharon, but not Nancy either, I swore I'd never tell her. And none of his employers. He could get away with that because he never had a criminal record. The longer he went without telling anyone, the deeper he buried the past and the more shameful it was to him. Least, that's how it seemed to me."

Sheldon sighed and his shoulders rounded. Rafe's past, it struck me, had also been Sheldon's burden all these years. Rafe once told me how good it was to have a brother, that his had stuck by him when it mattered. Never did I imagine he meant something like this.

"If it'd happened to me," Sheldon said, "I'd have told Nancy. Better to fess up and get it over with. She'd have understood, at least over time. But Sharon, she's ... more proper, in a way, more straitlaced. It would've disgusted her. She'd have seen it as rape, child molesting, what have you, and she would never look at Rafe again. Doesn't help that nowadays this sort of thing, sex with a minor and all, is practically worse than murder. Back then it was a scandal, but now, Christ almighty, a dirty secret like this comes slithering out of your past and it's a Jesus media circus. The police ransack your house looking for kiddie porn, you're not allowed to set foot near a school, people spit at you, slash your tires, spray-paint your house. It's the end of your career for sure. It's the end of life as you know it. You're done."

He took a deep breath and let it out slowly, and he turned to me, his eyes red-rimmed and bleary, heartbroken. "That's why he did it, Will. Whether she meant to or not, that grade A shit-disturber made a complaint, and whoever investigated it would have to dig into his background to see if he'd harassed anyone before. It wouldn't take much. It's public record that he lived in Cape Breton until he was nineteen, and the newspaper articles are all there just waiting for someone to stumble on them. To hell with the newspapers — there are families, plural, in Braelorn who'd spill every detail of his so-called sexual molestation and criminal behaviour the minute some suit shoved a microphone in their face. They're like everybody else nowadays, they want their fifteen minutes on TV."

"Fuck," I said. "Fuck." It was my total contribution to Sheldon's hour-long narration.

"He worked so hard, Will. I wish you could've seen it. So hard. Every day I lived with him that man drove himself. He punished himself for what he did. And the thing is, what he did, it wasn't even wrong. Not in my books it wasn't. Fuck the law, fuck what other people say. It was sex. They both wanted it, they both got off on it. It was the most natural thing in the world. End of story."

I thought about that. Thought of the four girls I had sex with during school, the first when I was fourteen, half a year older than Amber, the year my mom died and Lisa down the street comforted me, the year of my first flight lesson. Was it wrong for us to have sex? I thought of all the women I've slept with since, not one of them because of love, not until Sharon. Did that make it wrong?

Sheldon ran a hand over his brow. "It seems so unfair, so ... cruel. After all those decades, for it to come back and paint him into a corner. Right when Sharon and him were gonna take another run at it. Right after he hurt her so bad by leaving. Christ, think how she'd be if all this came out. It'd pull the guts right outta her. You know, if he was alone he could've handled it, I think he could. Moved to the States maybe, started a new life. But Sharon. He'd die before letting that woman think she'd lived all those years with some kind of perverted rapist." He stopped. "Ah, Jesus. I guess that's what he did."

FORTY-TWO

January

JANUARY 2, the start of the new year, the end of the story.

The story of Rafe is all I could think about yesterday. I brought it home with me from Sharon's, I slept with it through yesterday afternoon, I sat with it and got shit-faced again last night. What to take from it all, I still don't know. The only thing I'm certain of at this point is that no amount of vodka or beer can make the story of Rafe sit more comfortably with me.

It snowed this morning, before I woke up with this thudding hangover, my second in two days. Just a couple of centimetres, enough to give our green-and-grey city a rare dusting. When I opened my eyes and saw the sharp white light through the blinds I'd forgotten to close, I vowed I would see Sharon before the day is over. She texted me yesterday to say Sheldon and Nancy had gone home as planned, and again this morning to ask ever so casually what I've been up to. I don't blame her for worrying. We've never gone this long without talking.

But first I need coffee. I've been at Sharon's so much lately that the cupboards are bare, so I pull on yesterday's clothes and prepare to hit the street. On the way out I knock on Melody's door, she always has good organic beans on hand, but there's no answer. To my surprise I'm disappointed. She'd be welcome company right about now. I hope she's in some park catching snowflakes on her tongue or doing some other goofy thing. I hope her scumbag boyfriend got her something nice for Christmas.

Out on the street, the biting air plus the novelty of snow helps straighten me out some. Three blocks from Starbucks, the nearest coffee shop, the snow changes to sleet-laden rain. In less than a minute it plasters my hair to my skull, soaks my pant legs, and puts a cushion of water under every step. The bright white sky greys up and everything goes dim even though there's another half hour to morning. I look toward the downtown highrises and the North Shore mountains, usually a striking sight from this part of Commercial Drive, but they're covered in cloud, the sky a woollen watch cap over the city's brow.

I tuck my chin inside my Helly Hansen jacket, a garment that has more than outlived its waterproof years, and trudge through the slush, wishing I had re-waxed my hiking shoes. It's cold, in that damp, seeping way peculiar to Vancouver in January.

The Starbucks comes into view, its broad green canopy dripping dregs of snow. In the dry patch below, instead of patio chairs, which someone has seen fit to remove from the elements, is a pile of coats and blankets. As I near, the pile shifts. Inside it, or more accurately underneath it, sits a man, his bony hand thrust out for money.

Look at him, I tell myself. This is not the day to pretend another human is invisible. But he doesn't return my gaze, nor does he speak. He just sits there, a slumped scarecrow with his arm out, waiting.

I don't know why, because homeless people are pretty much a fixture in my neighbourhood, but I am riveted by this man. The thick rain sheets off me and the chill pushes through my skin, but I can't move. Neither, it seems, can he. He keeps his hand extended, unwilling, I guess, to give up hope that I'll put something in it.

Where do you come from? I want to ask him. Where is your family? I stand so long in front of the ragged man, his hand held out to me, that my head starts to pound and his features blur and a kind of trance comes over me. Instead of the man's face I see my mom's, fresh and open, from the engagement photo Dad keeps beside his bed. I see Ernie, head thrown back as he cackles at one of his own jokes, and Sheldon, bowed mournfully in the car. I see Melody's cloud of hair, and Andy on the sand watching the girls go by. I see Nathalie in a temper, hurtful, also hurting. I see Sharon, her eyes warm, accepting, and wounded. And I see, as I always do, Rafe.

Where does your story begin? I want to ask this man. What events lined up, and in what order, so that you landed here in a pile of castoffs instead of flying a plane or investigating a crash, or being in bed with your lover or at the park with your child or inside this Starbucks sipping a mocha? Was it something you did? Was it something done to you? Or are you both a victim and an agent, in a ratio too tangled to measure?

As usual these days I have no answers. In fact, I barely understand the questions. So I do the only thing that feels right: I take off, headed nowhere, shoes slapping the sidewalk, face stinging from the sleet, amazed at all the things I can't reconcile—the sterile, cookie-cutter exterior of the Starbucks, and the real-life bundle of truth outside it, and the lives and loves that are lost and redeemed and in some cases lost again. I take off and all the mysteries come with me. Today I don't block them out. Today I leave none of them behind.

EPILOGUE

NO MATTER HOW LONG you've been in the business, there's something exhilarating about the lead-up to fire season. After too many months living on your own schedule and, for some of us, in your own head, it's a relief to get back to the routine. Clocking in at West Air every day, doing practice runs, getting the lowdown on everyone's winter, guessing what kind of summer we're in for — resuming the familiar rhythm gets you primed for later, when the real action comes.

For me this year fire season kicks off early. Today, before any actual wildfires break out, before the on-call periods start, I will hop in my vehicle, crank up the tunes, and speed along the highway that connects this motel in Quesnel to the place where he went down.

I still think about him, more now that work's started up. Going through the days of training and prep without him is like learning all over again that he's gone. I'm not the only one who misses him. Once in a while the other pilots turn nostalgic and roll out the remember-when stories. When they do, I stay quiet. For me, remembering Rafe Mackie is a more complicated business than recalling a career of crazy stunts and bull's eyes.

When I think about him, I think how perfectly he planned the end, and how well he hid his tracks. A surprising number of people take their own lives in airplanes, and that's not counting terrorist hijackers. I googled the subject over the winter and was amazed at the reasons behind it — debt and lost love are big ones, but there's also jealousy,

379

depression, job loss – as well as the many ways people go: slamming into mountains, diving into fields, plowing into buildings if there's a chance of taking out a cheating spouse or no-good family member at the same time. For Rafe, flying to his death was an ideal way to end it. No one would suspect, and no one does, and he got to go out the way he wanted – in the cockpit, full speed ahead, reputation intact. It's a chance not many people get.

What also became clear over the winter, as I took apart the puzzle and put it together again, is that Rafe's decision to die, probably like most suicides, came not from one motivation but from many. The publicity that would dog him, the shame he'd have to wear, the labels of sex offender and pedophile that people would slap on him without giving two shits or a moment's thought to the circumstances – all that horrific fallout was part of it. But not the biggest part. His transgression, if that's what it was, took place in the distant past, and he'd lived too decent a life since then and was too well liked by friends and colleagues for that particular wave to sink him. Knowing Rafe, once the media circus died down he'd recover, he'd find a way to ride it out. I'm not even sure he'd have to disappear like Sheldon suggested.

No, the main trigger for Rafe's decision was Sharon. Sheldon had that part right. Rafe had wounded her profoundly with the affair, and I know Rafe – he couldn't bear to do it again. She'd be tainted by the scandal by association, but more than that she would forever see Rafe as a liar of the worst sort: one who had conned her from the beginning. She would have to redraw every image of him, re-evaluate their entire marriage, and admit to herself and everyone else that she'd been appallingly deceived. Better that she feel the quick stab of his death, a loss she could recover from, than the lifelong torment of the truth. Better he die as a man who loved his wife than live as a man who destroyed her.

In the end Rafe had to protect the woman he adored, he had to fix his mistakes as best he could. He had to because that's who he was, a protector and a fixer. He'd made the exact same decision early in life: to salvage his parents' future by going away from them. The difference this time is that he had to leave for good.

Sharon left too. First on a two-week cruise around the Caribbean. She wasn't talking in her sleep at New Year's — she really did it, and she went by herself even though her sister badly wanted to go along. Then once she got home, tanned, serene, and more beautiful than I'd ever seen her, she put her affairs in order and moved back to Toronto.

She did her best to let me down gently. It was early February and she was just back from the cruise. I was giddy to see her, like some pathetic puppy wagging my tail. We'd texted while she was away, but only a little; she needed time to clear her head, she'd said. We met at her place the day she got home and I couldn't stop touching her — her shoulder, her hair, her hand. I'd missed her so much that I ached. A rare winter sun had come out — I remember how it steamed the water from the pavement and the roofs. We sat in her kitchen with the window cracked open, the breeze filled with this intense perfume. The witch hazel, Sharon said. It flowers in winter.

Then she spoke the words that strike fear into the hearts of all men: "We need to talk."

The cruise had given her time to think, she said. As soon as her friend Rachel listed the townhouse for sale, she was moving back east to be near her sister and friends. She didn't belong in Vancouver, she never had. But I needed to know that I was the best thing that had happened to her here. I had healed her, she said. Those were her exact words, I know because I repeated them for days afterwards. She told me I'd find someone wonderful for the long haul, someone my own age who could go hiking and surfing with me and have kids with me, someone who didn't like Celine Dion. She said the last part so I'd laugh. She always knew when things were in danger of getting too heavy.

Over the next few weeks my heart took a fresh wallop every morning I opened my eyes to a bed without her in it. For a while I got reacquainted with the club scene and the toxic table d'hôte, enough that Melody got concerned and started bringing me untouchable items again, like tabbouleh and marinated kale. Sometimes I'd ask her in, if it wasn't too late and she didn't have plans with her new boyfriend. If I was sober we'd play Scrabble or watch some dumb movie on TV.

If I was wasted she'd make me drink water or tea, and then she'd sit cross-legged on the floor and listen while I slurred and slobbered. She's a good listener, Melody. Still a know-it-all, but it turns out she actually does know a lot about certain things, like how to look after yourself and keep your mind open.

On the worst days after Sharon left, when I was most out of it or so hungover I couldn't leave the apartment, I'd argue with her, out loud. I told her I didn't want anyone else. I didn't want the glossy nighttime girls with their heels and makeup. I tried to talk to them, but they all seemed so young and shallow and boring. I didn't want kids, I would tell her. I didn't care about that kind of life as long I could be with her. It didn't matter if she hated the outdoors and listened to shitty music. We had something bigger than all that and she couldn't just throw it away. And I loved her. That was always my clinching argument. It was the cliché that summed up all the clichés, but it was the truth. Now that I know what love feels like, how fierce it is and how deep it goes, how it will have its way with you no matter what, the mere fact of it seems enough to settle any argument. Only it's not.

As the winter dragged on and Sharon stayed away, and I gradually examined all that had happened, I came to see that she was right, at least about some of it. I still miss her, every day, and I still love her. I still want to take care of her, like Rafe asked me to in his letter. But I know that what grew between us, even though it was beautiful and profound, was no basis for a life together. Not because of our ages or different lifestyles, or the whole thing about kids, which I'm not even sure I want, but because of secrets. From the moment I crossed that woman's threshold, I was hiding the truth from her, and the hiding only grew. She kept things from me too. Some of them I know now, others I'm sure I don't.

Secrets. There's a seductiveness to them. They're deep and dark, they take hold in the most intimate parts of us. But in the end they're like roots near a foundation — the bigger they grow, the more damage they do. There's little I'm certain of anymore, but there is one thing: after today I'm done with secrets.

I'm still working on my life after Sharon. Who knows what shape it'll take? For now it's about getting back to the job, falling into the routines, staying healthy. Seeing more of my dad and less of the clubs. Staying open inside, like Melody says, instead of closing down. It's about climbing back into the Aerostar, Ernie and me reading the terrain below and knowing exactly what to do. And it's about the flying. Always, it's been about the flying. Everything that's worth doing, every feeling you have that's real — to my mind, it comes down to letting go and trusting in flight. To be part of a force so powerful, intoxicating, and potentially uncontrollable, to let it lift you high above the ordinary world, to say yes to the freedom of it and also the danger — that's what makes life worth living. All you can do is give yourself over to it, body and soul. That's what I plan to do, for as long as I can swing myself into the cockpit, for as long as the air holds me up.

Today, though, it's time for the fire. I check my backpack. Inside it: a large bottle of water, camp fuel, a wad of newspaper, a lighter. And the letter, of course, the creased page that's gone shiny from handling, and the envelope it came in that night that changed my life. What's a fire without fuel? Everything I need is here.

Outside the motel it's brewing up clear and warm, a good day to put the top down on the Honda S2000. I want the wind on me as I floor it down the highway.

When I get to the right place, I'll leave the car on the shoulder — no way is that baby going anywhere near the bush — and hike the rest of the way in. I've got the lat-long from the investigation report, but I'll know the spot when I see it, even though this time I'm not viewing it from the air.

I'd thought about asking Ernie how to make the next part mean something, whether setting it on fire is enough or I should dribble a little water to make steam or what. He's more up on ceremonies than I'll ever be. But in the end I decided to keep it private and not think about other people's traditions. As long as the words go up in flame, that's what matters. And as long as I shut my eyes, this time on purpose, to remember and accept. This is just for me, after all. And for Rafe.

Author's Note

The 2013 British Columbia wildfire season around which this novel is built is depicted fictionally, with no attempt to reflect actual circumstances that year. All fires, weather, aircraft incidents, firefighting personnel, and other details connected with the 2013 season are products of my imagination.

The catastrophic wildfires of 2003, including the McLure and Okanagan Mountain Park blazes, are a matter of public record. In this novel some details of those fires, and all portrayals of specific people who fought them, are made up.

West Air Flight Services is a fictional company, and the people who work there are fictional creations. Any similarity to actual people, living or dead, is coincidental.

Decidedly *not* fictional is the fact that year after year, teams of courageous individuals put themselves directly in the path of wildfires, whether from the air or on the ground, to protect land, property, animals, and citizens. We the protected owe these individuals an unrepayable debt for taking on such perilous work for the public good.

Acknowledgements

I am continually astonished at how lavishly people will donate their time and expertise, and how cheerfully they will prop up the spirits of an aspiring and at times flagging novelist.

For reading portions of the manuscript and offering invaluable specialized feedback, thank you to Iva Cheung, Ann Doyon, Mallory Eaglewood, George Heath, and Travis Shelongosky. I am indebted to Ray Horton, recently retired from Conair Aerial Firefighting in Abbotsford, BC, who warmly and patiently led me through the duties, offices, and aircraft of aerial firefighters and who offered insights (and corrections) galore on the manuscript. I consider these reviewers my partners in authenticity and clarity. Any errors, stumbles, or misrepresentations are my own.

Thank you to Ann Carmichael, retired harassment investigator, who in the 1990s hired me to edit and write reports and eventually trained me in complaint investigation.

Huge thanks to the readers who helped me shape and reshape this complex story: John J. Barr, Tanya Dare, Marie Heath, Andrew Peck, Robert Perch, Sue Safyan, Robyn So, and the late, great, forever-missed Graham Young. Gwen Martin, whose editing instincts are impeccable and whose brain is as large and good as her heart, cracked a problem no one else could. To the many friends, family, work partners, and fellow writers who buoyed me up when literary prospects dragged me low, I am profoundly grateful. Words cannot properly acknowledge Lois Richardson and Barbara Tomlin, the kindest readers, editors, cheerleaders, and friends a writer could hope for.

For advice and help with publishing, agenting, and other aspects of the long business of getting this book between covers, I am grateful to Caroline Adderson, Jesse Finkelstein, Sally Harding, Eve Lazarus, Sharon McInnis, Barbara Pulling, Stephanie Sinclair, and John Vigna. For creating the covers and the design inside them, I am again in awe of the visionary Natalie Olsen. And for supplying the know-how, encouragement, and support, both technical and moral, that every author dreams of receiving from their publisher, I thank the tireless (and bison-friendly) crew at NeWest Press: Matt Bowes, Claire Kelly, Christine Kohler, Carolina Ortiz, Meredith Thompson, and the incomparable Leslie Vermeer, who once again proved that few experiences equal the pleasure of being edited by a consummate pro.

Finally, for the life of passion and flight and all-round adventure he has given me, I extend my hand to Travis Shelongosky, private pilot and retired air accident investigator, without whom this book would not exist.

Frances Peck worked for three decades as an editor, ghostwriter, and educator before returning to her first love, writing fiction. Her debut novel, *The Broken Places*, was named a *Globe and Mail* best book of 2022 and was a finalist for the Rakuten Kobo Emerging Writer Prize. She lives in North Vancouver, British Columbia. Learn more at **francespeck.com**.